THE
RULE-BREAKER

BY
RHONDA NELSON

MILLS &
BOON

First published in Great Britain 2013
by Mills & Boon, an imprint of Harlequin (UK) Limited,
Eton House, 18-24 Paradise Road, Richmond, Surrey TW9 1SR

© Rhonda Nelson 2013

ISBN: 978 0 263 90335 5

14-1213

Harlequin (UK) policy is to use papers that are natural, renewable and recyclable products and made from wood grown in sustainable forests. The logging and manufacturing processes conform to the legal environmental regulations of the country of origin.

Printed and bound in Spain
by Blackprint CPI, Barcelona

A Waldenbooks bestselling author, two-time RITA®
Award nominee, *RT Book Reviews* Reviewers' Choice
nominee and National Readers' Choice Award winner,
Rhonda Nelson writes hot romantic comedy for the
Mills & Boon® Blaze® line. With more than thirty-
five published books to her credit, she's thrilled with
her career and enjoys dreaming up her characters and
manipulating the worlds they live in. She and her family
make their chaotic but happy home in a small town in
northern Alabama. She loves to hear from her readers,
so be sure to check her out at www.readrhondanelson.
com, follow her on Twitter @RhondaRNelson and like
her on Facebook.

For Ollie, my sweet, neurotic little fur baby,
who sits at my feet from the first word on the page
until the last. That, dear readers, is dedication.

Prologue

Mosul

ELI WESTON NOTED THE Bible, the rosary and the bottle of Jack Daniel's on his friend's bedside table with a burgeoning sense of disquiet. Not that all three items didn't make regular appearances on Micah Holland's table—they did—but usually it was only one or two, not all three together.

That knowledge, combined with the increasingly blank expression on his friend's face, made the hairs on the back of his neck rise.

Eli emptied his pockets and dropped heavily onto his bunk. "Another day in paradise," he muttered, shooting Micah a smile. "You been back long?"

Micah shook his head. "Nah."

A beat slid to three. "You look tired."

He knew his friend hadn't been getting much

sleep, especially over the past two weeks. It was understandable, given what had happened. War was hell, and this war, in particular, had been fought in ways that boggled the mind. They'd been trained to fight other soldiers, to honor the rules of war, but this enemy didn't play by those rules and thought nothing of strapping explosive devices onto pregnant women and then sending them into a hospital.

That's what Micah had witnessed two weeks ago—what he'd tried to prevent—and he hadn't been the same since. Not that Eli blamed him, but...

He hesitated, not wanting to cross a line, but not wanting to see Micah deteriorate any further. They'd met in basic training, had been friends since Jump School. There were a lot of blood and bullets under the bridge. And if the situation were reversed, he knew Micah would try to counsel him, as well.

"Listen, man. There's no shame in talking to someone. I know you—"

Micah whirled on him, like a reanimated corpse, his eyes blazing. "You know *nothing*," he spat. "Nothing. So don't insult me by giving me the standard line. I've got to sort this out my own way and the only person I have to talk to about it or square it with is the man upstairs." He jerked his head heavenward, gave an ironic little laugh, one that, for reasons which escaped him, made Eli nervous. Micah released a heavy breath. "Just leave it, Eli. I know you mean well…but I'm handling it."

Rather than irritate his friend further, Eli merely nodded. But whether Micah wanted to admit it or not, he needed help. And if he wouldn't get it on his own, then Eli had every intention of making him by other means. One word to the right person would set the ball in motion.

Finally, he nodded. "Yeah. Fine." He arched a brow, pretending as if the exchange never happened. "You want to go get something to eat? I'm about to head over to the mess hall."

Micah shook his head. "No, thanks. I'm not hungry."

Eli heaved a silent sigh, then stood. He'd reached the door when Micah's voice stopped him.

"Eli?"

He turned expectantly.

Micah opened his mouth, then closed it. He seemed to be struggling with what he wanted to say, a myriad of expressions flashing rapid-fire over his tortured face. Finally, he muttered, "You're a good friend."

Eli swallowed, gave him an up nod. "So are you, man." Then he slowly walked away.

He'd made it to the front of the barracks before he heard the gunshot. And he knew before he'd frantically retraced his steps back to the room

Oh, Jesus. He dropped to his knees and gathered up his friend. *Sightless eyes, so much blood, rosary still in his hand.* "Micah! Dammit to hell," Eli sobbed, rocking him back and forth, his voice broken. "Oh, Micah, what have you done? What have you done?"

1

Eight months later...

Captain Eli Weston glanced at the invitation again, grimaced then tossed it back into the passenger seat of his rented truck as the city limits sign loomed into view. His belly clenched with dread, and tension inexplicably tightened his fingers on the steering wheel.

He *so* didn't want to do this.

In fact, Eli could confidently say that if he could choose any place on earth he wanted to be right now, Willow Haven, Kentucky, would undoubtedly occupy the dead-last position on his list.

Not because it wasn't a perfectly lovely little town, the quintessential Southern burg with lots of antebellum homes, majestic oak trees and a festival for every food group. Not because he could think of a million other things he'd rather do on his much-needed, too-short leave. He'd seen enough war—enough of the ravages of it, more specifically. Not even because he'd be working on the memorial for his late, beloved friend, Micah Holland.

It was the damned *lying* he most dreaded.

He'd been doing it for the past eight months, insisting to every superior officer who'd interrogated him about Micah's death that his friend had been cleaning his weapon when it misfired, that he'd actually witnessed the accident.

Accident, of course, being the key word.

Lies, all lies. And they knew it, too. But they couldn't prove it, so his "eye-witness" account stood.

And it was because of that account that his friend's parents had been able to confidently bury their beloved oldest son in hallowed ground, believing his death was an unhappy circumstance, not a deliberate act by his own hand. Having lost his own father to suicide, Eli was well-acquainted with that particular brand of grief and had decided within seconds of Micah's death to spare the Hollands that aspect of the misery, to do everything he possibly could to preserve his friend's memory and military legacy. Micah had been one of his best friends and a damned fine soldier. He'd been like a brother. Eli swallowed, his throat suddenly tight, an inexplicable anger welling inside of him.

It was the least he could do, really.

Well, that and sling a hammer, he thought, glancing once more at the invitation in the passenger seat. Honestly, had Sally, Micah's mother, not called and pressed him into coming to help build the Micah Holland Memorial in the heart of the town square, Eli wouldn't have come. He'd have simply begged out of the event or made up an excuse as to why he wouldn't be available— being deployed, in that sense, had its advantages.

But when Sally had told him that they'd simply plan the event around his leave, *his* schedule, he knew he wasn't going to be able to get out of it. And considering how good the Hollands had been to him—they'd practically taken him in as one of their own as soon as he'd graduated—he could hardly refuse. Eli's own family tree had withered and died with the death of his father, so being brought into the Holland fold had filled a void he'd scarcely realized was there.

Sally was the quintessential Southern mom. Her love language was food and nothing made her happier than a full table and full bellies. There was always a cake on the covered stand, cookies of some sort in the jar and cold iced tea in the pitcher. His lips quirked. And the emergency casserole in the freezer, of course, should she need to quickly provide a meal, either for her family or for someone else's.

Carl Holland was a farmer with a degree in Agriculture from Auburn University—and had two Toomer's Oaks grown from seedlings standing in the front yard. He had a deep affection for things grown in the soil. He was wise and patient, slow to anger and quick to laugh. Big and burly, with skin darkened from years spent in the sun and hands that were callused and scarred, Sally called him her Gentle Giant, GG for short, a sweet term of endearment that never failed to make Eli smile. He did now, remembering, and the action felt strange, almost foreign.

Probably because there hadn't been much to smile about in recent months.

Truthfully, though he'd never considered a career outside the military, he had to admit he'd been growing increasingly dissatisfied since Micah's death. He couldn't seem to shake the sense that his feet weren't so much on the right path as *stuck* to one instead. Bound by the very rules and regulations he used to appreciate, relish even. Micah had often joked that while he'd never met a rule he didn't *break*, Eli had never met one he didn't *like*.

Too true, he knew.

But rules established order and the absence of order was chaos. And Eli *hated* chaos. That word virtually described every foster home he'd lived in after the death of his father and the mental decline of his mother. The sweet, smiling woman he remembered from his early childhood had disintegrated into a vacant-eyed stranger who had to be reminded to eat, to bathe, and had to be told that she even had a son who needed to do those things, as well.

"Fragile," they'd called her, when she'd been taken to the psych ward at their local hospital in Twisted Pines, Georgia.

"Irrevocably broken," he'd later realize.

He drummed his thumb against the steering wheel, biting the inside of his cheek as the familiar sense of regret trickled through him. He'd need to go and see her before he reported back to base, Eli thought with a stoic twinge of dread. Not that she'd know him, not that she'd care. But he would do it, anyway, because it was the right thing to do, because she was the only family he had.

Furthermore, though he often spoke to her doctors and care team at the assisted living facility she called home—the one he paid for—a personal visit would remind them all that he was more than just the person writing the check. He was her son and, though he barely knew her, he loved her all the same.

Not that he was suspicious of any kind of abuse. He wasn't. Having heard horror stories about mental hospitals and nursing homes, he'd researched dozens of potential facilities before settling on Marigold Manor. It offered the best in security and care, and smelled more like flowers than antiseptic. Which was a plus if you asked him. To this day the faintest whiff of bleach conjured up images of slumped over bodies too medicated to move, most particularly his mother's. It had been a nightmare. He'd been twelve at the time. Old enough to know that her treatment was horribly wrong, but not old enough to do anything about it. Powerless.

Awful.

That was no small part of the reason he'd entered the ROTC program. With both sets of grandparents dead before his own birth and no close family, he'd known that he'd need the funds and the security to take care of his mother.

And he had, since he was eighteen years old. Two jobs, sometimes three, during college, then beyond graduation active duty had done the rest.

Duty, Eli thought. Would he ever escape it? And if he could, would he really want to? He released a long breath and slowly entered the town square. Those were questions for another day. A humorless laugh bubbled up his throat.

Or never.

As expected, the little hub of Willow Haven was abuzz with activity. Shoppers strolled along the freshly swept sidewalks, peering into windows as the regular walkers smoothly weaved in and out around them. Lots of flowers he couldn't name bloomed from overstuffed planters and hanging baskets, and red, white and blue banners hung from various eaves, proclaiming the Micah Holland Memorial Dedication for the coming weekend. Another knot of dread landed in his belly and a pinch of pain constricted his chest as the image of his bloodied friend rose instantly in his mind.

It haunted him, that image.

And the slightest thing could bring it back. The sound of a gunshot, a whiff of Jack Daniel's, even a laugh similar to his friend's. It would catch him unaware, yank him unwillingly back into that wretched moment when he knew his friend was gone. At some point he was going to have to tell Gage the truth, Eli thought, wincing from the reminder. The third member of their "three amigos" crew, Gage Harper had been running a covert mission when Micah had died. Knowing that Micah had been struggling, Eli imagined Gage already suspected the truth but, out of respect or fearful of the answer, hadn't asked.

He'd tell him, of course. At some point. In the near future, in all probability. And, God, how he dreaded it.

He'd become too damned acquainted with dread, Eli thought. In fact, he was so accustomed to it at this point, he was beginning to wonder if he'd know how to function without it, without the disquieting tightening of his gut or the ever-present whisper of uneasiness along his spine.

A group of men, Carl among them, of course, were busy driving stakes into the ground and pulling string, marking off the dimensions for the gazebo. Eli had yet to see the plans, but had been told the design had been rendered by Micah's ex-fiancée, Shelby Monroe. He hadn't quite worked out how he felt about that—had never been able to work out how he felt about *her,* for that matter. Not that anything beyond passing friendliness was in order—he'd be damned before he'd poach on a friend's territory—but somehow the prickling of his skin, the inexplicable jump in his heart rate and the unwelcome stirring in his loins didn't strike the *strictly platonic* note.

It was odd, really, how well he knew her without really knowing her. He'd been able to read her from the get-go, had been able to discern the thoughts behind the furrowing of her sleek brow, the upward quirk of her ripe lips, the twinkling or dimming of her pale green gaze.

That especially sensitive perception had also allowed him to work out some other things, as well. Like the fact that Micah had been more heavily invested in her than she'd been in him. He wasn't judging. Even now, he wouldn't. It happened. Micah and Shelby had been high school sweethearts who'd let things cool during college, when they'd both dated other people. They'd reconnected after a bad breakup—hers—and had stuck it out for quite a while. But it had ended six months before Micah's death.

Despite being desperately in love with her, Micah had drunkenly admitted after she'd broken things off that he'd taken advantage of the situation. He'd offered her a shoulder to cry on, then pressed his advantage by proposing before she was ready. "Because she would have said no if I'd waited," he'd explained. "And I just wanted her for my own. She was my It Girl," he'd said, smiling sadly. "I met her and—" he'd shrugged fatalistically "—that was it."

Eli had a grim suspicion he knew what that felt like. Because despite the fact that he'd known that she was and forever would be off-limits, to his eternal shame and chagrin, Shelby had had a similar effect on him. For reasons which escaped him, he'd been judging every girl he'd met against her for the past six years. She'd become the reason he wanted to visit the Hollands and the reason he'd desperately needed to stay away.

It was bad business all the way around.

To complicate matters, he suspected that he was partially responsible for the split. The last time he'd come home with Micah had been for his parents' anniversary party. In honor of their 30th, Carl had rented the old Wickam plantation, then hired caterers, decorators and a band because he'd said he didn't want Sally having to deal with anything more stressful than the invitations. When she began agonizing over the guest list, Carl had taken matters into his own hands and put an announcement in the local paper, inviting the whole town. Eli grinned. Problem solved.

The wine and booze had flowed freely, the food had been plentiful and delicious, and the band hadn't miss a single note. Watching the couples dance, most particularly Carl and Sally, had had the most peculiar effect on him, Eli remembered now. Seeing the love between the two, the affection and familiarity, had made his chest ache and a bizarre sense of…emptiness had swelled in his belly. It had been an odd, mildly troubling sensation because it smacked of regret and loneliness, neither of which Eli had ever allowed himself to feel.

Regret was pointless and the benefit of the military was the constant company.

At any rate, Shelby had witnessed his momentary…weakness? Confusion? Hell, whatever it was, mortifyingly, she'd seen it from across the room and even now, he could still remember the slight arch of her blond brow, the question form in her too perceptive green eyes.

Eli had merely looked away, then proceeded to drink entirely too much. He'd danced with every single woman in attendance—and a few who weren't so single, he'd later been told—and had pretended that nothing had happened, that he was fine, that he wasn't envious of his friend or of his friend's family. He'd laughed, he'd joked, he'd flirted and most importantly, he'd avoided *her*.

Looking back, that was his biggest mistake. If he'd simply behaved normally, she wouldn't have known that she'd seen something he hadn't wanted her to see. There would have been room for doubt. But he hadn't. What he'd done, he'd later realize, for all intents and purposes, was wave a red flag in front of bull.

She'd waited until he'd stepped outside for some air, then made her move. He'd felt the air change, heat and charge. A wind kicked up, rattling the leaves on the hundred-year-old live oaks, bringing her scent closer. A mixture of fresh rain and gardenias. Summer, his favorite season.

"What's wrong with you, Eli?" she'd asked, straight to the point as always. Directness was typically a trait he admired, but that night, it had grated on his nerves. "You're not acting at all like yourself."

He'd chuckled humorously, then taken another pull from the drink in his hand. "You think you know me well enough to make that call?"

She did, damn her.

She paused, gave him one of those disconcerting considering gazes, then said, "I do, actually. Does that bother you?" she'd drawled. "That you're mysterious but not necessarily a mystery? Not to me, anyway."

His heart had begun to pound, but he'd managed an unconcerned shrug. "Why would it bother me? It's bullshit."

She'd chuckled knowingly. "Oh, I have struck a nerve, haven't I?" She'd moved closer, as though sharing a secret, then cast a meaningful glance back at the house. "They're sweet, aren't they? They adore one another, and are so obviously, achingly in love, even after all these years."

Something in the tone of her voice made him look at her and it literally hurt, because she was so lovely, because she was so close, because she belonged to someone else. The night breeze toyed with the ends of her hair, blowing a wisp across the sweet swell of her cheek. Long lashes curled away from her eyes, revealing a wistful gaze that tore at him. She'd hugged her arms around her middle and was staring through the window, watching Carl and Sally take another turn around the room. The pearls Carl had given her gleamed around Sally's neck.

"They are," Eli had agreed, then looked away because, though he loved them, it was painful to watch. "Just think," he'd said, an inexplicable edge entering his voice. "That'll be you and Micah someday. Although I have to wonder if the tableau is going to be quite the same."

He shouldn't have said it. To this day, he still didn't know why he said it.

From the corner of his eye, he'd watched her attention shift to him, could feel the weight of her gaze, the full benefit of her regard. "What's that supposed to mean?"

"Nothing," he'd said, trying to backpedal, wishing like hell he could draw the words back into his mouth.

"No, it's not nothing," she'd insisted. "What the hell do you mean by that? You think Micah and I don't have what it takes to make a thirty-year marriage work? Is that what you mean?"

"I don't mean anything," he said, ashamed of himself. "Just forget it. I'm sorry. I've had too much to drink." That, at least, was true, if not a good excuse.

"You didn't answer my question."

"And here's the upside of not being your fiancé—I don't have to." Tension humming along every nerve ending, he'd flashed a smile at her, then turned to walk away, but she'd grabbed his arm.

"Listen, Eli, I don't know what your problem is, but—"

She shouldn't have touched him, Eli thought now. If she hadn't touched him, he would have been able to hold it together, he wouldn't have reacted as instinctively or as impulsively as he had.

He'd whirled on her and backed her up against the tree, crowding into her personal space. He'd startled a gasp out of her, her eyes round with surprise…and something else, something he ached for but didn't want to see—a flicker of longing, one so intense it nearly sucked the air from his lungs. He'd seen glimpses of it before, of course, but never this strong. And certainly never this close.

"The problem isn't what you don't know," he'd said, his voice low and fierce. "It's what you *do* know. What we *both* know."

Her gaze had dropped to his lips, torturing him, then bounced back up and tangled with his. She'd swallowed carefully, lifted her chin even though he could see the rapid fluttering of her pulse beating in her neck, betraying her bravado. "Oh, and what's that?"

"Let's just say that the level of affection in a relationship has to be equally weighted in order for it to succeed. And from where I'm sitting, the scales seem woefully unbalanced."

She'd stared at him, a hint of sadness poisoning the truth in her pretty gaze. "And you're an expert on relationships, are you? To my knowledge you've never had a girlfriend, just a string of one-night stands." It was true, but he'd always avoided examining the reason behind the behavior. He grimly suspected he wouldn't like the answers he found.

"Tell me I'm wrong, then," he'd told her, lessening the distance between them even more. This was wrong—so wrong—but he couldn't help himself. He couldn't make his body retreat when she was this close, when the scent of her twined around his senses and the sound of her quickened breath made his own lungs labor to keep up. It took every particle of willpower he'd possessed to keep from kissing her, to keep from falling into the sweet heat of her body and losing himself completely to her.

"I wish that I could," she'd said, wincing with regret, her voice low and broken. A kaleidoscope of emotion moved in and out of focus in her light green gaze. "Life would be so much less complicated if I could. If I didn't want—"

He'd stilled, his senses sharpening. "Want what, Shelby?"

In answer, she'd looked hungrily at his mouth, released a shallow breath, then leaned forward and kissed him. Tentatively, at first, almost reverently, as though she'd been waiting a lifetime to taste him and didn't want to ruin it by hurrying.

Shock and sensation detonated through him, delaying his reaction. Her lips were unbelievably soft, ripe and pillowy, and the taste of lemon clung to them, remnants of an iced cookie he'd watched her eat earlier. A little sigh had slipped from her mouth into his and, for whatever reason, the relief he'd heard in that sound had enflamed him more than anything else ever had or ever would. It was bittersweet and rang with surrender. The next thing he knew, his hands were framing her face, deepening the kiss. Her arms had wound around his neck and the best sort of tension had hummed through her body, the kind that proved she'd wanted him as much as he'd wanted her.

He would have taken her right there, against the damned tree, against reason and honor and logic and loyalty…had Micah not chosen that exact moment to walk out onto the front porch and call her name.

"Shelby?"

They'd broken apart like a couple of school kids caught making out in a coatroom, then stared at one another for the briefest, most horrible instant when shame polluted the moment between them.

She'd left him, and returned to Micah's side, where she belonged. But even then he knew she wouldn't go through with the wedding. Not because of him, exactly—desire was fickle and fleeting—but because the minute she'd admitted the truth to him, she'd been left with no other choice than to act.

That's how truth worked.

And considering that he was here, perpetuating a lie to protect the memory of his friend, he supposed dishonesty used the same mode of operation.

With a sigh dredged from his soul, he pulled

into a parking space, grabbed his tool bag from the passenger floorboard and exited the truck. The sooner he got this over with, the better. Considering she hadn't even been able to look at him during Micah's service, he fully expected Shelby to keep her distance. That, at least, was a blessing. Because, while he could lie to his superior officers, lie to fellow soldiers, lie to the grief counselor, lie to Micah's parents and little brother and everyone else he was likely to come into contact with while he was here…he wasn't sure he could lie to her.

Because, like she'd said, she knew him too well.

2

"HE'S HERE," MAVIS Meriweather announced breathlessly from her position at the storefront window. "Merciful heavens, I'd recognize that especially fine ass anywhere," she said, humming appreciatively under her breath. "It's hot today. You think I should take him a bottle of water?"

Shelby Monroe ignored the kamikaze butterflies swarming in her belly at this news and glanced indulgently at her assistant. "He just got here, Mavis," she drawled. "He's hardly had time to work up a sweat."

The "he" in question was Eli Weston, of course. Just the thought of him conjured more feeling—most of it conflicted—in her rapidly beating heart than could possibly be good for her.

Nothing new there, damn him. She should have known...

Mavis pretended to swoon and braced a be-jeweled hand against the wall. "Sweat," she murmured, blinking slowly. She shook herself and sent Shelby a scolding look, her perfectly drawn on brows furrowed with chagrin. "You ought to know better than to say things like that when I'm in this condition."

"This condition" being hornier than a teenage boy with his first skin magazine. Mavis's hormone replacement therapy had gone horribly awry. Either she was especially sensitive to the medication or she was on the wrong dosage. Regardless of the reason, the drugs were having a hyper reaction in Shelby's older friend and, as such, had resurrected her flatlined libido with disturbing results. A former Vegas showgirl who'd dated A-list celebrities and famous politicians, Mavis had never married—had said she considered it an invasion of her privacy—and had always been a charismatic force of nature. But a desperate-to-get-laid Mavis had the makings of a natural disaster.

"Have you talked to Doc Anderson?"

Mavis turned away from the window and fanned herself. She'd recently gone from blond to red, a shade that suited her. "I have an appointment next week."

It wasn't soon enough if you asked Shelby, but she supposed it would have to do. "Maybe he can get you sorted out." One could hope, at any rate.

She harrumphed under her breath. "The only thing that's going to get me sorted out is an obliging man, preferably one with an especially large penis and more stamina than intelligence."

Startled, Shelby's needle missed the buttonhole and pricked her finger. She winced and inspected the damage, thankful when she didn't see blood. She'd hate to bleed on this fine piece of vintage chenille. She was putting the finishing touches on a custom romper for Lilly Wilken's little girl. It was excellent work, if she did say so herself.

And she did, because she was a first-rate seamstress. She'd learned at her grandmother's knee and had taken to the craft like a fish to water. While other little girls had been playing with dolls and Easy-Bake ovens, Shelby had been learning how to sew. She'd gotten her own machine at ten and had started making her own clothes shortly thereafter.

Never one to follow the trends, Shelby had been happier with her own designs than anything she could buy off the rack. She'd always had a firm sense of self, knew what looked best on her own body and could tailor-make anything that struck her fancy. Thankfully, it wasn't long until other girls were knocking on her door asking her to help them find their own personal style, as well. She'd gone to college on a partial home economics scholarship and was able to pay for the rest with the modest inheritance her grandmother had left her.

Armed with a business degree—with a minor in fashion merchandising—she'd returned to Willow Haven, bought the old dry goods store on the town square and converted it into her own shop, which she'd named *In Stitches*. The front room showcased her own custom designs, the back housed the working area, where she kept three full-time seamstresses employed, and she'd converted the upstairs space into an apartment, which was presently part of Mavis's employment package.

But whereas business might be good, her personal life was in the toilet.

Between Micah's death and the guilt she felt over breaking off their engagement—not to mention the guilt she carried over what had happened between her and Eli the night of Carl and Sally's anniversary party—and the threatening letters she'd been getting for months, the last damned thing in the world she needed to complicate things more was Eli Weston, here in the flesh. She swallowed, her throat suddenly tight.

He blamed her—or at least considered her a contributing factor—she knew. How could he not? After what had happened? Though the official line from the military had cited an accidental death, Shelby knew that hadn't been the case.

She knew…because Micah had written her prior to his death and told her so.

She hadn't received the letter until several days after Micah's passing, but even then she'd suspected. Though she'd broken their engagement six months before his death, they'd still kept in touch. Hell, they'd been friends since grade school. Just because the romantic relationship was over hadn't meant that she'd stopped caring about him, that she hadn't wanted the best for him. And he'd been struggling, she knew.

Eli, she imagined, had known it, too.

Shelby had been so consumed with grief and regret that she'd hadn't even been able to look at him during Micah's service. She'd been too afraid of what she'd see there. And she blamed herself enough as it was. Not specifically for Micah's death—the sole purpose of his letter was to keep her from blaming herself—but the pain she'd inflicted on him, the guilt of longing for Eli… She owned that and suspected she always would.

Eli, she imagined, would, as well, which made facing him all the more difficult.

But there would be no avoiding him here and, considering that she needed his help to try and figure out who was sending the letters, she'd better pull herself together.

She released a shaky breath, thankful that her

hands were steady even though her nerves were stretched thinner than a razor's edge.

Thankfully, Sally had insisted that Eli be a part of the building and dedication of the gazebo going up in the center of the town square. A tribute to Micah, their fallen hometown hero. Because she'd always been good with a pencil, Carl had asked her to draw up the design. He'd told her it would mean a lot to the family, to Micah. In light of the breakup, she wasn't certain it was completely appropriate, but Carl and Sally had been too good to her over the years for her to be anything other than helpful.

To show their appreciation to everyone who was participating with the construction, Micah's parents were hosting a dinner every evening until the project was complete and Shelby had been told her presence was expected. "Micah loved you," Sally had told her. "And we love you. It would mean so much to us for you to be there."

Rather than argue, Shelby had simply nodded. She had no intention of doing anything that was going to cause Micah's family any further distress. They'd been through hell. That playful light behind Carl's eyes had dimmed, Sally's smile had resurfaced a few weeks ago, but it never moved past her lips, and poor Colin—their "little surprise," Sally liked to say—at thirteen, was caught at that awkward age where he was too young to truly cope and too old to allow himself to cry. He'd grown sullen and remote, a shadow of the happy, energetic boy she'd known. It was so sad.

And she would never, ever reveal the truth. No matter how many letters she received.

Which was why she needed Eli's help. As Micah's best friend, he could snoop around with less suspicion than she could. Willow Haven was a small tight-knit community. It wasn't just likely that she knew the sender—it was a certainty. Any questions she asked on her own behalf were going to throw up a red flag and potentially allow the truth about Micah's death to become public. She couldn't let that happen. Any questions Eli asked, as Micah's best friend and a Willow Haven outsider, wouldn't be as conspicuous.

It was odd, really. The letters had started the week after Micah's funeral and she'd received one every week since. Each one just as cryptic as the last, the notes were always short and to the point.

I saw you. I know what you did. I'm going to tell.

It wasn't the gun that killed him, it was you. I'm going to tell.

How can you live with yourself, knowing what you did? I'm going to tell.

And the latest? The most disturbing?

You deserve to die. It should be you *in a coffin beneath that heavy dirt. I'm going to tell.*

It chilled her, this last letter. Possibly because it seemed so matter-of-fact, so stark. She'd never given much thought to dying or what exactly it meant to be buried. She'd never considered that the earth above a coffin would be heavy or how wretched that would make her feel. Just thinking about it had made her want to rush down to Rosewood Cemetery, where her parents and grandparents were buried, and claw the earth away from their coffins, then move them into an aboveground crypt, much like the ones she'd seen in New Orleans. Irrational? Costly? Yes, but she couldn't seem to shake the idea.

Any more than she could shake the memory of Eli's kiss—the blazing desperation and desire in his pale hazel gaze—from her mind. It stuck there. Haunted her. Mocked her. Shamed her.

Enflamed her.

She should have never followed him outside that night, Shelby had told herself a million times. She'd known if she danced too close to the fire she was going to get burned. And the kicker? The horrible truth? If she had to do over again, she'd probably do the same damned thing. Because getting burned was better than being numb.

And she'd never realized she was numb until Eli touched her.

Had there been a spark of something prior to that? Yes, God help her, as unwelcome as it was undeniable. Shelby had tried pretending that it didn't exist, then chalked it up to Eli's mysteriousness, that intense direct stare that occasionally left her feeling as if he'd opened her head and taken a peek inside. She'd tried avoiding him, not avoiding him, looking for faults…everything. Nothing had nudged that niggle of awareness, that lingering longing that stirred in her gut.

That's why she'd ultimately broken it off with Micah. Because until Eli had kissed her, she'd been able to pretend that her affection and long history with Micah were stronger than something as small and insubstantial as the idea of someone else, of Eli. Because until he'd kissed her, that's all it had been—an idea.

She'd so been wrong. Wrong for ever allowing things with Micah to rekindle, then progress to a proposal. He'd been safe and familiar, and she'd been vulnerable and lonely. He'd picked her up, dusted her off and loved her, as always.

She'd desperately wanted to love him back. And she did, to a point. But never as much as he cared for her. Never with the same sort of intensity. He'd known it, too. Freely admitted it. But he'd never cared, so long as they were together.

She tied off the final stitch, then reached for her scissors and trimmed the thread. It was hard to reconcile a world he was no longer a part of, to know that she'd never see his smile or hear his laugh again. That had been the best thing about Micah, Shelby thought, a pang tightening her chest. His laugh. It had been joyful and uninhibited, infectious. She missed it most of all.

"You look odd, Shelby," Mavis remarked. "Are you all right?"

Shelby blinked and gave herself a little shake. Despite being extremely self-absorbed, Mavis could be disturbingly observant. "Yes, of course."

"Well, aren't you going to walk over there and say hello? He was Micah's best friend, after all, and he's using his leave to volunteer. I think it would be rude and inhospitable for you to ignore him." She shot Shelby a pointed look. "Like you did at the service."

Shelby stored her tools, then carefully folded the romper. She felt a blush creep up her neck. "I was understandably preoccupied," she lied. "And so was he."

"Maybe so, but he kept glancing at you and you never once looked his way. Say what you will, but I know that your actions were deliberate. It would have been less noticeable had you simply acknowledged him." She frowned. "I've never known you to be so unkind. It was so unlike you. I can only conclude that I'm not in possession of all of the facts and that you had your reasons." She paused. "However wrong they may have been."

Subtle as always, Shelby thought. But Mavis

was right. He was hurting, too, and she'd been a coward. As nerve-wrecking as it would be, this was her chance to make it right. Besides, she needed him.

Shelby stood, set the romper aside and smoothed the wrinkles out of her dress. "If you'll cover the store, I'll walk over there right now."

Mavis beamed approvingly at her. "Of course I will."

Shelby glanced at her pet and store mascot, then clicked her tongue. "Come on, Dixie," she said, then watched her eighty-pound pot-bellied pig lumber up from her hot-pink satin-covered bed in the corner. She bent down and clipped the leash to her rhinestone collar, then straightened her custom-made tulle skirt and matching bow.

Mavis merely rolled her eyes. "I swear she's gained more weight just since yesterday. How much bigger is she going to get?"

"It doesn't matter," Shelby told her. "That skirt's got an elastic waist."

"That's not what I meant and you know it. She's *huge,* Shelby. If she gets any bigger, she's going to need her own zip code."

Shelby smiled and scratched the top of Dixie's head. "Nonsense. "

When she'd moved out of the upstairs apartment and bought the house a block from the square so that she could have more room and a yard, Shelby hadn't counted on being lonely. She'd loved the idea of having more room, of having a little garden to tend, flowers to grow. But she'd barely been in the house a week before she'd decided that a pet— which she'd never had, because her grandmother had been allergic—was in order. A puppy, more specifically. Rather than buy a designer breed, she'd opted to go to the animal shelter.

She'd walked in knowing exactly what she'd wanted—a soft, cuddly, energetic puppy which would grow into a loyal companion. To everyone's surprise—most especially her own—she'd walked out with Dixie.

The little pig had been abandoned outside the shelter months ago, when the owners had evidently realized that she wasn't going to stay tiny and cute. It was a common misconception, which had resulted in thousands of the little animals being dumped in shelters all across the country. Knowing that the various dogs and cats would eventually be adopted, and that Dixie's chances were extremely less likely, Shelby gave in. The thought of leaving her there, trapped in that five-by-five box, was simply more than she could bear.

There'd been a learning curve with the pig— try finding *that* kind of food on the pet aisle at the Piggly Wiggly—but with the help of her vet and the internet, Shelby had adjusted…and couldn't be happier. Dixie had personality in spades. She was leash and litter trained, and extremely smart. Shelby grimaced. So smart, in fact, that she'd learned to open the fridge, which was why it was now locked tight with bungee cords. Hardly a permanent solution, but she could only tackle one thing at a time.

And right now, she had to deal with the return of Eli Weston.

Shelby opened the door and allowed Dixie to lead her out onto the sidewalk. The late-morning air was sweet with the scent of sugar coming from Lola's Bakery next door, making her mouth water. The phrase "blessing and a curse" sprung immediately to mind. If she didn't lay off the donut holes, she was going to have to start putting additional elastic into her skirts, as well, Shelby thought, making a mental note to eat a bowl of oatmeal before leaving for work in the morning. There. She already felt thinner.

Careful to use the crosswalk, she made her way across the street onto the green in the middle of the square, Dixie trotting along happily beside her on her short stumpy legs.

"Morning, Shelby," Walter Perkins said, tipping his hat at her, a smile on his lined face.

"Morning, Walter."

Dixie rooted at the ground, but Shelby jingled her leash, distracting her from whatever had caught her fancy. The pig knew better, but that didn't stop her from trying. There was only one area that Dixie was allowed to dig and burrow in and that was in the fenced-in area in the backyard. It was her own personal mud hole, complete with a kiddie pool filled with water for cooling off.

In the process of mixing concrete, Hank Malloy stopped and looked up at her, a grin leaping to his lips. "I swear, Shelby, every time I see you with that hog I start craving barbeque."

Used to the jokes, Shelby smiled. "She's a pet, Hank, not a pulled pork sandwich."

Hank's comment had attracted the attention of the rest of the group, but it was Eli's gaze she felt the most. A skitter of heat tripped along her spine and a sizzle of awareness made the backs of her thighs tingle. Her mouth went dry and her stomach decided this would be the perfect time to launch a career in gymnastics. It did a few backflips and somersaults, making her momentarily queasy.

"Shelby," Carl called, waving her over, a big smile wreathing his tanned face. "Look who's here," he said, happily clapping Eli on the back.

Left with no other choice, she mentally braced herself and looked at him then. Her lungs seized and rush of warmth spread through her body, concentrating in her palms and the arches of her feet. Every hair on her head lifted, then settled, making gooseflesh race down her arms despite the heat, and her insides vibrated so hard it was nothing short of miraculous that her teeth didn't chatter.

Sweet mercy...

His gaze was familiar—a glorious mixture of bright greens and pale browns—but heart-breakingly guarded and undeniably sad. Day-old golden stubble clung to his face, emphasizing the hollows beneath his high cheekbones, shading the stark line of his jaw. Dressed in work boots, worn jeans and a navy blue t-shirt that showcased the best pair of shoulders ever, he'd apparently arrived ready to work.

His lips—quite possibly the sexiest mouth she'd ever seen—tilted into something just short of a smile. "Shelby," he said, his voice the same rough-ened baritone she remembered. "It's good to see you." His gaze dropped to Dixie and a disbeliev-ing frown appeared on his face. "And your...pig."

"That's right," Carl said, chuckling softly at his reaction. "You haven't met Dixie yet, have you?"

He shook his head, then winced and rubbed the back of his neck. "No, I can't say that I have."

That's because she'd gotten her pet after Micah died, but rather than use that horrible frame of reference, she quickly changed the subject. "So you've just gotten in?"

He nodded. "Just a few minutes ago."

"Have you had a chance to look at the plans?"

"Not yet," he told her. "Carl was just about to

show them to me." His gaze tangled with hers. "You drew them?"

She shot a glance at Carl, who'd stepped away to speak with another volunteer. "Carl insisted."

He followed her gaze, seemingly reluctant to look at her, and winced sympathetically. "He's good at that," he murmured.

"It was good of you to come," she told him, awkwardly tucking a strand of hair behind her ear. "They appreciate it."

His gaze found hers once more, lingering for the briefest of seconds. "I know they do." He jerked his head toward the activity. "I'd better get back to it."

Equally startled and stung that he had so little to say to her—not that she didn't deserve it, she knew—Shelby reached out a hand, but stopped just shy of touching him. "Eli—"

He hesitated, his shoulders tight with tension, then turned and arched a dark golden brow.

"Could we catch up at dinner?" she asked. "There's something I'd like to talk to you about."

A shadow passed behind his gaze so quickly that she couldn't read it and, though his expression never changed, she could tell that he was reluctant to continue their conversation. "Sure," he said. "I'll see you at Sally's."

And he might, Shelby thought, but getting him to talk to her was a different matter altogether. A lump swelled in her throat and the little kernel of hope she'd clung to withered and died.

She'd been right. He did blame her for Micah's death.

3

WELL, THAT SURE AS HELL could have gone better, Eli thought, watching Shelby and her *pig,* of all damned things, walk back toward her shop. So much for thinking he was ready to face her again, that he could look at her and not want her with every damned fiber of his being.

His best friend's "It Girl."

Talk about breaking a rule. He mentally snorted. Somehow he didn't think that was the kind of rule Micah had been referring to.

"Only Shelby," Carl remarked, following Eli's gaze. He shook his head. "Everybody else looks at that pig and sees a pork roast. She looks at it and sees a pet."

Eli felt his lips twitch. "I have to admit it's the best dressed pig I've ever seen," he conceded. Actually, it was the *only* dressed pig he'd ever seen outside a story book—the *Three Little Pigs* had been one of his favorites as a child—but it was the truth all the same. And it wasn't enough that she had to dress the pig—she had to make sure their outfits were color-coordinated, as well. The yellow skirt and matching bow on Dixie's head perfectly matched the flowers on Shelby's dress.

And naturally, because she'd made it herself, that dress showcased the very best her body had to offer. Beautiful lush breasts, a tiny waist—one that he could easily span with both hands, an unbelievable turn-on—and especially generous hips. She in no way resembled the starved praying mantislike figures that were so popular on the covers of today's fashion magazines. She was toned but curvy, her shape reminiscent of a 1950's pin-up model. Completely, utterly feminine.

But more than how she looked, it was the way she moved that never failed to captivate him. There was something so innately graceful about the way her body went about the everyday ordinary things. The tilt of her chin as she listened to someone, the easy slide of her ripe lips into a smile, the rhythmic swing of her hips as she walked. The fabric hung like air in that sweet spot high enough on her thighs to be sexy, but not so low to be inappropriate and it fluttered with an exaggerated little pop with every step that she took.

Mesmerizing.

And a quick glance around the square con-cluded that he wasn't the only man who'd noticed. Irrationally, that made him want to roar and break things, preferably a few jaws. It was ridiculous the way she affected him, the way he'd wanted to feast his gaze on her, catalogue every little detail about her face the instant he'd seen her again. Every mole and freckle, every dip and hollow, every eyelash around those amazing green eyes. Eyes that were so clear a green they put him in mind of a piece of stained glass he'd one seen in a store window. And the hesitancy and vulnerability he saw lurking in that remarkable gaze? Awful…especially knowing there was nothing he could do to remove it. Much as it pained him, he had to stay away from her.

He'd failed Micah by not getting him the help he needed sooner—he could not fail him in this, too.

Shelby Monroe, no matter how tempting, was off-limits.

He felt Carl's gaze—one that was shrewd as well as kind—and gave himself a little shake. "You were going to show me those plans?"

"Are you sure you want to get started?" he asked. "I figured you'd want to go to the cabin and get settled in."

Rather than impose and stay at the house—where the only available room had been Micah's—Carl and Sally had offered to put him up at the family cabin out on Holly Lake, for which he was eternally thankful. Aside from not wanting to disturb the shrine that had no doubt become Micah's room, he and Micah had always stayed at the cabin together when he'd come in for a visit. A lot of laughter and beer had passed their lips out on that front porch overlooking the water. While it was going to be odd to be there without Micah, he knew he'd be much more comfortable there…and so would Sally and Carl.

Eli shook his head. "No, sir. I came ready to work. I'll go out there when we finish up for the day. It'll give me a chance to settle in and shower before coming back for dinner."

"If you're sure," Carl said, a question in his voice.

"I'm sure."

The older man nodded. "All right, then. Let's take a look at the plans." They walked over to what Eli imagined was command center, where a tent, a couple of tables and a few chairs had been set up. Coolers of cold drinks and various platters of snacks—Sally's work, he knew—sat on one, and a printout of the drawing as well as what looked like the volunteer schedule lay on the other.

A thought struck. "Where's Colin?" Eli asked. He'd expected Micah's little brother to be on-site throughout the entire project. Despite the differences in their ages, the two Holland boys had been exceptionally close and Colin, he knew, had hero-worshiped Micah.

Carl hesitated. "Probably off with some of his friends," he said. "I thought he'd want to help out with this, but he didn't have a lot to say when I asked him to come down here with me this morning. Said he'd already made plans."

Eli frowned, mildly surprised. "How's he holding up?"

"Not good," Carl confessed, lowering his voice. "In fact, I was hoping that maybe you could talk to him. He's always looked up to you, kind of sees you as an extension of his brother."

Eli didn't know about that, but now that he thought about it, he was surprised that Colin hadn't been around this morning, if for no other reason than to see him. They'd always gotten along well and had a good rapport. Eli had no illusions of taking Micah's place, but he'd kept in touch with Colin since Micah's death, hoping to build a better relationship with the boy. He'd made that promise to Micah years ago, long before the disaster in Mosul. In return, Micah had promised to oversee the care of his mother should anything happen to him.

"I'll certainly try," Eli told him.

Carl nodded, relief relaxing the tension around his eyes. "Thanks, Eli. We'd really appreciate it."

That settled, Eli bent forward and inspected the design.

It was not at all what he'd expected.

"Wow," he murmured, stunned.

"It's something, isn't it?" Carl asked, seemingly equally proud and pleased. "That's why I asked Shelby to put it together. Most everyone knows she can sew like nobody's business, but not many people realize that, had she not followed in her grandmother's footsteps, she would have pursued a career in architecture."

He whistled low and continued to marvel at the design. "I'm not so sure she didn't miss her calling." He looked up at Carl. "This is amazing."

Carl beamed, his eyes crinkling at the corners. "Not your typical town square gazebo, that's for sure."

No, it certainly wasn't. Rather than the quaint white shape with lots of fancy fretwork and gingerbread trim, Shelby's design more resembled something from one of Tolkien's novels, but more modern. Shaped like an octagon with a steep-pitched shingled roof complete with a weather vane, the plan called for natural material left in its raw shape.

Taking inspiration from the town's namesake, Shelby had incorporated lots of corkscrew willow branches in place of spindles, giving it a fanciful flair. Old gas lamps inside and out would provide ample lighting, and a fire pit, surrounded by a fountain, would take center stage. A row of wooden benches lined the inside walls, giving plenty of seating and recessed, glassless windows added additional character.

"We're going with a concrete floor, so it'll be easier to clean and maintain," Carl told him. "But we're going to stain it and stamp it with willow leaves so it'll look more like a forest floor."

Eli merely shook his head, almost at a loss for words. "It's incredible."

"Micah would have loved it," Carl remarked, a palpable ache in his voice. "And that's what counts."

Yes, he would have, Eli thought. Micah had always said he'd wanted to build a bigger version of the cabin, had planned on logging the lumber himself. Shelby no doubt knew that, too, and had managed to create something that would honor her former fiancé, but capture the spirit of the town, as well. It was a delicate equation to balance, but she'd managed it beautifully.

His gaze strayed to her shop across the street. Though the windows were crowded with well-dressed mannequins featuring her designs, he caught a glimpse of her behind the counter and felt a bolt of warmth land in his chest and spread through the rest of his body, most particularly his groin. Awareness slid down the length of his dick, making him shift to find a more comfortable position. He gritted his teeth as need bombarded him, that of the relentless variety, the kind that he imagined ruined kings and started wars.

He was about to mount the biggest battle of his career, Eli thought…and God help him, it was with himself.

SHELBY WAS JUST ABOUT to lock up and close the shop when the bell above the door tingled, heralding the arrival of another customer. Though she typically didn't mind staying late—and had been known to meet clients down at the store after hours in order to help out in a fashion emergency or to accommodate a schedule—today wasn't one of those days.

She was emotionally wrung dry after her reunion with Eli this morning. She'd also had a steady stream of clients in and out all day, and she had just enough time, if she left now, to go home and freshen up before heading over to the Hollands' place. As a result, she was not happy when she looked up and even less pleased when she saw who was standing there.

Katrina Nolan.

Micah had briefly dated Katrina during college, before he and Shelby had reconnected, and Katrina, who'd never been one of Shelby's biggest fans, positively hated her now. She'd never set foot in Shelby's shop, never spoke to her and had glared white-hot daggers at her during Micah's service. Sally had told her that Katrina had tried to rekindle things with Micah when their engagement ended, but that Micah hadn't been interested. Shelby hadn't been the least bit surprised—that Katrina had made the effort, or that Micah hadn't been interested.

Katrina had recently gone to work for the local paper and fancied herself some sort of small-town Lois Lane. She was constantly digging around in people's trash, had supposedly paid spies to troll the beauty parlor and post office for juicy gossip, and just generally made everyone uncomfortable. It was widely suspected that the only person Katrina had any real dirt on was the editor of *The Branches,* Les Hastings, because any other paper would have fired her by now. Shelby didn't have any idea why the woman was here, but knew that it wasn't to plan a sleepover.

This wasn't going to be good. A skitter of foreboding tingled down her spine.

Shelby didn't ask if she could help her because she didn't want to. She lifted a cool brow. "Yes?"

"I didn't catch you at a bad time, did I?" Katrina asked, completely unrepentant.

"Actually, you did. I'm closing in—" she glanced pointedly at the clock above the door "—two minutes."

Katrina's lips slid into a hard smile. "Not to worry," she said. "What I have to say won't take that long."

Shelby returned the same insincere grin, the kind that Southern girls learned to perfect from the cradle. "Wonderful. Because I've got to get over to Sally and Carl's for dinner and it would be rude to be late."

The dig landed, making Katrina's mouth harden. While the whole town might be invited to the dedication of the memorial, only the people Carl had picked to help build and design it were invited to their home. Willow Haven was a small town, so there were very few people *not* on that list…but Katrina was one of them. Mean? Petty? Yes.

But very satisfying all the same.

"Yes, I wouldn't want to keep you. Funny how that's worked out," Katrina mused, strolling forward. She stopped and picked up a sundress—one of Shelby's favorites—then grimaced as though she'd smelled something bad and returned it to the stand. "Even when you aren't part of the family—and never intended to be—you still manage to have a seat at that table." She looked up, her gaze almost triumphant, knowing. "I wonder if you'll still have that spot when they find out that Micah's gun didn't misfire, that he killed himself because of you."

A cold sweat broke out over the back of Shelby's neck and her throat went instantly dry. She'd wondered if it had been Katrina sending the letters, but it had seemed out of character. Katrina, as evidenced, wasn't sneaky. She was direct. She liked to play with her victims before pouncing.

"That's not true," Shelby told her. "And if you spread that malicious gossip or attempt to print it—if you hurt the Hollands…" she said, her voice cracking with anger. "I'll—"

A bark of laughter erupted from Katrina's throat. "You'll what?" she taunted. "Sew my mouth closed? Save the righteous indignation. I'm not going to ruin my own reputation just to destroy yours—that'll just be a bonus—but make no mistake, I've got a reliable source who was in Mosul when Micah died. Nobody there believes his gun misfired, no matter what the official report says."

So the military hadn't been able to prove otherwise, but *she* thought she could? Of course she did. Arrogant, bitter bitch.

Another smug smile turned Katrina's lips. "As it happens, the one and only witness to Micah's death arrived today and will be here for the whole week. I'm especially looking forward to spending some time with him over the next few days, picking his brain," she added coyly, as though "picking his brain" was a euphemism for screwing him senseless. "Surely I won't be stepping on your toes, will

I, Shelby? Since he was Micah's best friend and all? Or have you staked your claim there, as well?"

She was fishing, Shelby knew, needling her, looking for a reaction. But it didn't keep her blood pressure from racing toward stroke level or her anger fully in check. The idea of this mean-spirited opportunistic tramp flirting with Eli for any reason made a red haze settle over her head and the desire to pull all of her hair out from the roots suddenly hit her.

But she would not give Katrina the satisfaction. She would not betray an inkling of unease, a hint of disquiet. Shelby summoned her best you-poor-deluded-fool smile, then walked over and deliberately opened the door. "Eli's a friend," she said, glad that her voice was level. "Now get out."

Left with no choice but to leave, Katrina aimed another infuriating little grin at her and made her exit. Shelby turned the lock behind her, flipped the signed to "Closed" then sagged against the door. She sighed, feeling a little sick.

Well, that certainly wasn't a complication she'd foreseen. And it was all the more reason she needed to talk to Eli...especially before Katrina could.

The Rancher's...

4

"YOU'RE SKIN AND BONES," Sally admonished, piling another giant helping of mashed potatoes on Eli's already full plate. She tsked under her breath. "You eat up, now. There's plenty more where that came from."

Carl leaned over, a grin tilting his lips. "She's convinced that you've lost weight since we last saw you and is determined that you find it again while you're here. Get ready," he warned him. "She's going to help you carbo load. She's already planned the menu."

Startled but touched, Eli watched Sally make the rounds, adding more food to everyone's plate. She was a pretty woman with short silver hair and kind blue eyes, an open face and a lovely smile. She'd been a knockout in her day, as evidenced by the wedding photo on the mantel, and Eli could easily see why Carl had been so drawn to her.

"I appreciate it, Carl, but I haven't lost any weight."

"I didn't think so, either," he said, taking a sip of tea. "But don't tell her that. I'm looking forward to those banana pancakes in the morning."

Eli chuckled and inclined his head. "Duly noted."

"If you're handing out more potatoes, don't forget me, Sally!" Hal Jones boomed from the opposite end of the table, making those unfortunate enough to be seated near him shy away and wince, most notably Shelby, who nearly dropped her fork. Hal was one of those regrettable people who desperately needed a hearing aid, but refused to get one and his favorite word was "Huh?" Conversation with him was painful, but he was an ace carpenter and one of Carl's oldest friends.

Determined to keep from staring at Shelby— who'd traded her yellow printed dress for a lavender one with pretty cream-colored lace accents—he cast a glance around the rest of the massive table, taking in the contented scene. Because the Hollands enjoyed entertaining, Carl had made the long dining room table himself. Made of hickory he'd personally milled, the beautiful but functional piece easily sat twenty-two. It was the biggest dining room table Eli had ever seen and he'd never visited the Hollands when it hadn't been full.

Old blue Mason jars filled with wild flowers dotted the center, along with several butter dishes, bread baskets, gravy boats and salt and pepper shakers. The bulk of the food resided on a huge built-in sideboard, which also housed Sally's good china. She'd been collecting it since she got married, Micah had told him once, and it was tradition to get her a new piece each year for her birthday. "The only thing Mom likes better than new cookware is new dishes." He'd need to make a note of the pattern and Sally's birthday so that he could continue the tradition for Micah, Eli thought absently.

As though he'd spoken the name aloud, he felt Shelby's gaze on him once again. He knew that she wanted to talk to him and, while he was curious and desperate to just hear the sound of her voice, Eli had decided that anything more than passing conversation just wasn't going to happen. He was here at the request of Micah's parents, to honor the life and memory of his friend. Lusting after her in private was bad enough—doing it out in the open, when he was already struggling to hold it together—was out of the question.

He simply—sadly, irritatingly—didn't trust himself.

Take now, for instance. Though they'd only

shared a brief "hello" and a "pass the salt, please," Eli could tell that she was anxious about something. Probably the conversation she thought they were going to have. Her smile, while genuine, was strained and there was a tightness around her eyes that seemed more pronounced than earlier. He didn't know what had happened since he'd first seen her this morning, but whatever it was had rattled her. Hard. Every instinct he possessed screamed at him to comfort her, to offer some sort of support…but he couldn't.

He didn't dare.

Because those selfsame instincts also made him want to press his lips against her gorgeous mouth, then lift the flirty hem of her dress and fill his hands with her lush rump. The need to take her—every single part of her—and make her his was somehow more potent, more intense than it had ever been before. It slithered through him and tightened every muscle, infected every cell, hammered away at him until he could practically feel every blow against the weakening will of his resistance.

"You're in his seat," Colin said.

Eli turned, his gaze meeting the younger Holland's. Other than a mumbled greeting, the boy hadn't made any effort to speak to him. Eli wasn't certain what exactly he'd expected, but this definitely wasn't it. Other than Carl, who'd gone still and turned to look at his son, thankfully no one else had heard the oddly toneless remark.

Mildly taken aback, Eli set his fork aside. "Your mom asked me to sit here, Colin, but I'd be happy to move if it bothers you."

"I didn't say it bothered me," the boy replied, lifting his chin, though Eli definitely got the sense that the remark was untrue. "It's just weird. I'm used to looking across the table and seeing my brother. And you're not him." *And never will be* hung unsaid in the air between them.

Ah, Eli thought. So that was the problem. Colin had clearly mistaken Eli's concern and regard for Micah's family as a ploy to try and replace him. And given that the Hollands wouldn't build the memorial without him and had treated him like the proverbial prodigal son since he'd arrived today, Eli could see where the boy might get the wrong impression.

"You're right about that," Eli said, grimacing ruefully. "Micah was much better looking."

The lighthearted comment evidently struck the right note, because Colin's lips twitched and a flash of humor lit his haunted gaze. He looked so much like his older brother, Eli thought. Dark brown hair and eyes, the same longish nose. Colin hadn't quite grown into his yet—his face still held the roundness of youth—but he would and he'd be every bit the ladykiller his brother had been.

Carl darted him a grateful look, seemingly relieved that the tension had eased.

"What time are we going to get started tomorrow?" Eli asked.

"Breakfast is at six and we'll start at seven. I know that's early, but we need to take advantage of the good weather while we've got it. There's some rain moving in later in the week and I want to pull the wire, plumb the fountain and lay the lines before then."

Eli glanced at Colin. "You gonna make it tomorrow? We could use an extra pair of hands. And better music," he added under his breath.

Carl grinned. "What, Eli? Not a fan of big band tunes?"

Eli smiled, hesitating. "In small measure," he said. "But more than an hour becomes psychological torture." Jeremiah Winston, the oldest of the crew, had brought his antiquated boom box and collection of old cassette tapes and liked to play it *loud*.

It had been hell.

Colin hesitated, but gave him an up nod. "I can come out for a while. I'll put a playlist together."

Pleased that they seemed to be making some sort of progress, Eli forked up another bite of mashed potatoes. "What do you think of the design?"

"Don't know yet. I haven't looked at it." He

stood and pushed his chair away from the table. "See you in the morning."

"Colin, where are you going?" Sally called in dismay. "What about dessert? I've got blackberry cobbler and homemade ice cream."

"I don't want any," he said without turning around, then left and mounted the stairs, presumably to his room.

Eli glanced at Carl, concerned, and arched a questioning brow.

"Believe me," the older man said, his expression grim. "This was progress."

If that was the case, then clearly Colin was having a much harder time of it than he'd thought. Another unwelcome flash of resentment sparked, making his fists tighten, but he tamped it down, fought it back. Micah hadn't been in his right mind when he'd made the decision to end his life—logically, Eli knew that—but he still couldn't help the increasingly frequent bursts of anger at his friend for the mess he'd left behind. The people who'd been so hurt by his death. Irrational, he knew, but there it was.

And here he was, perpetuating the lie, protecting his adopted family—his gaze slid to Shelby—and burning for her.

Thank God Carl and Sally had filled the fridge and the cabin with plenty of alcohol, Eli thought. He was damned sure going to need it.

Eli leaned forward, caught Carl's eye. "I'm going to skip the dessert and head on out," he said with a small wince, his voice low. "Can you make my excuses to your lovely wife, please?"

Carl merely grinned. "Don't want her shouting at you from across the room, do you?"

Eli bit the inside of his cheek. "Not particularly, no."

His grin widened and he nodded once. "I understand. You slip on out and I'll see you in the morning."

Eli slid away from the table, preparing to make his silent exit, when Carl's expression grew more serious, making him pause.

"It means a lot, you being here," the older man said, his gaze warm and sincere.

Eli's throat tightened. "Wouldn't have missed it."

And in that moment, he realized it was the truth.

HE'D LEFT.

She didn't know whether she was more shocked, hurt or angry. Her fingers cramped around her fork from squeezing it so hard and her jaw suddenly ached, a result of her tightly clenched teeth.

Correction, Shelby thought, her eyes narrowing dangerously—she did know which emotion had taken top billing. She wasn't merely angry...she was furious. Granted she hadn't behaved as well as she could have at Micah's service, but she'd offered an olive branch this morning. If for no other reason than their shared friendship—which definitely strained the definition of the word, she knew—he still shouldn't have sneaked away as if she was some pesky ex-girlfriend who wouldn't leave him alone.

How galling.

Shelby had kept an eye aimed at the dining room entrance in the event that Eli had merely gone to the restroom, but when ten minutes passed and he didn't rejoin the group she'd realized with a sickening sense of disappointment that he'd left.

Without saying goodbye, without speaking to her, when she'd specifically told him that she needed to talk to him.

Especially now, she thought, remembering the unpleasant visit from Katrina. If she got to him first…

Growing angrier by the second, Shelby made a valiant effort to remain pleasant. She smiled through the dessert round, through Carl's heart-felt tear-jerking thank-you speech, then insisted on helping Sally with the cleanup. Every fiber of her being longed to bolt, to get into her car, drive out to the cabin—where she knew Eli was staying—and then ask him what the hell his problem was.

With her, specifically.

If he wanted to freeze her out and have nothing else to do with her, fine. But he ought to have the damned balls to give her an explanation to her face. The length and nature of their…friendship? Relationship? Hell, she didn't know. It defied labeling. Whatever it was demanded that much, at least.

She fully intended to do that, too, just as soon as she'd helped Sally get the kitchen and dining room back in order. She'd tried to shoo her away, of course, but Shelby wouldn't have it. She knew the older woman was tired—cooking en masse was hard work—and that she'd be feeding the same hungry crew first thing in the morning. Shelby simply couldn't leave her with this mess.

"Eli seems very reserved, doesn't he?" Sally mused, rinsing a plate to load into the dishwasher. A furrow of concern wrinkled her brow. "He barely smiled tonight. Did you notice?"

She had, but made a noncommittal sound as she continued to sort leftovers. Sally lived by the more-is-more philosophy when it came to food, and made certain that she never ran out of anything. Thankfully, she had the Tupperware collection to back it up. "I'm sure he was just tired," she said. "It was a long drive from Georgia and he put in a full day's work."

Sally hummed under her breath. "True," she said. "But I think it's more than that. He seemed tense and ill-at-ease. I hope that he doesn't doubt his welcome," she went on. "That he doesn't think that because we've lost Micah he's no longer a part of the family." She turned then and shot her a warm smile. "And that goes for you, too, young lady," she told her, her eyes twinkling with affection. "Micah brought the two of you into our lives and we love both of you. He's gone—" her voice cracked "—but you and Eli aren't, and the truth of it is…we need you." Her misty, emphatic gaze held Shelby's. "Never doubt it."

Feeling a lump lodge in her throat, Shelby nodded. She'd needed to hear that and was so thankful that Carl and Sally had still held her in fond regard after the breakup. While Sally had admitted that she'd been initially disappointed, she'd later confessed that she was happy Shelby had called things off instead of proceeding out of some misguided sense of obligation. It was easier to end an engagement than a marriage. An ounce of prevention was worth a pound of cure and all that.

Funnily enough, that's something that her grandmother used to always say and hearing the old adage from Sally had made her miss her gran more than ever. It also compounded the realization that she'd really come to depend on the Hollands as part of her adopted family since her grandmother's passing.

Having lost her parents at two years old to a car accident—an exhausted truck driver fell asleep behind the wheel and veered into their lane—she'd grown up with her widowed paternal grandmother.

Louisa Hillenburg Monroe had been a remarkable woman. A seamstress by trade, she'd been servicing Willow Haven and the surrounding areas since her early twenties. She'd been a founding member of the local community theatre and worked the *New York Times* crossword puzzle in ink. She was smart and fearless, interesting and forward-thinking. The same hands that could so skillfully create a length of lace finer than a butterfly's wing could just as easily shoot a clothespin from the line at a hundred yards. A faint smile turned her lips, remembering.

She'd been amazing, her grandmother, and there wasn't a day that went by when she didn't miss her, didn't think about her. She'd died during Christmas break Shelby's sophomore year. At her beloved sewing machine, of course. Heart attack. Shelby still struggled with that. Gran had been the picture of health. Fit and trim, a routine walker, she'd attended regular yoga sessions at the local health club. She'd been fine, hadn't complained of any pain, fatigue or shortness of breath. Here one moment, gone the next.

"You're going to rinse the gold leaf right off that plate," Sally teased, jarring her from her thoughts. She frowned, concern lighting her eyes. "You all right, honey?"

Shelby nodded, offering a smile. "I'm fine. I was woolgathering."

"No worries," she said, seemingly satisfied with the answer. She grimaced in sympathy. "I do a lot of that myself these days."

That was certainly understandable. Shelby couldn't begin to imagine the pain the Hollands were going through. The death of a loved one was terrible enough, but losing a child? Could it possibly be any worse? Having no children of her own yet, she didn't know, but could only speculate that it would be the worst kind of grief.

Sally loaded the last of the cutlery into the machine, then filled the dispenser with a dishwasher tab and closed the door. While she wiped down the sink and countertops, Shelby stored the various containers of leftover food into the massive double-doored refrigerator and then swept up.

She loved Sally's kitchen. It was huge, with lots of white glass-paned cabinets, an old farmhouse sink and new custom granite countertops. Herbs grown in her garden hung from a pot rack which doubled as a light fixture and the scent of rosemary and sage perfumed the air, mixing pleasantly with the smell of lemon cleaner and oil soap.

A buttery saffron colored the walls and her collection of antique crockery lined the cabinet tops. The ceiling was covered in copper pressed-tin tiles and battered wide-plank pine blanketed the floors.

An antique pot-bellied stove, which always had a fire burning through the fall and winter months, sat in the corner. Modern farmhouse chic, Sally liked to call it, and Shelby completely agreed. It was warm and functional, the true heart of the house.

"Are you sure you don't want to take anything home?" Sally asked her. "A plate for lunch tomorrow?"

Shelby winced and shook her head. She'd be having a salad for lunch tomorrow. If she let Sally feed her every meal she'd be bigger than the side of a barn. She worked hard, but sewing was a sedentary job and didn't burn off nearly as many calories as she'd like. As such, she'd taken up running three days a week to help combat her insatiable sweet tooth, but she wasn't one of those runners who actually *enjoyed* it. The serious ones, who shared their mileage and times through social media and bought fancy running clothes.

Ha. As if.

She ran because she had to, because the exercise gave her the most bang for her buck, so to speak, but she had no desire to enter a marathon, run faster or longer or anything else. It was strictly a calorie burning tool, an "if I run for thirty minutes, I can have a slice of pie with dinner" sort of thing.

"I'd better not," Shelby told her. "Isn't lasagna on the menu for tomorrow night?"

Sally grinned. "It is. With caramel cake for dessert."

Shelby inwardly moaned with delight. Sally's caramel cake was legendary—it had won the blue ribbon at the state fair for the past several years in a row. It was to-die-for. A diet assassin.

Sally hesitated for a second, her warm gaze becoming serious. "Shelby, I have a favor to ask."

"Of course. Anything."

"I want you to go out of your way to really spend some time with Eli this week," she said. "I couldn't help but notice that things were strained between you at the service and—"

Oh, hell. "Sally, it was a—"

"Difficult time, I know," she finished for her. "But you and Eli were the two people outside our family who meant the most to my son and I think it would pain him to know that y'all had a falling out."

Shelby swallowed. "But we haven't had a falling out."

Sally's gaze softened. "I couldn't help but notice that you didn't speak this evening."

"It was his first day back in town," she said, using the only excuse that came to mind. "We haven't had a lot of opportunity."

"I understand that, but make the opportunity. Please. For Micah's sake, if not for mine."

She'd planned on doing that, anyway, Shelby

thought, but having to do it to put Sally's mind at ease—particularly considering her feelings for Eli—was definitely a sticky wicket. Furthermore, the fact that he'd ignored her this evening and left without saying goodbye had clearly upset Sally, which was a mean thing to do, all things considered. Her temper flared once more, further igniting her irritation.

Eli might not want to talk to her, might not want to help her, might blame her for the breakup and the resulting heartache that it had cost his friend in what turned out to be his final months...but he was just going to have to get over it.

At least until this week was over. *Then* he could go back to ignoring her.

For the time being, the Hollands were going to have to come first.

5

It was her. He knew it.

So much for trying to avoid her.

Eli chuckled low, the sound rife with irony and dread, then brought the bottle to his lips once again. He was drinking Southern Comfort—appropriate, considering that was the only form of relief he was likely to get during this godforsaken week from hell. That must have been why Carl had left it for him—he must have anticipated that Eli would have to self-medicate.

Water sloshed against the side of the tub and splashed onto the back porch as he deliberately shifted into a more relaxed position. It didn't matter that he was wound tighter than a two-dollar watch, that the mere thought of Shelby sent a bolt of heat directly into his groin.

Perception, naturally, was key.

How did he know it was her who'd pulled into the driveway? From the back porch, no less? The particular sound of her car door? The crunch of a light-footed person across the gravel? Those keen senses honed by years of specialized military training?

He snorted.

Nothing that sophisticated, unfortunately. It was the tightening of his gut, the prickling of his skin across the nape of his neck, the slight hesitation from the moment the car motor turned off until the driver decided to exit the vehicle. As though she was steeling herself, preparing to face him.

That's what had given her away.

"I'm back here," he called, before she could mount the front porch steps. He might as well get this over with, Eli thought. He'd known a reckoning was coming, that she wouldn't be ignored.

That's why he'd started drinking the minute he'd gotten here.

She hesitated once again, then resumed movement and changed direction. Eli closed his eyes and prayed that she'd be in something other than that damned dress she'd had on earlier today. It was short and…flouncy. Not the least bit inappropriate—this was Willow Haven, after all—but somehow managed to be sexy as hell all the same. It hugged her curvy frame, showcased her healthy tan and moved when she did. The hem fluttered just so with every swing of her hips, a silent "take me" with each step she took.

It was infuriatingly, unnervingly *hot*.

And of all the women in the world…*her? Really? Still?*

A startled "Oh," made him open his eyes, his gaze instinctively shifting toward the direction of the sound.

He mentally swore. Just his luck—she was still wearing it.

Pale green eyes rounded in surprise, her lush mouth mimicking the action. As if he needed another reason to look at her lips. Sheesh. It had been hell avoiding her at dinner, watching her plump mouth slide around her fork. It was fascinating to watch a woman who loved the taste of food eat, Eli thought. She didn't just push it around on her plate, torn between what she should have versus what she wanted. She *savored. Enjoyed.*

It was hot.

"Evening, Shelby," he drawled, taking another pull from the bottle in his hand. The light from the back porch illuminated her achingly familiar face, while dusk settled over the lake and a hum of crickets sang in the background.

She blinked, her gaze sliding gratifyingly down his bare chest. It would have slid farther, he was sure, had the water not gotten in her way. She swallowed a couple of times, blinking a few more. "You're naked," she said hollowly.

He grinned at her, the alcohol making his smile loose and easy. "It's called bathing. I highly recommend it."

A flash of anger lit her gaze, painting color on her cheeks. "I'm familiar with the practice, smart ass." She gestured awkwardly. "I just don't know why you're doing it on the back porch."

He shrugged, unconcerned, and took another pull from the bottle. "It's where the tub is."

"There's a shower inside," she said tightly. "Could you get out of there? I need to talk to you, remember?" she prodded tightly. So much for the hesitancy he'd noted earlier, Eli thought. He should have known that it wouldn't last, should have realized that deliberately avoiding her wouldn't put her off, but would, conversely, make her that much more determined.

Whether it was her imperious put-upon tone— as though she were the one being imposed upon— or the circumstances surrounding this unholy relationship and even unholier attraction, he couldn't say, but he did exactly what she asked him to do.

He shrugged lazily, set the bottle aside, then stood. Water sloshed over the sides and sluiced down his body. He pushed his hair back from his face, careful to flex his biceps in the process.

He arched a deliberate brow. "Anything for you, Shelby. Happy now?"

She blinked wide, inhaled some garbled little sound between a squeak, a gasp and a choke, which he found intensely gratifying, then snatched the towel he'd brought out with him from a nearby chair and hurled it at him.

"I'm going inside," she announced, looking everywhere but at him. "I'll wait for you in the living room."

Eli took his time drying off, then anchored the towel loosely around his hips before following her in. The alcohol had worked wonders for his mood, but very little for the tension creeping back into his belly. Awareness, warm and potent, coiled through his stomach, then advanced lower, circling and settling into his groin. He gritted his teeth.

This was why he'd been avoiding her, Eli thought. Because simply by virtue of *breathing* in close proximity to him, she spun him tight. Made him want to lift the hair off the nape of her neck and press his lips against the hollow, slide his tongue along her jaw, dip it into the delicate shell of her ear then flip her skirt up over her lovely ass, bend her over and bury himself in her sweet, tight heat. He wanted to lose himself inside of her, wanted to hold on to her and forget about everything else.

But there would be no forgetting, he knew. He could *not* let that happen.

Rather than put on clothes, which he knew was what she expected, Eli sauntered into the living room and dropped heavily into a chair, the bottle dangling loosely from his fingers. More to torment her than himself, because in coming here she'd forced the confrontation. He could have miserably gone on avoiding her, had she simply left things alone. He broodily considered her, took in the straight line of her back, the tense set of her small shoulders. Despite the bravado, she was ill-at-ease. Nervous. His lips slid into a droll grin.

No doubt it would pass.

Cool air from the ceiling fan swirled over him, lowering the temperature of his heated skin. Having wandered over to the mantel to inspect pictures, she turned when she heard him and arched a brow, her gaze dropping deliberately to the towel, then finding his once more. "Wouldn't you like to go put on a pair of pants?" she asked, her voice flinty.

He shrugged. "I'm comfortable."

She swallowed, her green gaze lingering briefly on his chest. "I'm not."

Good. "Was there something you wanted, Shelby?"

A stutter of air leaked out of her lungs, her eyes fixated on the bulge building beneath the towel, then she blinked and gave herself a little shake. Girding her loins, he thought, while his own felt as if they'd been cast into hell.

She crossed her arms over her chest, inadvertently plumping her breasts. His dick stirred. "Your help, as a matter of fact, but we'll get to that in a minute."

Eli frowned. His help? Help with what?

She bit her lip, paused, piquing his curiosity. "Listen, Eli, I know that my behavior at Micah's service was…less than warm," she said haltingly. "And I'm sorry for that. I was a coward and I didn't want to face you, not after what happened at the anniversary party and then the breakup." She twisted the cord of her purse nervously around her fingers, tightening until her knuckles turned white. "Guilt is a powerful thing, but it's no excuse for rudeness." She hesitated, her gaze tangling with his, her chin firming. "That said, I did come over as soon as you arrived today and asked to speak with you later. I wouldn't have asked if it hadn't been important. Then you bailed. And Sally noticed."

Shit.

"She'd noticed the tension between us at the service, as well, and now she's worried. I'll own what happened at the service, but you sneaking away tonight without so much as a 'Hi, how've you been?' That's on you, chief."

Much as he'd love to argue with her, Eli knew she was right and he felt like an ass. In trying to control his rampant lust for Shelby, he'd inadvertently caused Sally worry and anything that heaped more stress onto Micah's mother was just not cool. He swore under his breath, then passed a hand over his face, suddenly very weary.

"I'm sorry," he said with a sigh. He looked up and caught her gaze. "That was not my intention."

"And just exactly what was your intention?"

To avoid you. But he couldn't very well say that, could he? Still, she knew. He could tell. Her eyes glittered knowingly and the slightest curve of her mouth suggested he hadn't fooled her at all.

"To get through this," he finally told her, which was the truth, if not all of it. "With my sanity intact," he added with a significant grimace. He lifted the bottle to his lips for another pull, winced when the alcohol burned his throat.

Shelby studied him for a moment, her keen gaze holding his, looking for hidden meanings and untold secrets. It unnerved him, that stare. He always got the feeling she was peeking right into his head, plucking the thoughts from the so-called safety of his mind. No one had ever been able to do that. Not any foster family, close friends or even old lovers.

He'd been safe...until her. That's what made her so dangerous.

"Keeping your sanity presumes your sane," she

said, her eyes twinkling. "Which is debatable." She paused, her humor fading, and sent him another measured look, one that made him slightly nervous. "As for getting through this, that's where I need your help."

So she'd said, and from the suddenly anxious line furrowing her brow and the grim set of her mouth, she was definitely concerned about something. That was rare enough that his antennae twitched. In his experience, Shelby was a lot of things, but Chicken Little wasn't one of them. She was quick to laugh, quick to cry, quick to anger and quick to forgive. Her feelings, whatever they were, hovered at the ready just beneath the surface. It was one of the things he loved about her. Whatever her response, it was always genuine.

And she was genuinely worried.

He silently offered her the bottle—his peace offering—which she took with a grateful quirk of her lips, then settled onto the couch with a sigh. She picked her end, the one closest to him, where she'd always sat when he visited. Her gardenia scent drifted to him, familiar and stirring.

"What's wrong, Shelby?"

She smiled sadly. "A better question is what's right."

"That bad?"

She looked up at him, her expression grave. "Pretty bad."

A finger of unease slid down his spine and he arched a brow, silently encouraging her to go on.

He watched her set her shoulders, steel herself then release a small breath. "I've been getting anonymous letters since the week after Micah's funeral."

He blinked, stunned. What the hell? All senses on alert, Eli leaned forward. "Letters? What kind of letters?"

"Vague, cryptic letters. I hadn't planned on coming out here tonight, so I didn't bring them, but they're just weird."

"What do they say?"

She pushed a hand through her hair. "Things like 'I saw you. I know what you did. I'm going to tell.' And 'It wasn't the gun that killed him, it was you. I'm going to tell. How can you live with yourself, knowing what you did? I'm going to tell.'"

Eli felt his eyes widen as shock detonated through him.

"But this last one was the worst," she continued. She swallowed, the muscles working in her slim throat. Her troubled gaze found his. "'You deserve to die,' it said. 'It should be you beneath that heavy dirt.'"

Jesus. Ordinarily Eli considered himself a pretty good problem solver, but at the moment he didn't know where to start. He was stunned, reeling. *I know what you did? I'm going to tell? It wasn't the gun that killed him, it was you? You deserve to die? Heavy dirt?*

What in the name of all that was holy did this person see and, more importantly, who were they going to tell? Definitely cryptic. Definitely disturbing. His gaze swung to Shelby, whose hand trembled around the bottle. And definitely wrong.

"Have you contacted the authorities?"

She shook her head. "At first I just thought it was someone who was angry at me for calling off the engagement. I was rattled, but not too concerned. But as time has worn on and the letters keep coming…" She lifted her shoulders in helpless shrug. "I don't know what, if anything, they saw, and I don't know who they're going to tell. But I can't risk too much poking around because I don't want to look guilty of anything and I don't want Carl and Sally to be further hurt."

He completely understood, but she couldn't let this go on. She needed to go to the police, which is exactly what he told her. "I'll help in any way I can while I'm here, but this is a matter for the police. You need to report this."

She winced and he inexplicably braced himself. Clearly, there was more. "I agree," she said. "But it's too late now."

"Too late? Why?"

"Because Katrina Nolan came by to see me this afternoon just before I closed and she said that she has a source in Mosul who insisted that, despite the official report, Micah's gun didn't misfire while he was cleaning it, that he killed himself. Because of me," she added, her voice cracking.

Nausea and anger boiled up through him and he pushed to his feet. "Shelby, that's—"

"She's working for the local paper, she smells a scandal and she hates me." Another small shrug. "If I go to the police now and tell them that I've been getting these letters, she'll find out and she'll dig deeper."

His eyewitness account stood, but there had definitely been talk—there always was—and, depending on who her source was, this had the potential to get really ugly. And hurtful for the Hollands.

All that lying, all that insistence and his refusal to change his story would be for nothing if she brought that shit here and stirred it up. It would ruin everything, Eli realized, the worst case scenario running through his head. It would devastate the Hollands, taint Micah's service, spoil the memorial gazebo and everything it would stand for. And for what? A story? From a bitter, jealous woman who couldn't stand that she'd never been first in Micah's heart?

He remembered Katrina. She was one of the in-between girls Micah had dated—translate: disposable—when he and Shelby had initially

split. He'd never liked Katrina. She was hard…
and sneaky. A bitch.

And to think he'd imagined his biggest problem
was going to be controlling himself around Shelby.

"We can't afford to let her dig, Eli," she said.
"We can't let her find out the truth."

The truth? His head swiveled slowly to face
her, another blow of dread landing in his suddenly
tense belly. Her gaze was sad when it met his.

Sad…and knowing.

Bloody hell. She knew. Of course she knew.
And he was a bastard because it was a terrible relief to know that he wasn't the only one, that he
could share the burden.

"The truth?" he asked, not because he needed
confirmation, but because it was expected. Because this scene had to play out. Because, while
she did need his help, she also needed to share the
weight of the secret.

She recognized the ploy for what it was, chided
him with her gaze. "You know the truth."

Yes, he did. But how did she? How could she
possibly know?

"He wrote to me," she confessed in answer to
his unspoken question. "He was afraid that I'd
blame myself and he didn't want me to think that
it was my fault." Tears welled in her eyes and she
picked at a loose thread on the couch, then lifted
her shoulder in a slight shrug. "That was Micah.

Protecting me, loving me, thinking of me…till the very end."

Yes, he had, Eli thought. Shelby had a way of inspiring that sort of devotion. He ought to know… because he was half in love with her himself.

6

Looking both relieved and shaken, Eli released a long breath and pushed his hands through his wet hair, making the short, tawny golden waves on top of his head spike in odd angles. He should have looked ridiculous. She swallowed, a barb of heat twisting low in her sex.

He…didn't.

Shelby licked her lips, struck by the sheer masculine perfection of his towel-clad body. At six foot four, he was tall—a particular turn-on for her—and every inch of that especially large frame was loaded with well-honed, mouthwatering muscle. She'd seen him in swimming trunks in the past, so his bare chest and legs weren't anything she hadn't witnessed before. But seeing him in the towel, knowing that it wasn't *actually* clothing and could so easily fall off, well, that was another matter altogether.

Though it was wholly inappropriate given the conversation they were having, she found herself fascinated with the width of his shoulders, the delineation of his muscled arms and impressive pecs. The swirls of hair barely dusted his chest, then arrowed low, where a treasure trail disappeared beneath the edge of the towel. An errant bead of water clung to the right of one flat male nipple and she wanted to lick it, taste the saltiness of his skin, slip her fingers along his ribs, play them like a harp. If she played the harp. Which she didn't, but why would that matter?

Longing rose up inside of her, welled until she could scarcely catch her breath. She could feel it pressing in against her diaphragm, crowding the air right out of her lungs. A hot, steady throb pulsed in the heart of her womb, making her feminine muscles clench and her nipples tingle behind the sheer fabric of her bra. She smothered a whimper, which she considered an improvement, since she'd had to suffocate a wail when she'd first stumbled upon him in the bath. Sweet heaven.

Hard muscle, sleek masculine skin, heavy-lidded golden eyes...

No one had ever affected her like this.

No one had ever made her want to abandon social rules and common conventions, made her want to abandon good sense and sound judgment. She'd never looked at a man and immediately, instantly thought of nothing but white-hot, down-and-dirty, back-clawing, clothes-tearing *primal* sex. The sort that guaranteed the survival of the human race.

She'd wanted him before—felt that increasingly insistent pull before—but never more strongly than she did now. Because Micah was gone? she wondered. Because, theoretically, nothing stood in the way? She didn't know. She only knew that the intensity of it shocked her...shamed her, considering what she was here to talk about.

Her former fiancé. His best friend.

Her gaze bumped into his. It was hot, his pupils dilated, darkening the gold, deepening the green. A muscle ticked in his tense jaw, jumping spasmodically, interrupting the otherwise smooth planes of his face. She imagined a cable between them, crackling with electricity, drawing them closer and closer together.

He turned abruptly and walked to the window, purposely putting some distance between them, she knew, torn between being thankful that he had the strength and saddened because a part of her wanted him to snap the way he had the night of the anniversary party.

It had been rare, that momentary loss of control. A sight to behold, all that passion simmering just beneath the surface.

Because Eli Weston didn't let himself lose control. He always kept his head and did the right thing. How odd that the thing that she most appreciated about him was the one thing she wished he'd abandon *right now.*

"When did he write to you?" he asked without turning around. His voice was even, but an undercurrent of…something…resonated all the same.

"The letter was dated October 12th, but I didn't receive it until the 22nd."

Eli turned and shot a look at her over his shoulder, a frown clouding his brow. "But that was—"

"Several days prior to his death, I know," she finished. Shelby hesitated, choosing her next words carefully. "I…I don't know what he waited for, Eli—the right moment or the nerve to do it, or maybe to decide how he was going to do it— but his mind was made up and I don't think anything anyone could have said to him would have changed it."

Eli shook his head, his nostrils flaring. "I should have acted sooner," he said. "I should have forced him to get—"

Shelby hung her head and chuckled softly, tears pricking the backs of her lids. "He said you'd say that," she told him. "That you'd second-guess yourself, but that ultimately you'd see the truth, that you had a way of looking past the bullshit and seeing what was real."

Eli's lips quirked tiredly and a small bark of laughter rumbled up his throat. "Maybe so, but not in this instance. Bastard," he mumbled under his breath. "Wish he'd sent me a damned letter."

"Would you like to read mine?" she asked him, surprising herself. But he was the only person she'd ever be able to share it with and if reading it lessened any perceived guilt on his end, then all the better.

Eli glanced up, seemingly startled, his gaze darting to hers. "You don't think Micah would care?"

Shelby considered her response, then shook her head. "Ultimately, no. He wrote me so that I wouldn't blame myself, and he made sure that it was you who found him." She lifted a shoulder. "If that's not trust, then I don't know what is."

He stilled, his expression fixed, but stark. It was obvious that he'd never connected that particular dot and Shelby's heart ached for him. What the hell had he been thinking all these months? How much did he blame himself for what happened? Better still, how much could she have spared him had she simply summoned the nerve to face him at the service?

He finally nodded. "I'd like to read it, if you're sure you don't mind."

"Not at all. Why don't you drop by my house

tomorrow evening after dinner? That would give you a chance to read all of the letters."

Though she knew that he would help her, if for no other reason than to protect the Hollands, he still hesitated and that hurt. She felt her shoulders droop and she let go a small breath. Was it always going to be like this between them? Shelby wondered. One step forward, two steps back?

He nodded, his face passive. Stoic. "That sounds like the best place to start."

It was really their only place to start, but she didn't see what good pointing that out would be. "In the interim, I think you should avoid Katrina. The longer you can stall her, the better." The idea of thwarting Katrina lifted her mood considerably.

Eli's eyes rounded. "Oh, I have no intention of avoiding her."

Shelby blinked. "I'm sorry, what?"

"I'm not going to avoid her," Eli repeated. So she had heard him right. Damn.

"Why not?"

"Because, in the first place, if I'm the go-to source and I can shut this whole 'investigation' down with a single conversation, then that's the most expedient option."

A well-reasoned, sound argument, Shelby thought. But she still didn't like it.

"Second, if a simple conversation isn't going to shut her up, then I need to find out what she knows—or what she thinks she knows—and I need to get her to name her source."

"She's not going to give that up," Shelby told him. "She's horrible, but she's not stupid. I'm not even convinced that she's got a source. It's entirely possible that she's just trying to stir up shit."

He crossed his arms over his chest and inclined his head. "If that's the case, then we need to know that, too. Regardless, I'm not going to be able to avoid her."

He was right, she thought, grimacing. Balls.

Eli's lips slanted marginally. "You really can't stand her, can you?"

She couldn't, but it was more than that. She couldn't stand the thought of her using Micah's own friend to ruin his memorial and hurt his family, couldn't stand the thought of her flirting with Eli, touching him in any way or sharing so much as a smile with him. She could practically feel her nails growing, preparing to scratch. It was ridiculous. Eli wasn't *hers,* dammit. Still...

Shelby merely shrugged, tamped down her irritation. "What's there to like?"

His eyes twinkled, the first real light she'd noted since he'd gotten back into town today. "Not much, from what I've observed."

Mollified, she relaxed a bit. "That's good to know," she said. "Because I got the impression she intends to seduce the information she wants out of you."

He laughed incredulously, his eyes going wide. "Oh, is that right?"

Shelby nodded, pleased that he seemed to find the idea so amusing. "Just giving you fair warning."

His gaze tangled with hers, a smile lingering on his lips. A beat slid to three as the silence stretched between them. Awareness sizzled along her nerve endings, twisted around her middle. "Noted but unnecessary," he said, his gaze skimming her face, stalling hungrily on her mouth. "I'm not interested in her."

A breath stuttered out of her lungs. "I figured you had better taste."

He didn't move, but she could feel his presence pressing in on her, surrounding her. He smiled. "You know me better than anyone else, right?"

She used to think so, but now? She wasn't so certain. Still, it was a loaded comment, one that made her acutely aware of the last time they'd had this conversation and, more significantly, what had happened after it. Longing rose up inside of her, making her skin prickle with heat, her palms ache for the touch of his skin. Need bombarded her, relentless and potent. She bit back a whimper and struggled to focus.

Shelby stood, jerking her thumb toward the back door. "I'd better go."

While she still could. Before she did something she couldn't take back. Not that she'd want to…but he might, and that would be unbearable.

OPERATING ON THREE hours sleep and a mile-high stack of pancakes, Eli slogged through the morning, determined to work off his carbohydrate-induced comalike state and aimed a grateful nod at Colin, whose upbeat playlist kept him from crawling into the cab of his rented truck and falling asleep. Thanks to Maroon 5 and Flogging Molly, he was able to keep up with Carl, who was working tirelessly alongside him. Despite the breeze, sweat beaded on his brow and his shoulders stung, evidence of an early sunburn.

Though he'd been convinced last night that he'd worked and drank enough to sleep like a rock, Shelby's unexpected, bomb-dropping visit had wound him so tight he'd spun for hours after she'd left.

Truthfully, finding out that Micah had written to her prior to his suicide wasn't a shock. He should have known that his friend would do that, particularly considering the timing. He wouldn't have wanted Shelby to blame herself and Eli knew beyond a shadow of a doubt that their breakup wasn't in any way a contributing factor to Micah's downward spiral. He'd actually come to terms with the breakup—had seemed to be half expecting it, truth be told.

What he hadn't been able to come to terms with was being powerless while insurgents strapped a bomb onto a heavily pregnant woman and sent her into a hospital—to the children's ward, the miserable SOBs, to maximize the horror. Wiping the remains of her unborn baby from his face was undoubtedly Micah's tipping point, the place he couldn't come back from. He'd had nightmares for months afterward, waking up screaming and sobbing, clawing at his face.

Eli couldn't imagine… And he'd witnessed his own share of terrible things.

No, the existence of a letter hadn't been what rocked him. Even learning that she'd been getting threatening letters hadn't knocked him too far from center. Was it concerning? Yes. A game-changer? No. And he had every intention of helping her find the culprit and setting that straight. Other than Shelby and his family, Eli could confidently say that he'd known Micah Holland better than anyone else and he knew that Micah would be livid if someone was blaming her, in any way, for his death. He'd help right that wrong.

For Micah, and for Shelby.

Even learning that, impossibly, he wanted her now more than ever wasn't too disturbing. It only stood to reason that he'd want her more now. He'd been wanting her more with every breath for the past six years and the only thing that had enabled him to act with a modicum of honor—the anniversary party notwithstanding, of course—was knowing that she was Micah's, that she was taken. And now that they'd broken up and Micah was gone…

Yes, God, yes, he wanted her even more. To his eternal shame and regret, he did.

He didn't have any idea how he was going to keep his hands off of her, how he was going to help her—spend time with her—and *not* take her.

Especially when he knew she wanted it, too. Wanted him, too.

It was there in her eyes, the raw need and emotion, the desperate desire. It was in the shallow breath that trembled between her ripe lips, the fast flutter of the pulse at the base of her throat, the heat he watched rise beneath her skin when he looked at her. Or better still, when she looked at him. He could still feel the hot slide of her gaze over his body, linger on his shoulders, move down his chest, then lower still where he'd stirred behind the towel. How could he not, when she'd stared at him like that? Like he was her own personal porn star.

He'd *never* had a woman look at him like that. Not with the same sort of single-minded yearning he saw in Shelby's pale green gaze.

Talk about a turn-on. It was nothing short of a miracle he hadn't had an *equipment malfunction* right then and there.

Thankfully, the conversation had turned to Micah—just like it always would—and Shelby had made that "trust" remark, which had completely, unwittingly upended him. He'd always assumed that Micah had made sure that he'd found him because he'd wanted Eli's protection, because he'd counted on Eli to protect his family from the truth.

Quite honestly, though it pained him to admit it, there were times when he really resented his friend for the burden, for leaving him with the mess of his death, the memory of his death. He'd already dealt with his share of suicide—which Micah had known—because he'd been the one to find his father. The older Weston had hung himself from an eave in the barn. And like Micah, he'd made sure that Eli would be the one to find him. He'd been eleven at the time, his "boy-man" his father had always called him, because he'd been eerily mature from a very early age. And perhaps his father had known his mother wouldn't have been able to cope.

Still, mature or not, the man had been his father, and seeing him dangling from that that rope… It was odd what the mind chooses to note or to focus on in a time of crisis. Eli couldn't remember his father's face at all—a gift if there ever was one—but could still recall his socks, of all things. They'd been cream with little black diamonds on them, and the elastic had given in the right one, making it bunch around the top of his dad's penny loafers. Or "penniless" loafers, as his mother used to call them, because his dad had never inserted the pennies into the slit on the top of the shoe.

He smiled, remembering. He'd completely forgotten about that until now. Strange…

At any rate, was that why his dad had made certain that he found him? Because he trusted him with his death? Or had he simply been thoughtless, too far gone to care whether his eleven-year-old son discovered him or not?

He'd never wondered why until last night, until Shelby's comment had forced him to consider it. Revisit it.

As if there was a day when he didn't think about that day, about his mother, about Micah, about the countless others he'd lost to war? Death haunted him, Eli thought. Stalked him.

He was damned tired of it.

"Thinking heavy thoughts?" Carl asked, startling him out of his somber reverie.

Eli blinked, chagrined. "Just thinking," he told him. He pulled a handkerchief from his pocket and mopped his face, resting a booted foot against a two-by-four.

Rather than further question him, the older man merely nodded. "Thinking's good, so long as it's productive. Don't get too caught up in thinking about whys and what fors. Some things don't have an answer on this side of heaven," he said. "Sometimes a man just needs to move forward, no matter how hard it is, so that others will follow him." Carl looked away, his gaze landing on Sally, who was presently—God help them—unloading lunch.

Eli nodded. "I understand."

Or at least he thought he did. In other words, the memorial was a marker, beyond the funeral, to help push Sally on through to the other side of grief. And given that Carl would do anything for his Sally, Eli completely understood that.

"Do you think it's going to help?" he asked him.

Carl was thoughtful for a moment, his lips rolling around the toothpick stuck in the corner of his mouth. "I honestly don't know," he finally said. "But I had to do something and this is what she wanted." He paused. "She's worried about you and Shelby," he continued. "She insists that y'all had some sort of falling out."

Oh, hell. "We haven't."

Carl's too perceptive gaze caught Eli's and held. "See to it that you don't, please. You and Shelby have known each other a long time and my son loved both of you. History is important, Eli. You, of all people, ought to know that."

He did and, though he appreciated the reminder, he didn't need it.

Carl expelled a relieved breath. "There," he said. "I told her I'd mention it to you and I have." He grinned at him, clapped him on the back. "Duty fulfilled."

Eli chuckled.

"Duty aside, though, on a personal note, I'd really appreciate it if you'd spend some time with Shelby this week. She's carrying a lot of guilt over the breakup and, though there's no ill will or hard feeling on our part, there are those in this town who haven't been so forgiving." His pointed gaze landed just to the left of Eli's shoulder, forcing him to shoot a glance in that direction.

Katrina Nolan was making a beeline straight for them.

"I try to see the best in everyone," Carl remarked. "But when it comes to that one, I'm still looking."

"Afternoon, Mr. Holland, Eli," Katrina said, acknowledging them each in turn. "Looks like things are moving right along."

Carl nodded curtly. "Yes, they are. If you'll excuse me, I need to…" Get the hell away from her, it would seem, Eli thought, watching Carl amble toward the other side of the square.

Katrina barely noted Carl's departure, but instead turned a calculating look on Eli. She placed a hand on his arm and leaned in, as though they were much better acquainted than they actually were.

"Listen, Eli, I'm reporting for *The Branches* and I'd like to get your perspective on Micah's death and the memorial." She slid a finger down his arm. "I was hoping I could pick your brain over lunch?"

His flesh crawled where she touched him and, even if Shelby hadn't warned him, he would have been suspicious of Katrina's motives. She was purposely crowding into his space and there was a purely malicious glint in her eye that was beyond disguising.

Drawing on his high school drama club reserves, Eli managed to return her smile. "Sure. I wouldn't pass up an opportunity to honor my friend's memory."

And he'd be damned before he'd let her malign it.

7

"HONEST TO PETE, SHELBY, if I don't get some relief soon, I'm going to do something unforgivably stupid."

Her mind snarled into a hot ball of rage, Shelby wasn't in the mood to listen to Mavis lament the state of her elevated hormone level or the amount of sex she *wasn't* getting.

Her face presently glued to her front window, she'd watched Katrina put Eli in the crosshairs, then move in for the kill. Though she couldn't make out anything they were saying, reading Katrina's body language was a whole other matter. She'd sidled into Eli's personal space, then casually placed a hand on his arm, sliding her finger down the length of it, as though measuring his penis.

It was enough to make her hurl.

After a moment, she'd watched Eli smile, then

Katrina had looped her arm though his and aimed a triumphant smile in her direction as they'd made their way over to Sarah's Diner, presumably for lunch.

"You haven't listened to a word I've said," Mavis complained as she tacked a button onto a top. "Don't you even care who I'm tempted to do?"

"What," Shelby absently corrected. "And no, not at the moment."

"No, *who,*" Mavis insisted gravely. "Who I'm going to do. See? You aren't listening."

Shelby forced herself away from the window and, with effort, relaxed her jaw. She'd warned him, she told herself. She knew why he'd obviously agreed to go to lunch with that woman. She knew that he wasn't the least bit interested in Katrina. There was absolutely nothing to be concerned about, on any level. And yet…

"Ah," Mavis breathed knowingly, spying Eli and Katrina framed in Sarah's window. "I see what's got your knickers in a knot. What's she up to, you reckon? Is she just yanking your chain, or is it something else?"

Shelby resumed her seat and picked up her antique bobbins from the pillow, determined to channel this excess energy into something productive. Handmade lace, rendered a strand at a time via dozens of individually threaded bobbins, required enough concentration to hopefully calm her mind.

It was a lost art, one that had nearly died out altogether after the industrial revolution, but was slowly—thankfully—seeing a resurgence.

"It's both," Shelby muttered. She told her friend about Katrina's visit last night and the veiled threat she'd leveled. Mavis didn't know the truth about Micah's death, but she knew enough about Katrina to know that the spiteful journalist wasn't interested in the truth—she was interested in a story.

Mavis's expression blackened. "I wish I knew what she had on Les Hastings. Then we could put a permanent end to her reign of terror," she said.

Shelby stilled as a thought struck and her gaze swung to Mavis's. "Isn't Les in your Scrabble Society?"

"Yes," Mavis admitted suspiciously. "He's quite the wordsmith. And he's fit and attractive and frighteningly smart. It's a pity about that speech impediment," she said, frowning thoughtfully. "He's quite striking until he opens his mouth. Elmer Fudd doesn't do it for me, I'm afraid."

"But could he?" Shelby asked slyly.

Mavis gasped. "Shelby Justine."

She knew she was in trouble when Mavis used her full name, but she pressed on, anyway. Mavis had mentioned Les many times before and Shelby knew that her friend respected him. "You're the one who was going on and on about who you were going to do. Surely whoever you've sighted can't be any more desirable than Les."

"Clark Upton," she admitted glumly. "I swear, I think he knows I'm in some sort of compromised state. He's been at the park the last three mornings when I've been on my walk."

That was rather industrious, considering Clark had accidently shot off three of his toes in a hunting accident and had trouble walking at all, much less for exercise. Clark was a nice man, but he was wider than he was tall, and wasn't known for being the sharpest tool in the shed. Additionally, Clark had earned the nickname "Stump" in high school, the moniker given to him from fellow football players who'd shared a field house shower with him.

Indeed, Mavis was desperate if she was considering taking Stump for a lover.

"Les has always had a thing for you, Mavis," Shelby needled. "And he's got all of his toes."

Mavis's gaze turned inward, speculative. "You're right," she said. "And I'll bet he's hung like a horse."

"Mavis."

She blinked innocently. "What? It's a pro, right? While we're listing them."

She'd never be able to look at Les again without mentally "neighing" at him, Shelby thought, snickering under her breath. At her laugh, Dixie lifted her head off her pillow and looked at Shelby.

Deciding that a trip or a treat wasn't in order, she immediately relaxed once more.

"What are you laughing at? It was your idea!"

"It was a suggestion, that's all. If you're not going to be able to control yourself until you can see Doc Anderson, then why not take advantage of the situation? Why not see what secrets you can pull out of Les?"

Mavis was quiet for a moment, her head cocked in thoughtful consideration. She was much quicker to share the details of her love life than to actually share her body, despite her bawdy behavior. "I rather like Les," she confessed. "He's smart and well-read. He's interesting. And if Katrina does have something on him, then I'd like to see him off that hook."

Shelby nodded. "I agree."

Mavis straightened. "This is a workable solution to my problem," she said. "I won't take advantage of him. Merely explain my dilemma and see if he's interested in…alleviating some of my tension." She shrugged. "And if he happens to share what, if anything, Katrina has on him, then all the better."

Shelby grinned. "So you're going to seduce Les?"

"No," she corrected. She snagged her purse, pulled a compact from the inside pocket and freshened her lipstick. It was red, naturally. "I'm going to proposition him. Men do it all the time," she said. "I don't see any reason why I can't be as honest."

Why, indeed? Shelby thought, secretly admiring her older friend. She was horny. She wanted to get laid. She was taking a proactive step toward that end, one that men did with a lot less forthrightness and impunity all the time.

"Go, Mavis," Shelby told her, impressed.

"Go yourself," she said, arching an imperious brow. "I'm not the only one with quivering lady bits. Your hormones are every bit as sensitive as mine are right now and the solution to your problem is only in town until the end of the week. You'd better make some hay while the sun is shining, chickie. You'll regret it if you don't."

Blushing to the roots of her hair, Shelby lifted her chin and returned to her lace-making. "I don't know what you're talking about," she lied. It was pointless, but felt necessary.

"Well, well, would you look at that," Mavis said distractedly. "Eli must have eaten something that Katrina wanted. She's licking it off his mouth. Enthusiastically."

Shelby's head shot up and she darted toward the window, where Mavis stood. *"What?"* she breathed, sickened. "That conniving bitch!"

Mavis chuckled knowingly, while Shelby peered across the square into the diner window, where Katrina sat alone. A quick scan of the green revealed that Eli had returned to work.

Shelby shot a scowl at her friend. "That was sneaky."

"But effective," Mavis countered with a knowing smirk. "Why can't you just admit that you're attracted to him, that you've always been attracted to him?"

If only it were that simple. That easy. "Because I shouldn't be," she admitted, swallowing tightly. "Because I was engaged to his best friend."

Mavis tutted sympathetically and laid a hand on her arm. "And those were all valid reasons… until you broke off the engagement," she said. "But what's stopping you now? We don't choose who we're attracted to any more than we can choose who we love."

Shelby watched Eli pull a water gun from his back pocket and tag Colin in the back of the head with a quick squirt, then hurriedly hide the little weapon before Colin could see him. Scowling, the boy looked around, searching for the culprit, then rubbed the back of his head before returning to work. Eli did it again, but couldn't keep from laughing, which tipped his hand. She watched Colin's sullen face transform into a big smile—one so like his older brother's—then watched him laughingly promise what she imagined could only be retribution. It was good to see the boy laugh and judging from the expression on Carl's face, he definitely agreed.

"How long have you known?" she asked.

Mavis blinked. "Known what? That you have feelings for Eli?"

Shelby sighed and nodded.

Mavis simply shrugged. "Since you first met him," she said. "But I have an eye for that sort of thing. My grandmother was a matchmaker, you know. She, too, could spot chemistry. And you and Eli Weston have that in spades. Take it from an old woman," she said, sounding suddenly tired. "You're a fool if you squander it."

Shelby sighed, torn. "Is that the overactive hormones talking or the benefit of experience?"

Mavis laughed softly, her eyes twinkling. "Probably both. But it still applies."

BECAUSE HE'D BEEN ABLE to practically feel Shelby's gaze boring a hole into the back of his head while he'd lunched with Katrina—gratifying, he had to admit—Eli decided that he should probably walk over to her store and give her an update. Honestly, he was a little surprised that she hadn't hurried over to the green the instant he'd returned to grill him about it, but the stream of customers in and out of her store must have prevented it.

He told Carl where he was going, which garnered a pleased smile, then made his way over. He spotted Shelby through the glass door and his heart gave an inexplicable little jump. She smiled when she saw him, her lush lips tilting into a pleased smile as he opened the door and stepped inside. She was behind the counter, ringing up a sale. "This color looks gorgeous on you, Katie," she said. "I think cherry is definitely your signature shade."

Eli smiled as a blushing Katie passed him on her way out the door, then turned, looked at Shelby and arched a brow. "Signature shade?"

"Yes," she said. "It's the color that looks the best on you, defines your personality. When I put together the rest of Katie's summer wardrobe, I'll include a splash of it on every outfit." She lifted a shoulder. "I'll bring it in either as part of the fabric or in the accessories—it really doesn't matter, so long as it's there—and will add a punch of it to everything so that it becomes her 'signature shade.'"

Intrigued, Eli studied her. Today she'd pulled her hair up in a flirty ponytail and secured it with a wide pale pink satin ribbon, dotted with little daisies. Today's dress was sleeveless, fitted to the waist then flared out in tiny pleats. It, too, was pale pink, like the early dawn he'd witnessed over the lake this morning, and the hem was finished in a pale yellow.

Ah...

"Yours is yellow," he said. Hell, no wonder she reminded him of summer, of warmth.

She grinned, seemingly pleased that he'd noticed. "Lemon chiffon, to be exact, but yes, definitely yellow. It's my happy color."

He glanced at the pig, who wore a similar bow around her neck and a glittery pink skirt. "Dixie's, too?"

Shelby grimaced. "Brown is more her style, but she wears enough of that as it is. Mud," she clarified at his blank expression.

Eli felt his eyes widen and he chuckled. "Oh, right."

The phone rang. She winced, then shot him an apologetic glance. "I'll only be a minute. You'll wait, right?" she asked so anxiously his conscience pricked. His self-preservation tactics had hurt her more than he'd realized.

He nodded, then cast an appreciative glance around the inside of her shop while she took the call. It was so…Shelby. Bright, whimsical and organized. Racks and racks of her handmade custom designs filled the space. Lots of different colors and textures, dresses, tops, pants, scarves and the like. Dozens of vintage mirrors and heavy frames filled with old sewing patterns lined the walls. Shades she'd obviously designed herself hung from various bulb lights around the room, offering color as well as light. Pouffe chairs and footstools outfitted a single corner, presumably where beleaguered shoppers waited to try things on.

Shelby was more than just good at what she did—she was passionate about it. Every detail, down to the old wooden thread spools which served as cabinet door knobs, told him so.

"Sorry about that," she said as she replaced the receiver. "Madeline Martin lost a button and needs a replacement."

"This is really something," he said with a significant glance around the room. "I'm impressed."

"Thanks," she said, her eyes warming with pride. "It's been a lot of work, but it's worth it."

"I can tell." He heard voices coming from the back, then the whine of a sewing machine. He lifted a brow.

"My elves," she teased. "In addition to myself and Mavis, I've got three full-time seamstresses. I'm putting together an online store, so I'm trying to get some stock built up before we launch."

Eli smiled. "Going global, huh?"

She laughed nervously. "That's the plan. I want to serve a bigger audience," she said. "But I don't want to grow so much that I can't do things the way that I want them done. I know all of my clients, have a personal relationship with them. I don't want that to change to the point that I lose what makes me different."

"And what's that?"

"I don't just design and make clothes—I put together an entire style based on age, body type, a signature color and personal preferences. Granted I do quite a bit of off-the-rack stuff—universal designs—but ultimately, my custom clothing is what makes my services so unique. Typically, it's a service only the wealthy enjoy, so I try to keep things affordable."

He could certainly see that simply based on her own clothes. He'd never seen another woman dress as well as Shelby did. She had a firm grasp of what looked good on her and capitalized on that information by tailoring every stitch of clothing on her body. Even her underwear, Micah had once mentioned.

The idea made his groin tighten.

"Well," she prodded, propping her elbows on the counter. "I couldn't help but notice that Katrina cornered you this morning."

One would hope, since she'd been staring at them, Eli thought, smothering a smile. He nodded. "She did. And you were right, she's definitely digging. I've agreed to go by her place this evening so that we can talk a bit more in private."

Shelby stilled, her eyes flashing. "You *what?*"

He'd anticipated that little development going over like a lead balloon, but he hadn't anticipated how much he'd enjoy her reaction. "It's necessary, Shelby," he said, leaning against the counter. "She thinks she's got something and I have to know what that something is. I can't let her keep digging around. If she asks too many questions, the Hollands are going to hear about it and that's the last damned thing we want, right?"

The adorably mulish set of her jaw didn't change, but her eyes grew less wary, resigned. "Right," she agreed. "I just don't trust her. And I *hate* that she's doing this, that she's using Micah's death to torment me and potentially hurt Carl and Sally."

Torment her? By flirting with him? Is that what she meant? Or was it something else? *She hates me,* she'd said, he remembered now. Because of Micah? Eli wondered. Probably. No doubt because Shelby always had what Katrina wanted.

And if Katrina suspected Shelby wanted him…

Flattered, he squashed a grin. No wonder Shelby looked ready to pull her hair out. "I'll only stay long enough to get the information we need," he said, hoping to mollify her.

"And then you're coming directly to my house, right?" A line emerged between her brows. "Or do you think you should come to mine first, so that you can see the letters, perhaps look for some evidence of involvement at Katrina's?"

Eli frowned. "Do you think Katrina's involved?"

Shelby bit her lip consideringly. "My gut says

no—it's not her style—but I don't think we can we completely rule her out, either."

Eli ultimately agreed with Shelby's opinion. Given the way Katrina was flirting with him—verbal humping, really—she didn't seem like the kind to do anything in secret. She was off-puttingly…bold.

"I'll come by your place first," he told her.

"Sounds like you'll have a busy night," she remarked tartly, still endearingly perturbed. It was ridiculous how much that pleased him, how much knowing that she was actually jealous made his chest puff with pleasure.

Eli grinned. "You sure green isn't your signature color?"

Color bloomed instantly beneath her cheeks and she looked away, obviously embarrassed. "Ha-ha. Very funny."

He thought so. Still smiling, Eli pushed off from the counter and headed for the door. "I'd better get back to work. See you this evening."

"I'll save you a seat," she said.

Confused, he turned and arched a brow.

"At the dinner table," she clarified. "Sally made me promise to make you feel welcome."

His grin broadened. "Do I get to define welcome?"

She snorted and rolled her eyes. "No."

He shrugged, feigning disappointment. "Damn. I knew it was too much to hope for."

But he hoped, anyway. And that was more dangerous than the ever-present need hammering through his blood.

8

WHEN MAVIS MERIWEATHER had dropped by his office this afternoon and requested a private audience at his house this evening, Les Hastings couldn't have been any more surprised.

Women, for the most part, regrettably, didn't seek his private counsel.

Born with a speech impediment no amount of therapy had corrected, Les had learned at an early age that listening would serve him better than talking, and that he communicated best via the written word, which was why he'd started *The Branches,* Willow Haven's daily newspaper.

Resigned to a quiet life filled with old jazz, Alfred Hitchcock movies and a personal library that rivaled some of the best in the state, Les had found that a fine tumbler of scotch and a good book could fulfill the majority of his needs.

Except sex, of course, but that wasn't something he'd ever had much luck with.

Women liked to be wooed with pretty words, and a man who couldn't pronounce his *r*'s and whose attempts at conversation closely resembled a popular Looney Tunes character who was on a perpetual "wabbit" hunt, didn't "woo" well. While he didn't necessarily like it, he'd nevertheless accepted his fate. This was the hand he'd been dealt, so this was the one he was forced to play.

While he'd occasionally arranged for an escort service on those rare instances when he'd traveled out of town, a recent experience had cut off that particular avenue of fulfillment. He didn't pay for sex so much as the soft touch of a women's hand, the feel of a plump breast beneath his palm. Things lots of other men took for granted, could easily find at a roadside dive or hotel bar. For free. He'd tried those avenues, as well, but never with any luck. The instant he spoke, it was over.

It was terrible, that moment, when he watched interest flee and pity emerge.

That's why the escort service had been the perfect solution. He arranged everything online, established some ground rules, kept conversation to a minimum and tipped generously. Did he long for an affectionate touch? Prefer to make love than simply exchange bodily fluids?

Yes, but he'd given up on that, as well.

As such, he'd resigned himself to celibacy and even convinced himself that, much like the Benedictine monks of long ago, he'd devote his time and energy to a greater purpose. He'd make knowledge his mistress. He'd take the noble high road.

And then Mavis had casually dropped by and the floor—not to mention the high road—had disappeared from beneath his feet.

Because Mavis was...extraordinary.

A former dancer who'd dated famous baseball players and politicians, Mavis had packed more living into her twenties than most people did in a lifetime. She was one of those women who changed her hair color with her mood, but still managed to look natural. She was tall and curvy, with breasts so luscious they should come with a warning label.

Hell, *she* should come with a warning label.

Her eyes were startlingly blue, the clearest aquamarine, and her bone structure was delicate and fine, like a piece of Limoges porcelain. She wasn't just beautiful—she was a showstopper. Combine those qualities with an innate sensuality, a razor-sharp wit, a fiendishly clever mind and a command of the English language that would make Shakespeare weep and she became his perfect woman.

And he'd wanted her—desperately, pathetically—for the past forty years.

Having known her for that long and having moved in the same social circles for the past several years, Les had spent a good deal of time with Mavis. He couldn't claim to know her better than anyone else, but he'd observed her enough to think that he knew her better than most.

And the glint he'd seen in her eye today had been new and keen. It had held an unmistakable interest he'd almost discounted as wishful thinking. Until she'd leaned across his desk—displaying her lovely cleavage to its best advantage—and pressed a kiss against his cheek.

Mavis Meriweather was *flirting* with him.

Either hell had frozen over or the Almighty had decided to pay him an unexpected kindness.

Regardless, some sort of divine intervention was at work and, as such, he was torn between euphoria and terror.

The doorbell rang, heralding her arrival. With a bracing breath and one last gulp of alcohol, Les pushed from his chair, made his way to the front entrance and opened the door. He inclined his head and gestured her inside.

"Goodness, Les," she said, her gaze darting around his entrance hall. Like his library, it, too, was filled with books. They lined the walls, were stacked casually on tables, supported various vases, spines out, to better display their artistic gilt letters. A stained-glass fixture hung from the ceiling and a worn oriental rug blanketed the floor. "This is beautiful. It's not at all what I was expecting."

He felt his gaze widen, trying to decide if he should be insulted.

She gasped through a smile, then turned to look at him, her eyes sparkling. He felt that grin all the way to his toes. "Oh, dear, that didn't come out right, did it? I merely meant that I'm pleasantly surprised. I knew that you were a reader, but this—" She gestured widely, seemingly at a loss for words. "This is incredible."

If she was impressed with the foyer, then his library was really going to slay her. He nodded his thanks, ushering her deeper inside the house then pushed a glass-paned pocket door open and followed her through.

She stopped short, inhaling delightedly. "Oh, my…"

Having converted the formal living room and dining room into one long room lined with bookshelves and anchored with fireplaces on each end, Les was especially proud of his space. Littered with antique furniture, old maps and atlases, the room was filled with the things he loved. The classics, of course, an extensive collection of poetry, hundreds of biographies and histories from all over the world, not to mention hundreds—possibly thousands—of fiction novels.

He watched her wander over to a shelf, peruse the titles offered there. She slid a finger over the spine of Sir Arthur Conan's Doyle's *A Study in Scarlet.*

She turned to look at him and lifted a brow. She was so pretty it hurt. "A first edition?"

He nodded, smiled as if it were a no-brainer.

She grinned. "Of course it is. You founded the Baker Street Boys, didn't you?" Her forehead wrinkled. "Odd that this book should be bound in blue linen, isn't it? Scarlet would have been more appropriate."

"The UK edition was," he said, careful to avoid the *r*'s as usual.

She smiled at him, her lips curling fondly, and inclined her head.

Les made his way to the liquor cabinet and gestured to a bottle. "Wine?"

She winced and shook her head. "Got anything stronger?" she asked hopefully.

For courage? he wondered. He grinned at her and lifted a cut glass decanter. "Scotch?"

"That'll do it," she told him. She strolled over to an armchair, the leather creaking as she settled in. Dressed in a breezy linen dress the color of cranberries, she looked like Christmas had come early, tart and delicious.

Mouthwatering.

Les made his way to where she sat and handed

her a glass. Her elegant hand curled around the tumbler and she watched him as she took a drink, her eyes peeking at him over the rim. It was sexy, that look, and he hardened instantly, nearly to the point of pain.

"You have to be wondering what I'm doing here," she said, glancing up at him, almost as if she were curious about it, too.

Les found her gaze and held it, then damned near swayed from shock when a spark of yearning flared in those remarkable blue eyes. "I've thought of little else," he admitted. "What do you need, Mavis?"

Her eyes had dropped to his mouth. Ordinarily, he would have wondered if he'd tripped up and used a word with an *r* in it, but he knew he hadn't. He'd always been especially careful around her. Furthermore, she wasn't looking at his mouth as though he'd made a mistake—she was looking at it as though she wanted to taste it. Her breath came in lengthened shallow breaths and her pupils had dilated. Classic signs of desire and, since she was looking at him, logic demanded that she... desired him.

He locked his knees to keep them from wobbling.

"I need a lover, Les," she said baldly, in typical Mavis form. "And I'm here because you're a gentleman. You're interesting, attractive, intelligent and discreet. This would be a friends-with-benefits sort of thing, strictly physical." She arched a brow. "What do you say? Are you interested?"

Les studied her a minute. Though he was relatively certain her request was legitimate, years of being cautious, of examining motives, was too ingrained to ignore. Satisfied that hell had definitely frozen over and that she was some sort of benevolent angel come to life, he carefully set his glass aside and just as carefully unbuttoned his cuffs and rolled them up. He dropped to his knees in front of her, slid his hands beneath her dress and firmly grasped her thighs, startling a gasp out of her in the process, then gently jerked her forward. The scent of her hot sex drifted to him, the musky scent of woman, and he inhaled deeply as he slid his nose up her thigh.

"God, yes," he breathed.

MORE NERVOUS THAN SHE could recall being in recent memory, Shelby forced herself to sit quietly and wait for Eli. Dinner at the Hollands' had gone well and, on the whole—other than Colin, who seemed more surly than usual—the atmosphere in general was more relaxed. Shelby couldn't help but notice that Carl and Sally seemed especially pleased that she and Eli were on seemingly warmer terms. She'd caught a shared look between the two she wasn't entirely certain she'd been meant to see.

It had been significant, almost calculating, and more than a little self-satisfied.

In other words, odd.

She'd saved him a seat, as promised, and the tension humming between them proved to be a constant distraction. She was acutely aware of every move he made, the innocent brush of his shoulder against hers, the way his long fingers wrapped around his glass, the muscles moving beneath his skin as he did something as innocent—as mundane—as lifting his fork to his mouth.

And his mouth…

It was a little full for a man, but wide and carnal and so sinfully wicked it made her squirm in her seat every time she'd looked at it. And when he smiled…it was sexual magic. Nothing short of panty-melting.

A knock sounded at her front door, startling her out of lust-fogged stupor. Dixie did her dog impression by quickly lumbering up and trotting to the door, pressing her snout against it and sniffing loudly.

Shelby rolled her eyes and nudged her out of the way. "Chill," she said. "It's not the pizza delivery guy."

"I could have brought a pizza," Eli said, his lips curled into a sheepish grin. Hands shoved into his pockets, he wore a pair of faded jeans and an ochre T-shirt that brought out of the highlights in his golden eyes, accentuated the deeper tones in his tawny hair. Tension tightened his shoulders, haunted the fine lines around his eyes, suggesting that he wasn't as relaxed as he seemed, either. He bent down and scratched between Dixie's ears, earning instant piggy love and devotion.

"Careful," Shelby warned. "That's one of her erogenous zones."

Eli looked up. "Really?"

Shelby chuckled and shook her head. "That was too easy."

"How was I supposed to know?" he asked, settling on one end of her couch. He cast a look around the room, taking in her decor, noting the exits. "I'm not familiar with the pig-pet model."

"She's been spayed," Shelby explained, handing him a glass of wine. "Otherwise, she'd pee all over the house, spreading her scent. Not to mention the PMS," she added with a significant grimace. "From everything I've read, it can get really bad."

"Pig PMS?" He shot her a skeptical look. "You're yanking my chain again, aren't you?"

"Not at all."

He took a sip from his glass, let the wine settle over his tongue before swallowing appreciatively. "You learn something new every day," he said, his gaze landing on the pictures on her mantel. There were several. Some of her parents, her grandparents, Dixie, but the snapshot he lingered on was of her and Micah and him.

It had been taken at the lake, after a day spent waterskiing. Micah stood between them, an arm slung around both their shoulders. She and Eli had just shared a joke Micah had missed and he'd wandered up while they'd been laughing. Sally chose that exact moment to insist on a picture, so Micah had moved in between them and they'd all grinned. She and Eli were still smiling over the joke and Micah was smiling because he'd been happy that day. He'd been happy most of the time, which had made his suicide all the more painful. He must have gone to a really dark place and lost the light, Shelby thought now.

Eli gestured to the picture, his face somber. "It's still hard to believe, isn't it? That he's gone. That he went the way he did."

She swallowed, nodded. "It is. I would have never dreamed that he'd…" She couldn't say it, couldn't finish. "He was always so happy, and even when he was angry, he was still good-natured." She hesitated. "He didn't elaborate, in the letter," she said. "He just said he'd been unable to stop something and that the damage was unbearable, that he couldn't 'un-see' it." She glanced at him, bit her lip. "Do you know what happened?"

His jaw tightened and he gave her a curt nod. "Are you going to make me tell you?"

"No," she said. She wouldn't make him relive something so terrible that it drove their friend to suicide. "But if you ever *need* to tell me, I'll listen."

He turned to face her, his expression stark, pained. "You'll regret it," he said. "But...thanks."

It wasn't until that moment that Shelby realized the sheer magnitude of the burden Micah had put on Eli. In addition to finding him, he'd had to lie to protect him, to protect his family—repeatedly, she imagined, because even she knew "his gun misfired" was often code for suicide—and carry the weight of whatever it was that put Micah there. And now he was here, building the memorial, doing the next right thing, and Katrina Nolan was trying to take that away from him.

Her fingers tightened around her glass as another bolt of anger rocketed through her.

It quickly fizzled out, though, when she realized she was doing the same damned thing—giving him a problem to fix.

"Listen, Eli," she said, turning to look at him. "If you can sort out Katrina, I'll take care of the letter writer." She wearily rubbed a line from between her brows. "Micah gave you plenty to do without me adding to it and I—"

His eyes flashed and he straightened. "You're not adding to anything," he said, his voice suddenly hot. His expression blackened and he pointed to the mantel. "All of this—every damned bit of it—is on *him,* you understand? *You* didn't do this. *He* did."

She could feel his anger, his frustration. It rolled off of him in waves, pounding into her with its intensity. "I understand that, but you don't have to—"

He bolted up from the couch, walked to the mantel and shook his head. "Yes, I do. I do have to do it. For him, yes, because he'd absolutely flip a bitch if he knew someone was blaming you for this. He'd expect me to take care of it, because that's what friends do." He turned to look at her, his face a mask of anguish. "You know what his last words to me were? 'You're a good friend, Eli.'" A bark of awful laughter erupted from his throat. "A good friend? Yeah, right. I'm the good friend who didn't get him the help he needed. I'm the good friend who couldn't keep him from putting a gun in his mouth. I'm the good friend who's been lusting after his fiancée for years. Even now— *even now*—it's all I can do to keep my hands off of you. He's *dead* and it doesn't make a difference. God help me, I still want you. Good friend?" he repeated incredulously, eyes wide. *"Really?"* He shook his head, passed a hand over his face. "What bullshit. But I'm trying to be now, and you know what? I resent it. I'd like nothing more than to thrash the hell out of him for this, to read him the fucking riot act."

Chest constricted so tight she could barely breathe, Shelby didn't know where to start. It wasn't just Eli being Eli—he was looking for absolution.

For all the wrong reasons. And it explained *so* much.

"I'd better go," he said, heading for the door. "I'll look at the letters tomorrow night."

Shelby hurriedly stood. "Eli, wait."

"Shelby, please," he implored without looking at her. He rested his forehead against the door, closed his eyes. "I need to do this. Let me do this."

Finally, she nodded and he left.

But this conversation was far from over.

9

FEELING A BIT LIKE A ransom victim who'd narrowly escaped his captor, Eli waved a final goodbye at Katrina and slid behind the wheel of his truck.

He exhaled a mighty breath, then quickly backed out of the driveway, wincing as his tires squealed against the pavement. With any luck she'd decide he was a badass and wouldn't come to the correct conclusion that he was that damned desperate to get away from her.

Good Lord…

She'd been stuck to him like flypaper from the instant he'd walked through her door, had been forced to move from the couch to the chair when she'd crowded him. He'd lost count of how many times he'd disentangled his hand from hers, and had successfully dodged her lips on three separate occasions.

Of course, when she'd come to the door in a threadbare t-shirt—without a bra—and in a pair of shorts that left the bulk of her ass hanging out, he should have turned around right then and left.

He didn't, because he'd wanted to sort this out once and for all and, while he wasn't completely certain he'd been able to do that, he was confident that she'd merely heard a rumor, that her source hadn't been anyone officially associated with the investigation.

Shelby had been right—Katrina was fishing… and she definitely hated her. Like Shelby, he believed that the woman was simply trying to stir up shit and had decided that the best way to do that was through him. She'd kill two birds with one stone—take something she suspected Shelby wanted, which was him based on her behavior tonight, and ruin her reputation with the Hollands.

"I just think that it's odd that Shelby broke the engagement off and six months later Micah's gun 'misfires,'" she'd said, her voice rife with skepticism.

"What you think is odd, I think is simply unfortunate timing," he told her. "Micah's death had absolutely nothing to do with Shelby. I was there. I know what happened."

She considered him. "I know you do," she said. "And I wish I believed you."

If she'd hoped to intimidate him, she'd been

sadly mistaken. He'd been questioned by men *much* more frightening than her.

Eli had merely shrugged, as if he didn't give a damn, and truly—ultimately—he didn't care what she thought. She could think whatever the hell she wanted to, but the instant she started sharing her suspicions and it affected the Hollands, she was going to wish that she'd kept her vicious mouth shut.

"You don't have to believe me," he said. "But before you drag Micah's memory and service through the mud and upset his family with *your* suspicions and no proof, I'd think very carefully. Slander's not nearly as difficult to prove nowadays."

"I don't intend to slander anyone."

Eli dropped the amiable good-old-boy routine. "You've just indicated that you think I'm a liar. If you print a contradictory opinion to my eyewitness testimony, then you'll be making it official." He'd shrugged, pinned her with a level gaze. "And if that happens, you'd better hope that paper you're working for has good insurance because I can assure you you'll need it."

"There's no need to get—"

"Listen, Katrina, anytime a soldier dies off the battlefield, there's talk. I won't say there isn't. But you're barking up the wrong tree. And frankly, given yours and Micah's past relationship, I would have thought you'd be concentrating on what a wonderful guy he'd been, not trying to start a fire where there's no flame."

Her eyes had widened and a knowing spark had entered her gaze. "You've been talking to Shelby."

"She's a friend." He kept his voice even, neutral.

"That's what she said." She'd hummed under breath, her eyes narrowing. "But is that all she is?"

Dangerous territory. "Is this for an article or are you just curious?"

"I'm curious."

He should have told her it was none of her damned business, should have played it off, muttered some vague answer, but he couldn't, knowing that Katrina was only interested in hurting her, knowing that she'd wanted to use him to that end.

He smiled at her and shrugged helplessly. "She's my It Girl," he said, then turned and walked away.

ELI CONSIDERED GOING back to Shelby's house—he didn't like the way he'd left things between them—but ultimately decided that he was too raw and wrung out to finish their discussion. It had been wrong of him to dump all of that onto her, then simply walk away, but it was either that or take her—to bed, on the floor, against the wall or any variation thereof—and once that was done... he was done for.

There would be no going back.

His It Girl, indeed, Eli thought, making the final turn that would take him out to the cabin. Fatigue dragged at his limbs and he longed for a hefty dose of alcohol and a cool soak in the tub overlooking the lake. They'd gotten a lot done today, having piped in all the water and gas lines, finished the frame and began the tedious process of lining up the willow branches around the perimeter.

Though he hadn't anticipated enjoying himself or the work, Eli had been surprised to discover that he did. He liked the pleasant ache in his muscles at the end of the day, the evidence of hard work and something to show for it. He'd been on construction crews during the summers while he'd been in college, but hadn't appreciated the labor the way he did now.

Thankfully, he seemed to have a knack for it, was able to look at a plan and instantly visualize the best way to put it together. Considering his overall dissatisfaction with his chosen career path, it was nice to discover that there was an alternative; one that actually excited him. His contract expired in three months and, though he'd been pressured to re-up, Eli had resisted.

He noted the lights shining through the living room windows before spotting her car.

Shelby.

His heart rate accelerated, pumping his blood more swiftly toward his groin and his fingers tightened against the steering wheel as anticipation shot through him. See? This was what happened. His mind might be convinced that avoiding her and not taking things to the next level was a good idea, but his body obviously disagreed. It betrayed him with every breath into his lungs, every determined push of the overheated blood in his veins.

He should have known she'd be here, Eli thought. He should have realized that she'd have to have the last word, that she wouldn't be able to leave things alone.

All right, Eli thought, feeling a muscle jump in his jaw. If she wanted a reckoning, then she'd by God get one.

Micah had encouraged him to stop following the rules, to start breaking a few instead. Though he doubted this was exactly what his friend had in mind, he was going to get his wish because Eli was about to blow *this* particular rule all to hell and back.

And he was certain that doing the wrong thing was never going to feel more right.

THE SWING OF HEADLIGHTS across the window and the sound of popping gravel signaled Eli's return. Shelby had been waiting for nearly an hour and had been getting increasingly anxious with every second that passed.

She knew Eli well enough to know that he

wouldn't want to discuss what happened at her place this evening, but he ought to know her well enough to know that she wouldn't be put off. He'd lost it—which he so rarely did—and given her a glimpse into what he was going through, what he was feeling.

She was familiar with guilt enough to recognize it, but she hadn't expected that he'd take on so much of it, especially on account of his feelings for her, for what happened at the anniversary party. Had he forgotten that *she'd* kissed *him,* not the other way around?

He might have snapped, but it had been her who'd ultimately broken.

She heard his feet mount the steps, cross the porch then the door opened. Looking resigned but dangerous, his lips twisted into something that fell well short of a smile, he nodded at her. "You've got a key?"

"No," she said. "I gave it back more than a year ago. But I know where the spare is hidden."

He poured himself a tumbler full of whiskey, then lifted the glass and took a healthy swallow. His eyes, when they met hers, were hot and angry, and an eerily banked energy, much like the calm before the storm, crackled around him. Her skin prickled with as much warning as desire and she lifted her chin.

"Any luck with Katrina?"

He sauntered into the living room, but didn't join her on the couch. He was keeping his distance. His gaze slid like fire along her legs, her breasts and over her lips before it bumped into hers. "Is that what you really want to know, Shelby? What you came here for?"

"I want to know a lot of things," she said, resisting the urge to squirm. Heat coiled in her middle and flooded her womb. "But you know why I'm here."

A bark of fatalistic laughter leaked from between his lips and he shook his head and his eyes widened significantly. "Yes. Yes, I do."

"Then let's get to it, shall we?" Waiting on him had given her an opportunity to consider what she wanted to say, so she was ready for him. "For someone who is normally so damned perceptive, you've really missed the mark this time." She leaned forward. "Micah told you that you were a good friend because you *are*. You—"

Predictably, he exploded. "How can you say that when you know—"

Shelby pushed determinedly to her feet. "When I know what? That you couldn't get him to get the help he needed? We both know Micah Holland was so stubborn he wouldn't have crossed the street if he didn't want to, even if there was a naked woman holding a cake on the other side. Holding yourself accountable for his behavior is wrong on so many levels, I don't even know where to start."

"He wasn't in his right mind."

"I know," she said pointedly. "Because if he'd been in his right mind, he wouldn't have killed himself. It was hard enough to reason with him under normal circumstances. Thinking that you could have done more is noble, but flawed."

"Noble?" he parroted, his voice harsh. He stalked toward her, his eyes smoldering with desire and frustration, longing and helplessness. "Was it noble when I cornered you under that oak tree and told you that I knew you didn't care for Micah as much as he did for you? Was it noble when I showed you how I felt? How I've always felt? When I kissed you?"

Her heart hammered in her chest and she swallowed, her gaze tangling with his. He was mere inches from her face, his expression fierce and tormented. She could smell his cologne, something warm and musky with a clean finish. "You didn't kiss me," she told her, her gaze boring into his. "*I* kissed *you*. Because I'd wanted to do it for years, because I was tired of fighting it, because you were there and so close and I was afraid I'd never get another chance." She felt a sad smile slide over her lips and she expelled a little breath. "So you can shrug that albatross off your neck, Eli. That one's on me."

He shook his head. "No, if I hadn't pushed you—"

"You're wrong. You didn't tell me anything I didn't already know. I cared deeply for Micah and I'd wanted things to work because he was a good man who loved me. I tried, I really did." She bit her lip, hesitated. "But I couldn't make myself feel something that…just wasn't there. Not the way it should have been. It wouldn't have been fair. To him or to me."

"Maybe so," he said. "But it doesn't change the fact that you were my best friend's fiancée and—"

Irritation spiked and she snapped. "And you were my fiancé's best friend! I *know*. I get it. It's wrong. It's shameful. It's inconvenient." She whirled away and threw her hands up in power-less frustration. "There. Feel better?"

Something shifted in his golden eyes. "No."

"Good. Neither do I. Because knowing all of that doesn't change anything, does it? It doesn't make me want you any less."

"You think I don't know that?" he bit out, his voice a low growl. "Why the hell do you think I've been avoiding you? Why I've tried to stay away? But everywhere I turn—everywhere I look—there you are. On the square, at the Hollands' place, on my back porch—" he gestured wildly "—and in my living room." His brow folded, pained. "You're killing me, Shelby." He started toward her. "I give up. I quit. I can't fight anymore."

His surrender was bittersweet. "Oh, no," she said, backing away when every cell in her body wanted to advance. "I'm not going to be another one of your regrets. I'm not going to be another guilt stick you can beat yourself up with."

She wanted him—God, how she wanted him— but not like this. Not when he'd look at her afterward and see another mistake.

He kept coming, his blistering gaze fastened on her mouth, until her back hit the wall, startling the breath out of her. "Then you should have stayed home."

She felt her eyes widen. "But—"

"Shut up, Shelby," he said, his big hands landing on either side of her head, his mouth a mere agonizing, seemingly eternal, inch from hers. "So there's no confusion, this time *I'm* going to kiss *you*."

And, mercy, did he.

His lips were sure and deliciously bold when they met hers, a confident lush slide across her own that instantly melted her insides and made her stomach drop and then rebound. Her breath left her in a stuttering whoosh and she closed her eyes, savoring the perfection of the moment.

His hands still braced on either side of her head, so that only their mouths touched, he tangled his tongue around hers, curling and diving in long, masterful stokes that made her feminine muscles clench and her panties set fire. Her breasts tingled and plumped, growing heavier with each increasingly wonderful slip of his lips over hers, and with every probing lap of his tongue, she felt a corresponding sensation deep in her sex, making her body alternately tense and relax. Impossibly it felt as if his mouth was in *both* places, which weakened her knees and liquefied her bones.

Though his mouth was self-assured and unhurried, she could feel the tension buzzing around his big frame, the quake of his arms as they stayed planted beside her head. It was almost as if he was deliberately not touching her, which was infuriating, but strangely erotic. She longed to feel his hands against her skin, the warmth of his body against hers. She wanted to taste him all over, to lick a path up the side of his neck and sample the soft skin behind his ear.

Unable to stand it any longer, Shelby lifted her hands, snagged the front waistband of his jeans and tugged him to her. His reaction was swift and gratifying. As though she'd inadvertently thrown a switch, his control snapped.

Without warning, he growled low in his throat, then picked her up, his hands going beneath her dress to her rump. Pleasure whipped through her, pulling a gasp from her lips, and she instantly wrapped her arms around his neck and her legs around his waist. The hot, hard length of him nudged her aching sex and she inhaled sharply, then pressed herself against him.

It wasn't the least bit subtle, but damned effective.

Ultimately, she just didn't care. His big hands were kneading her ass, his hot mouth was against her throat and every nerve ending in her body was painfully aware of him.

Just him. Eli. *At last.*

She clawed at his shirt, determined to get her hands on his bare skin, while he stumbled and bounced them around the living room, completely, wholly lost in her. In that moment, she owned him and nothing—nothing—had ever felt so important or more thrilling. They dislodged a picture from the wall and knocked over a metal urn of dried flowers, before he finally swept a lamp from the table and set her on top of it.

He made quick work of the row of buttons down the back of her dress and she shrugged her shoulders out of it while he whipped his shirt over his head.

Glorious muscle draped over masculine bone. Sleek, supple skin...

She blinked drunkenly, intoxicated by him, high on need, wasted on desire.

Breathing hard, his golden eyes feasted on

her bare breasts, before tasting them, his thumbs brushing their undersides while his fingers splayed over her quaking ribs. His hot mouth closed over a nipple and suckled, making her sex fist and beg.

In answer, she cupped him through his jeans, thrilled when he hissed against her skin, then loosened the snap and lowered the zipper. He was hot and hard and, sweet merciful heavens…*large*.

He quaked when she touched him, then found her other breast and slipped a hand beneath her dress, his clever fingers slipping along the inside of her thigh until the crease, then dipping over, expertly brushing her swollen clit through her panties.

She jerked, shocked by sensation, and shamelessly widened her legs. She needed him there. *Now.*

Hot and hard and fast and deep.

"They snap," she breathed brokenly against his chest, licking the defining ridge beneath his left pec while stroking him with her hand, her thumb grazing the thick crown of his penis. "My panties. At the sides. Take them off."

He popped one side and smiled against her. "That's ingenious."

Ordinarily she would have been flattered, but now wasn't the time to get distracted. She felt the other side give way, then the slide of his long fingers over her slickened nether lips before he pushed one deep inside.

He jerked in her hand, hardened even more. "Jesus, you're tight."

She spasmed, her muscles grasping at him. Shelby groaned and bit her lip.

She was going to die if he didn't take her, if he didn't—

To her whimpering displeasure, he stilled and swore hotly. "I didn't bring any condoms. I didn't think—"

"I'm healthy and I'm protected. You good?"

"I'm good."

She scooted forward and guided him to her entrance, sucked a breath through her teeth as he nudged against her, then inexplicably found his gaze. His eyes were heavy-lidded, blazing with golden heat and roiling with emotion. He was beautiful, magnificent in his masculinity. And so, so dear.

Then, with as much tenderness as desperation, he wrapped his powerful arms around her, and kissed her as he entered her in one blisteringly perfect thrust. Every muscle in her body rejoiced in relief, in recognition, in bliss and she came instantly, crying out as the sweet, redeeming storm of release thundered around her.

10

It was a good damned thing he was holding on to her, Eli thought, as Shelby's tight, hot channel squeezed greedily around him. Little white spots danced behind his lids, his knees weakened and, though he hadn't "detonated on impact" so to speak, since his early teens, he came hellishly close to doing just that.

Because she felt so good. Better than good. Better than great. Better than anything he'd ever felt in his life. She was eager and responsive, her keening cry as she clung to him the most beautiful sound he'd ever heard in his life. Her need sharpened his own; they sparked off each other until they were little more than two flames curling around each other.

Anchoring an arm around her waist and one on her hip, Eli drew back then pushed into her again, burying himself to the root. He was mindless with desire, bent on nothing but her pleasure, on making her his, focusing solely on what was happening between them.

He'd been thinking about this for years, dreaming about losing himself inside of her, filling his hands with her breasts, smelling her sweet skin, tasting those unbelievably carnal lips…but nothing could have prepared him for the genuine article.

She was exquisite, beyond compare.

Rosy-tipped breasts, flushed skin, the ripe curve of her ass…

At some point she'd taken her hair down and the long tendrils hung loosely around her small shoulders. Her mouth was swollen from his kisses, her eyes had darkened to a deep jade and her lids hung at half-mast, as though they were too weighted with pleasure to fully open.

She held on to him, her hands sliding over his back, his ribs, then she raked her nails gently down his chest, grazing his nipples in the process and the little sting of pain sent a bolt of heat directly to his groin, surprising him with its intensity. He plunged in and out of her, over and over, harder and harder until sweat dewed on her body and the mewling groans coming from her throat grew more pronounced. She tightened around him once again, squeezing his cock so hard he had to bite the inside of his cheek to keep from coming.

Not yet, dammit.

He'd deliberately kept his hands off of her when he'd kissed her because he'd known—*known*—that when he touched her, that would be it. He'd lose it. And he had. Instead of taking her to bed, like he'd dreamed of doing—or hell, even lowering her to the floor, which would have made more sense— he'd ricocheted off the bleeding walls until he'd found the little table and sat her there. The back edge of the table hit the wall and the legs squeaked across the floor with every thrust into her, every frantic push into her achingly tight little body, but he didn't care. Couldn't. Because everything he had, everything he'd ever been or ever would be, was wrapped up in her.

She bent forward and licked his nipple, blew on it, sending gooseflesh skittering across the small of his back, then she reached around him and grabbed his ass, squeezing it with a possessive growl of delight that made him want to beat his chest and roar.

He pumped harder, his balls tightening, heralding the first flash of orgasm. He could feel it gathering force in his loins, strengthening like a tropical storm over the gulf. Lightning bolts of pleasure struck him, electrifying every cell in his body, and need thundered through his blood. She bent forward again, lightly sinking her teeth into the tiny sensitized nub of his nipple and he *exploded*.

Release blasted through him, rocking him to his core, shaking his foundation. Every muscle alternately froze then melted, making him tremble and shake against her. She held on to him, then bent forward and sucked hard on his shoulder while tightening rhythmically around him, her feminine walls drawing every ounce of pleasure out of him, while her mouth mimicked the intimate act.

Bloody damned hell...

He'd died and gone to cock heaven, Eli thought, as the last vestiges of release pulsed through him.

She pressed a kiss against him, then drew back to look at him. Her eyes sparkled with sated desire and her lips curled into a satisfied smile. He felt that grin set like a hook in his chest and tug. He was doomed, Eli thought. But he'd figured that out a long time ago.

Her eyes widened significantly and she exhaled a lengthy breath. "Oh, my God. That was..."

"Epic," he finished, smiling down at her.

"Wicked good," she added.

He lifted her up and helped her down off the table, stupidly delighted when she wobbled a little on her feet. His clearly weren't the only knees that were malfunctioning. "Long overdue," he improvised.

Her eyes warmed. "The prologue."

He liked the sound of that, Eli thought, smiling. "What do you say we finish this conversation in the bathtub?"

She grinned. "You get the towels and I'll get the booze."

Ten minutes later, they were settled at opposite ends of the old cast-iron bathtub, her feet resting on either side of hips. "This wasn't exactly what I had in mind," Eli said broodily. He'd wanted her to lean back against him, let him hold her. "But I have to admit this position has its advantages." Her head rested against the lip of the tub, her bare breasts playing peekaboo with the water. She looked relaxed and gorgeous, innately sensual.

"I wanted to be able to look at you," she told him, running her fingers along the inside of his calf. "I have to be able to see your face. It's the only glimpse I get into your head."

He snorted, took a pull from the bottle they were sharing. "What are you talking about? You're always in my head. Most of the time it's damned uncomfortable," he admitted grimly.

She smiled, seemingly pleased.

"And you like that, don't you? You like winding me up so you can watch me spin," he said.

Her gaze tangled with his. "You don't spin enough," she said, startling the hell out of him. "You keep everything so tightly locked down that when you finally let go, you have absolutely no control. You're a pressure cooker," she explained, as though that was supposed to make sense.

He arched a skeptical brow. "A pressure cooker?"

"Yes. You do your best work under pressure. It's your element, what gives you control. You're fast and efficient and are more comfortable at boiling point. But when your regulator gets jammed and you don't have any way to let off the steam, you explode." She grinned widely. "And it's *awesome*."

Much as he hated to admit it, disturbingly, her analogy made sense. He did like to be in control—years of not having any would do that to a person. That's what had always scared him about Shelby. She was the only person who'd ever been able to make him lose it.

It was terrifying. And wonderful.

"You know what I like best about watching you spin?" she asked, her tone light.

He wasn't altogether certain he wanted to find out. "I'm sure you'll tell me," he drawled.

"It's what comes out of it. It's you, unfiltered. Genuine."

He laughed uncomfortably. "I'm beginning to wonder if I should be lying on a couch."

She playfully flipped her foot, splashing him with water. "Go ahead and make fun," she said. "But you know I'm right."

She was, damn her.

She shifted, scooting forward until she strad-dled him. He settled his hands at her waist, looked up at her. Moonlight cast a halo around the back of her head and her creamy skin gleamed in the night. She was warm and wet and beautiful and… *everything,* he realized with a short breath. He ached, looking at her. Burned.

She framed his face with her hands, her thumb stroking his cheekbone. Her touch was reverent, awed. "Do you know how long I've wanted to do this?" she asked, her voice low and foggy. "Just touch you." She leaned forward and slipped her nose along his jaw, breathing him in. "Just feel your skin beneath my hands."

Heat pooled in his loins, rousing him instantly, and she slipped over the length of him, undulat-ing her hips.

"Are you going to be okay with this, Eli? Really?" She shifted, taking the engorged head of his cock barely into her body, and waited. "Be-cause if you're not, then you need to tell me now," she said. "I don't want to wake up in the morn-ing and see any regret or guilt on your face." She rested her forehead against his. "I couldn't bear it. It would break my heart."

She was breaking his right now. He hated that he'd made her doubt him, that she wasn't sure of him, even after what had just happened between them.

Was their history complicated? Yes. Did he

wish they would have met under different circumstances? Possibly. But considering he probably would have never met her at all without Micah, then that didn't seem quite right, either.

He would be lying if he said there wasn't a small part of him that still felt odd about moving in on Micah's girl, knowing how he'd felt about her. But Micah was gone and staying away from her—denying them both—wasn't going to bring him back.

"I guess what I'm asking, Eli, is…am I safe with you? Can I trust you to want me enough? At least for this week?"

He nodded, his throat tight. "You're safe with me, Shelby."

He heard her sigh, felt the tension melt out of her body and she seated herself fully onto him, taking the whole of him deep into the heart of her. She was his water nymph. His goddess. His It Girl. He gritted his teeth as pleasure knifed through him, then gathered her close and kissed her deeply, with every bit of feeling he possessed.

Whether or not he was safe with her was another matter altogether.

MAVIS MERIWEATHER HAD lost her virginity at sixteen to a handsome college football player who would go on to become a state senator. That experience had lasted a grand total of three minutes—

including the clumsy, slobbery foreplay—and had left her wondering why everyone was so mysteriously desperate to do it. It had been awkward, uncomfortable and messy.

While she would go on to take other lovers, some of them more talented than others—and a great deal of them famous—Mavis could count her bona fide, vaginal orgasms, brought about by an actual penis without any digital interference, on one hand.

Or at least she could—until yesterday.

When she'd made the impulsive decision to proposition Les, she'd never dreamed that he'd end up being the best lover of her life. That the unexpected confidence in his touch would enflame her more quickly than a hot flash. She'd never imagined that she'd sing the hallelujah chorus from his armchair while he lapped at her mythical g-spot with his tongue, or that she'd spend the rest of the evening sprawled naked on his Aubusson rug, drinking thirty-year-old scotch while he suckled her breasts in between the shaggings.

Rug burn, Mavis thought. At her age. She bloomed with pleasure.

Wasn't it wonderful?

Honestly, when he'd deliberately rolled up his cuffs, then slid his hands beneath her dress, over her thighs, then gave her that little tug, she'd nearly had an immaculate orgasm right then.

There was something to be said about a man who didn't hesitate, who *acted,* instead of *reacting.* It had been thrilling the way he'd taken control, hadn't tried to pretty the business up with flowery words or insincere promises. It had been strictly about good sex, pleasure in exchange for pleasure. He'd wanted her—rather desperately, it seemed—and had made sure that she knew it, that she felt it.

There was nothing more gratifying for the ego than being desired and, considering she'd been feeling less and less desirable over the years— getting old was hell—Les's reaction had been especially heartening. Making love was nice, but every once in a while a woman just wanted a good old-fashioned fucking, and that's exactly what he'd given her.

Repeatedly.

In multiple, anatomical positions.

And with any luck, he was going to do it all over again tonight.

This arrangement could end up working well, Mavis thought, as she tidied a rack of clothing. Les was an interesting man whom the world had treated unkindly because of his condition and, while she hadn't been unkind, she had to admit that the speech impediment had, initially, prevented her from taking a closer look at him.

Her mistake.

Les was interesting, well-read and good-looking,

and there was something especially attractive about the effort he put into communication. He had the most expressive face she'd ever seen and she could easily get more out of conversation with him, just by watching him, than any other man she'd ever met. He deliberately chose his words, because he had to, but that meant that he actually *thought* about them first. Another item on the pro list. And she suspected there were going to be many, many more.

WELL, WELL, WELL, Shelby thought, looking at the soft smile playing over Mavis's lips when she and Dixie walked into the store. She set her purse and sewing basket on the counter, then turned and grinned. "You look…remarkably relaxed."

Mavis's smile brightened and a soft blush rose beneath her cheeks. Shelby nearly did a double take. Mavis? Blushing?

"I take it Les accepted your proposition?"

She nodded. "He did."

"And?" she prodded.

"And that's all you need to know."

Shelby blinked, her jaw dropping. "What? You mean after months of listening to you whine and complain about the sorry state of your sex life and the miserable pool of appropriate single men with any stamina in this town, you're not going to dish?

You're not even going to tell me how it was? You? The reigning Queen of TMI?"

Mavis paused, seemed to consider. "All right. It was the best sex of my life," she said. "If there was a Golden Penis Award, he'd win it, hands down, no question."

Shelby bit the corner of her lip. "The Golden Penis Award," she repeated, smothering a snicker. "Really?"

She had a candidate in mind for that, as well, Shelby thought, her belly fluttering at the thought.

"Really," Mavis insisted. She gave Shelby a shrewd look, then a knowing smile tugged on her lips. "You look remarkably relaxed, as well," she said, throwing the words back at her. "Dare I hope I wasn't the only one getting an itch scratched last night?"

Shelby bit her lip, tried to squash an immediate, telling grin, but failed miserably. "I did," she admitted. "But don't tell anyone."

Mavis frowned. "Why not?"

She hesitated. "Because I'm not sure where this is going, how we're going to resolve things at the end of the week, and I don't want to upset Carl and Sally."

"You think Carl and Sally will mind? They've considered you a daughter for years. Your happiness is important to them, Shelby, and if you've found that with Eli, they'll support you. I'm sure of it."

"I know that it is, but I was engaged to their son and—" she lifted her shoulders in a helpless shrug "—and Eli was his best friend. It's possible that they'll consider it a betrayal." She released a breath. "And it's not worth risking if, at the end of the week, we decide—or he decides—that there's no future for us. I live here," she said, gesturing around her store. "My life is here. And he's a career soldier."

"So was Micah," Mavis replied.

"Yes, but his family is here and he'd always planned on coming home." She grimaced. "Eli's family history is vague," she said, her brow creasing. "I know that his father passed away when he was little and, if his mother is still living, then they don't have a good relationship. He's always come here on leave and never mentioned visiting any other family."

Which was odd, really, Shelby thought now. Strange that she'd never really thought about that before, but it wasn't like he'd simply appeared, fully grown. She'd never heard him mention his parents at all, or bring up any childhood memories for that matter. The only reason she knew that his father was dead was because Sally had mentioned it once in passing, one of those "bless his heart" comments.

"So what do you want to happen at the end of the week?" Mavis asked, her eyes kind.

Shelby bit the inside of her cheek, felt her chest fill with emotion, warm and tingly. She hugged her arms around her middle and felt a wobbly smile tug at her lips. "I want him to go AWOL."

Her gaze twinkling knowingly, Mavis grinned. "I figured as much."

Honestly, she couldn't think about the end of the week without a big lump of dread forming in her throat. She knew what she wanted—she wanted him. She had wanted him for what felt like forever, and last night…

Last night had been more than she could have ever hoped for, ever anticipated. Considering the level of physical attraction, the fact that they'd had blazingly phenomenal, knock-the-world-off-its-axis sex wasn't a surprise. She would have been more surprised if they hadn't.

But it had been *so* much more than that. She hadn't just longed for his touch, she'd longed for *him*. She'd wanted *him*. Touching him, tasting him, feeling his big hard body plunging into hers…it had been bittersweet, a relief so profound that she'd felt tears prick the backs of her lids and her body melt with emotion. It was almost as if something inside of her recognized some counterpart in him and now that she'd found whatever that was, nothing else—no one else—would ever do.

And while she knew that Eli definitely wanted her and cared for her, she wasn't altogether certain that his feelings for her would trump the duty he felt he owed to Micah's memory. Last night had been a huge step forward, she knew. She'd been afraid to look at him this morning, terrified that, despite the fact that he'd assured her he wouldn't have any regrets, she'd see the guilt and self-recrimination in his dear face, anyway.

Thankfully, she hadn't.

She'd awakened to a magnificent wall of muscle at her back, his thigh slung over hers, his loosely curled hand over her breast. She'd known the instant he'd awakened because he'd stilled, seemingly surprised, then had leaned over and pressed his nose into her hair, breathing her in.

He'd been happy, and nothing could have thrilled her more.

Would things ultimately work out for them? Would Carl and Sally be okay with it if they did? Could they keep the memory of Micah without it casting a shadow on their relationship? Truthfully, she didn't know.

She only knew this—he was hers until the end of the week and she had every intention of taking advantage of it.

"Oh," Mavis said, frowning. "I forgot." She picked up an envelope Shelby hadn't noticed from the end of the counter and handed it to her. "This had been slipped beneath the door when I came down this morning."

Shelby's heart began to pound and a sickening dread rose in her gut. She didn't have to read it to know what it was, could tell from the block lettering on the outside, addressed to her. Until now they'd been coming through the mail. But evidently whatever they'd wanted to say couldn't wait until tomorrow.

"Shelby?" Mavis queried, concerned. "You've gone pale. What is it? What's wrong?"

Shelby released a shaky breath and, hands trembling, opened the letter, revealing a fuzzy picture of her and Eli from last night. In the tub. Oh, God…

Traitorous whore. You'll be sorry. I'm going to tell.

Shelby sucked in a breath, squeezed her eyes shut as nausea pushed up the back of her throat.

Having peered around her shoulder, Mavis gasped. "My God. Shelby, what is this? Who sent you this?"

"I don't know," she said. But whoever it was had clearly seen them and was hell-bent on ruining her.

11

"ELI WESTON THREATENED me last night," Katrina announced from the doorway.

Debating the merit of sending Mavis a bouquet of flowers—old-fashioned, he knew, but he thought she'd appreciate them—Les smothered a sigh and looked up. "Oh?"

"I want to run the Micah Holland story," she said, stepping in and closing the door behind her. A tremor of irritation surfaced. He hadn't issued an invitation, but evidently she thought she didn't need one. "I sent it to you last night. Did you read it?"

"No, I was busy."

Her brows shot up. "Busy? Really?" Her lips twitched with condescension. "Playing Scrabble again, were you?"

Les couldn't help the faint smile that pulled at his lips. "No."

"Then what could have possibly been more important than reading my story?" she asked, feigning confusion. "Because I was under the impression—and thought you were, too," she said, her voice hardening, "that what I want you to do supercedes anything that you want to do."

Walking into that hotel room in Louisville and finding her there was the worst thing that had ever happened to him, Les thought, feeling his temper rise. Katrina was a cunning, ruthless bully with no discernible moral character. He loathed dangling over her barrel, but as of yet, he hadn't figured out a way to maneuver himself off of it. Telling the world that she was a call girl wouldn't ruin her reputation because she didn't have one—or a good one, at any rate.

But telling the world that he paid for sex was another matter altogether.

He was a city councilman, and his reputation as an honorable businessman had been hard-won and had taken him years to establish. While other daily newspapers were going out of business all over the country, his still enjoyed a thriving print circulation. He'd limited online content, slashed advertising prices and, after much deliberation, added a gossip column.

He refused to run anything inflammatory—

which was why Katrina had been determined to get her story the old-fashioned way—and vetted every article that went into each issue. Occasionally, he'd post blind riddles to the epublication, then bury the clues in the print edition, fostering cross-promotion between the two.

In short, he'd worked hard to build this life and having this opportunistic viper try to take it from him galled him to no end. He'd given her the job to keep her quiet and had secretly hoped that would be the end of it.

He should have known better.

"They're dedicating the Memorial on Friday," she said, smiling as if it were a foregone conclusion. "Let's run it then, capitalize on all the hype."

"I will not," Les told her. "I would be hesitant to print it, even with authentication."

Which he'd explained to her already. He wasn't in the business of capitalizing on other people's grief and didn't intend to start now. Whether Micah had committed suicide, as Katrina suspected, or died from a misfired weapon, the fact remained that Carl and Sally had lost their son. Either that point was completely lost on Katrina, or she didn't care. Intuition told him it was the latter.

Katrina's nostrils flared and she planted her hands on either side of his desk. "You will," she said. "Or you'll regret it." She smirked. "Or in your case, *wegwet* it." Smiling triumphantly, she pushed away and coolly made her exit.

ELI KISSED SALLY ON THE cheek. "Thanks for dinner," he told her. He feigned a wince. "I'm going to need to buy those jeans with the elastic in the waist if you don't stop feeding me like this."

Sally beamed at him. "You're working hard. I'm just keeping you healthy."

He wasn't certain that fried chicken, black-eyed peas, mashed potatoes, green beans and banana pudding were exactly "healthy," but they were damned good.

"You'll be around for breakfast, right? I'm making a new casserole, with biscuits and sausage gravy."

In other words, fat with a side of fat, Eli thought, his lips twitching. He'd be willing to bet the casserole was full of cheese, too. He nodded. "I'll be here."

"Why don't you stop by and pick up Shelby? She's always been a fan of my biscuits."

If Shelby hadn't asked him so innocently, he probably wouldn't have thought much about her request, but it was almost…rehearsed? "I'll give her a call and see if she'd like a ride," he said, feeling an odd frown inch over his brow.

"Excellent!" she enthused.

A thought struck and he jerked a finger toward

the stairs. "Mind if I pop upstairs and say hi to Colin before I go?" he asked.

Colin hadn't made it to the square today, though he'd assured Eli that he'd be joining them again. He'd missed dinner, as well. While Eli knew that most teenagers were typically moody, Colin's erratic behavior seemed almost schizophrenic. One minute, he'd be laughing and cutting up, making jokes with everyone. The next, scowling and sullen, pissed at the world.

Sally nodded, her eyes softening with gratitude. "Sure," she said. "I heard him come in late last night, but he hasn't been down for a meal and when GG asked him about going to the square, he'd said he didn't feel like it." She paused uncertainly. "I don't want to make him go, but I wonder if we're doing him any favors by giving him a pass."

Eli wished he knew. Giving her another squeeze, he mounted the steps to the second floor. Micah's room was straight ahead, the door closed, and the sight of it made Eli flinch, knowing that he'd never sleep there again.

Colin's room was at the opposite end of the hall and his door was shut, as well. It was eerie.

Eli approached it and knocked softly. "Colin?" He could hear the faint sound of music—more Floggy Molly by the sound of it—but nothing else. He waited a minute, before trying again, a little louder in the event that Colin had his earbuds in.

He'd just decided to try the door when it abruptly opened.

"What?" the boy demanded, glaring up at him.

Slightly taken aback—Colin had been reserved with him at times since Eli had arrived, but never openly rude—Eli stared down at him. "I just wanted to see why you didn't come to the square today. You'd told me you'd be there," he reminded him.

Colin lifted his chin. "I didn't feel like it."

Right, Eli thought, feeling his jaw tighten. Carl and Sally might be at a loss on how much rope to give him, but Eli wasn't opposed to jerking a knot in his ass. Yes, he was a boy. Yes, he was hurting. Guess what? Life could be painful.

"Man lesson number one," Eli told him. "Do what you say you're going to do."

Colin blinked, evidently surprised at Eli's reaction, then his expression blackened with derision. "I didn't ask you for man lessons. I've got a dad for that."

"And you're damned lucky that you do," Eli said, unable to hide the edge in his voice. "So how about showing up tomorrow and helping him out? Or are you going to continue to let everyone else do it? Let everyone else build the memorial to *your* brother?" He lifted a shoulder. "It's your call, chief, but you're the one who's going to have to live with it." He nodded once. "Think about it."

Colin's eyes narrowed and his face screwed up in anger. "Don't tell me what to do. I don't have to—"

"Man up, Colin," he said, shooting him a firm look. "It's time."

Because he was too old and too dignified to stand around and argue with a thirteen-year-old, he turned on his heel and descended the stairs.

His shoulders weighted with fatigue, his eyes lined with concern, Carl waited for him at the bottom. "Well?" he asked. "Any luck getting through to him?"

Eli merely shrugged, sighed. "I guess we'll see tomorrow."

"I wish I knew what to do," Carl told him, casting a troubled look upstairs.

Eli swallowed, clapped him on the back. "You're doing everything you can," he said. "And Colin might not appreciate it now, but he will."

That was the trouble with lucky people—they'd never seen the other side of the coin.

"Thanks, Eli," Carl told him. "You're a good man."

Eli momentarily froze, shaken at the comment. No one had ever said that to him before, ever, least of all someone he admired and respected. Pride crowded into his chest, so foreign he almost didn't recognize it. His ears buzzed and his throat went dry.

Carl Holland thought he was a good man…

now. But would he hold that same opinion when he found out about his relationship with Shelby? Eli would like to think so, but ultimately, who knew?

That was a bridge he'd just have to cross when the time came, he thought. He just hoped like hell he wouldn't have to burn it.

JAW SET SO HARD SHE WAS listening for the resulting crack, Shelby watched Eli's expression go from confused concern to blistering anger in the space of about sixty seconds, which was exactly how long it took him to thumb through the letters. He glanced at up at her, obviously trying to rein in his temper before speaking.

"This is all of them?"

Seated at her kitchen table, Dixie at their feet, Shelby nodded. "This—" she pointed the newest one with the picture "—is the one that came today. Mavis found it on the floor. Someone had shoved it under the door."

"And the rest arrived in the mail?"

"They did," she confirmed. "Postmarked locally." She leaned back and pushed her hair away from her face. "I'll admit that they've been vague, but disturbing. But knowing that this person is actually watching me, saw us…" She shook her head. "It's got me a little creeped out."

So much so that instead of spending the night at the cabin again, she'd insisted they stay at her place. She'd ridden out and picked him up, and they'd left his truck in the driveway so that it would look as if he was there, alone. Meanwhile, she'd closed every blind in the house.

Explaining the letters to Mavis hadn't been fun, but had been necessary, all things considered, and she'd sworn her friend to secrecy about them. She hated not telling Mavis the complete truth—she'd left out the circumstances of Micah's death—but she just couldn't do that. She and Eli were the only people who knew what really happened and it *had* to stay that way.

Thankfully, Mavis had been distracted when a gorgeous bouquet of white calla lilies arrived for her—from Les, of course—and had let the issue drop without further comment.

"Had the picture arrived on its own, I would have assumed that Katrina was behind this," Eli said. He made a face. "I can certainly see her hiding in the bushes, spying on people." He frowned, then shook his head. "But with the letter...I just don't think so. I don't think it's her."

Shelby didn't, either. And honestly, she didn't expect to hear anything else out of Katrina. Eli had thwarted her advances—which had to be infuriating for her, Shelby thought with vengeful glee—and had threatened to sue the paper if she intimated in any way that he hadn't told the truth. And regardless of whatever Katrina had on Les

Hastings, he was an honest man. He wouldn't print anything that couldn't be verified from multiple sources. She grimaced.

Unfortunately, by ruling out Katrina, that left the "suspects" column on their clue sheet empty. She'd received the occasional tut-tut aren't-you-sorry-now? look from various people after Micah's death, but no one had been unkind. And she sure as hell had never been called a whore.

Eli scanned the letters again, his forehead creasing into a puzzled scowl. "These just don't make sense. This 'I'm going to tell.'" He looked up at her, cocked his head. "Tell what to whom? It's almost like a nah-nah nah-nah boo-boo sort of thing. Juvenile." Something shifted in his expression and his gaze sharpened.

"What?"

Eli looked up at her, hesitated. "It's probably nothing."

"What's nothing?" she asked grimly.

He looked at the picture again. "This looks like it was taken with a cell phone, doesn't it?"

"Yes," Shelby said. "But why is that important? Everyone carries a cell phone nowadays."

"It might not be important at all," he said vaguely. "I'm just thinking out loud."

"You're not thinking that clearly, or else I would know who you suspect," she pointed out, annoyed at his reluctance.

His mouth twitched, evidently finding her irritation amusing, which naturally irritated her more. She pushed back from the table and headed for the door. "Fine," she said. "Don't tell me who you think called me a whore. I'll just—" She yelped as he scooped her up from behind and threw her over his shoulder.

"You'll just what?" he asked, a chuckle in his voice as he walked unerringly into her bedroom and dropped her onto the mattress. He followed her down, lifted her hands over her shoulders and pinned her down.

"This isn't going to work," she lied. "If you think that a blatantly masculine show of strength is going to make me forget that I'm mad at you and that…" His nose slid along the side of her jaw and he pressed against her suggestively, making her gasp.

"What was that?" he murmured, his voice low and husky.

A helpless laugh escaped her as need swept through her. She was melting beneath him, putty in his hands. "You don't…play fair," she said brokenly, her breath stuttering out of her lungs as he did it again, that hot, hard suggestive thrust of his hips against hers. She opened her legs and rose up to meet him, squeezing his fingers.

She felt him smile against her throat. "Haven't you heard? I'm breaking all the rules now."

She rocked her hips against him again. Two could play at this game, dammit. "Am I a rule?"

He chuckled again, then sighed into her ear, sending goose bumps racing along her overheated skin. "A rule? No. You're the exception to every rule."

She smiled against him and pressed her lips to the side of his head, desperate to feel more of him. "Hmm. I sound powerful."

"Are you going to abuse it? Or will you trust me? Let me handle this letter business?"

Ah... "You did this on purpose, didn't you?" she accused, her eyes widening in mild outrage. "You knew that if you got me into bed and blew in my ear you'd be able to get exactly what you wanted."

He drew back and looked at her, his golden eyes twinkling with humor, yet hot with need, and he grinned, completely unrepented. "A man has to play to his strengths," he said. "Can I help it if you can't keep your hands off of me?"

She laughed and squeezed his fingers significantly. "Who has a hold of whom?"

"Semantics." He bent forward and kissed her, his skillful lips sliding expertly over her own. Heat boiled up beneath her skin and she groaned. "You know you want me."

God help her, she did, Shelby thought.

"You never answered my question," he said, letting go of one of her hands so that he could unbutton her shirt. He popped the front closure of her bra, baring her breasts to his heated gaze, then rolled her nipple between his thumb and his forefinger, bringing it to a fuller peak, before pulling the aching bud into his mouth and suckling hard.

Her eyes all but rolled back in her head and her back arched off the mattress. They were wearing too many clothes, Shelby thought. "You asked a question?"

He shaped his hand around her breast, massaged it, then licked at her again. "I did. I think you should say yes."

He scooted down the length of her, flipped her skirt up over her thighs, tore her panties off then hooked her legs over his shoulders and set his wicked mouth against her sex.

Her eyes widened as shock and sensation tore through her and she fisted her newly freed hands into the coverlet. Her neck bowed off the bed and it was all she could do to keep her hips still, to keep from grinding against his talented tongue. He lapped and licked and suckled, drawing hard on the delicate hood of her clit while simultaneously tugging at her nipple.

She came, hard. *"Yessssssss!"*

Eli quickly shrugged out of his shirt and shucked his jeans and underwear, then dragged her by her feet to the edge of the bed and plunged into her, sending another wave of unbearable pleasure cascading through her.

Masculine pleasure clung to his smile as his hands found her hips and he rocketed into her once more. "See? That wasn't so hard now was it?"

She grinned and tightened around him. "Oh, I don't know. It feels pretty damned hard from my position."

He chuckled low, his gaze rife with humor and something else, something that made her heart skip a beat. "You're something else, you know that?"

She nodded once. "Damn straight. I'm the exception to every rule."

And he'd become a rule breaker. Clearly they were meant for each other…and she desperately hoped he reached the same conclusion.

12

SNIFFING A SINGLE FLOWER from her bouquet, a smile curling her lips, Mavis rang Les's doorbell and waited impatiently. She'd decided that yesterday was simply an aberration, a fluke, that she'd been so desperate to get laid that she'd imagined how good it had been, how many times he'd brought her to climax.

It couldn't have possibly been as fantastic as she remembered, she'd concluded and, even if it was, then he wouldn't be able to repeat the performance.

The door opened and Les, looking smart in a French blue oxford cloth shirt and a pair of worn jeans, did a head-to-toe perusal of her frame, his attention lingering on her legs, the curve of her hips, her breasts, before finally finding her gaze.

The look in his eyes—enigmatic, hot and intense, and the same shade as his shirt, which she'd never noticed before—made the air thin in her lungs and her pulse rate leap into an irregular rhythm.

He silently offered her his hand, escorting her over the threshold, then closed the door behind her and swiftly backed her up against it, the heat of his body surrounding her as his lips descended to hers. He kissed her fiercely, probing the tender recesses of her mouth with certainty and expertise, his tongue sliding provocatively over hers.

He'd win the Golden Tongue Award, too, Mavis thought dimly, the blood hammering in her ears as it rushed through her. A flash fire of heat ignited in her limbs, spread through her body so swiftly she felt as if she were going to self-combust...and he'd only kissed her.

The thought had no more formed then fled, when his hand found the knot of her wrap-style dress and he loosened it, baring her right there in the foyer. He licked the seam around the top of her bra, tracing the curve with his tongue while his hand reached boldly into her panties, cupping her mound, circling it with his warm, wide palm.

Her head fell back against the door and she moaned, her eyes fluttering shut, the bloom hanging forgotten in her hand. She bit her lip as his hot mouth closed over her breast through the sheer fabric, suckling her, the fabric abrading her nipple, while a clever finger parted her weeping folds, swept at her clit and then slipped deep inside her body. She tightened around him, cried out.

"Les, please…"

In answer, he pulled her forward, drawing the dress completely off in the process, then bent her over a low chair. She felt his finger slide down the middle of her back to the tune of the whine of his zipper.

"Look," he said, his voice low and controlled.

Mavis glanced up, noted the leaning mirror against the wall right in front of her. But it was the reflection of the woman in it that thrilled her. Her pale skin was flushed, her lips swollen, her breasts covered with black lace. He stood behind her, the thick swell of his penis riding high on her rump. He pinned her with his gaze, much like a butterfly tacked to a display board, then swept her panties to the side and pushed into her in one long, sure stroke.

His gaze never left hers, held it firmly as he pumped in and out of her, his hands braced on her hips.

She couldn't have looked away if she'd wanted to.

Her breath came in ragged little puffs as her feminine muscles tightened around him, bore down as she came nearer and nearer to climax. He reached around and stroked her throbbing, engorged clit, then pressed a thumb against the rose-bud of her bottom.

Mavis felt her eyes widen as the most powerful orgasm she'd ever experienced burst through her. Her mouth opened in a soundless scream, her body quaked and she hung her head, too weak to support it on her own.

"Look at me, Mavis," he said gruffly, and she did, because she needed that connection, realized that he'd made her watch so that she could see herself the way he saw her. Beautiful, desirable, a carnal creature.

He thrust harder, grasped her hips and again and pistoned in and out of her as though the very hounds of hell were on his heels. His tight balls slapped against her rump and he hardened further, nudged deeper then buried himself the root and wrapped his arms around her middle as he emptied himself into her. A thick rush of warmth burst into her channel, setting off another sated tingle of pleasure.

"Look at you," he said, his eyes smoldering and earnest. "A goddess."

Mavis swallowed, moved by the compliment as much as she was by his lovemaking. She quirked her lips and released a small sigh. "I do like to be worshipped."

Hours later, after she'd done some reciprocal worshiping in the form of a lengthy blow job and a harder ride—honestly, the man's stamina was incredible—Mavis lay on the rug at the foot of Les's bed and watched his lovebirds play in their antique Victorian cage while he sipped champagne from the small of her back.

"They're beautiful," she said, enjoying the bubbles against her skin, his hot mouth against her. "What are their names?"

She felt him smile against her. "Bonnie and Clyde."

Mavis laughed and shot him a look over her shoulder. "Bonnie and Clyde? Seriously?"

Les smiled. "Watch them. You'll see why."

Intrigued, Mavis turned around and did just that. Clyde flitted around the cage, moving from one shiny object to another, then settled in at their food bowl and started kicking the seeds out. Every once in a while he'd stop and cock his head at Bonnie as if to say, "You see this? I'm a badass." Bonnie would fluff her feathers and preen and gradually moved closer until she, too, joined him in removing every bit of food from their bowl. Once they were finished, they took turns chasing each other from perch to perch until they reached the very top of the cage, then cuddled close, wrapping their necks around each other.

Mavis turned, stunned. "She follows him into trouble, then they make out. Like a couple of teenagers." She shook her head. "Wow. Did you watch them before you named them or did you just get lucky?"

"I watched," he said.

She wasn't surprised. "You watch a lot, don't you?"

His blue gaze was steady, seeming to wonder if there was a hidden meaning in what she'd just said. Finally, he lifted a shoulder. "People fascinate me," he said. "Especially you." He released a small breath, a cloud moving behind his eyes. "Which is why I need to tell you something that is likely to come out by the end of the week. It's best if you hear the news from me. I only hope that you won't judge me too critically."

Mavis felt her brow wrinkle at his grim tone, the reluctance she heard in it.

She sat up, drawing his silk robe with her and turned to face him. "What's wrong, Les?"

By the end of the conversation, she knew exactly what Katrina Nolan thought she had on Les—who'd called her Kat to avoid the *r*'s, which she'd found oddly endearing—and his noble answer to her threat, even if it meant losing his reputation.

"If you don't want to see me again, I'll abide by your wishes," he concluded, ever the gentleman. Which was so incongruous when she considered only a few minutes ago he'd been eating strawberries from between her legs.

He was fascinating, Mavis thought. She was merely opinionated with an interesting past.

"Why would I not want to see you again?" she asked. "Do you think I care that you've occasionally used an escort service?" Her eyes widened in blinking astonishment. "Have you forgotten that I asked you to have sex with me and I wasn't even so nice as to offer to pay you for it?" she said, her lips curling into a smile.

He grinned, almost sheepishly. "I'm cheap."

Mavis leaned forward, slid a finger down the side of his cheek, affection welling in her chest. "You're the best lover I've ever had, Les," she said. "And it's going to take a lot more than an old romp with a call girl to get rid of me." She paused, then bit her lip. "That said, I'm not fond of sharing."

In fact, the idea of him doing with another woman what he'd been doing with her made her distinctly ill.

"I'm afraid I'm going to have to insist on exclusivity," she said. "Is that going to be a problem?"

He leaned forward, grabbed the back of her neck and kissed her, and she discerned the faintest trembling in his hand. For whatever reason, that unsteadiness moved her more that she would have ever imagined.

"No," he said. "I belong to you."

Relief swept through her. "Good," she breathed.

"And don't you worry about Katrina," she said. "I'll take care of her."

And she would.

Though he completely ignored Eli, Colin was at breakfast the following morning and shadowed his father around on the site, determined to outwork everyone else involved in the process. He measured and cut willow branches, hauled shingles up the ladder, carried debris to the small Dumpster the city had arranged for them on-site, and generally did everything that was asked of him and more. Occasionally, he'd send Eli a mutinous glare, but as long as Colin stepped up for Carl, he was willing to overlook it.

What he wasn't willing to overlook, however, were the letters the boy had been sending Shelby, particularly this last one. Did he know for sure that Colin was the person behind them? No, not yet. But he strongly suspected that he was. Between the childish tone of the notes and the reference to "heavy dirt," which was something Colin had referred to after the funeral—he'd remarked upon how he hated it, hated that Micah was under there—Eli was relatively certain that Colin was the guilty party.

Thankfully, Shelby hadn't figured it out yet. She'd always cared for Colin and he knew that she'd be crushed to discover that the boy was angry at her for hurting his brother.

Additionally, given that Colin hadn't exactly been warm to him, either, over the past year and half, Eli was relatively certain he'd figured out what Micah's little brother had seen and grimly suspected that he'd witnessed what happened between him and Shelby at the anniversary party.

It explained the kid's hostility all the way around.

But before he could confront him and try to set things right, he needed proof and he suspected he'd find it on Colin's cell phone. Getting it would be the tricky part.

Carl joined him for a drink in the tent and cast a glance at the darkening sky. "Rain's moving in," he said. "If it holds for another hour, John will have the roof finished."

Eli winced. "It'll be close. Those clouds are coming pretty fast."

Carl nodded at Colin, who was busy covering the remaining willow branches with a tarp. "I don't know what you said to him, but it worked."

He chuckled. "It wasn't anything profound, I'm afraid. I just told him to man up."

The older man shook his head. "Simple enough. Good advice."

Having spotted them in the tent, Colin finished

up and joined them, which he'd done every time he'd noticed Eli talking to Carl. "What now, Dad?"

"We need to gather the tools up before the rain sets in," Carl told him. "But take a break first. Your mother will be disappointed if all those cookies she sent this morning aren't gone."

"I'll get one later," he said, shooting a look at Eli, who was working on his third cookie. He turned to walk away.

"Colin," Eli called. "Would you mind if I use your cell phone for a minute?" He grimaced. "My battery died."

The boy hesitated, but then grudgingly handed his over. "Sure."

"Thanks," Eli told him. "I'll give it right back."

Pretending like he needed a little privacy, Eli moved to the corner of the tent and quickly pulled up Colin's photos.

Bingo.

He'd taken several of him and Shelby in the tub, but thankfully the bulk of them were too fuzzy to make out. Eli deleted them, anyway. It was rude, not to mention an invasion of privacy, to take someone's picture without their consent.

He called Shelby, watched her answer the phone in her shop. "In Stitches," she said. "Can I help you?"

Eli lowered his voice. "Oh, I think you can."

She turned toward him and he watched her face light up with a smile. "Eli? What are you doing?"

"We're knocking off early because of the rain. Any chance you can leave Mavis in charge and play hooky with me?"

"I think that can be arranged. What did you have in mind?"

"It's a surprise."

Her grin widened. "You don't know yet, do you?"

"It'll be great, I promise. I'll pick you up in an hour."

Smiling, Eli walked over and returned the phone to Colin. "Thanks, man. I appreciate it."

Colin's gaze was suspicious. "Who did you call?"

"Shelby," he said. "I promised her I'd go to the police department with her this afternoon. With the rain coming, I wanted to let her know I'd be finished here early."

He frowned. "Police department? Why?"

Eli glanced around, pretending to confide something he was only sharing with Colin. Which he was. "She's been getting letters from some psycho since your brother's funeral. He's stalking her, from the sounds of it, and that's a class C felony." Whether that was true or was doubtful, but it sounded good and it had the desired effect. Colin's eyes rounded.

"That bastard's going down," Eli said. "Micah would be *livid*. He and Shelby might have broken up before he died, but they were still close. History, you know? It's not always good, but it doesn't have to be, right?" He slapped the boy on the upper arm. "Keep it to yourself, okay? If your mom and dad got wind of it they'd be really upset. And they've got enough on their plate."

Colin nodded, seemingly distracted. "Right. Yeah. I won't say anything."

No, he didn't think he would. Eli snagged another cookie on his way out of the tent and popped it into his mouth, fighting a smile. He'd let Colin stew on that for a little while, then they'd have a good old-fashioned "come to Jesus" discussion about why it was wrong to send horrible letters to women in general, and Shelby in particular.

In the meantime, he had a date to plan.

13

"THIS WAS A STROKE OF GENIUS," Shelby said, as she curled into Eli's side, the pleasant aftermath of release still tingling through her. "And to think that only an hour ago you didn't have a plan."

She sensed his smile. "I'm good at improvising."

"You're good at everything," she said, pressing a kiss against his chest. She snuggled deeper against him, listening to the rain pound the metal roof of the old fire tower and watching it come down in a steady sheet over the edges. Treetops loomed around them on all sides, giving the impression of their own treehouse retreat, one that was romantic and away from prying eyes. Eli had packed blankets, pillows, a basket of beer and left over chocolate chip cookies, courtesy of Sally.

A thought struck and she propped up on her

elbow to look at him. "You know what just occurred to me?"

His lips twitched and he turned his head to look at her, his eyes golden and sated. "What?" he asked, a hint of suspicion in his voice.

She smiled. "Technically, this was our first date."

A hint of pleasure warmed his gaze. "It was, wasn't it?"

Shelby manufactured a concerned frown. "I guess that makes me easy, doesn't it?"

Eli's chuckle moved through her and he slung an arm over his forehead. "There's absolutely nothing easy about you, Shelby," he said. "You are wonderfully complicated, an eternal puzzle. It's one of the things I love most about you."

"Wow," she breathed, her toes curling as happiness spread through her. "An insightful compliment and I didn't have to wind you up to get it out of you. We're making progress."

"Am I going to get a reward?"

"Didn't you just get one?"

"Not for the insightful compliment," he said. "You just wanted me."

She playfully pinched him. "Hey."

"I wanted you, too," he said. "So we're even." He turned to look at her, searched her gaze then slid a finger along her cheek. "Thanks for letting me read your letter," he said. "I…I needed to hear some of what Micah told you."

Shelby had silently handed it over last night after they'd made love for the second or third time—she'd lost count—then had quietly left him alone with it. She'd found it folded up, lying on her dresser when she'd returned to her room and they hadn't spoken about it…until now.

She swallowed. "I'm glad that it helped."

He looked away, staring at a place on the raw-beamed ceiling. "My dad hanged himself when I was eleven," he said, his voice strangely toneless. "I found him, too."

Shelby sucked in a silent breath, horror bolting through her. *"Eli…"*

"That thing you said, about Micah trusting me enough. I hadn't been able to look at it like that and—" His arm tightened around her. "Thank you."

Rather than risk answering and interrupt him, Shelby merely squeezed him back and waited, hoping he'd reveal more. There were so many questions she wanted answered, but she wouldn't pry, not when she knew it would cause him pain.

"I still don't know why my Dad did it," he continued. "He didn't leave a letter, didn't seem to have any problems, none that I can remember, anyway. It had been a day like any other. He came in from work, ate dinner, watched the news and then helped me with my homework. I was learning fractions," he said, his smile faint. "And then, when we were done, he said he needed to check on something in the barn and, if he wasn't back before Andy Griffith came on, I was to come and get him." He stopped stroking her arm. "It was so I'd be the one to find him, not my mother, and so I wouldn't have to walk out there after dark."

Jesus. Tears pricked the backs of her lids and her throat stung. What a horrible, horrible thing to do to a kid. How damned selfish.

"My mother broke down and never recovered," he said with an awful chuckle. "She's in a facility in Georgia. I'll go and see her before I report back to base, but she's not going to know who I am. She hasn't since it happened."

Her chest ached, it squeezed so hard. "I'm so sorry, Eli," she said, knowing that the words were inadequate but unsure of what she could offer. "Where did you go after that?" she asked. "Who took care of you?"

"I was in foster care until I was eighteen. Since I didn't have—don't have," he corrected, "any other family."

Well, that explained why he never talked about his parents, explained why he spent his time on leave and holidays with the Hollands. *They'd* become his family. And she certainly knew how that felt, because since she'd lost Gran, they'd adopted her, as well.

They were both orphans, welcomed into the Holland fold by virtue of Micah.

"I miss him," she said, her voice stretched thin with emotion. She turned her face into his chest. She didn't have to explain who she was talking about. Eli knew.

He hugged her tight and she felt his hand tremble against her. "I do, too."

A sob broke loose and she cried then. He held her, grieved with her as the rain continued to pour from the sky, almost as though weeping for their lost friend, as well.

When the last tear fell from her cheek, she tilted her chin, found his lips and kissed him with every ounce of feeling she possessed. The desperation and desire, the fear and longing...all of it. She poured her heart out and then some.

Don't leave me, I love you, love me back.

She rained kisses over his face, peppering them along his achingly familiar jaw, the corners of his mouth, the soft skin at his temples, the slope of his brow, then crawled on top of him, relishing the feel of his big, hard body beneath hers. She straddled him, then slowly lowered herself onto him, her breath wheezing out of her lungs in a low, sibilant hiss. She claimed him with every roll of her hips, every determined rock of her body.

Mine, mine, mine...make me yours.

How was she ever going to let him leave? Shelby thought. How was she ever going to let him go?

ELI BRACKETED HER wicked hips with his hands and watched as Shelby worked herself against him. Her hair hung in a long blond curtain around her shoulders, her pouty nipples sat like puffs of pinkened whipped cream on her rounded breasts and her waist was tiny, then flared into those unbelievably fantastic hips.

She leaned back, taking him deeper, then stretched her arms over her head, let her eyes flutter shut, sank her teeth into her bottom lip—as though it was too much, the pleasure too intense to bear—and rode him hard.

Sweet merciful hell, Eli thought, gritting his teeth. She was hot and tight, and the sleek contraction of her muscles grabbed greedily at him, hanging on to him, creating the most delicious friction between their joined bodies. Her breasts shook on her chest, absorbing the force of his thrusts, and he rose up, cradled her back and pulled one delicious nipple into his mouth.

She cried out and rode him harder, the need for release chasing her further and further to that goal.

"Oh, yes. Please. Right...there. Oh, *dammit.* I need— I want—"

Without preamble, Eli flipped her over onto

her back, spread her wider and plowed into her, hard. Desire hammered brutally through him and he passed that stark desperation onto her, plunging deeper and deeper, sating himself into her with every frantic thrust of his hips. His cock hardened further, driving him mad, as she repeatedly fisted around him. He held on to her, wrapping her close, felt her tight nipples brush against his chest with every move of their bodies.

It was *amazing* how good that felt.

How her soft, womanly body made him feel powerful, strong, indomitable.

But she was the strong one, Eli thought, because she'd brought him to this. With a single touch, an achingly sweet kiss against his cheek, the slide of plump breasts against him, her weeping, slickened sex along his cock and then that perfect instant, when she'd greedily welcomed him into her body.

"Come for me, Shelby," he said, angling deep. "Let it go."

She did. Her mouth opened in a long, keening wail, her muscles went rigid, locking around him as her back left the blanket and she quaked, shook, as the orgasm ripped through her, dragging her to that place of sublime perfection.

Seconds later, he joined her there. He pushed hard and held, every muscle in his body going weak. His vision blackened around the edges and his heart pounded so hard it was a miracle it didn't rupture against his breastbone. He sagged against her, kissed her shoulder, levered up and looked down into her painfully dear face.

There she was, Eli thought. The exception to every rule. The woman he was hopelessly, irrevocably in love with.

It was time to talk to Carl, Eli decided. Time to man up and let the chips fall where they may.

Because all he wanted was to fall into her forever.

MAVIS PARKED HER CAR at the curb in front of Katrina's house, opened her umbrella—rather regrettably, because she loved the rain, loved the way it felt against her skin, the sound of it, the smell of it—then calmly made the trek up the front walk to her door.

Katrina's unsmiling face appeared when she opened it. Evidently, she'd checked the peephole and knew who was waiting on the other side.

"Mavis," she said.

Mavis closed the umbrella and shook it, then breezed past a startled Katrina into the house. Clearly—astonishingly—Katrina must have made decent money on her back, which Mavis didn't have an opinion on one way or the other, except in how it affected Les. The smallish living room was decorated with nice furniture and decent art work—none of it to her taste, naturally, but she recognized quality when she saw it. A laptop with a small web cam attachment sat on her coffee table. Considering that Katrina was wrapped up in a pretty robe, Mavis gathered that she'd interrupted something. She turned and lifted a brow.

"I didn't invite you in, Mavis," Katrina said tightly.

"And yet that didn't stop me." She glanced at the laptop. "Entertaining a client through the wonder of technology?" she asked.

Katrina's eyes widened. "What?"

"Don't play coy, dear. You're not good at it."

Her eyes flashed. "I don't know what you're talking about."

"You're a piss poor liar, as well, then. In your line of work, that must be a detriment."

"My line of work? I'm a journalist. I don't have to lie."

Mavis laughed and shook her head. "Journalist? Really? You cover weddings and the occasional traffic accident. You're hardly a journalist. But that wasn't the work I was talking about."

"I don't have time for this, Mavis. If you've got a point, then get to it."

All right, then. She would. She leveled a look at Katrina. "Les isn't going to run the Micah Holland story," she said, and had the pleasure of watching the younger woman's eyes nearly bug out of her head, before they narrowed into angry, suspicious slits. "You're going to quit your job at *The Branches,* effective immediately, and you're not going to tell a single living soul that Les used to occasionally frequent the escort service you work for."

Katrina shook her head, her eyes sparking shock and derision. "I'm not, am I? And just who the hell is going to stop me?"

Mavis lifted an unconcerned shrug. "I am," she said.

Katrina snorted and crossed her arms over her chest. "You're out of your mind."

"Occasionally, yes," she admitted. "But more significantly, I'm meaner than you, and if you attempt to ruin Les, then I'll ruin you."

"How? By telling everyone in this backward little burg that I'm a call girl? Go ahead," she taunted. "I couldn't care less."

"Right now, maybe," Mavis told her. "But someday you're going to meet someone—away from this 'backward little burg' because no one here likes you—and you'll convince the poor miserable sod to marry you." Mavis strolled to a table, picked up a piece of crystal and idly inspected it. "You'll have a big wedding, a wonderful honeymoon and then you'll settle down, have a couple of sweet little children, join the PTA and the Junior League and do all the things that you pretend to abhor, but secretly long for. You'll finally fit in. You'll get comfortable, you'll be happy—" she turned to look at her "—and *that's* when I'll tell your secret." Mavis offered a pitying smile, watched a little of the starch leave the girl's spine. "You see, Katrina, you're shortsighted. Right now, you don't have anything to lose because you don't care about anything. You're young and stupid. But that will change, and when it does, I'll be waiting. And I'll destroy you then, the same way you're threatening to destroy Les now." She arched a brow. "Am I making myself clear?"

"Crystal," Katrina ground out.

Mavis beamed at her as though she were a dim student who'd just had a lightbulb moment. "Excellent. Now call Les and quit. And apologize."

"What?"

Mavis gestured casually with her fingers. "Go on. Do it now."

Looking as if she'd just eaten a plate of shit— which, for all intents and purposes, she had— Katrina reluctantly did as Mavis instructed.

She disconnected and glanced up, an odd expression on her face. "Why do you care so much about Les's reputation?" she asked. "What's he to you?"

Mavis smiled and lifted her chin. "He's the finest man I've ever known, the best lover I've ever had and he's the man I intend to marry."

The image of Katrina's gaping jaw entertained

her all the way to Les's house. He was waiting at the curb for her, umbrella in hand, when she arrived.

"How?" he asked simply once they were safely inside, his face a mask of astonished disbelief and relief.

Mavis merely shrugged. "It was simple enough," she said. "I simply explained that she wouldn't always have nothing to lose if her secret was revealed, and that I'd wait until I was certain that she was the happiest she'd ever been in her life, and then I'd ruin it for her."

His lips twitching, Les cocked his head in mild astonishment and poured her a glass of scotch. "A diabolical solution," he said, seemingly impressed. "Well played. Thank you."

"You're welcome." She took a sip, hesitated, her bravado slipping. "There's something else," she said, heat billowing up beneath her skin as his gaze drifted boldly over her. He lifted her hand, bussed the back of it with his lips then turned it over and pressed a hot, open-mouthed kiss into the center of her palm.

Her knees quivered, the tops of her thighs quaked and burned.

Good Lord, this man...

As usual, his gaze clung to hers, showing her how she affected him, never letting her forget how much he wanted her. How on earth had she lived in town with this man the majority of her life and not realized that he was the *only* one for her?

He arched a brow in a silent question, encouraging her to go on.

She gestured to his back porch. "Do you mind if we go outside?" she asked. "I love the rain."

His fingers threaded through hers, as though he was reluctant to let her go, Les nodded and opened the door. Rain hammered the porch rooftop, pounded the lush green grass and made his flowers droop. He obviously spent a great deal of time out here, she thought, noting the comfortable chairs and small table. Jasmine grew in an arbor on the end of the porch, perfuming the sweet air, and another stand of it covered a small gazebo farther into the yard. It was lovely, almost like a park.

"I like this," she said. "It's lovely."

She felt his gaze slide over her face, settle on her mouth. "I know a thing or two about lovely."

All right, Mavis thought. It's now or never… and never wouldn't do. "Les, I'd like to amend our agreement again, if it's all right with you."

He stilled, looked up at her, his expression guarded. "Amend it? How?"

She sighed softly. "I've decided that simply promising exclusivity isn't going to be enough for me, after all. I know that I'm the one who approached you, then set the rules, and then changed them, and now I'm wanting to change them again——" she shrugged helplessly, looked up at him from beneath her lashes "——but the idea of you ever being with another woman, ever so much as *looking* at one the way you look at me, makes my mind turn black with rage," she said, her voice cracking with anger just thinking about it. "I'm jealous by nature," she admitted. "So…" More terrified than she'd ever been in her life, she left her chair and knelt before him, startling him, as she squeezed his hand. "I guess what I need to know is…will you marry me?"

Heat and happiness warred for room in his gaze, then he lifted her up, swept her into his arms and hauled her through the rain out to the jasmine gazebo. He carefully set her down, letting her slide along the length of his body, then laid her down in the sweet, wet grass, cocooned beneath the fragrant vines and slowly, deliberately pressed a reverent kiss against her lips while he thrillingly yanked the sash of her rain coat open.

She was naked beneath it.

"You haven't answered me," she said, resisting the urge to preen beneath that hot stare. He sat back on his haunches, unbuttoned his shirt in that slow but methodical way of his then opened the snap at his jeans and freed his manhood. It jutted proudly from between his thighs, huge and wonderful and hard for her.

He entered her in one, fierce stroke, tearing a guttural, "Yes," from his lips. "God, yes. A thousand times *yes*."

14

"I'D LIKE TO BEGIN BY thanking you all for being here today," Carl said, standing proudly with Sally and Colin at the entrance of the newly finished gazebo.

Eli longed to grab Shelby's hand, thread her fingers through his, but had decided that it would be better to speak with Micah's father about his feelings for Shelby after the dedication service.

"As you all know, Sally, Colin and I all lost a beloved member of our family nearly nine months ago, our oldest son, Micah. Micah was born and raised in Willow Haven, was christened in Our Lady of the Willows Catholic church, attended school here, played football for the Bobcats and, after college, went on to serve proudly for the United States Army. We love him, we miss him, and wish to honor his memory today by dedicating this beautiful gazebo—" he gestured widely with his hand "—to him, and to all the other veterans our fair town has produced and will continue to encourage."

A round of applause rang out and Carl waited patiently for it to subside.

"I'd like to personally thank each of you who gave your time and your talents for this endeavor, especially my son, Colin," he said, wrapping an arm around the boy. "And to a man who isn't my son by blood, but of the heart, Eli Weston."

A lump swelled in Eli's throat and he nodded his thanks at Carl.

"While Sally and I were never blessed with a daughter, we found one in Willow Haven's own Shelby Monroe. Though she and Micah decided to honor each other truthfully by ending their engagement, to us she was a part of our family and always would be. She designed this lovely structure for our son and for that, we are eternally thankful."

Eli felt her tremble next to him, watched her swipe a tear away from the corner of her eye.

"So, without further ado," he said, handing the scissors over to Colin for the ribbon cutting. "To Micah Holland, our son, your friend…a hero."

Colin's chest puffed with pride as he turned and snipped through the pretty yellow ribbon, and a collective cry of joy and applause rang out as the local high school band struck up a tune. The group disbursed, loading plates with food that Sally and her army of local cooks had prepared. Yesterday's rain was gone and the sun shone brightly overhead, lightening the glorious blue sky.

Both Sally and Carl found him and hugged him tight. "We're so glad that you were here," Sally told him. "It's meant more than you'll ever know."

It had to him, as well, for different reasons. While Carl and Sally shuffled toward the food line, Eli watched Colin stalk away from the square and head toward the direction of the Catholic church.

He knew exactly where the boy was going.

Eli caught Shelby's gaze, nodded to Colin's retreating figure and watched as realization dawned. She gestured significantly to Eli, encouraging him to follow the boy.

Eli purposely hung back for a minute, giving him a good lead, then quietly took off after him. Predictably, he found him at the foot of Micah's grave, part of the yellow ribbon dangling from his hand. He wiped his face with the back of his hand.

"This sucks, bro. I didn't want a damned memorial. I want my brother back."

His throat tight and clogged with emotion, Eli stepped out from behind a tree. "I'd like my friend back, too, Colin, but that's not the way it works."

Colin turned on him, eyes hard and wet with unshed tears. "Shut up," he shouted. "You have no right to call him a friend. I saw you!" he exploded. "I saw you with her! He trusted you!" Colin came at him, fists wailing against Eli's middle, and Eli let him pound away. "How could you? Bros before hoes, man. I'm thirteen and even I know the code!"

Eli grabbed his arms, forced him back. "Shelby isn't a whore, Colin. No more letters, you understand?"

He blinked. "You knew it was me?" He jerked away from him. "Did you go to the police?" he asked, his eyes widening in alarm.

"No," he said. "I didn't."

Colin seemed to wilt and shook his head. "I just don't understand," he said. "He was your friend. He loved you. And he loved *her*," he said, his voice hard.

"That's right," Eli said. "And I'm not going to pretend that what you saw between me and Shelby meant nothing, because it did. We all loved each other, Colin, which I know is confusing for you because it's been confusing for us, as well. But what you have to realize is that Shelby didn't break things off with Micah because of me. She did it because she knew that she didn't care for Micah as much as he cared for her. She didn't want to marry him knowing that the affection was unbalanced between them."

"She broke his heart."

Eli hesitated, winced. "She bruised it, but he

knew how she really felt, and he loved her enough to let her go, because he cared enough for her that he wanted her to be happy." He paused. "And if Micah could do that, don't you think you should be able to?"

He might as well be talking to himself, Eli thought, the truth crashing into him. Micah would have wanted her to be happy and, ultimately, he wouldn't have given a damn where that happiness came from.

Colin twisted the ribbon around his fingers, then looked up. "Do you really think that's what he'd want?"

"I know that's what he wanted," Carl said from directly behind them.

Startled, both Eli and Colin turned around.

"Because he told me so," Carl finished. He laid a hand on his son's shoulder. "Listen, Colin, I know this is difficult to understand—there are things that just simply aren't going to make sense until you're older—but Micah told me years ago that if anything ever happened to him, to give his blessing, and mine," he added significantly, "to Shelby and Eli." A faint smile tugged at his lips and his gaze lingered on Micah's headstone. "He said he was too selfish to get out of the way on his own, but if providence intervened, to make sure that they stopped denying each other." Carl glanced at Eli. "Why do you think Sally and I have been pushing you two together all week, why we insisted that you come here? We're honoring our son's wishes," he said, his voice thick. "And ensuring that the pair of you stay in the family."

Overwhelmed with emotion, his eyes burning, Eli walked over and wrapped his arms around Carl, who hugged him back just as tightly. "He wanted you to be happy, too," Carl said. "My son was a good man."

"He was," Eli told him. "The best."

Carl drew back, looked at him, unspoken gratitude in his kind eyes. "Thank you for being there for him," he said. "What happened in Mosul…" He shook his head. "That was bad business, a load no man should ever have to carry. Pregnant women, dead babies…"

Eli stilled, a question forming. Did he know, then? But how could he know?

Carl slung his arm around Colin's shoulder. "Come on, son. We've got a lot of food to eat." He glanced at Eli. "And you should probably find Shelby, shouldn't you? Don't you have something to ask her?"

MAVIS STROLLED UP, her fingers threaded with Les Hastings. "Where's Eli?" she asked, glancing around.

"He's gone to speak with Colin," Shelby told her. "My letter writer," she added significantly.

Mavis's eyes rounded right along with her lips. "Oh. *Oh.* Right."

"I'm sure Eli will sort it out."

"I'm sure he will, too," she agreed. "By the way, I'm giving notice."

Stunned, Shelby felt her jaw drop. *"What?"*

"Oh, I'm not quitting," Mavis quickly assured her. "I meant for the apartment. I'm moving out."

Shelby didn't understand. "Moving out? Moving where?"

"1230 Windmere Street," she said.

Windmere Street? But that's where... She gasped, a smile sliding over her lips. She glanced at Les, who looked more than a little thrilled with the idea. "You're moving in with Les?"

She nodded, pleased. That was a big step for Mavis, who'd always insisted that cohabitation had nothing to offer other than additional dirty laundry and more food preparation. That her friend was willing to do it for Les meant that she was genuinely smitten with him.

"Yes, I am," she said. "But not until after we're married. He's a gentleman, after all, and is determined that we do things properly." She frowned thoughtfully. "Though I should probably add that *I* proposed to *him* and insisted that I make an honest man out of him."

"M-married?" Shelby repeated faintly. "Mavis you're going to give me heart failure," she admonished, laughing delightedly. "When are you getting married?"

"A week from Sunday. I'll need a dress. I was hoping you'd—"

Shelby squealed and threw her arms around her. "Of course! Congratulations!" Excited, she hugged Les, as well, startling a chuckle out of him.

"Thank you," he said.

Mavis's eyes rounded. "Oh, did you hear the news?"

"There's more?"

"Yes, Katrina Nolan has decided to leave town. She has a feeling her options will be better in a bigger city."

Hmm. That was good news. She saw Mavis's hand at work there and nodded at her, acknowledging her job well done. "I'm sure…someone, somewhere…will be sorry to see her go."

Mavis glanced past her shoulder and she nodded. "I know someone who's going to be sorry to see him go." She leaned in. "A word of advice— don't let him." And with that parting comment, the pair of them turned and strolled away.

Anticipation making her nerves jump, Shelby pivoted to find Eli swiftly approaching. "Hey," he said, smiling down at her. "Is there somewhere we can go talk?"

Shelby nodded. "My shop? I'm technically closed, so we should have some privacy."

His fingers at the small of her back, Eli followed her across the street to the door. Her hands shaking so hard she could barely insert the key in the lock, she eventually managed to let them in.

"Let's go back here," she said. "I've got a little break room."

While she'd always been good at reading him, she couldn't draw anything from his expression, his tone, and it was making her crazy. She'd seen Carl head toward the cemetery, as well, and knew that Eli had to have spoken to him. And without Carl's approval…

Shelby would like to think that he would be willing to risk the Hollands' regard for her, but she just didn't know. And she wasn't even certain she could ask it of him, knowing that, like her, he had no other family.

The minute they were through the door, she turned around and looked at him. "Well? What happened? With Colin and with Carl?"

Eli released a breath. "Colin did see us the night of the anniversary party," he told her. "He was understandably confused and upset and gave me the 'bros before hoes' speech."

Shelby felt her eyebrows wing up her forehead. "What? I—"

His lips quirked and he stepped forward, taking her hand. "He realizes that you're not a whore and, more importantly, he realizes that Micah loved you so much that he'd want you to be happy, regardless of who you were happy with." He expelled a pent-up breath, his golden gaze deepening with emotion. "And it turns out…he wanted that person to be me."

Shelby sank onto the couch, her legs unwilling to support her. "What?"

"He told Carl," Eli said, sitting beside her. He laid their joined hands on his knee, absently stroked her fingers. "That's why they've been pushing us together this week. Because Micah *knew,* Shelby—he knew—and he told his dad that he was too selfish to give you up on his own, but if anything ever happened to him, to make sure that we were together, that we had his blessing." He cleared his throat. "Their blessing."

Numb with shock, her stomach quivering, Shelby felt her eyes fill with tears. *"Micah,"* she breathed. "Only Micah."

He squeezed her hand. "And I'm glad that we've got his blessing, that we have the Hollands', but it wouldn't have changed anything if we hadn't." His gaze tangled with hers. "I love you, Shelby." He gave a helpless little laugh. "I've loved you for years. You're my It Girl, too."

Bubbles of happiness fizzed through her, emotion overwhelmed her. "Your it girl, too?" she asked, confused.

Eli grinned. "That what Micah used to call you.

He said that once he met you, that was it." He lifted a shoulder. "I know exactly what he meant, because the same thing happened to me. You smiled and…that was it."

Shelby rested her head against his. "What are we going to do, Eli? I don't want you to go."

"And I don't want to go, but I have to," he said, her heart squeezing at his words. "But I'll be back in three months, when my contract is up, and I want to marry you in that gazebo you designed and I helped build for our friend. Will you do that, Shelby? Can you wait three more months?"

Shelby wrapped her arms around his neck, joy whipping through her, the promise of a future she never imagined she'd have suddenly lying out before her.

"I'd wait three more years if you asked it of me," she said.

"So that's a yes. Yes to marriage. Yes, to the gazebo."

She nodded. "It is," she breathed against his lips, then sealed the promise with a kiss.

Epilogue

Three months later...

HAPPIER THAN HE COULD have ever imagined that he'd be, Eli waited impatiently inside the gazebo for Shelby to make her appearance, Colin standing beside him.

He'd given his power of attorney to Shelby while he'd been away and she'd used that authority to move his mother to a facility closer to Willow Haven. Though his mother still didn't know who he was, she sat in the audience, in a wheelchair and smiled at everyone who passed by.

It meant a lot that she was there.

The band finally—blessedly—struck up the wedding march and then she was walking toward him, a vision in white, Carl escorting her. Though he knew she'd be disappointed that he wasn't absorbing every detail of the dress she'd been working on for months, Eli could only look at her face. She was gorgeous. Glorious.

His.

Looking lovely as always, Mavis followed behind her…leading Dixie, who'd also been garbed in white tulle, a garland around her neck.

Eli chuckled and shook his head. Only Shelby would bring a flowered pig to her wedding.

Carl gave him her hand, then reached out and squeezed his shoulder. "You be good to her or you'll answer to me."

"I will," he said.

He looked down into her smiling face, her green eyes clear and alight with happiness. "You brought a pig to our wedding," he said, careful not to move his lips.

Shelby merely grinned. "I'm the exception to every rule, remember?"

Yes, Eli thought. Yes, she was.

* * * * *

**Is there anything sexier than a hot cowboy?
How about four of them!**

New York Times bestselling author
Vicki Lewis Thompson is back in the Blaze® lineup for
2013, and this year she's offering her readers
even more…

Sons of Chance

Chance isn't just the last name of these rugged
Wyoming cowboys—it's their motto, too!

Saddle up with

I CROSS MY HEART
(June)

WILD AT HEART
(July)

THE HEART WON'T LIE
(August)

And the first full-length
Sons of Chance Christmas story

COWBOYS & ANGELS
(December)

Take a chance…on a Chance!

COWBOYS
& ANGELS

BY
VICKI LEWIS THOMPSON

First published in Great Britain 2013
by Mills & Boon, an imprint of Harlequin (UK) Limited,
Eton House, 18-24 Paradise Road, Richmond, Surrey TW9 1SR

© Vicki Lewis Thompson 2013

ISBN: 978 0 263 90335 5

14-1213

Harlequin (UK) policy is to use papers that are natural, renewable and recyclable products and made from wood grown in sustainable forests. The logging and manufacturing processes conform to the legal environmental regulations of the country of origin.

Printed and bound in Spain
by Blackprint CPI, Barcelona

With gratitude to Dana Hopkins for her steady hand on the editorial reins and her most excellent tweets.

Prologue

December 24, 1989
Last Chance Ranch

A WHITE CHRISTMAS was all well and good, but some-body had to shovel the snow off the front porch, and Archie Chance had appointed himself caretaker of that chore. His wife, Nelsie, had tried to talk him out of it, but he was the logical guy for the job. Everyone else was busy wrapping presents and cooking food.

In the ninth decade of his life, Archie could still wield a mean shovel, whether he was mucking out a stall or clearing a path through the snow. He rather enjoyed both jobs.

After bundling up in a sheepskin jacket, earmuffs and his Stetson, Archie took a pair of gloves out of his coat pocket and opened the massive oak door. Yeah, it was cold out this morning, but he'd endured worse. Frigid winters were a fact of life in Jackson Hole.

The snow shovel was kept handy by the door all winter. Archie picked it up, scooped up a load of snow and was about to throw it over the porch railing when the ranch foreman, Emmett Sterling, called out to him. The tall cowboy made deep ruts in the snow as he plowed his way from the barn up to the house.

Archie emptied the shovel and leaned on it as he watched Emmett approach. "Nelsie called down to the barn, didn't she?" The phone connection to the barn was a recent addition, and right now Archie didn't care for it.

"She might've."

Archie blew out a breath, which created a substantial cloud in the air. "Look, I'll be fine out here. My back hasn't bothered me in quite a while."

"And Nelsie wants to keep it that way." Snow crunched under the tall cowboy's boots as he mounted the steps. "Especially seeing as how it's Christmas tomorrow. She doesn't want you putting your back out right before the big day. Can't say I blame her."

Archie considered his options. He was Emmett's boss, so he could refuse to turn over the shovel. But Emmett had interrupted his own chores in the barn to come up here and help, so sending him back down would mean more wasted time.

Archie also realized that if he insisted on shoveling and happened to reinjure his back, he'd look like a stubborn jackass. Nelsie would be ticked off, and making her mad wouldn't help the celebration of Christmas any.

"Much as I hate to admit it, you make a good point, Emmett." With a sigh of resignation, Archie relinquished the shovel.

"I'd be obliged if you'd hang around and keep me company," Emmett said. "Conversation makes the job go faster."

"Be glad to." Archie laughed. "Nothing wrong with my jawbone." As he brushed the snow off the porch railing and leaned against it, he thought about the kindness inherent in Emmett's invitation, as if he knew Archie had come outside partly to enjoy the crisp winter air. Emmett was less than half Archie's age, but he understood people better than most anybody Archie knew.

"I hope you don't fault Nelsie for calling me," Emmett said as he tossed snow over the railing. "She just cares about you, is all."

"I know that. She's a good woman, and I'm a lucky man to have someone like her fussing over me. It's just…"

"You don't want to be fussed over." Emmett dumped more snow into the yard.

"You got that right. And I like to think I can do everything the same as I always did. She knows I'm touchy that way, and she doesn't nag me. Not much, anyway."

"You said it yourself, Archie. She's a good woman, and you're a lucky man."

Archie heard the note of longing in Emmett's voice. Emmett's wife, Jeri, had decided ranch life didn't suit her and had divorced Emmett a couple of years ago. She'd taken their young daughter, Emily, back to California with her.

Although Emmett could have fought that, he hadn't. Instead, he made do with sporadic visits from Emily. Archie thought it was a shame the marriage hadn't worked out. Emmett would have made a good family man.

Archie didn't get too many opportunities to talk

privately with Emmett, so he decided to make use of this one. "You can tell me to mind my own business, but I can't help wondering. Have you ever thought of remarrying?"

"Nope." Emmett kept shoveling.

"Sorry if that was too personal."

"It wasn't." Emmett propped the shovel on the porch floor and leaned on it while he looked over at Archie. "I didn't mean to sound like it was. I just don't have any interest in marrying again."

"Why not?"

Emmett paused, as if considering his answer. "Mostly it's about Emily. All my spare cash goes to my daughter, and any woman I hooked up with would rightly conclude she came second to Emily. Not many would accept that, and if they wanted to have children, what then? I wouldn't start a new family when I still have Emily to think of."

"The right woman would understand."

Emmett smiled. "Maybe. But if that's so, I haven't found her yet."

"Well, I hope you keep looking."

"I hate to disappoint you, Archie, but I'm not looking. The kind of woman who would be happy with a cowpoke in my situation is a rare breed. I seriously doubt I'll ever marry again."

1

Present day

CRAMMED INTO THE small backseat of Watkins's king cab, Trey Wheeler thought about the wedding he would soon be a part of. He'd worked as a horse trainer at the Last Chance Ranch for a few months, so he didn't know the groom, Emmett Sterling, all that well. But Trey could tell the ranch foreman was majorly stressed about his upcoming nuptials.

His fiancée, Pam Mulholland, ran a B and B down the road from the Last Chance. She seemed like a nice lady, but when it came to this wedding, she wasn't making things easy on Emmett. Even a newcomer like Trey could see that.

Pam was wealthy and Emmett was not. Although Emmett was crazy about Pam, he'd allowed their financial differences to keep him from proposing until the previous summer, when a shyster had blown into town and shown interest in Pam. Emmett had thought it prudent to take her off the market before he ended up losing her forever.

But Pam, who'd been previously married to a cheating bastard, wanted the wedding of the century this time, and she'd reserved the entire Serenity Ski Lodge in Jackson Hole for a Christmas-themed celebration. Trey was thrilled because Pam had hired him to play guitar for the ceremony along with Watkins, a seasoned ranch hand and the husband of Mary Lou Simms, the ranch's cook. Trey had caught a ride up to the Serenity resort with Watkins and Mary Lou, who were as eager for several days of celebrating as everyone else. Everyone, that was, except the groom.

Trey edged his guitar case aside and leaned toward the front seat as they navigated the snowy road leading to the resort. "Do you think there's a chance Emmett will bail and ruin everything?"

"No," Mary Lou said. She'd tamed her flyaway gray hair under a furry hat. "I've known Emmett Sterling for a lot of years, and he's considerate. He might not like this operation, but it's what Pam wants, and he loves her."

"That's a fact," Watkins agreed. "And the Chance family has gone to some trouble to hire temporary help so we could all get up here and stay a couple of days after the wedding. Emmett wouldn't mess with that kind of generosity."

"I hope not." Trey looked out at the snowy landscape. "I know how much everybody's looking forward to this, including me."

Watkins grinned as he glanced in the rearview mirror. "You gonna try skiing, cowboy?"

"You know, I might. I mean, thanks to Pam, it's free, so why not?"

"That's what I'm thinking," Watkins said. "At least the bunny slope, right, Lou-Lou?"

"At least. I used to be pretty good, but I haven't skied in years. I hope it's like riding a bike and it'll all come back to me once I suit up."

Watkins sent her a fond glance. "I can't wait to see you all decked out. I'll bet you'll look great in goggles."

Mary Lou laughed. "No, I won't, you old flatterer, but I appreciate the thought."

Trey got a kick out of those two. They were both in their fifties, and Watkins had been after Mary Lou for years. She'd resisted the idea of tying the knot until about eighteen months ago, but now that they were married, they both seemed deliriously happy. It was very cute.

The truck approached a curve, and Trey sucked in a breath, as he always did when he came to this part of the road.

"You okay back there?" Watkins glanced in the rearview mirror again.

"Yeah. This is where I had my accident last spring. It always gets to me a little bit."

"I'm sure it does." Mary Lou looked back at him, her gaze sympathetic. "You could've died."

"I would've died, if that woman hadn't come along." *His angel*. For the millionth time, he asked himself why she'd come to his rescue and then left before he could thank her.

He'd been heartbroken after getting a Dear John letter from Cassie, who'd moved back east to attend law school and had fallen for someone there. In the predawn hours, he'd lost control of his Jeep on this curve. Pure misery had kept him from fastening his seat belt, so when the Jeep flipped, he'd been thrown into a snowdrift.

As cold as it had been that morning, he could easily have died from exposure. But his angel had shown up, pulled him out of the snow, taken him to the hospital and left. In his dazed state, he only remembered a halo of blond hair, blue eyes and a soft voice. He also thought she'd come to his hospital room once to check on him, but he'd been really out of it and might have dreamed that.

After he'd recovered, he'd tried unsuccessfully to find out her name. His search had yielded nothing. If she'd given it to the hospital personnel, it had disappeared somehow. Nobody could help him.

Without a name, his chances of finding her dropped considerably. He couldn't even describe her very well, other than her blond hair and blue eyes. Lots of women in the Jackson Hole area had blond hair and blue eyes. She also might have been a tourist, which meant she could live anywhere. People from all over the world visited Jackson Hole.

He wasn't even sure he'd recognize her if he saw her on the street. But her voice haunted his dreams, and he thought he might know the sound of it if he heard it again. More than once he'd stopped a blonde walking down the sidewalk in Jackson and asked her something lame, like directions to the nearest burger joint, so he could listen to her voice. None of them had sounded like his angel.

He'd begun to think she might have been an honest-to-God angel instead of a real woman. He didn't really believe in such things, but that would explain her sudden appearance at his hour of need and why she'd vanished into thin air after rescuing him. Still, he kept looking and listening, hoping that he'd meet her again so he could express his gratitude.

In the meantime, because he owed his life to her, he'd wanted to do something to commemorate her rescue. She might be a caring woman who didn't want to be identified, or she might be a spirit sent down from heaven. In either case, she was his angel.

After much thought, he'd chosen to have an angel's wing tattooed on his left biceps in her honor. Whenever he looked at it, he was reminded that he was one lucky son of a bitch to be alive. In the months that had followed the accident, he'd also realized that Cassie had not been worth dying for. He was ready to move on. Unfortunately, the woman who had made that epiphany possible had vanished without a trace.

ELLE MASTERSON LOOKED forward to having the Last Chance Ranch folks at Serenity for a long weekend while the foreman and his lady got hitched. She'd been warned by management that these would not be experienced skiers, but teaching beginners was her first love. With no other guests to take care of, she'd build her schedule around whatever they wanted, beginning first thing in the morning.

Before then, she needed to finish her Christmas shopping. Rather than head into Jackson, she'd decided to see if she could find something for her favorite cousin in the Serenity resort gift shop. The items were pricey, but she'd get an employee discount.

The shop wasn't busy. The only customer was a tall cowboy, probably part of the Last Chance bunch,

who had his back to her as he glanced through a se-
lection of postcards on a rack near the door. Samantha, a fun-loving, curvaceous redhead, stood behind
the jewelry counter at the far end of the store, and Elle
headed in that direction.

"Hey, Elle! What's up?" Samantha seemed eager
for company.

"I need something pretty for my cousin Jill. A necklace, maybe. She likes turquoise, but she also likes
nature-themed stuff, like wolves and—"

"My God, it's you! I recognize your voice!"

She whirled toward the speaker. The tall cowboy
who'd been shopping for postcards stood at the end
of the jewelry counter staring at her as if he'd seen a
ghost. One glance into his brown eyes and she knew
why.

Trey Wheeler looked completely recovered and perfectly healthy. He also was as drop-dead gorgeous as
she'd remembered. Like most cowboys, he wore his
hat indoors, the brim pulled down a bit so it shadowed
his eyes and gave him an air of mystery. He'd also left
on his sheepskin jacket, but he'd unbuttoned it, which
provided a glimpse of his physique.

The guy was built like a defensive end—slim hips,
broad shoulders, powerful chest. She wondered if he
was still hung up on Cassie, the woman he'd called
out for at the hospital, the woman he'd begged not to
leave him.

He swallowed. "So you're real, after all." His voice
was husky with emotion.

"Did you think I wasn't?" Then she considered
what shape he'd been in after the accident. He'd suf-

fered from exposure and a concussion. He might have thought she was a hallucination.

Samantha spoke up from behind the counter. "Could one of you fill me in? Sounds like there's a story here."

Elle turned to her. "This gentleman flipped his Jeep into a snowbank last April, and I took him to the hospital."

"Then you disappeared," Trey added. "I've been searching for you ever since. Where did you go?"

"Argentina."

His eyebrows shot up. "You live there?"

"Six months out of the year, starting in April. Then I'm here for six months. I'm a ski instructor."

He nodded slowly, as if fitting the pieces together. "That explains why I didn't run into you around town. But I wish you'd left your name and contact information. You saved my life. I wanted to show my appreciation for that."

"Wow, Elle." Samantha gazed at her. "You're just like the Lone Ranger!"

"My thoughts exactly." Trey seemed to have recovered his poise. He walked forward and held out his hand. "But now that you're unmasked, allow me to introduce myself."

She knew his name, but didn't want him to know that she knew, so she kept quiet.

"I'm Trey Wheeler, horse trainer out at the Last Chance, and I'm exceedingly grateful for what you did."

She grasped his large hand. His grip was firm, warm, and...sexy. Tingles of awareness shot through her. "You're welcome. I'm glad I happened along."

She tried to extract her hand, but he held it captive as he smiled down at her. "Not so fast. I still don't know your name."

"Elle Masterson." The continued physical contact jacked up her heart rate.

"Nice to meet you at last, Elle. Buying you dinner doesn't seem like much of a payback, but it's a beginning. Are you busy tonight?"

She scrambled to get her bearings. Trey Wheeler was a fast mover. She should have anticipated such an invitation, but she hadn't. "Sorry, but I make it a policy not to date resort guests." She smiled to take the sting out of the rejection.

"I get that, but this isn't a date. It's a thank-you dinner for saving my life. That's significantly more important than a date."

"So you'll take me to dinner and consider your obligation to me fully satisfied?"

He grinned. "I didn't say that."

Her heartbeat ratcheted up another notch. He had a killer smile going on, and he was employing it to maximum effect. He seemed determined to charm her, and he was accomplishing his goal.

But she followed her personal rule about not dating guests for many reasons. All sorts of complications could arise, including getting fired for unprofessional conduct. Every resort she'd worked for had agreed it was a good policy, although some were more relaxed about the issue than others.

And even if she didn't have a strict policy against dating guests, she'd be wary of dating this one. Catching a guy on the rebound wasn't her idea of fun. She took a deep breath. "I'm sorry, Trey, but dinner isn't a good idea. I understand that you want to thank me in some way, but anyone would have done the same under similar circumstances. Your gratitude is very sweet, but you don't owe me for doing the right thing."

"I think I do, but if dinner won't work, I'll come up with something else."

"No, really. That's unnecessary. Knowing that you're all recovered is enough of a reward for me."

His brown gaze was warm as it swept over her. "I admire your modesty, but this is important to me, and I'm not the kind of man to just let it go. You'll be hearing from me. See you later, Elle." He touched the brim of his hat and walked out of the shop.

She stared after him, her pulse hopping around like a Mexican jumping bean.

"You should have accepted his invitation to dinner," Samantha said.

Elle turned. "You know I don't believe in getting cozy with a guest."

"Yeah, but he has a point about the special circumstances. Besides, not many guests look like him. He's one hot cowboy. I say he's worthy of a little rule-bending."

"Let's think about this for a minute, Sam. He's not simply a guest. He works at a ranch in the area, which means he won't be completely gone come Tuesday afternoon."

"Even better! Then he'll stop being the kind of conflict of interest that bothers you so much."

"No, but…" Elle felt ridiculous putting her reservations about Trey into words. She'd sound paranoid, or at least presumptuous. She didn't know him at all, so she couldn't predict how he'd behave in a relationship.

Yet she'd heard his heartbroken plea to Cassie, obviously his former lover. Cassie might be old news by now, but Trey didn't strike her as the type who'd be fine with dating a woman who spent half the year in Argentina. He seemed too intense for a casual affair.

Casual affairs were all she allowed herself because she had such a great life following the snow. She didn't want to tie herself down to one place or one man. Not yet, anyway.

Maybe in a few years she'd grow tired of the traveling. At that point, someone like Trey would be a possibility. But he wasn't right for her now, no matter how fast her heart beat when he was near.

Samantha frowned in obvious disapproval. "I know what it means when you tighten your jaw. You're going to reject this yummy man's advances, aren't you?"

Elle consciously relaxed her jaw and smiled at Sam. "Yep. But you're welcome to him, if he appeals to you that much."

"Oh, he does, but I don't stand a chance. He only has eyes for you."

"That's silly."

"No, it's incredibly romantic. Did you hear what he said? He recognized your *voice*. That means he carried the sound of your voice around in his head for months while he searched for you. The memory of you *haunted* him. How great is that?"

Elle rolled her eyes. "You really should ask him out. You're obviously into his brand of drama."

"You should be, too. A Prince Charming like him doesn't come along every day of the week. You may look back on this later and realize you screwed up a golden opportunity."

"Maybe I will, Sam, but the timing is way off." She gazed at her friend. "He may be a prince, but I'm not ready for a fairy-tale ending."

2

TREY ENJOYED A rowdy dinner with everyone from the Last Chance, including the prospective bride and groom. Once Trey understood the layout of the resort, he realized that his spur-of-the-moment invitation to Elle might have been impractical. The formal dining room had been appropriated for Last Chance people, which left the coffee shop and the bar for private meals. Neither of those places suited Trey's image of treating Elle to a special dining experience.

During dinner, the hotel manager passed around sign-up sheets for resort activities. Trey had never skied a day in his life, but he signed up for lessons when he saw that Elle was listed as one of the instructors.

For eight months she'd been a mystery woman he couldn't forget, but other than her voice, her eyes and that halo of blond hair, he'd known nothing about her. She could have been a teenager or a senior citizen, short or tall, plump or skinny, plain or pretty.

And now he knew. She took his breath away. How amazing to think that Pam and Emmett's wedding had brought him face-to-face with Elle Masterson, his angel. Hearing her voice had been a jolt. Seeing her standing there in all her glory had made him feel as if Christmas had come early this year.

Oh, yeah, he wanted to get to know her better. He thought she might want the same thing. Her blue eyes had sparkled with interest when she'd looked at him, so even though she'd thrown up roadblocks, he would persevere. That flash of sexual attraction had been decidedly mutual.

He understood why she'd be wary of getting involved with a resort guest, but he'd only be in that category for a few days. If he laid the groundwork now, he could build on it later, when he was no longer a guest.

Something had clicked for him the moment he'd rounded that corner in the gift shop and laid eyes on her. She might think coincidence had made her drive past where he'd swerved off the road, but now that they'd met, he wouldn't call it coincidence. He'd call it destiny.

After dinner, he and Watkins checked out the wedding ceremony venue, a large space with exposed beams and warm wood paneling. In daylight, when the ceremony would take place, the curtained windows would look out on pines and ski slopes. The candlelit reception in the evening was scheduled for the adjoining ballroom. Trey and Watkins would play then, too.

"It'll be real nice," Watkins said, looking around the room where the wedding would take place. "The acoustics should be decent, too. I'm glad they carpeted the floor."

"Did you want to practice tonight?"

"Nah, let's not." Watkins smoothed his handlebar

mustache. "There's a country-and-western band playing in the bar, and Mary Lou wants to dance. She
doesn't get to do that whenever I'm playing, so this
will be a treat for both of us. She's probably already
in the bar ready to boot scoot."

"Before you go, I wanted to tell you something."

Watkins, who was a good six inches shorter than
Trey and at least fifty pounds heavier, glanced up at
him. "What's that, son?"

Trey liked that Watkins called him "son." Trey's
folks were both gone, his mom from cancer and his
dad in an oil rig accident. Although Trey had come
to grips with not having living parents, he reveled in
the family atmosphere of the Last Chance and appreciated how Watkins and Mary Lou had taken him
under their wing.

"I've found her," he said. "My angel. She works
at the resort."

"No kidding!"

"She's one of the ski instructors, and her name is
Elle Masterson."

"Well, I'll be." Watkins stroked his mustache again.
"What's she like?"

"Perfect."

"Hold on there, cowboy. No woman's perfect. You
know how I feel about Lou-Lou, but I'd be the first
to admit she's not perfect. Don't go setting some lady
on a pedestal. You'll regret it."

"You're right." Privately, Trey didn't think so. "But
Elle is darned close. And she likes me. I can tell she
does."

"Then why didn't she identify herself when she

hauled your ass to the hospital? Something's not adding up here."

"I know, and I mean to get to the bottom of that. But the main issue is her principles. She doesn't believe resort employees should get involved with resort guests."

Watkins nodded. "She must be a sensible woman, then. You can't have that kind of thing in a fancy establishment like this. You need to respect her wishes on that."

"I will. And I do. But don't you think this is a special case? She saved my life. And she likes me. I hate to waste time on rules and regulations in this situation."

Watkins smiled. "You're talking about four days, right?"

"Well, yeah, but—"

"It's not a long time, son. I know at your age it seems forever, but trust me, those four days will go by fast."

"I suppose." Once again, Trey didn't agree with Watkins. After eight months of searching for his mystery woman, he'd finally found her, and she was wonderful. He was eager to explore the possibilities, and they'd both be staying under the same roof, so to speak. He couldn't imagine how time spent that way would go by fast.

"You don't believe me." Watkins clapped a hand on his shoulder. "That's okay. But don't go back to your room and stare at the ceiling all night. Get your guitar and come down for a drink. I know these guys who are playing, and they'd probably let you sit in on a set or two. It'll be good practice."

"Sure, why not?" Given that his hands were tied when it came to Elle, he couldn't think of a better way to spend the evening.

AFTER A QUICK supper in the employees' dining room, Elle climbed the stairs to her room on the second floor of the staff's quarters. A printout of the next day's schedule had been left on her desk, and she picked it up. No big surprise, Trey had registered for her group lesson first thing in the morning.

She was one of three ski instructors employed by Serenity, but Annalise had been given the weekend off because these guests wouldn't need advanced lessons. Elle and her colleague Jared could handle the Last Chance group, who were mostly all beginners.

Switching Trey to Jared's group would make an issue out of the situation, so she'd leave the schedule as it was. But she had to smile when she noticed that Jared had all women except for a guy named Watkins, and she had all men.

Besides Trey, Elle would be working with Alex Keller, Nash Bledsoe, Jeb Branford and two of the Chance brothers, Gabe and Nick. Elle hadn't met any of them, although she certainly recognized the names of the Chance boys. There was a third brother, Jack, but apparently he wasn't into skiing lessons.

All the men except Alex Keller had checked the beginner box on the sign-up sheet. Alex had checked the box indicating he had some experience, which meant he might be willing to help the others. All in all, it should be a fun morning. She loved taking nonskiers and turning them into enthusiastic fans of the sport.

As she considered whether to hit the sack early

to be ready for tomorrow's activities, her cell phone chimed. For some reason, Amy, the bartender on duty tonight, was calling her. Elle picked up her phone. "Hey, Amy."

"Unless you're in your jammies already, you should get yourself down here."

"I was almost in my jammies. What's happening?"

"One of the guys from the Last Chance is performing with the band and he is *hot*. I know you're a country fan. Come down and I'll put you to work behind the bar so you'll have an excuse to hang around."

Elle had become enamored of country music in the past year, and hearing it live was always a treat. Besides, she didn't feel tired enough to go to bed yet. "Thanks, I'll be right there." Disconnecting the phone, she ran a comb through her hair, reapplied her lipstick, popped a mint and grabbed her room key. She'd helped Amy behind the bar a few times before, and she liked the job.

On her way downstairs, she breathed in the scent of Christmas. Serenity went all-out this time of year, and she liked spending the holidays here. Each guest room door had its own fresh wreath, complete with a couple of cinnamon sticks tucked into a big red bow.

Staff members didn't get wreaths, but they were all given small trees to decorate. Hers was sitting in a corner of her room, waiting for her to get busy with lights and ornaments. Until she did, she could enjoy the fifteen-foot blue spruce in the lobby, which sparkled with lights and elegant glass balls. Pine boughs, pinecones and festive ribbons decorated the check-in desk.

The bar opened off the lobby, so the music drifted

toward her as she walked past the Christmas tree toward the heavy double doors inset with stained glass.
Someone was singing in a husky baritone that tickled
her nerve endings.

"Going in to hear our new star?" called Ralph from
the front desk.

"Yeah, I'm told he's pretty good. Amy is letting me
help behind the bar."

Ralph laughed. "Have fun. The women tell me he
looks pretty good, too."

"I'm just here for the music, Ralph."

"That's what they all say."

As Elle grasped the brass handle and opened the
door, she had a premonition about who this sexy country singer might be, but she discounted it. The universe
wouldn't be so generous as to give the bodacious Trey
Wheeler a great singing voice, too.

Obviously the universe was exactly that generous.
Sitting on a stool in front of the mike, strumming his
guitar and crooning a solo love song, was the man
she was determined to avoid, the man every woman
in the room was fixated on. The rest of the band was
silent, not that they would have been noticed if they
had decided to play backup.

Trey's face was shielded by the lowered brim of his
hat, and he seemed completely absorbed in his music.
He cradled the guitar in his lap. One booted foot rested
on the floor and the other was propped on a rung of
the stool. His supple fingers moved up and down the
guitar's polished neck in a sensuous dance as his voice
flowed over her, intimate as a caress.

Lost in a daze of feminine appreciation, she stood
motionless in the doorway. The atmosphere in the

room was electric. Nobody laughed. No glasses clinked. Trey had them all in the palm of his hand.

Then he looked up, as if he'd sensed her come in, and he gazed straight into her eyes.

Her breath caught. He was no longer singing to some unidentified lover. He was singing to her. The passionate lyrics spilled from his lips with such longing that she took a step closer. His slow smile told her he'd noticed, and she halted, embarrassed by how he'd hypnotized her.

Mercifully, the song ended before Elle lost all sense of propriety. After the raucous applause died down, Trey stepped back and the band launched into a lively swing tune. Another guitarist moved up to the mike to belt out the lyrics, and Elle hurried over to the bar.

Amy, who wore her dark hair piled on top of her head, grinned at her. "Told you."

"Yes, ma'am, you did." Elle lifted the hinged part of the bar and scooted inside. "The thing is, I kind of know him already."

"You *do?* Then you get dibs. But if you don't want him, then— Oh, crap. I see orders coming in. We'll talk later."

The next twenty minutes were a flurry of drink orders and washing glasses. But at the first lull, Amy brought up the subject immediately. "So how do you know him? Please tell me he's an old family friend and you think of him like a brother."

"I wish." Elle told her about last spring's incident involving Trey, and their chance meeting in the gift shop today.

"My God, that means he wrote that song about you! He introduced it by saying he'd been rescued by an angel. That totally explains why he focused on you for the last part of the song."

"He wrote it about me?" Elle's cheeks warmed. "That's sort of…"

"Romantic. It's romantic, Elle. Seems like you hooked him good by going all mystery woman on him for eight months. I envy the hell out of you. He's mighty fine."

"I wasn't trying to hook him."

"You did, anyway. Don't look now, but he's coming over here and he looks determined."

Elle turned, and sure enough, Trey was striding toward the bar carrying his guitar case. Her breath hitched. "Maybe he wants a drink."

"I think he wants you, *chica*."

Elle had to admit Amy was probably right. The heat in Trey's eyes was unmistakable.

He set down his guitar case and leaned on the bar. "I didn't know you'd be here, Elle."

"Amy needed some help."

Amy glanced away, but was unsuccessful at muffling a snort of laughter.

"Hmm." He didn't appear to be buying that. "I'm glad you did, especially because I happened to be singing your song."

"I…I didn't realize you were a musician." Her resistance to this gorgeous man was fading fast. No one had ever written a song about her. She liked to think she wasn't susceptible to such romantic gestures, but the butterflies in her stomach signaled otherwise.

"Could we go somewhere and talk?"

"You're not going to play anymore?"

He shook his head. "That's enough for tonight."

"Amy might need me to stay."

"Nope," Amy said. "Thanks for the help, but I can handle it."

Elle took a deep breath. "Okay, then. We can go out in the lobby. There are some comfy chairs in front of the fire."

He seemed about to comment on that suggestion, but then he didn't. "All right. Lead the way." But the minute they were out the door, he put a hand on her arm. "I'd rather go somewhere more private than the lobby."

She turned and looked into his eyes. That was a big mistake. The intensity reflected there, combined with the lingering effects of his song, tempted her beyond reason. She shouldn't surrender to his magnetism, but resisting it was proving difficult.

He lowered his voice. "My room?"

She shook her head. "Sorry."

His gaze sharpened. "Then tell me where I can find you."

Dear God, she was considering the possibility of inviting him to *her* room. She shouldn't do that. She really shouldn't. But if they were alone, she could explain why she didn't want to get involved with him. She could mention his ravings about Cassie.

He was right that they needed privacy for that kind of conversation, and the options were few. They couldn't very well take a walk in subzero temperatures. But if he came to her room, they could speak freely and clear the air once and for all.

Yeah, right. Their meeting might go that way, but if she didn't keep a tight rein on her libido, it might go another way, too. He was one potent cowboy. The thought of being along with him made her quiver.

"Please, Elle," he murmured. "We have a connection, you and I. We need to talk about it, figure a few things out. At least I do."

She let out a breath. If they didn't settle this now, it would hang over them all weekend. "Okay. My room, then. But we shouldn't be seen going there together." She quickly gave him directions.

"I'll drop off my guitar and be there in a few minutes."

She nodded. Heart racing, she hurried out of the lobby and down the hall toward the staff quarters. This was insanity, but then, Trey was making her insane—insane enough to risk being alone with him.

Nothing had to happen if she maintained control. That might be easier said than done, though. She was playing with fire when it came to an emotional man like Trey. Adrenaline fueled her steps as she ran up the stairs.

Once in her room, she straightened up the place, although judging from Trey's intense focus, he wouldn't care if the room was trashed. She cared, though. She'd been a military brat, and her parents' neat-freak habits were deeply ingrained. Order and discipline had been her watchwords since childhood.

Trey's sentimental approach to life both fascinated and frightened her. His ability to stir an emotional response in her was a warning signal that he could disrupt her carefully managed existence. But he couldn't knock her off-kilter unless she allowed it. So she'd just have to stay in command of the situation.

WHEN TREY HAD packed for the weekend, he'd used his
trusty duffel, as always. Maybe, just maybe, he had
some condoms tucked in a side pocket of that duffel. He probably shouldn't be thinking about that. He
shouldn't, but he was.

The whole time he'd been talking with Elle in the
lobby, she'd given off sparks. If he had to guess, he'd
say she was affected by his song about her. That was
okay with him. He'd written it months ago as an expression of joy and gratitude, but it seemed as if everything he wrote came out sounding like a love song
in the end.

He sensed that her argument against dating him
wasn't as strong as it had been this afternoon. The
tide had turned in his favor, and if, in the privacy of
her room, the heat started building…well, he didn't
want to be without the means to follow through. A
condom didn't take up much room in his pocket, and
if he didn't need it, no harm done.

He might not find a stash in his duffel, but it had
been his traveling companion during his relationship

with Cassie. Chances were good some were still in
there. Funny how the thought of Cassie didn't bother
him anymore. She'd never have been happy with a
cowboy who planned to stay in Wyoming for the du-
ration.

The aroma of fresh pine greeted him as he fit the
key card into the door to his room. At some point he'd
track down Pam Mulholland and thank her for treating
everyone to a weekend at this plush resort. He'd fully
expected to bunk with someone at the very least, but
Pam had reserved separate rooms for each of them.
What a luxury.

Pulling his duffel from the closet, he checked the
side pocket and hit pay dirt. He took one condom and
left the rest. Then he reviewed the directions she'd
given him.

His hat would only be in the way, so he left it in his
room. Once he was in the hallway again, he decided
that maybe he should head toward the staff quarters
by a roundabout route. If anyone questioned him, he'd
pretend to be lost. If she'd established a policy of not
dating guests, she wouldn't want anyone to know she'd
invited him to her room.

In the end, he managed to actually get lost. Feeling
like an idiot, he retraced his steps and by a stroke of
luck didn't encounter anyone as he roamed the halls.
Eventually he found her room and rapped softly.

She opened the door dressed in the same outfit
she'd had on when they'd parted. Apparently, she
hadn't decided to slip into something more comfortable. He had no idea how this meeting would go, but
at least they'd be able to talk without any danger of
being overheard.

"I'd about given up on you." She scanned the hall-way before whisking him inside.

"I got lost." He hated admitting it, but that was better than letting her think he'd dillydallied around.

"Really?" She closed the door and leaned against it. Her breathing seemed a little fast. "My directions were pretty straightforward."

"They were, but I wanted to confuse anyone who might see me walking the halls, so I took a different route and ended up confusing myself, too." He wasn't breathing normally, either. Being alone with her in a room with a bed was messing with him.

She looked amazing. He hadn't paid much atten-tion to what she had on before, but now he was in-tensely interested. She wore black jeggings and cute little boots that were fashionable but useless. A light blue sweater with a V neck clung to her breasts. Gaz-ing at her caused his groin to tighten.

"So you deliberately tried to keep your destina-tion a secret?"

"Yeah."

"Thank you." Her expression softened. "I appre-ciate that."

"Judging from what you said earlier, you wouldn't want anyone to know I'm here."

She nodded. "But I'm not as worried about that as I am about…other things."

"Like what?" She was still leaning against the door and he was a good ten feet away, his back to her cur-tained window. He cut the space between them in half and would have moved even closer, but she put up her hand like a traffic cop.

"Hold it right there, cowboy. You were right when you said we need to talk."

He couldn't help smiling. "We do, but I'd rather not have to shout."

She mirrored his smile. "It's a small room. You were hardly within shouting distance. Just stay right there for now, okay?"

He did. Never let it be said that he forced his attention on a woman. Her eyes told him she was as revved up by their proximity as he was, but he'd let the situation unfold naturally.

Her chest heaved, which made her breasts quiver. "You probably can tell that I'm attracted to you."

"God, I hope so. Otherwise I've lost my ability to recognize interest when I see it." He was gratified when his comment made that flame ignite in her eyes once again. Her lips parted, and she looked so ready for a kiss that he considered ignoring her command to hold his ground.

"We need to talk about Cassie."

That cooled his jets. *"Cassie?"* He couldn't have been more shocked if she'd mentioned ties to the Mafia. "You know her?"

"Not at all, but I came to see you after you were admitted to the hospital, and you kept asking for her. You…uh…begged her not to leave you. You were quite emotional."

Embarrassment washed through him, and he scrubbed a hand over his face as if to erase the color he knew would be there. "She's totally out of my life. At the time when I rolled the Jeep, I was still upset about the breakup, but I'm over her."

"Are you sure about that?"

"Yes. I'm not the kind of guy who would hit on a woman if I was still in love with someone else. I don't use one person to get over another person." How he hated that she'd heard him moaning over Cassie. But he couldn't change what had happened eight months ago, and he really wouldn't want to. The accident had brought them together.

"I'm willing to accept that you're not that kind of man. But that's not the only thing worrying me."

"Then what else?" If there were more obstacles, he hoped to remove them. Discovering whether he and Elle had a chance of building a relationship was his top priority.

"Judging from the way you reacted to breaking up with Cassie, you were deeply in love with her."

"I certainly thought I was, but I've figured out it never would have worked. I've made peace with that." He had a sudden insight. "Is that why you didn't leave any contact information? You thought I was in love with someone else?"

"You *were* in love with someone else."

"I suppose so." He shoved his fingers through his hair. "But I'm not anymore, and I'm extremely interested in you, so I don't understand why we're talking about Cassie."

"I just need to know something. Do you usually get that involved when you're in a relationship?"

He sensed this might be a trap, so he took a moment before he responded. "Sometimes I do, yes." That wasn't quite accurate. He had a tendency to surrender his entire heart to the woman in his life, which left him bruised and battered when the love affair ended. But he didn't know how else to be.

"Getting deeply involved with me wouldn't be a good idea."

"Are you married?" He imagined some Latin lover down in Argentina and wanted to hit something.

"No, and I don't expect to get married for a long, long time."

"That's fine with me, but just for the record, why the repetition of the word *long*? Do you have something against marriage?"

She pointed a finger at him. "See? That's what worries me. I'll bet you're looking for happily ever after."

"Eventually, yeah. What's the matter with that?"

"Not a thing, except…well, I'm just not into that routine."

"Okay."

"I'm looking for 'happy right now.'"

He desperately wanted to touch her. If he could kiss her, this conversation would be unnecessary. She was worrying about things that wouldn't matter for quite a while. When April arrived, they could deal with this issue. Talking about it tonight was a waste of valuable time. "I can work with happy right now."

"You were awfully quick to say that, Trey. I'm not convinced you mean it, especially if you've been thinking about me for months and you even wrote a song about me."

He gazed into her blue eyes and curbed his frustration. Maybe she had a point. Now that he'd discovered that his angel was a beautiful woman, he could be guilty of romanticizing the connection between them and falling in love with the idea of her. Yeah, that sounded like something he'd do.

Blowing out a breath, he shoved his hands in his

pockets so he wouldn't forget himself and reach for her. "It's possible I've attached too much meaning to this chance encounter because of Pam and Emmett's wedding after what happened last spring. But damn it, when a gorgeous woman appears out of nowhere and saves your life, that's gonna make an impression."

"You were delirious. I doubt you saw me all that clearly. You couldn't have known how I looked."

"That's true. I've thought about how dazed and confused I must have been. You could have been seventy-five and missing all your teeth and I wouldn't have known the difference."

She smiled at that.

"But you seemed like some sort of angel with your halo of blond hair, which was lit up somehow."

"From the headlights of my truck, no doubt."

"Probably. I also remembered your beautiful blue eyes, which are as beautiful as I thought they were, by the way."

"Thanks." Her cheeks turned pink.

"But I especially remembered your voice—soft, caring, soothing. I'm a musician, so sound means a lot to me. Your voice, which is also sexy as hell, has been part of many dreams these past few months."

The color in her cheeks darkened. "Oh."

"Now let me ask you something."

"Fair enough."

"Did you ever think of me after that?"

She met his gaze, even though she continued to blush furiously. "Yes."

"Often?"

"Often enough." She drew a quivering breath. "But that whole bit about Cassie made me decide you were too intense for me, so I thought it was better that we'd lost touch."

"And now?" He probably shouldn't have asked that, but the gleam in her eyes made him bolder.

"Oh, Trey. You do turn me on, but I'm so afraid that—"

"Don't be afraid." He pulled her into his arms and lowered his head. He was done talking. "Don't ever be afraid of me."

KNOWING FULL WELL that she was doing *exactly* what she'd vowed not to, Elle gave up the fight. But he was so appealing, so determined, and…oh, dear God, the man could kiss. His mouth covered hers gently at first as he settled in with velvet pressure that was just enough to make her want more. Pulse racing, she cupped the back of his head and parted her lips, inviting him to take as many liberties as he wanted.

And he obviously wanted. He deepened the kiss with a sureness that made her gasp. There would be no retreat now. She'd planned to stay in control, but that plan was scrapped the moment she surrendered to the thrust of his tongue. When he splayed his fingers over her bottom and pulled her against his rigid cock, she moaned in excitement.

Clothes became the enemy. She tugged at the snaps of his Western shirt, needing to touch him without any barrier. His breathing roughened when she slid her palms up the furred planes of his muscular chest.

Lifting his mouth a fraction from hers, he chuckled. "I'll take that as a green light."

"Extremely green." She reached for his belt buckle. "I want you naked and I want you now."

"That means we have matching goals." Returning to that most excellent kiss, he slid a hand under her sweater and unfastened her bra with one quick movement.

Things progressed quickly after that. His ability to kiss was matched by his talent for ridding her of her clothes. She completely lost track of her mission to unbuckle his belt.

A girl could be forgiven for being distracted when a hot cowboy expertly slipped off her sweater and put his mouth there…and there…and *there*. She whimpered as he took her nipple between his teeth and tugged. This was going to be good. Very good. She'd worry about the emotional consequences later.

As she adjusted to the wonders of being topless and very well caressed, he moved on, divesting her of her jeggings, panties and boots. After that, well, he *really* took liberties with where he put his clever mouth. And his agile tongue.

Her knees threatened to give way as he drove her insane. "I'm…going to fall…"

"Not on my watch." Scooping her into his arms, he laid her down on the bed and proceeded to finish what he'd started, which meant she had to grab a pillow and press it to her face to muffle the sounds of her heart-pounding orgasm.

The pillow provided some measure of privacy, too. No man had ever produced such an uninhibited reaction in her, and she was a little embarrassed. Here she'd been worried that *he* was too intense, and she was the one bringing all the drama. But wow. Just… *wow*.

The mattress shifted as he climbed off the bed. The

clank of his belt buckle hitting the floor told her that he was completing the task she'd abandoned. One boot thudded to the floor, then another.

Moments later, the mattress dipped again, and he tugged at the pillow. "You under there?"

"Yes."

"Are you hiding?"

"Yes."

"You must be part ostrich, then. They hide just like that, everything exposed but their heads."

That mental image was enough to make her jerk the pillow away and meet his gaze. "Hi."

"Hi, yourself." He slowly combed her hair back from her face.

As she soaked up the warmth from his smile and his amazing brown eyes, she was comforted, but as he continued to look at her, comfort morphed into arousal. Her breath caught.

"What?" He stroked her cheek with one finger. "Why did you gasp like that?"

"I…" Her face felt hot, but the heat didn't stop there. It shot through her, making her ache in a way she hadn't known was possible. "I still want you."

"That's convenient." He cupped her face in one hand and leaned down to feather a kiss over her lips. "I still want you."

"Did you bring any—"

"Yep. Just in case." Foil crinkled, and then he was back, dropping more soft kisses on her mouth as he moved over her.

"Good man." Wrapping her arms around his broad back, she rose to meet him, and they came together as if they'd been doing this forever. No fumbling, no miscues. One sure thrust, and they were locked in an age-old embrace.

"Mmm." His hum of praise vibrated against her mouth.

She couldn't have said it better. He fit her perfectly, his hard cock stretching her just enough to make her want more. She hadn't had a lot of lovers, but none of them had felt so absolutely right.

That scared her more than a little. She wanted this kind of perfection someday, but she wasn't ready for it now. Too late. Trey was here, buried deep inside her, and he had started to move. *Sweet heaven.*

If she'd thought they were a nice combination while stationary, they were a spectacular event when in motion. He began slow and easy, giving her time to catch his rhythm. She didn't need any time. Instinctively, she knew him, knew his moves.

"Open your eyes."

She did, and discovered he was looking down at her as he rocked forward and back, forward and back. Each roll of his hips brought her climax nearer. He made it seem effortless, as if he could love her this way for hours, yet surely he must be struggling to hold back. If so, he gave no indication.

"Your eyes are getting darker," he murmured.

The coil of tension within her tightened another notch as she held his gaze. "That's because…" She gulped. "Because I'm close."

"I know." A flicker in his eyes betrayed his excitement, although his pace never altered. "I can feel it."

"You don't have to hold back."

"But I want to hold back." His breath hitched, but

his strokes remained unhurried. "I want to watch you come."

"What about—" She moaned and clutched his hips. How she wanted this, needed this! "What about you?"

"Later. You first." He pushed forward, putting pressure at the critical spot. Then he slid back and pushed in again.

"I need the pillow." Panting, she struggled to hold back her orgasm. "I need it now."

"Use my hand." He covered her mouth gently.

With that, she erupted in a climax that shook her from head to toe. She clutched his hand and pressed it tight against her mouth. Her hips lifted toward the pleasure, and he continued thrusting. She kept coming, her cries captured in the palm of his hand. At last, her body shaking, she sank back onto the sheet. But little aftershocks continued to roll through her.

"My turn." He moved faster, now. Slipping his hands under her bottom, he held her as if knowing she didn't have the strength to do it herself.

Amazingly, she wasn't finished. His rapid strokes brought her right back to the edge, and when he hurled himself over with a deep groan, she followed with a gasp of surprise. As she clung to him and gulped in air, her dazed mind kept returning to one simple truth. She'd started an affair with Trey Wheeler, and keeping it under control would take all her willpower.

4

TREY HAD A million things he wanted to say to Elle as they lay wrapped in each other's arms, but he chose not to say any of them. Actions spoke louder than words, anyway, and their actions tonight in this bed were shouting about the possibilities ahead of them. He'd let her think on it, and he sure as hell would, too.

Going into this, he'd had high expectations. The reality of making love to her had shot way past those expectations, and he suspected the lovemaking would only get better with time. A relationship was built on more than sexual attraction, and he knew that, so the next step was getting better acquainted somewhere other than in bed.

Tomorrow they'd be together for the skiing lesson, with other folks around. He was glad they'd been to bed first, though, so neither of them had to waste time wondering if and when sex would happen. The *if* part was settled, and the *when* would be every chance they had.

He didn't think he was being egotistical to assume that. She'd responded more enthusiastically than any woman he'd been with. She'd want more of that, and heaven knows he would, too. She was incredible. His body had never felt so energized, so damned complete.

But he held off telling her all those things, especially because she was getting drowsier by the second. He'd wondered earlier if she'd notice his angel wing tattoo once his shirt was off, but she hadn't. Just as well.

He wasn't sure how she'd feel about it, jumpy as she was about commitment. Tattoos were permanent, although they did fade with time. Still, Elle might not like the fact that he planned to carry a reminder of her forever, no matter how their relationship turned out.

He stayed with her until she drifted off to sleep. Then he slipped out of bed, dressed quietly and left her room, locking the door behind him.

As he started down the hall, he saw a woman walking in his direction. There was no escape. As they drew closer to each other, he recognized Amy, the bartender. He had no idea what time it was, but she'd probably just gotten off work and was going to her room.

When they met, she smiled at him. "You look worried."

"I am worried. It's obvious where I've been, and I don't want the word to get out."

"I won't rat on you, if that's what you're concerned about."

"I appreciate that."

"But after the introduction to your song tonight, followed by you and Elle leaving the bar together, I predict you won't keep this liaison a secret very long."

Trey sighed. "I don't want to embarrass her. Apparently she has this ironclad rule, and—"

"It's her rule, and she has the right to break it. I can't speak for everyone, but I won't tease her."

"Thanks. And, listen, I also want to thank you for asking Elle to help you behind the bar tonight. That turned out really well."

Amy laughed. "I can see that it did. FYI, your shirt is buttoned up wrong."

"Oh." Trey glanced down and sure enough, she was right. But he couldn't very well fix it right here in front of her. He'd do that after they parted ways. "Anyway, I hope you weren't slammed with orders after we left."

"I wasn't slammed with orders in the first place." Amy's smile widened. "I didn't really need her help. I told her to get her butt down there so she could listen to a hot cowboy sing with the band."

"Really?"

"Really. She loves her some good country music. I had no idea all this other stuff was going on with you two."

"Huh. So my music did have some effect on her."

"I'd guarantee it. Of course, you were having some effect on all the women in the room. Have you thought of doing anything with that gift?"

"Nah. I love training horses. The life of a professional singer doesn't appeal to me at all. Local stuff is all I care to do."

"Too bad. I know it's competitive, but I think you could make it if you wanted to give it a try."

"That's nice to hear, but it just doesn't interest me."

"All righty, then. Guess I'll be going off to bed. See you tomorrow."

"You bet. And thanks again." Trey continued down the hall. So Elle was susceptible to his music, was she? That was a bonus he hadn't counted on.

Amy thought he should do something with his gift. Apparently, he already had. And he'd continue to use it to charm his angel until she figured out they had something special going on.

CARRYING HER SKIS and poles in a zippered bag in one hand and two clipboards in the other, Elle walked out to the bunny hill a little before nine, the time appointed for the beginner lessons. She prided herself on always being on time, but this morning she'd been more motivated than usual.

Jackson Hole had trotted out one of its famously perfect winter mornings. A cobalt sky arched over pine forests crisscrossed with ski runs. Sunlight turned the snow into a rhinestone-studded carpet.

Elle couldn't imagine a more beautiful setting than this one. She'd bounced out of bed with the kind of energy she'd had as a kid. Breakfast had tasted like gourmet fare, even though it was her usual yogurt and fruit combined with strong coffee.

She had plenty of reservations about letting Trey into her life, but for the short term, he'd made her feel as if she'd spent a day at the spa. Her body hummed with awareness knowing she'd see him very soon.

She was already planning ahead, looking for opportunities for them to be alone so that she could feel his magic hands, taste his exotic kisses and feel the thrust of his…well, yes. Definitely that, too. She got hot thinking about it.

He was scheduled to play for the rehearsal dinner

tonight, but after that…he'd be all hers. She'd had a short conversation with Amy in the employee cafeteria, and Amy had mentioned meeting Trey in the hallway. Amy wouldn't gossip, but she'd warned Elle that Trey's song and his subsequent exit from the bar with Elle would fuel rumors.

Probably. She wasn't going to let worry about fallout dampen her mood today, though. She'd enjoyed the most thrilling sex of her life last night, and the man responsible for that would be at the bunny hill any minute. A little voice in her head warned her that she was flirting with disaster, and she ignored it.

Jared was already there. Leaning her gear against the side of the ski hut they used as a base of operations, she walked over to him. "Ready for the newbies?"

"Absolutely." With his lean, muscular body, Jared fit the image of a sexy ski instructor. He inspired confidence in those he coached with his brilliant smile, which flashed often in a face tanned by constant exposure to sun reflecting off snow.

Women found him irresistible, but Elle had never heard about any liaisons with guests. She decided to ask him about that. "I know the ladies hit on you all the time. Have you ever…?" She wasn't quite sure how to state it so she wouldn't offend him.

Jared winked at her. "Elle, you know perfectly well that a gentleman doesn't discuss his affairs."

"So you have had them!"

"I didn't say that."

"You didn't have to. If you'd walked the straight and narrow, you would have told me. But you hedged."

Jared studied her with dark eyes that hinted at his

Mediterranean heritage. "Why do I get the idea this isn't an idle question?"

"Because it's not, obviously. I've never done anything like this before, and I want to know how much potential trouble I could cause myself."

"Does this have something to do with the singing cowboy?"

She stared at him. "How did you know it was him?"

"Sweetheart, *everybody* knows."

"They do not." She couldn't believe word had traveled that fast. "You're making that up."

"Nope. The Last Chance crowd is well aware that he searched high and low for you following his accident last spring. Add in his revealing performance at the bar last night and the two of you leaving together, and it doesn't take a genius." He surveyed her. "If I needed any confirmation, all I have to do is look at you. You're bright as a penny that just popped out of the U.S. mint."

Elle groaned. "He's signed up for a lesson this morning, along with five other guys from the ranch. Are you saying they'll all know?"

"It's a safe bet."

"Great. How am I supposed to handle *that?*"

"It won't be a problem."

"How do you know? I think it could be a huge problem. Teasing, innuendoes, stuff like that."

"Obviously, you don't know much about cowboys, Elle. I suppose you wouldn't, because they don't come up here much. You've never had a reason to understand the culture."

"What culture?"

"Cowboys have a code of honor. I'm not saying

all of them do, but it's expected of the Last Chance bunch or they're sent on their way. Those guys might give each other grief, but they would never knowingly embarrass a woman, especially a woman connected to one of their buddies."

"How do you know so much about it?"

Jared smiled. "That's what you learn if you stick around during the summer and hang out at the Spirits and Spurs in Shoshone. You should try it sometime."

"I follow the snow."

"I've heard you say that, but doesn't it get monotonous?"

Elle shrugged. "I'm an army brat. Staying in one place all the time is what would get monotonous for me. Besides, skiing is what I do."

"It's what I do, too, but I take a break in the summer." He glanced over her shoulder. "Looks like our students are on the way. Prepare yourself."

"What for?" Elle turned around and had to fight to keep from laughing. The women were all outfitted in typical water-resistant skiwear they'd probably bought in Jackson or in the resort ski shop. The men were a different story. They had the required skis, boots and poles. But they'd dressed for a day riding the range, not a morning on skis. All of them wore jeans, sheepskin jackets, leather gloves and Stetsons.

No, wait. One man was outfitted in ski clothes, a short, barrel-chested guy sporting a handlebar mustache. She'd bet he was the one signed up with the women in Jared's group.

"Good luck," Jared murmured.

"It's only the bunny slope. Shouldn't matter." She counted the men as they approached, and her gaze locked momentarily with Trey's. He grinned, and she couldn't help grinning back. She hoped he felt as great this morning as she did.

But her quick head count gave her seven men instead of six. One of the Last Chance group must have changed his mind and decided to try the sport after all. She wondered if they'd communicated on the dress code or if they'd all come to this Western-wear decision of their own accord.

"Good morning, gentlemen, and welcome." She handed one clipboard to Trey, who'd reached her first, his long strides betraying his eagerness. She gave the other one to the next man, who also wore a mustache, although not of the handlebar variety. "If you'll pass the clipboards around and fill out the required liability form, we can get started. While you're doing that, you can also introduce yourselves."

"I'm Trey Wheeler." He said it as if he'd never met her before. No one smirked or made a comment.

"Gabe Chance," said the man with the sandy mustache.

A green-eyed man next to him spoke up. "Nick Chance."

"We brought him along 'cause he's a veterinarian," Gabe said. "If we break anything, we're covered."

"Good to know, but I'll do my best to make sure that doesn't happen." Elle turned to the next man in the semi-circle.

"Jack Chance."

"Ah. So you decided to join your brothers, after all." Even semi-isolated at the resort, she'd heard of Jack Chance, oldest of the brothers, part Shoshone and acknowledged spokesman for the Chance family in Jackson Hole.

Jack's dark eyes flashed with humor. "I blame tequila shots and my potential ex-buddy Nash Bledsoe here." He glanced over at the cowboy standing next to him. "We have a sizable bet riding on my ability to stick it out this morning."

"I see." This lesson was shaping up to be a memorable one.

"I'm Alex Keller," said a fair-haired man.

"You're the one with some experience," Elle said.

"A little. I'm no expert."

She'd believe that, since he'd chosen to dress in jeans like the rest of them.

"And I'm a total beginner," said a freckle-faced cowboy who looked like the youngest of the group. "Jeb Branford, at your service, ma'am."

"It's great to meet all of you." She smiled at them. "But I have to ask, why the jeans and cowboy hats?"

Alex glanced around the circle. "Told you guys she'd wonder about that."

"We don't own skiing gear," Gabe said. "Seemed kind of silly to buy it for one time."

"True, but you could have rented something."

"That's what Watkins did," the freckle-faced guy named Jeb said. "Mary Lou made him. But the rest of us agreed that those ski pants and puffy jackets look sort of...unmanly." Then he flushed. "I mean, the outfit suits you, ma'am, but we're...we're cowboys."

"Fair enough." Elle bit back a smile. "You should be fine for the bunny slope, but—"

"Damn, is it *really* called the bunny slope?" Jack looked pained.

Nash clapped him on the shoulder. "'Fraid so, Jack, old boy."

"I was hoping that was just you being cute, Nash."

"It is, in fact, the bunny slope," Elle said. "If any of you graduate from the bunny slope, you might want to rethink your outfit. Wet denim can get pretty uncomfortable."

"Which will only be a problem if we fall down," Jack said.

Alex, the one who knew better, smiled. "Good luck with that, Jack."

Jack gazed at him, his expression serenely confident. "Time will tell, won't it? When this is over, we'll compare butts and see who has the dry one."

Elle ducked her head so they couldn't see her expression. If Jack, or any of them, thought they would stay upright throughout this lesson, they were in for quite a surprise. She might have to put on a ski mask so they wouldn't catch her dying of laughter.

"All righty!" She glanced around the group. "After you've signed the form, go on over to the bench and put on your skis. I'm about to put mine on, so if you want to come over and watch how it's done, you're welcome. I'm also sure Alex can help you with that."

Alex nodded. "I remember that much, at least. And something about a pizza wedge and a French fry."

Jeb peered at him. "Are we skiing or eating lunch?"

"Skiing," Alex said. "You'll get it when we start out. I just remember you never want to French fry when you should pizza wedge."

"Very good advice, Alex." Elle wondered if Trey would follow her as she walked over to retrieve her skis. She was grateful when he didn't. She wouldn't mind giving him a private ski lesson, but that would be flaunting their connection, and she didn't want that.

Once her cowboys were lined up with their skis and goggles on, she wished she could take a picture. She doubted Serenity had ever seen anything like it. Amazingly, they had managed to get in line without whacking each other's shins, but it was early yet. "Have any of you gone snowshoeing?" she asked.

Several nodded, including Trey. She filed that away for later. He might not be ready to ski with her by the end of the weekend, but they could take some snowshoes and trek to a private clearing for some quiet time together.

"This isn't like snowshoeing," she said. "Your skis are waxed on the bottom so they slide over the snow, which can be a good thing or a bad thing, depending on whether you're in control."

"That's what we're here to learn," Gabe said.

"It's the most important thing to learn." Elle positioned her goggles on top of her head. "Alex is right about the pizza slice and the French fry position. To slow down, put the tips of your skis together and the tails apart. The larger the pizza slice, the slower you'll go."

They all nodded.

"French fry position means your skis are parallel so you'll go faster. Keep your knees apart at all times. Pretend you're holding a basketball between them."

"Or a flake of hay," Jeb said. "I never played basketball, but I've tossed around plenty of hay."

"A flake of hay, then." Elle got into a basic skiing position. "And keep your knees slightly bent, like I'm doing now, and lean forward a bit. This is not a time to stand tall."

"Can we give it a try?" Nick seemed eager to get started. "The women have started up already."

"So they have." Elle noticed that Jared's group was on the towline headed for the top of the bunny slope. "Any questions before we follow them up there?"

Jeb raised his hand. "What about the falling down part? I know Jack doesn't plan to, but I might."

"Excellent question. If you fall, get your skis parallel to each other and below your body. Also, stay sideways to the hill. Use the slope to push yourself up. I'll be there to help you, so don't worry too much about it. You'll be fine."

"Count on it." Jack led off, and as he did, he called out, "Wagons, ho!"

On cue, the rest started singing the theme song from *Rawhide* as they marched in single file over to the towrope. Elle wished to God she had a video camera. Those cowboys were too cute for words. And one of them, the one she'd had naked in her bed last night, was the cutest of them all.

5

TREY COULDN'T SAY he was the worst skier in the bunch, but he wasn't the best, either. Alex had done this before, so he didn't count, but Jack Chance surprised them all. He took to skiing as if he'd been born with a ski pole in each hand. His jeans stayed dry. Figured. After all, this was Jack they were talking about.

Trey didn't have much natural ability for the sport, apparently, and on top of that, he spent more time watching Elle than practicing his pizza wedge and French fry moves. Clad in black ski pants and jacket, her sleek body was poetry in motion as she swerved among her students, giving tips and helping those who'd fallen.

He and the others, including Alex, had gone down at least once. Trey had landed in the snow twice so far, and both times, just his luck, Alex had come over to help him and make suggestions before Elle could. The third time, though, Elle happened to be closer to him than Alex was. She skied in his direction, moving with grace and efficiency.

About a yard away, she made what he'd learned

was a hockey stop—a quick shift sideways with parallel skis. It created a little spray of snow and looked impressive. He wanted to learn that, but he needed to master the pizza wedge first.

"Uncross your skis and scoot around so they're downhill from you," she said.

His goggles were bugging the hell out of him, so he shoved them in his jacket pocket. Then he untangled his skis and repositioned his legs downhill of his body. In the process some snow worked its way under the hem of his jacket. Damn, that was cold. She'd been right about wet denim, too. Ski pants were looking better every second.

Gliding toward him, she swooped down and plucked his hat out of the snow. "I'm sure you want this."

"I do." He abandoned both poles so he could take it from her and brush the snow off. "Thanks."

"I have to admit the hats aren't the worst idea in the world." She pushed her goggles up and gazed at him. "They stand up to the snow and they shade your eyes."

"Yeah, but we're all losing them like crazy." He put on his hat and tugged on the brim. "The bunny slope is littered with Stetsons."

Her laughter made her eyes sparkle. "Next time you can tie them on."

"Next time I'll wear something else."

"Does that mean you're willing to try this again?" Still balanced on her skis, she crouched down beside him.

If he attempted to do that, he would topple over. She was a superb athlete, and that turned him on. "Sure, I'll try again. So far I pretty much suck at this, but the company's great."

"What a nice thing to say."

"Yeah, well, I've been told I'm—" He paused and drew in a sharp breath as the sun emerged from behind a cloud.

"That you're what?"

"It's not important." He gazed at her, entranced by the image that had haunted him for eight months. "You look exactly the way you did when you pulled me out of that snowdrift, except it's the sun making the halo instead of your truck's headlights."

"At least this time you don't have a concussion."

"At least this time I know your name."

"You know a lot more than that about me, cowboy."

He looked into her eyes, and his pulse hammered in response to the desire he saw shining in those blue depths. "And I plan to learn a whole lot more." He was also becoming aroused. His swelling cock pushed painfully against a layer of cold, wet cotton followed by a thicker layer of cold, wet denim. "This isn't the best time to be having this conversation, is it?"

Her mouth curved and she glanced down at his crotch. "Probably not. I can imagine what those wet jeans must feel like."

"They're all that and worse. Any chance you'll come by and help peel them off when this is over?"

"Tempting as that sounds, it's not a good idea." She straightened and pulled her goggles down.

He spoke quickly, wanting to get vital information to her. "Incidentally, your manager, Carl, came looking for me during breakfast in the restaurant."

She lifted the goggles again. "He did?"

"Yeah. Someone told him the story about you rescuing me last spring, and he thought that was kind of cool." Tired of sitting in the snow, he used the slope as leverage and pushed himself upright. He wasn't totally steady, but he was standing. "He wanted to set my mind at ease. He doesn't see a problem with us socializing when you're off duty."

"Socializing." She smiled. "I guess that covers all sorts of things."

"Yes, ma'am, it does."

She held his gaze for a beat. "At the end of the lesson, you should soak in the tub for a while. Your muscles aren't used to this."

"Sounds like you want me to get naked."

Her eyes sparked with mischief. "It's not a bad idea."

"Got any more ideas?"

"I happen to have a two-hour break after this."

That news helped him generate a considerable amount of body heat. "I'm in room 124."

"Okay." Repositioning her goggles, she dug her poles into the snow. "See you then." She sped off to help another fallen cowboy.

He stood there wondering how in hell he was supposed to practice pizza and French fry when his cock was as rigid as a ski pole.

"Trey!"

He recognized Watkins's voice, although he couldn't see the guy. Using his poles to balance himself and wincing at the discomfort in his crotch, he turned cautiously to his right, where Jared's group had been practicing.

So far, the groups hadn't mingled. Trey suspected male pride was involved. The five married guys wanted to perfect their technique before they joined their wives, who had been working with Jared.

Watkins looked pretty damned confident as he stood on the slope in his peacock-blue ski pants and jacket. He'd opted for a matching knit cap, and though Trey could see the sense in that kind of headgear now, it still looked dorky, especially paired with the goggles. Maybe a different color would help.

"Check this out, my friend!" Watkins's grin made his handlebar mustache wiggle. He pushed off, his knees bent as they'd been taught. First he sashayed left, and then he sashayed right, followed by a perfect, snow-spewing hockey stop.

"That's great!" Trey was jealous, but he had no right to be. He'd been lusting after his ski instructor instead of focusing on the task at hand. "Would you be willing to show me how you did that?"

"Absolutely." Watkins used his poles to good effect as he skied toward Trey.

"Wait for me! I'm right behind you!" Mary Lou called out. Sailing over in their direction, she seemed as much at home on her skis as her husband. "Isn't this fun?"

"I'm not sure I'd use that word," Trey said.

Mary Lou looked him up and down. "Of course you wouldn't, dressed like you're heading down to the corral. Why didn't you wear the right stuff?"

"We all thought—"

"Never mind. I had the same argument with Watkins. He couldn't picture himself in ski pants, either."

"But you were right to talk me into it, Lou-Lou. I can move a hundred times better in these." He surveyed Trey's wet jeans. "That denim looks mighty soggy and uncomfortable."

"You have no idea."

"I have some idea. I fell in an icy river once. But maybe you can still learn, even wearing jeans."

"He can," Mary Lou said. "He's young and agile. If old codgers like us can pick it up, so can Trey, despite his wardrobe choices. Come on, son. Show us what you've learned so far."

Trey moved his skis into a good-sized pizza wedge and gradually narrowed it. He began to move slowly down the hill.

"That's it!" Watkins called out. "Good job! Now use your thighs to turn yourself slightly to the left."

"Knees apart!" Mary Lou yelled. "Butt tucked in!"

Trey wished they weren't making so much noise with this instruction, but he had asked them to help, so he'd endure the humiliation. And he actually made a turn.

"Now go the other way!" Being a singer, Watkins knew how to project, so the entire hillside of skiers was probably listening.

"Butt tucked!" Mary Lou wasn't a singer, but she had a good set of vocal cords on her, too.

Trey managed to change course without falling down, while Watkins and Mary Lou cheered. That would have been okay, except that others had joined in, which led Trey to believe he had collected an audience. Not his goal.

But if he had one, he might as well do his best. He executed another turn, and another. At this rate he'd be at the bottom before long.

Behind him, somebody started up a chant—*Wheeler,*

Wheeler, Wheeler. The volume grew as more people joined in. Damn it, this was plain embarrassing. He could fall down at any minute.

In spite of that fear, he was determined to finish with a hockey stop. A fellow couldn't have people chanting his name and then have the performance peter out at the end. Besides, one of those people watching had to be Elle, although he doubted she was chanting. That was more the kind of thing a bunch of cowboys would do to one of their own.

His timing had to be right. One more turn and then the hockey stop. He swerved left, pivoted the way he'd seen Watkins do it, and sent up a decent spray of snow. Cheers erupted as he teetered there for one glorious moment. Then he fell.

The cheers turned into one unison groan. Trey started to chuckle, and the more he thought about that juvenile display of showmanship, the harder he laughed. Good thing he was already on the ground, because doubled over like this, he never would have been able to balance on the damned skis.

Elle got to him first. "Trey! Are you hurt? Can you get up? What's wrong?"

He gulped for air. "I'm fine. Just…laughing my fool head off."

"Oh, good." She sighed in obvious relief. "When I saw you holding your stomach, I thought you'd done something to yourself, although I couldn't imagine what."

Grinning, Trey snapped the catch on his skis and took them off. "That was *almost* impressive."

"I was impressed."

"Glad to hear it. Is this lesson over yet?"

"As a matter of fact, it is. Your timing was perfect, even if your demonstration wasn't. Let me help you up."

"Thanks." He should be embarrassed that a woman was pulling him to his feet, but he'd already made a fool of himself, and he was glad for the support. She'd once hauled him out of a snowdrift, so she certainly had the strength to help him up now.

Besides, this way he got to hold her hand, even if they both had on gloves and he couldn't touch her soft skin. He would be doing that soon, though.

Eventually the rest of the skiers came down the bunny slope, all of them staying on their skis the whole way. They gathered at the spot where Elle and Trey stood. Trey accepted both congratulations and commiserations while they all divested themselves of their skis.

Jared made a megaphone of his hands and got everyone's attention. "I realize everyone will be busy tomorrow with wedding activities, but we can schedule another session the morning after that. How many are in?"

All hands went up, including Trey's.

"I'd advise the cowboys to acquire ski pants," Jared said. "You'll find them a lot more pleasant."

"I'll vouch for that," Watkins said.

"I've got twenty bucks that says Jack won't wear 'em," Nash said.

"You'd lose that bet, my friend," Jack said, "just like you lost the one today."

Nash made a face. "Don't remind me."

"But, Jack, you're the only one who didn't fall

down." Jeb's expression was filled with hero worship. "You don't need to worry about ski pants."

"I didn't fall down, but I'm here to tell you that my boys are *not* happy." Jack glanced around at his jeans-wearing companions. "The next time I come out here, my guys will be thermally protected and water-proofed. Count on it."

After the laughter died down, the crowd dispersed with much joking about frosty denim and shrinkage. Trey would have liked to confirm with Elle that they'd meet in his room when she was free, but she was having a long conversation with Jared. Trey decided to go back to his room and get free of the cursed jeans.

Watkins called out as Trey started toward the lodge. The barrel-chested cowboy had his cell phone in his hand.

Trey paused. "What's up?"

"I have a call from Pam." He put the phone to his ear and continued to talk as he approached. "Let me check with him, Pam. Should be fine." He put his thumb over the speaker and glanced at Trey. "As we might expect, Emmett's freaking out a little about all the fuss surrounding the ceremony."

"What fuss?"

"You and I haven't been part of it, but Pam's been in consultation with the chef about the menu because some items didn't come in as expected, and the flo-rist shipped the wrong arrangements and Emmett's coat doesn't fit quite right. You know, the usual wed-ding issues."

"If you say so. I've only been involved in one wed-ding, and that was when Sarah and Pete got married last August. I'm not what you'd call an experienced wedding person."

"The upshot is, Emmett is stressed. Pam thinks it'll help if we meet in the room where the ceremony will be held and give them a little preview of the music we intend to play. She thinks just listening to those songs he loves, songs he helped choose, will remind him of how great the wedding is going to be."

"I'm not sure that will work. It might make him more nervous than ever."

Watkins nodded. "It could, but she's running out of ideas short of plying him with whiskey."

"Isn't there a bachelor party for him tonight? We can get him toasted then."

"And we will, but it's quite a few hours between now and the bachelor party. Anyway, I think we should give it a shot."

"You bet. After all, she's rolled out the red carpet for all of us. Does she want us to do the preview now?"

"Yep. As soon as we can change out of our ski duds, or in your case, out of your wet jeans."

"Oh."

"You got something planned?"

"Not exactly, but…" Trey couldn't very well explain to Watkins what he'd scheduled for the next couple of hours.

"Something to do with our ski instructor, maybe?"

Trey's face grew hot.

"Look, ordinarily I'd put Pam off for a little while, but she sounded desperate. If you want me to go down there and handle it by myself, I will."

As a testament to his driving need for Elle, Trey considered that offer, but only for a split second. "No, that wouldn't be right. I'll go. Give me fifteen minutes to change clothes and grab my guitar. I'll meet you in the lobby."

"Thanks." Watkins squeezed his shoulder. "I know Pam is going to really appreciate this."

"I'm sure she will." Trey glanced back at Elle, who was still talking to Jared. How could he let her know the plan had changed?

Too bad he didn't have her cell number. He'd get it first chance he had, but for now he'd have to stop by her room and slip a note under her door. That wasn't great, but it was the best he could come up with on short notice.

Knowing he needed time to write and deliver the note before he met Watkins in the lobby, he made tracks for his room, which fortunately was on the first floor. He took off his gloves and jacket on the way there. That soak in the tub wouldn't be happening.

Inside his room, he tossed his coat on a chair and pulled off his clothes as fast as his cold fingers allowed. Then he grabbed a towel from the bathroom and rubbed it briskly over his chilled body. Ah, better. Not as good as a soak in the tub, and definitely not as good as making love to Elle, but he'd survive.

As he finished his rubdown, he heard a knock at the door. He wrapped the towel around his waist and checked the peephole. Maybe Pam had changed her mind and Watkins had come down to tell him. He could only hope.

Instead, he discovered Elle, still in her ski clothes, outside his door. He pulled it open. "I—"

"Don't talk." She hurried inside and began tearing off her jacket. "I have five minutes. Jared's driving into town to look at some new ski equipment for the lodge and needs me to go. The sale ends today. I couldn't get out of it." She dropped the jacket and knelt down to take off her boots.

"But you still want to—"

"Oh, yeah." She glanced up, and her blue gaze was full of fire as she dispensed with her boots. "I want to."

He dropped the towel.

6

Elle had known the sensible thing to do—cancel having sex with Trey. On her way to his room, she'd conducted an inner debate. Her sensible self had put up a really good argument about not appearing too eager.

Except she was eager, and not totally rational, either. A rational woman would have called his room to say she couldn't make it. The devil in her had whispered that it would be quicker to simply stop by.

Once she'd decided on that course of action, she'd begun to consider another one. Finding him wrapped in a towel had been the deciding factor. Seeing how quickly he reacted to her suggestion had told her she'd made the right choice.

She stood and shoved her ski pants and silk long johns to the floor. He, however, hadn't moved, except for the elegant rise of his cock. "You'd better get the—"

"Right." He spun away from her and headed for the closet.

She noticed a tattoo on his left biceps as he turned away. She didn't get a clear look, but thought it might be a wing of some kind. Now was not the time to ask about it, though.

She pulled her turtleneck over her head and dropped it on the pile of clothes at her feet. Crossing to his king-size bed, she threw back the covers, scattering decorative pillows everywhere. By the time she'd climbed in one side, he'd climbed in the other.

They met in the middle, his mouth hungrily seeking hers as he moved between her thighs. One quick thrust and he was there, right where she ached to have him. The pressure set off tiny explosions that reverberated through her.

His mouth lifted, hovering over hers. "Promise we'll have longer tonight."

Breathless with need and not caring that he knew, she pressed her fingers into his back. "I promise. But I need you now."

"I need you, too." He began to pump, first slowly and then faster. "So…oh, God…so much." His breathing grew ragged as he pounded into her with enough force to lift her from the bed.

She rode the whirlwind with him, arching her back and urging him on. "Yes, oh, *yes*. Keep doing that. Right there…right…" She came in a fiery rush, and he swiftly followed her into the flames with a deep groan of surrender.

She gulped for air. "So good."

"Yeah." He kissed her once, hard. "Tonight," he murmured as he levered himself away from her.

"Yes." Quivering in the aftermath of her orgasm, she forced herself to slide out of his bed. He'd already disappeared into the bathroom.

She'd loved every minute of that experience, but

she'd love every minute of a longer one, too. Jared's request faded in importance. "Should I text Jared and beg off?"

"No." He walked out of the bathroom, a study in masculine beauty.

"Are you sure?" She admired his chest, furred with dark hair, and followed the line of hair to his navel and beyond, where dark curls framed his semierect cock and impressive balls. Her body grew moist and achy all over again.

"I'm sure. I can't stay, either. Pam Mulholland asked Watkins and me to give her a preview of the wedding music."

"Now?"

"Yep. I'm meeting Watkins in the lobby. He may already be there."

"Whoops. We'd better get moving, then." As she stooped to gather her clothes, the humor of the situation made her smile. "You could have given me a rain check, you know."

"Are you kidding?" He opened a drawer and got out a pair of briefs.

"No." She dressed quickly. She'd rather not be here if Watkins got tired of waiting and came looking for Trey. "I would have understood."

"Lady, I'm no fool. Opening my door to find you ready and willing was a gift. I wasn't about to say no to an opportunity like that." He grabbed jeans and a shirt and put them on as he talked. "I'll be smiling all day."

"Better be careful. People will wonder what you've been up to."

"Are you worried about that?" He sat on the bed

and pulled on his boots. "What people think of us getting together?"

"I'm not super worried, but I'm not used to having everyone know my business." She hadn't realized that was a priority with her until now, but maybe that was a big reason why she'd always kept her personal life separated from work. Not dating resort guests, both here and in Argentina, had guaranteed her privacy.

"Then we'll keep it on the down-low." He stood and picked up his guitar case. "Ready?"

"Yes." She zipped her jacket. "If you're going toward the lobby, I'll go in the opposite direction."

"Before we leave, give me your cell number, in case you get some free time this afternoon."

She grabbed a pad and pen from his desk and scribbled it down. "I doubt it. Jared and I are scheduled to make a promo video for the resort's ski program. But just in case, let me have yours, too."

He tore off the bottom of the page she handed him, wrote his number and gave it to her. "And I need one more kiss."

"Make it a quickie."

He laughed. "I think we already did that." Setting down his guitar, he drew her into his arms. His kiss wasn't quick at all. He lingered and tasted, teased and nibbled.

She moaned softly and drew back. "No fair. You've stirred me up again."

"Just making sure you'll show up here tonight after the bachelor party."

"We'll meet in your room, then?"

"My bed's bigger."

"Good point."

A sharp rap on the door made them jump apart.

Trey mouthed the name *Watkins*.

"I'll hide in the bathroom and leave after you do," she murmured.

He nodded and picked up his guitar.

She put a restraining hand on his arm, stood on tiptoe and finger-combed his tousled hair into place. Now he didn't look quite as much like a man who'd been rolling around in bed with a woman. Then she retreated to the bathroom and listened as Trey apologized to Watkins for being late.

"Hey, no worries," Watkins said. "When you didn't show up in the lobby, I wondered if we had our wires crossed. Is everything okay?"

"Everything is great. Just had to warm up a little is all," Trey said as he closed the door behind him.

They'd been gone only a couple of seconds when Elle's phone, which she'd tucked in the pocket of her jacket, chimed. No surprise—it was Jared—but she was grateful he hadn't called a minute ago. She answered it with a cheery greeting.

Jared sounded slightly impatient. "I thought I'd hear from you by now."

"Sorry. Something came up." *Did it ever.* "I'll be down in the lobby in ten minutes." She'd have to race back to her room like an Olympian and freshen up in record time, but she could do it.

"Okay. See you then. Hurry. This kind of sale doesn't come around often. Carl's eager to cash in on it, and he wants you to check out the snowboards, since you've had more experience with them than I have."

Elle understood the urgency. The resort got a volume discount from this store, and a sale on top of that could save significant money. Usually she enjoyed shopping for winter sports equipment.

But as she flew back to her room and shucked her clothes for the second time, her thoughts were on the glories of making love to Trey. She expected that once the newness wore off, she wouldn't be so focused on him.

Their relationship was really only about sex, and that would get old eventually. It always had before with other guys. Elle wasn't even sure that she and Trey would have things to talk about if they weren't locked together in feverish delight.

He was a cowboy and she was a ski instructor, so their career paths had nothing in common. She had no knowledge of horses and all he knew about skiing he'd picked up this morning. She was well traveled thanks to her parents' military lifestyle and her own decision to spend six months on each side of the equator. Trey might be a globe-trotter, but she doubted it.

Frankly, she didn't care if he shared her love of travel and skiing. She wasn't looking for a lifetime companion and she'd made that clear. At least she hoped he wouldn't misunderstand her sexual eagerness for something deeper and more meaningful.

Maybe she needed to reemphasize her philosophy tonight. The sex was terrific, and she'd love to partake as often as possible while he was here, but that didn't mean she was falling for him. She'd look for any signs that he had a different idea about how things were working out between them.

If he did hope for more than sex from her, she'd have to break it off. Selfishly, she didn't want to do that. Sex had never been this good before. But she couldn't continue to indulge if she thought Trey would end up with a broken heart.

EMMETT WAS ALREADY in the room that had been designated for the wedding ceremony when Trey and Watkins arrived. Pam was nowhere to be seen, though. The decorating had begun, although no one besides Emmett was in the room now.

Trey thought it was a fine spot for a wedding—not too big and not too small. He estimated that about sixty folding chairs had been set up, with an aisle down the middle. Pine boughs were everywhere—over the arched windows and covering a trellis that would serve as the focal point for the ceremony.

Wine-colored ribbons were woven among the boughs, and the same color was used for cushions on the dark wood folding chairs and the runner down the middle of the aisle. The room looked classy and smelled wonderful, and Trey figured the staff wasn't even finished.

Emmett didn't seem to be enjoying the ambiance, though, as he paced in the back of the room. In his sixties, Emmett looked like the quintessential ranch foreman with his tall, lanky physique, clear blue eyes and carefully trimmed gray mustache. He was completely at home on the back of a horse or pitching hay into a stall, but he appeared ill at ease in a room filled with expensive wood paneling, thick carpeting and crystal chandeliers.

He spotted them and walked over immediately. "I'm glad you boys are here. I have this great idea, but I can't get Pam on board with it. I'm hoping you two can help me convince her."

Watkins set down his guitar case, and Trey followed suit. "What idea is that?" Watkins asked.

Emmett rubbed his hands together, betraying his nervousness. "Pam and I can fly to Vegas this afternoon, get married tonight, and fly back here tomorrow. Then we can all party, just like she planned."

Watkins stared at him. "Emmett, that's not going to work."

"No, it isn't," Trey added. "I'm the new guy, so I don't know all the history, but I can't see that happening."

"Why not?" Emmett's jaw tightened. "The main thing is the party, right?"

"Uh, no," Watkins said. "The main thing is folks witnessing the ceremony when you and Pam get hitched. They're all looking forward to that."

"I don't know why they want to sit through some boring ceremony." Emmett caught himself. "I don't mean to say your music will be boring, you understand. That will be first-rate. But you'll still play for the party when everyone can dance instead of being stuck in these rows of chairs."

"Watkins is right," Trey said. "They're looking forward to the ceremony itself. You and Pam are important to them, and they want to be part of this wedding. I don't think it'll work for you to fly off to Vegas."

"And I doubt Pam would go, anyway," Watkins added. "You can't get married in Vegas without a bride."

"See, that's where you two come in." Emmett began to pace again, waving his arms as he walked. "If you both tell her it's a great idea, she might listen. I've tried to get Emily on board, but my stubborn daughter won't hear of it. I've talked to Sarah and that didn't go well, either." He turned to Watkins. "I even tried talking to Mary Lou a few minutes ago. She popped in to see how the decorations were coming along. She's completely against the Vegas plan."

"That doesn't surprise me," Watkins said.

"It surprised me! You and Mary Lou got married on a damned Panama Canal cruise, for God's sake! You didn't go through all this foolishness!"

"You're right about the cruise." In a gesture that said Watkins was stalling for time so he could think, he took off his hat, still damp from the snow, and brushed a speck of lint from the crown. Then he repositioned the hat on his head and glanced up at Emmett. "I'm Mary Lou's husband, so I understand where you're coming from."

"I knew you would. You need to get me out of this circus. The party's okay. I'm fine with the party. It's standing up in front of a room full of people dressed in a coat that doesn't fit right, and saying those words, which should be private, in front of all those folks…"

"You and Mary Lou are alike in that. She didn't want a big deal, either, especially because we'd both been dodging the question of marriage for so many years."

"Exactly! Just like Pam and me. So why won't Mary Lou back me on this? She of all people should understand."

Watkins shook his head. "When you put it like that, I'm not sure I have the answer."

"Look," Trey said. "You can disregard me if you want, but maybe it's because Mary Lou can see it from a different angle this time."

Watkins turned to gaze at him. "That's smart think-ing, son. Plus we just had Sarah and Pete's wedding in August, which everybody, including Mary Lou, enjoyed so much. She might understand a little bet-ter now why it's important to let folks be a part of a wedding ceremony."

Emmett sighed. "You're saying I have to take one for the team, aren't you?"

"Well, and for Pam," Watkins said. "You love her, right?"

"I've loved her for years."

"There you go." Watkins smiled. "If saying her vows in front of all her friends and family will make her happy, then you gotta do it."

Emmett scrubbed a hand over his face and looked at them. "Guess so."

As if on cue, Pam walked into the room. "There you two are! Ready to play for us?" She was dressed in a cheerful red velour sweat suit, and not a blond hair was out of place in her chin-length bob, but her bright tone sounded forced.

"You know what?" Emmett walked over and put his arms around her. "We don't need a preview."

Her body stiffened. "Why not?"

"These boys will do a fine job. I don't think we need to worry about their performance. This wed-ding's going to be great."

Pam looked stunned. "It is?"

"Yep. I can hardly wait." He glanced over at Trey and Watkins. "See you both at the bachelor party to-night. In the meantime, I'm going to have a long and very private lunch with my fiancée."

"See you tonight!" Watkins picked up his guitar case and motioned to Trey. "Let's go, cowboy."

Trey grabbed his guitar and followed Watkins out of the room, but he couldn't resist glancing back at Emmett and Pam. Pam looked as if someone had just handed her the moon.

Her expression haunted Trey as he said goodbye to Watkins and walked back to his room. The covers on the bed and the scattered pillows bore mute testimony to the wild passion that he'd shared with Elle less than an hour ago. But it wasn't love that she felt for him.

If he was honest with himself, he'd have to say that no woman had ever looked at him the way Pam had looked at Emmett. They'd desired him, but they hadn't gazed at him with their heart in their eyes.

He'd imagined himself in love several times, but had he been? Or had he been in love with the idea of love? If so, then he needed to grow up. This emotion he felt for Elle seemed substantial, but he couldn't swear it was love. It could be gratitude mixed with her mystery-woman allure and his intense sexual attraction to her.

Watkins had known Mary Lou for years. Emmett had known Pam for years. Trey had known Elle for less than twenty-four hours. During that time they'd had some amazing sex, but not much conversation.

If he expected Elle to ever look at him the way Pam had looked at Emmett, then he needed to spend time getting to know her and letting her get to know him. That probably meant—and this was a slightly depressing conclusion—not having sex.

Or maybe they could have sex, because they both wanted to, and then they could have a long conversation. He wasn't even sure she'd be interested in having a long conversation with him. Maybe all she cared about was the sex. That thought was the most depressing of all.

If it was true, though, he might as well find out now. He'd started out wanting Elle in his bed, which was a goal any man with a pulse would understand. She was just that hot. But now he wanted more than that for the two of them.

Maybe he'd subconsciously had that goal all along, but until seeing Pam and Emmett together, he hadn't realized how much he wanted their kind of relationship. He didn't want to wait years for it, either.

7

THE SHOPPING TRIP to Jackson took much longer than
Elle would have liked, but Jared seemed in no hurry.
All thoughts of squeezing in an hour of alone time
with Trey disappeared. Once they returned to the resort, making the video sapped the rest of the day.

By the time Elle glanced at her watch, it was time
for the bachelor party to begin in the bar. Fred was
working the party, giving Amy the night off, which
meant Elle wouldn't be asked to help out. That gave
her no choice but to wait for Trey's call signaling the
end of the bachelor party.

She decided to use the time to decorate her Christmas tree, but the tree was small and her decorations
few. She liked Christmas well enough, but having two
parents in the military had meant that anything could
come up to derail the holidays—a move or a deploy-
ment of one parent or the other. Her mother and father
had never established family traditions. Flexibility
had been the key element for the Mastersons, and Elle
had grown up thinking traditions weren't necessary
to a happy life.

That made her the perfect employee for a resort that offered Christmas holiday ski packages. She worked straight through, which allowed both Jared and Annalise to spend a few days at home with their extended families. Her parents treated Christmas so casually that it seemed silly for her to fly thousands of miles to be with them for the holidays.

She hung the last ornament on her tree long before she could expect Trey to call or text, so she decided to turn on her computer and do a Google search for the Last Chance Ranch. Now that she'd met all three Chance brothers, she was curious about the place. She vaguely remembered that they sold horses, so they should have a website.

Wow, did they ever have a website! The images were spectacular, and she quickly realized why. Dominique Chance, Nick's wife and one of the skiers this morning, was a professional photographer. Elle had seen her work in the windows of a gallery in Jackson. Naturally Dominique would make sure the ranch and its paint horses were shown off to good advantage.

Elle lost herself in exploring the site, all the while picturing Trey there. She read the history of the place—how Archibald Chance had won it in a poker game during the Great Depression of the 1930s. The centerpiece of the ranch, a mammoth two-story log house with wings extending at an angle on each side, looked like something out of a movie.

During the summer months, the ranch house opened its doors to disadvantaged boys, eight per season. They lived and worked on the ranch from the middle of June to the middle of August. An application form was available on the site.

Elle found it significant that the charitable program was as prominent on the home page as the paints that were the ranch's bread and butter. She didn't know much about horses, but she could appreciate the beauty of the ones in the photos. One arresting image showed Jack Chance dressed all in black and mounted on a black-and-white stallion named Bandit.

No doubt about it, there was something very sexy about a square-jawed cowboy sitting on a powerful horse. She mentally substituted Trey for Jack in the picture. Yum. She could picture him racing across a grassy meadow, leaning over the horse's neck, his body in tune with the fluid motion of the horse.

She wouldn't ever see that, of course. She'd be in Argentina during the months that Trey could conceivably be riding the range doing his cowboy thing. They'd be thousands of miles apart, their short fling forgotten.

Maybe he'd find a cowgirl at that bar Jared had mentioned in the little town of Shoshone, near the ranch. She couldn't remember the name of the bar, so she typed *Shoshone* into Google and found it. The Spirits and Spurs was owned by Jack's wife, Josie, who'd also been on the bunny slope today. The bar, more than a hundred years old, got its name from the ghosts who haunted the place—miners and cowhands who'd bought drinks there for generations.

Even though she kept reminding herself that she would never set foot in the bar, she was intrigued. It also provided live music every night during the summer, another feature she wouldn't be able to enjoy. Trey probably played there, at least once in a while. She was sure that whenever he performed, he would attract the attention of both local girls and tourists passing through.

Did that knowledge bother her and make her jealous? Hell, yes. She had absolutely no right to be jealous of whoever caught his fancy, but the thought of Trey getting jiggy with another woman was decidedly unpleasant.

She'd have to work on that reaction. She couldn't very well plan to have a casual fling with the man and then expect him to be celibate for the rest of his life because he'd be spoiled for anyone else. Unfortunately, she was a little worried that she might be spoiled for anyone else after the incredible sex they'd had and promised to have again.

As if thinking about that activity prompted it, her cell phone pinged with an incoming text. She grabbed her phone eagerly. Winding down. Should be about 10 min. Will text when on my way.

Heat swirled through her. She thought she'd been calmly waiting for this text, but apparently not. The phone shook in her hand as she tried to reply with a simple OK, see you soon. She took a deep breath and managed to punch the right letters.

Now what? She had the sudden urge to take a quick shower. And shave her legs. She accomplished that in record time. As she dried off and lotioned up, she thought about what to wear. Nothing too revealing and sexy. Although that would be fun, she'd be walking the halls, where she might meet people.

But she certainly didn't have to put on underwear. Finally, she settled on jade-green yoga pants and a matching sweatshirt. Easy on, easy off. She got hot again thinking about that. She had some slip-on running shoes without backs. Those would do for her feet.

She put on a little makeup because, once again, she'd be walking the halls and could run into people who might wonder why she looked ready for bed. Ah, she was *so* ready for bed. Brushing her hair, she left it loose.

Her phone pinged again, and adrenaline rushed through her system a second time. She picked it up. On my way.

Heart racing, she texted him back. Me too. Pocketing her room key and her phone, in case she needed to set an alarm, she turned off all the lights and left her room. She didn't want someone to see a light in her window at three in the morning and ask her about it.

As she took the stairs to the first floor and walked through the double doors into the guest portion of the hallway, she saw a cluster of guys talking and laughing near one of the suites. They behaved in the jovial way of men who were slightly drunk. She thought she recognized the Chance brothers, who were with an older man she hadn't met.

They'd probably all attended the bachelor party. She hadn't thought about it until now, but Trey might be under the influence, too. Liquor usually flowed freely at such events. Could be an interesting evening.

The four men in the hallway were busy joking with one another. Although she'd have to walk past them, they might be too involved to notice her. She could only hope.

As she drew closer, she confirmed that the three younger men were the Chance brothers. The older guy had a handmade card stuck in his hatband that said Groom. Must be Emmett Sterling.

"Give me one good reason why I can't sleep with my fiancée tonight," he said in a voice that carried down the hall. Yes, he was definitely tipsy.

Nick Chance stuck one finger in the air and belted out, "Tradition!"

"It ain't mine," Emmett said with a grin. "So back off, boys. I'm goin' in."

"I'd advise against it." Gabe put a restraining hand on his shoulder. "You've slipped your little love note under the door, so we need to get goin'. I'm sure she told you about this program, buddy. She's a thorough lady, and she would've mentioned it."

"Yeah, but she was only joshin'."

Gabe glanced over at Nick. "You think she was kidding, bro?"

Nick shook his head. "Not when I talked to her. She wanted to be *A-L-O-N-E* tonight."

"Oh, she just thinks she does. I'll convince her different," Emmett said.

Head down to hide a smile, Elle walked faster. Maybe she could scoot past while they were arguing this delicate point.

"Emmett, this is why Pam got you a different room for tonight." Jack sounded reasonable and patient. "She wouldn't do that if she didn't mean it."

"But I still got a key for *this* one, and I know how to use it. I'll surprise her. She loves surprises."

Unable to help herself, Elle snuck a peek at the action. Emmett fished a card key from his pocket and started for the door. Feisty guy.

"Hang on, there, cowboy." Nick caught his arm.

"Sorry, Emmett." Jack plucked the key from his hand. "If we let you go through that door, our ass is grass. We promised Pam. The elevator's right down this way." With a glance at Nick, he took Emmett's other arm. "What d'ya say we mosey in that direction, just for fun?"

"Fun means moseying through that door. Bunch of spoilsports." But Emmett allowed himself to be turned.

That put all four of them on a collision course with Elle. She'd been too busy eavesdropping and hadn't moved fast enough. She smiled brightly, pretending that she had not been listening in on their exchange. "Hi there, gentlemen! Did you have a good time at the bachelor party?"

"We surely did." Jack turned to Emmett. "Emmett Sterling, our esteemed groom, I'd like you to meet our equally esteemed ski instructor, Elle Masterson."

"Nice to meet you, ma'am." Emmett touched the brim of his hat. "Thought about getting out there on the bunny slope, but Pam and I decided I might break something, which would mess up our honeymoon."

"I understand."

"Say, what's this I hear about you being the young lady who pulled Trey Wheeler out of a snowdrift last spring?"

Hearing Trey's name mentioned when she was on her way to have sex with the guy made her blush. "Fortunately I came along right after he flipped his Jeep."

Emmett nodded. "I'm mighty glad you did. He's a good hand and plays that guitar of his real nice, too. Kept us plenty entertained tonight."

"I'm glad." Dear God, how she wished that her

blush would fade, but Trey was a subject guaranteed to put pink in her cheeks.

"I assume you're free tomorrow afternoon and evening," Emmett said, "since we're your only responsibility and we sure as hell won't be out skiing then."

Carl had given her the day off, which wouldn't help her at all when it came to Trey, who would be at the wedding. "I thought I'd do a little skiing on my own," she said.

"Ah, you can do that anytime." Emmett waved a dismissive hand. "Come to the wedding and watch me get hitched. Ceremony's at two, but you'd best get there early and grab a good seat."

"Thank you so much, but I don't want to intrude." That much was true, but she wouldn't mind getting to hear Trey and Watkins perform.

"Emmett wouldn't ask if he didn't mean it," Jack said. "It's a great idea. We're all grateful for what you did for Trey. You'd be most welcome."

"Absolutely," Nick added. "You have to come. I'm sure Pam would want you there, too."

Gabe grinned at her. "It'll be the wedding of the century. You don't want to miss that, do you?"

She laughed. "Not when you put it that way. Thank you. I'll be there."

"Good. That's settled." Emmett looked pleased. "Now, before you go, I have an important question to ask. Normally I wouldn't discuss this in public, but I've had a few drinks, so my tongue's loosened up a bit. And you're a woman."

"Yes, I am. Excellent observation."

"A mighty pretty woman, at that. Anyway, as a

woman, what do you think of keeping a man and his fiancée apart the night before they get hitched?"

Elle glanced at Jack, whose eyebrows rose expressively. She understood his silent request that she help the cause, not hinder it.

As it happened, she was glad to. "I think it's sweet," she said, earning her a big smile from Jack. "Old-fashioned, maybe, but sweet. It gives you a chance to miss each other a little, and that will make the wedding night even better."

"Hmm." Emmett stroked his mustache. "Hadn't thought of that. Might be true. Guess I'm okay with it."

"If that's settled, we'd best be off," Nick said. "Big day tomorrow."

"Yep." Elle was more than ready to be on her way, too.

The men all said their good-nights and touched the brims of their hats in farewell.

"Thanks again for the invitation," Elle said.

"We'll be expecting you." Jack met her gaze. "Have a good night, Elle."

"Thanks." She'd probably imagined a gleam of mischief in Jack's dark eyes. As she continued down the hall, she told herself he didn't know where she was going. Yeah, right. Why else would she be roaming the halls at one in the morning if not to pay a call on the cowboy in room 124—the very cowboy they'd just been discussing?

AFTER ELLE'S EAGERNESS that morning, Trey halfway expected her to beat him to the room. Instead, he had time to straighten the covers on the bed and retrieve a couple of condoms from his duffel bag. He'd bought more in one of the resort shops devoted to toiletries and over-the-counter medicine.

When she still hadn't arrived, he sat on the bed and took off his boots. Then he stripped his belt from its loops and laid that on the dresser. After that, he had to stop himself from taking off everything else. Not cool. She might have caught him wearing only a towel this morning, but his showing up at the door like that again would lack class.

Yet he was too agitated to sit still. Laughing to himself, he thought of his original plan to have an in-depth conversation with Elle before getting naked. Good thing he'd shelved that idea. But he hadn't given up on the concept of getting to know her better, and vice versa.

Their current situation put a premium on having sex, because they didn't have the luxury of time. Maybe, after the wedding was over, they'd have that luxury. She'd still be working, though. He had a lot more questions than answers right now.

High on the list was wondering where the hell she was. He'd made the trip from his room to hers, even gotten lost, and it hadn't taken him this long. He glanced at his phone, both to check the time and see if she'd texted. Okay, she wasn't *that* late. His perception of time was skewed by his impatience.

At long last, the knock came. He hurried over and stubbed his toe on the desk chair. Swearing under his breath, he threw open the door.

"I got held up."

"Never mind that." He pulled her into the room, kicked the door shut and filled his arms full of warm, fragrant Elle. "God, you feel good." He rained kisses on her upturned face. "And smell good." He delved into her mouth. "And taste good," he murmured, lifting his head and changing the angle so he could go deeper.

Nudging off her shoes, she pressed her sweet body against his, and unless he was mistaken, she didn't have anything on under her yoga pants. He slid both hands inside her waistband and encountered her bare, sexy bottom. Not even a thong presented a barrier to his questing fingers.

His lips hovered over hers. "I like this decision."

"I wish you'd shown up in a towel."

"Didn't want to be repetitive and boring." He pushed the yoga pants down her hips and kneaded her sleek little derriere.

"Trust me, not boring."

"I'll keep that in mind." He reached between her thighs. "You're soaking wet."

She moaned softly. "Your fault."

"And I could drive nails with my cock."

Her laughter was breathless. "Maybe…" She gulped as he caressed her. "Maybe we should do something about that."

"Good idea." Cupping her bottom, he lifted her up. Her yoga pants fell to the floor as he cradled her against his jutting fly.

"Excellent move." She wrapped her legs around him.

He carried her the short distance to the bed and lowered her to the mattress. Then he followed her down and wedged his aching cock, trapped behind his fly, between her thighs.

She squeezed her legs tighter, and her voice was

ragged. "I'll bet…if you stayed right there…I could come."

"Want to?" He rocked his hips forward, pressing against her heat as he nibbled on her mouth.

She sucked in a breath. "I like the old-fashioned way."

"Then turn me loose. I'll take off my—"

"Can't wait that long." She relaxed her thighs and reached for the button below his navel. "Need you now."

Lust scorched a path straight to his groin. "Go for it." While she dealt with his zipper, he grabbed a condom on the bedside table. But when she pushed down his briefs and got both her hands on him, he groaned and nearly dropped the packet on the floor.

Desperation made him hold on to it. He ripped it open with his teeth, and she took over from there. He was breathing like a charging bull by the time she finished rolling it on, and then he was afraid he acted like one, too.

One of these times he would use more finesse when he engaged in this activity with her, but now wasn't that time. Now was about thrusting home with no hesitation or apology. Fortunately, she didn't seem to mind at all.

In fact, she seemed very pleased with his randy behavior, judging from the way she urged him on. She used some pretty earthy language to do it, too, and he loved that. She was no shy maid, his Elle.

Maybe he didn't know a lot of things about her, but he knew how she responded to sexual pleasure. She gave it everything she had, which inspired him to do the same. He didn't need to think about holding back and waiting for her orgasm, because she let him know it was right around the bend.

He could go headlong and seek the climax he craved. He could ride her with fierce energy because she asked him to. Hell, she begged him to. He could use the same four-letter words she used to describe the hot sex they were sharing.

She was, hands down, the best partner he'd ever had. Yeah, they'd have a conversation eventually, but he believed they were having one now. And this one counted, too. Oh, yeah, it counted.

She cried out and arched under him mere seconds before he came in a glorious rush that made him dizzy. They clung to each other and gasped for breath in unison. He didn't know what else they'd find in common, what other pleasures they'd share, but this…this was unbelievable. And so right.

8

"THAT WAS PLAIN FUN." Elle gazed up at Trey. It had taken them a while, but they were finally breathing normally again.

"Can't say I've ever had more fun in my life." Levering himself up on his forearms, he glanced down at her green velour jacket, which had remained zipped throughout. "But you must be ready to get rid of extra wardrobe items. I sure am."

"I suppose. I got a little sweaty under this thing, but the immediacy of it all was darned exciting." That was putting it mildly. She'd never done it when the guy had his pants on, or mostly on. "Thanks for indulging me."

"My pleasure. Literally. It turns me on that you couldn't wait. I also like that you got so graphic." His cock, still firm and tucked securely within her, twitched. "I'm still liking it, in fact. Keep talking."

She laughed. "It's a function of the moment. I don't normally use that kind of language."

"I figured not."

"So I didn't shock you?"

"Nope."

"You…you make me want to say those things."

"I do? Don't get me wrong. I love that you feel so uninhibited with me, but why?"

She had to think about that. "Maybe because our connection is so basic. And maybe because we didn't find out a lot about each other before we had sex."

"Huh."

"If I'd known more about your background, I would have wondered if I should use those words. Am I making any sense?"

An emotion flickered in his dark eyes. "Guess so. You're saying that we're all about the sex. No complications."

Well, yes, she was saying that, but she wished he looked a little happier about it. Because they craved each other with such intensity, she'd begun to believe this hot, temporary fling was working for both of them. "Is that a problem for you?"

His expression lightened immediately. "Hell, no. Only a fool would have a problem with incredible sex." Breaking eye contact, he drew down the zipper on her sweatshirt. "And the night is young."

"Technically, it's not." The cool air felt lovely on her overheated breasts. Under his gaze, her nipples tightened.

"I know, but we're just getting started." He grazed the tip of each nipple with his palm, and that whisper of a connection made her womb throb.

He glanced up. His voice was low and rough with awareness. "I felt that."

"I can't help it. When you touch me, I…" She moaned as he spread his fingers over her moist skin and pressed gently. A spasm shook her.

"Stay here."

"Oh, don't worry. I will." She couldn't move if the place caught on fire. She was too turned on.

Easing away from her, he left the bed. In moments he was back, and the lamplight gleamed on his naked body, which was as sweaty as hers. "This time, by God, we're going to take it slow."

She gazed at his erect cock and smiled. "You sure about that, cowboy?"

"I'm positive about that, lady. For starters, I want you to sit up, scoot back a ways and take your jacket off."

"Sounds as if you have a plan."

"I do."

Her body hummed with anticipation as she followed his instructions. She wondered if he'd called her *lady* on purpose, echoing her use of *cowboy*. Labels weren't as intimate as first names. Maybe he was going to be okay with keeping this arrangement casual, after all.

"Spread your legs."

"This is getting more interesting by the second."

"That's the idea." Throwing back the covers, he climbed in. He sat facing her, his legs apart, too. "Come a little closer. Prop your thighs on mine."

"Have you been reading *The Kama Sutra?*"

"I paged through it once in the library. Come a few inches forward so we can reach each other. I want you within kissing distance."

As she adjusted her position, she held on to his muscled arms for balance. She glanced at the tattoo. Maybe she wouldn't ask him, after all. Personal details were best left unexplained if she wanted to maintain a no-strings liaison with him.

"Perfect." Cupping her face, he leaned in for a kiss.

She decided to cup something a little lower. She might be within kissing distance, but that put him within fondling distance. She took a notion to make use of her close proximity to his family jewels.

Leaning back, he grasped her wrists and lifted her hands to his shoulders. "Not yet."

"What, there are rules to this game?"

"Yeah, kind of. Let's see how long we can stay like this, touching each other, caressing each other, but not coming."

"So the winner is the last one to cross the finish line?"

"That's right. If you hold off as long as you can, it's supposed to make your climax a whole lot more powerful."

She laughed. "More powerful than I've already had with you? Are you trying to kill me?"

"I'm trying to make this last a while. Each time we've gotten together, we've been so frantic for each other that we've gone straight for the easy climax. Let's slow it down a little. Play around. Get creative."

"Exactly. That's what I was trying to do."

"But we need to start at the top and work our way down. If you start *there,* we'll be done before you know it."

"Oh. Okay. I'm down with that." She gazed at him and realized that she'd never slid her fingers through his dark hair. Its wavy thickness invited a woman's touch.

He wore his hair on the longish side, although not quite collar-length. The style fit his musician persona.

Other than grabbing his head in a fit of passion, she hadn't spent much time fooling around with his hair.

Reaching up, she used both hands to comb it back from his temples. "Like this?"

He closed his eyes and sighed. "Like that."

"You have wonderful hair." She let the silky strands slip through her fingers. "You should take off your hat when you play guitar."

He kept his eyes closed, as if soaking up her touch. "I like wearing the hat when I play."

"Why?" Moving her hands to his forehead, she traced the path of each eyebrow. His brows were thick, too, and he had long eyelashes. She hadn't noticed that detail until now.

"Protection, I guess."

She didn't have to ask what he meant. Even though she'd never performed for anyone, other than in school plays when she was a little kid, she understood that it had to be somewhat scary unless you were an exhibitionist. Trey wasn't an exhibitionist, which made him vulnerable up there in front of an audience.

Yet he continued to write songs and play them for others. Something in him demanded expression, so he bowed to that demand but kept his hat on. His reason for doing that tugged at her heart.

Leaning forward, she placed a soft kiss on his lips. When she started to pull away, he captured her head in both hands and brought her mouth back to his. "More," he whispered.

She settled into the kiss, stroking his tongue with hers, shifting her angle, finding a better fit, melding her mouth with his, surrendering to the tactile joy of his supple lips. He groaned and thrust his tongue deep.

Without warning her core contracted. She pulled back, gasping. "Stop for a minute."

His dark eyes blazed with fire. "But I like kissing you."

"And I like kissing you, too. A little too much." She took a shaky breath. "I almost came just now."

The heat in his gaze intensified. "Good to know."

"It seems I'm not very talented at this game."

His eyes glittered. "Maybe we should change the rules and see how often I can make you come."

"That's no challenge." Her breathing slowed. "I think I understand the problem. I'm conditioned to come when you and I are naked together."

"Then I should be conditioned that way, too."

"No, because you're a guy. You're conditioned to have an erection whenever we're naked together." She gestured toward his cock. "Exhibit A."

"Can't argue that conclusion."

"But guys, at least the considerate ones, start training themselves to hold off their climaxes, because women tend to take longer. Am I right?"

"Right, except in your case, that's not true. You're a powder keg from the get-go."

"Well, yes and no. I used to take longer. Something about you really flips my switch."

He looked pleased with that information. "So you're saying that with another guy…"

"I would be awesome at this game. But now that you've set up this challenge, I'm determined to meet it."

He frowned. "I'm not sure this is such a good idea, after all. I didn't have the whole picture before, and I like having you conditioned to come whenever you're naked with me."

"But you said my orgasm would be more powerful if I can hold off."

"The *book* said that. But if you're happy with your orgasms as they are, then let's forget this program. The book could be wrong, you know."

He was adorable, and she couldn't remember ever joking around with a man in bed this way. "I *am* happy with my orgasms, but maybe I could be even happier. Come on, Trey. You set up some expectations. No fair abandoning the idea. It might work if I can resist your sexual magnetism."

He laughed. "You are sure good for my ego. I suppose we can have fun trying. So we're back to the original plan?"

"However you wanted to work it is fine with me."

"Then I can kiss you?"

"Sure. I'm ready now." She paused. "What happens after the kissing, so I'm mentally prepared?"

"Caressing above the waist."

"Okay." Her breasts tingled just thinking about that.

"Then caressing below the waist." His tone was casual, but his expression grew more intense.

"I have the advantage there." Moisture gathered between her thighs. "You're more accessible than I am."

"That's a matter of opinion." He surveyed her spread thighs. "You look damned accessible to me."

"No peeking allowed. I'm susceptible to those hot glances."

"Don't think it's only you with an issue. I just found out you're already wet down there. Now I'm harder than ever."

Her breath caught. She was ready to tackle him and forget this nonsense, but he'd aroused her competitive instinct as well as her sexual urges. "That's fair. Ready to start?"

"Oh, yeah."

"On three. One, two, three, *kiss*."

He swooped in. She should have known he'd play dirty. His tongue blatantly mimicked the act they were temporarily avoiding. She gave it right back to him, sucking on his probing tongue and moaning suggestively.

Her reward was listening to his increasingly labored breathing. Or was that her breathing? After a while she couldn't decide who was gasping louder.

She responded to that kiss as usual, which meant she felt the urge to surrender to that great feeling hovering within reach. She fought that urge, which was extremely unfamiliar, but interesting.

He was the one who broke off their kiss, which she scored as a point for her side. When she looked into his heavy-lidded eyes, she could see a battle going on. Chest heaving, he ran his hands over her shoulders in a light massage.

Poor baby. He seemed to be having trouble getting enough air in his lungs. She stroked his shoulders in return, but she used a firm touch. He had muscles that begged for a girl to dig in and appreciate all that manliness.

In spite of having to control her response to him, she liked this routine. She hadn't spent enough time running her hands over his sculpted body, and she was making up for it now. He quivered under her touch.

She glanced into his eyes and saw molten need there. "How're you doing, cowboy?"

A muscle twitched in his jaw. "Just fine. How 'bout you?"

"Fine, just…" Or not. He'd begun to fondle her breasts, and that…that could be trouble. His touch was all the more erotic because of the small calluses on the tips of his fingers. This man could also make a guitar sing with his talented caress, and knowing that excited her even more.

He watched her as he rolled her nipples between his thumb and forefinger. "Your eyes are getting dark."

She didn't doubt it. Her nipples seemed connected to her womb with a taut string, and when he squeezed them gently, it was as if he plucked that string. She began to vibrate.

He had the upper hand now. She would go down in flames unless—unless he was sensitive there, too. Placing both hands over his pecs, she began a slow massage. His heartbeat thudded against her right palm, and when she squeezed his nipples as he'd squeezed hers, the rhythm of his heart picked up.

His hands stilled and his jaw tightened. He closed his eyes and blew out a breath. "That's…good."

"Glad you like it." She continued to stroke his chest and play with his nipples. "You have an incredible body. I love doing this."

He remained motionless, as if she'd mesmerized him with her touch, and perhaps with her voice, too. The idea fascinated her, so she kept talking. "Your skin is like velvet under my fingers, like warm velvet that's been lying in the sun."

His breathing became uneven.

"I'd love to lie naked with you in a sunny meadow and see your skin gleaming in the light, your muscles rippling as you slide into me, your—"

"I want you." His hoarse voice betrayed how much. Tension radiated from him and his whole body trembled with the force of it. "I can't take this. I thought I could, but your voice…" He opened his eyes.

She gasped at the primitive fire in those dark depths. The need reflected there made her shake, too.

He swallowed. "There's a condom on the nightstand."

She'd won. And she'd done it by *talking* to him. Scooting back, she reached for the packet on the nightstand and ripped it open.

"Hurry."

"Yes." She glanced at his cock, where a bead of moisture gathered at the tip. Lowering her head, she licked it off.

"Elle." He grasped her head in both hands, pressing his fingertips into her scalp.

She didn't know if he'd meant to lift her away or urge her down, but in that split second she made her decision. She took him into her mouth and sucked hard.

With a tortured groan, he came, and she took all he gave her. When at last his shudders ceased, she released him, giving him one last intimate kiss.

"Oh, Elle." He lifted her up and pulled her into his lap. "Elle." His mouth found hers.

She wrapped her arms around his neck, and when he urged her thighs apart, she welcomed the firm thrust of his fingers. He caressed her with sure strokes, and the climax she'd resisted so fiercely surged forward with blinding speed. Her hips bucked, and she wrenched her mouth free as the impact of her orgasm left her gasping for air.

He stayed with her, pumping his fingers in and out as she moaned and shook in his arms. She didn't know if it was the best climax ever, but it was pretty damned wonderful. This delayed gratification might be worth exploring some more.

At last she lay still. Slowly she opened her eyes to find him gazing down at her with raw emotion. The intensity of it should probably worry her. But she felt so good, so completely and utterly satisfied, that she couldn't bring herself to be worried about anything.

She gave him a lazy smile. "I win."

9

ELLE HAD WON, all right. Trey knew exactly what she'd won, too—his heart. She'd unknowingly wooed him with her most powerful weapon. Her voice had stayed with him for months, and now he'd never forget it.

Earlier tonight he'd been treated to her honeyed voice speaking in very explicit language that had driven him wild. But that had been child's play compared to what she'd accomplished this time. Her sensual touch and seductive murmurs had woven a spell that had brought him to a fever pitch.

He hadn't merely wanted to have her. He'd wanted to ravage her. Holding himself in check had taken all his strength, and when she'd used her tongue to tease him, his control had snapped. He wasn't sure if she'd meant to finish what she'd started, but he would have given her no choice.

Whether she knew it or not, this level of intimacy had brought them to the soul-baring stage. But he didn't dare tell her that. She seemed to think she was less inhibited with him because they knew so little about each other. Maybe she'd convinced herself that they were having stranger-sex, where the participants were largely anonymous. She couldn't be more wrong.

Without realizing it, she'd already revealed so much. He knew she was both competitive and generous. She was more passionate than any woman he'd had sex with. She didn't back down from a challenge and she used her sense of humor to stay balanced. On top of that, she was honest, at least with him. Maybe not so much with herself.

He'd learned all that from making love to her. Although he didn't know everything about her, he knew enough to recognize someone with the potential to be a lifelong... He hesitated to admit how far his thoughts had taken him. Too far, probably, because she'd given every indication that she wasn't looking for anyone permanent in her life.

He fervently hoped she'd change her mind about that. His strategy would be to love the dickens out of her until she got used to having him around. That would include some old-fashioned wooing, because great as the sex was, they couldn't do it *all* the time.

Consequently, he'd come back to the room tonight prepared with a bottle of wine he'd bought at the bar and the leftover party munchies he'd asked the bartender to package up for him. He gazed into her flushed face. She did look happy. So far, so good. "What do you say to a picnic?"

She laughed and sat up. "I hope you're not suggesting we haul a blanket out into the snow."

"Nope." He thought about the picture she'd painted of lying naked in a meadow. Wrong time of year for that, but he'd remind her of the concept sometime soon. To make that fantasy come true, she'd have to stick around, though. He wasn't sure how well she'd respond to that idea.

"So where will we picnic?"

"Right here. In bed."

"I think we just did that."

"I mean with food and drink."

"Are you going to smear me with cream cheese?"

His cock, which logically should stay at rest for a while, twitched with obvious interest. "Great idea, but I didn't steal any cream cheese from the party. Hold that thought for next time."

"So you're suggesting an actual picnic."

"I am. Are you hungry?"

She tilted her head as if to consider that. "Yes, I am! Must be all the great sex. Whatcha got?"

He climbed out of bed and unearthed his stash, which Fred had packed into a paper bag. Thank God screw-top wine wasn't considered tacky anymore, because he had a bottle of red that wouldn't require a corkscrew. He pulled it out. "You up for this?"

"You bet. I love me a good malbec. But I thought cowboys liked beer."

"I happen to like both, but wine seemed to fit the occasion."

"What occasion?"

Finding you. "Having a chance to be alone and naked together."

"I guess that deserves a toast, now that you mention it. Want me to get us water glasses from the bathroom?"

"I stole glasses, too." He took two stemmed goblets from the bag. "Actually, that's not true. Fred thought I needed them."

"Did Fred know *why* you needed them?"

"Probably." He couldn't see any point in trying to disguise the fact that nearly everyone at the resort assumed he and Elle were getting it on tonight. "Do you care?"

"I'd better not care. The reason I was late involved meeting the Chance brothers and Emmett Sterling in the hallway. I think Jack knew exactly where I was going. Nothing much gets by him."

"That's a fact." Trey took out assorted crackers, pretzels and some chunks of cheese. "Were they all leaving the bachelor party? Is that why you ran into them?"

"They were talking Emmett out of spending the night with his fiancée after she specifically requested that he not do so."

Trey could picture that. He grinned. "Did they succeed?"

"I think so. They were headed up to Emmett's bachelor quarters when I left them. Oh, and Emmett invited me to the wedding and reception."

"He did? Excellent! I was afraid I wouldn't get to see much of you tomorrow. Will you dance with me?" This weekend was improving minute by minute.

"Won't you be playing the music?"

"Not constantly. Watkins and I can trade off, and we'll use some recorded music so we can have a break. We can definitely dance." And he could hardly wait to hold her in his arms on the dance floor. He had a feeling they'd be awesome together there, too.

"That would be fun. Gabe said it will be the wedding of the century."

"A wedding that almost didn't happen. Emmett

wanted to fly to Vegas this afternoon and sabotage the entire effort." Trey spread out napkins on the bed and dumped some of the goodies on them.

"You're kidding!"

"Nope." He accepted the glass of wine she gave him and leaned toward her. "Here's to you, me and a king-size bed."

"I'll drink to that." She touched her goblet to his. "But now tell me more about this Vegas thing. I can't believe it."

Trey carefully positioned himself on the bed so the picnic wouldn't be disturbed. "He's reconsidered that notion."

"Well, I should hope so! Talk about crazy. How could he think of doing such a thing after the preparation and expense?"

"He's not into all that. And Pam's money is paying for it."

"Oh." She nibbled on some cheese. "I did wonder where the money was coming from. I thought maybe the Chance family was footing the bill."

"No. If they were organizing things, they'd probably have suggested having it at the ranch instead. Pam was the one behind coming to the resort. She wanted everyone to get away from their place of work so they'd feel free to party."

"Makes sense." She picked up a cracker. "Great eats, Trey. Thanks."

"You're welcome." He added a sense of gratitude to her list of good qualities.

"I looked up the Last Chance on the internet tonight."

"You did?" He found that very encouraging. "What did you think?"

"It's gorgeous."

"The place is even prettier than it looks online. Dominique took some awesome pictures for the website, but nothing beats actually being there, working in that historic barn, training the registered paints they breed. I was really happy to get the job." He drank some wine while he thought about whether he should say what was on his mind. Aw, hell, why not? "You should come out and see it for yourself."

She studied him over the rim of her glass. "Why?"

Because I want you to fall in love with my world, and with me, that's why. He couldn't say that, either. He was censoring himself a lot, and he wondered how long his tolerance for that would hold out. "It's a landmark in Jackson Hole. Now that you've met the owners, you might as well take a look at the place, just to say you've been there."

"I'll keep that in mind." She picked up a cracker, put some cheese on it and popped it in her mouth.

He had trouble not focusing all his attention on her, which she wouldn't appreciate. But she looked so cute sitting on the bed with no clothes on, sipping her wine and eating her snack. He stored the image away. There was a chance this was all he'd ever have, and he needed to be realistic about that.

She finished her cracker and cheese. "Do you ever play guitar at the Spirits and Spurs?"

"I have, a time or two. Where did you hear about that place?"

"Jared mentioned it. He spends the summers here in Jackson Hole. God knows what he does to keep himself occupied and solvent all summer. He must pick up odd jobs. But apparently sometimes he drops in at the Spirits and Spurs in Shoshone." She drank more wine. "Do you think it's really haunted?"

He realized that she was intrigued by the ranch and the nearby town, but he didn't want to overplay his hand. She'd been motivated to check out the area online, but that could have been idle curiosity. It didn't mean she was ready to give up her summers in Argentina to be here. Or to be with him.

"I've never seen a ghost," he said. "I've never even sensed a ghostly presence. But I know those who have. Some think that Archie Chance, the Chance brothers' grandfather, shows up at the Spirits and Spurs from time to time. They say he used to hang out at the bar whenever his wife, Nelsie, went shopping in town."

"Probably no ghosts make an appearance in winter, though."

"Sure they do. Remember the story of Scrooge?"

"Oh, yeah." She looked thoughtful. "I admit to being fascinated by the idea of ghosts. I don't really believe in them, but still…"

He set his wineglass on the nightstand. "Elle, if you have the slightest interest in going to the Spirits and Spurs, I'll take you. I can't promise ghosts, but Josie decorates it real nice for the holidays. Not like Serenity, of course. But nice."

"Serenity's a little over the top, but I like it."

"Spirits and Spurs decorations are a lot simpler. There's a tree, and pine boughs and twinkling lights. Well, and Josie always hangs up mistletoe. She claims the customers expect it, but I think she's the one who likes it, personally."

"Maybe the mistletoe attracts ghosts."

"Maybe."

Elle looked eager for a moment, as if she might be considering his invitation. But then her expression changed and she shrugged. "I usually stick around here during the holidays so Jared and Annalise can have time off. I'll need to work."

"Even at night? Every night?"

"We have night skiing for the more experienced guests. Don't worry about it. Christmas is no big deal for me, really."

"You're not into Christmas?"

"There's not much point, in my case. I buy gifts for my parents and send them to wherever they're currently stationed, and a cousin and I exchange presents every year, but that's the extent of my involvement."

He didn't know what to say to that without prying into her personal business. Obviously seeing her folks during the holidays wasn't important to her. Mentioning that his folks weren't alive anymore so he had nowhere special to go during the holidays would be an unnecessary downer.

His special place was quickly becoming the Last Chance. He'd heard from Watkins all about how the family celebrated. Watkins loved holidays at the ranch. Consequently, Trey was really looking forward to Christmas Eve, when the Chances invited all the hands to the house for a big party. Christmas Day was nice, too, according to Watkins, because anyone was welcome to drop in from noon on, after the family members had opened presents and finished their Christmas breakfast.

Elle drained her glass. "More wine?"

"Sure, why not?" He finished his wine and held out his glass.

"It's good stuff."

"Not bad." He took a long swallow. "You know what? We should toast Emmett and Pam. Without them, we wouldn't be here."

"Good point. And I'm even going to the wedding tomorrow." She leaned over and clicked the rim of her glass against his. "To Emmett and Pam." She glanced at his arm as he raised his glass to his lips. "Trey, I promised myself I wouldn't ask you about your tattoo, but it's late, and we've had sex and wine, and I keep staring at it whenever you flex your arm."

He tried to ignore the sense of foreboding. Things were going so well, but this wasn't a topic he wanted to discuss yet. "Why do you suppose I have a tattoo? It's so ladies will fixate on my manly muscles."

"I've heard that's why guys get tattoos there."

"You've heard right."

"But why an angel wing?"

His pulse rate spiked. How to answer? "I needed a tattoo and I liked it better than the hula girl."

"I don't believe that's the reason. You're not the type to pick some random thing and have it inked on your body, not even to get women."

"How do you know I'm not?"

"Because… Well, I just know, that's all."

So she wasn't going to admit that she'd learned important things about him, too. Of course she had. They couldn't have been so intimate without her picking up on facets of his personality.

He thought about lying and saying that it was a generic symbol of his guardian angel. He wasn't in the habit of lying, but he didn't think she'd like hearing the truth. They had a fragile understanding, one that could be easily shattered.

But he had hopes for this relationship, fragile though it might be. Lying about his tattoo would be something he couldn't fix if they ended up together. Eventually he'd have to tell her why he had it, and then he'd be exposed as a liar.

So he chose to tell her the truth and accept the consequences. "As I mentioned before, I tried to find you after you saved me last spring."

Her expression turned wary. "Right."

"When I couldn't find you, I needed...*wanted*...to commemorate that lifesaving moment. I thought of you as my angel. Well, *an* angel, not necessarily *my* angel. So I got the tattoo."

Wariness had turned to shock. "So the tattoo is for *me?*"

"I needed something, Elle, something to express my gratitude for being alive, and your part in it. I chose this. It represents a twist of fate as much as anything."

She didn't seem to be buying that. "I'm not an angel, Trey. I'm so far from being an angel it's hysterically funny. I spew four-letter words when I have sex with you!"

"That's not the point." He reached for her, but she leaped off the bed.

"I think it's exactly the point. You've created some idealized image of the person who rescued you. She's an effing *angel*. Her wing is now a permanent part of your body!"

"I did that before I knew you." He left the bed, desperate for her to understand. "I wasn't even sure you were real! For all I knew, you were some heavenly being who'd swooped down to make sure I didn't die!"

"I am real, Trey." She picked up her yoga pants. "And human and fallible. I make mistakes all the time. One of them might be getting involved with you."

"Don't say that."

"I said *might*." She pulled on her pants. "The jury's still out on the question. But my initial impression, when I heard you calling out for your girlfriend, Cassie, was that you were a romantic soul who needed to find an equally romantic soul." She located her jacket on the floor.

He wanted to argue with her about being a romantic, but he thought she could be right. Who else but a romantic would have an angel wing tattooed on his arm? Who else would write a song about the angel who had saved him, and then actually perform it for other folks?

So, if they were ever going to have a future, which seemed less likely now than it had five minutes ago, she'd have to accept that about him. "Maybe I *am* a romantic guy," he said. "If I have that tendency, I've tried to downplay it because I sensed that wouldn't impress you."

"You've got that right." She zipped her jacket. "Sappy sentimentality doesn't work for me."

"Ouch."

"Sorry." She scanned the floor looking for her shoes. "That was a little harsh."

"It was a lot harsh. Is that how you see me? A sentimental sap?"

"No. At least not mostly." She found the shoes. "We've had some good, honest sex that wasn't sentimental at all. I'm on board with that. But when I discover that the angel's wing on your arm represents me, I get worried. You're expecting something from me that I'm not prepared to give." She shoved her feet into the shoes.

"Yet."

She whirled to face him. "What the hell does that mean?"

"Don't forget that I've made love to you, Elle. I've known you in a way that you may not even admit to yourself. There's a depth of feeling you may not acknowledge, but I feel it. Damn it, I was there, holding you, and I felt it!"

She gazed at him. "You're delusional." Then she turned and walked out of his room, closing the door quietly behind her.

He wished she'd slammed it. That, at least, would have shown some fiery emotion. He knew she had it in her. He'd experienced it firsthand.

But she was willing to pretend that her ordered life had no room for that kind of passion. He scared her because he threatened to upset the careful image she'd created of how things should be.

He didn't blame her for being confused. Although he had to read between the lines, he could guess that she'd been taught not to get attached to people or places. That might have been a by-product of being a kid with parents in the military, but he'd known others with that background and they weren't so fiercely independent.

The clue might be her lack of interest in seeing her parents for Christmas. Hell, if he still had parents, he'd make damn sure he traveled to wherever they were.

But she might have been taught through example to minimize the importance of family celebrations.

She'd told him that his emotional response to losing Cassie had kept her from maintaining contact. But although she tried to present herself as a person who didn't need those messy emotions, her joyful response to having sex with him said otherwise. He suspected she was hungry for a deep personal connection.

Maybe she'd sensed that she was making one with him and had panicked. He could go after her, calm her down. Instead, he decided to sit tight and see if she could stay away. He was hoping that she couldn't.

10

ELLE HAD A bad feeling she'd overreacted. But she needed time to think, and she couldn't think very well when in the presence of Trey's magnificently naked body, especially decorated with that exceedingly sentimental tattoo. Thankfully no one was in the halls as she hurried back to her room.

Once there, she went to switch on her bedside lamp and changed her mind. Instead, she turned on her Christmas tree lights. Then she flopped down on her bed and lay there surrounded by the soft, multicolored glow.

It reminded her of a Christmas many years ago, one she'd spent with her parents in Germany. She'd been in third grade, so she would have been eight. She'd begged for a tree that year, as she had every year.

They'd never had one, or even much in the way of decorations. Her mother had insisted that hauling ornaments around from place to place was ridiculous. Neither was she willing to buy new ones each time and discard them when they moved, because that would be wasteful.

When her mom hadn't budged that year, either, Elle had used money she'd been saving for a bike and bought a tree, a stand and ornaments. It hadn't been a very big tree, but she'd put it up in a fit of rebellion, determined that she'd enjoy the heck out of it.

That hadn't been easy when her parents had both made her feel silly for doing such a thing. They'd acted as if the tree was a nuisance, and she'd been told to take it down the day after Christmas. Putting it up and taking it down by herself had been a lot of work, and when they'd moved, her parents hadn't wanted to take the ornaments. In the end, she'd given them to a friend at school.

She'd always assumed her parents, especially her mother, were simply being practical. Now she wondered if that was the whole story. Neither of them made a big deal out of anything tradition-oriented, come to think of it. Not birthdays or anniversaries, either.

Elle had accepted their lack of interest in celebrating, along with the idea that wasting time and money on such things made no sense. They would laugh if they knew Pam Mulholland had rented out an entire ski resort for her wedding to Emmett Sterling. Elle saw something of her parents' attitude in Emmett.

What a shame it would have been if he'd succeeded in ruining this for his fiancée. Elle had always identified with the Emmett Sterlings of the world, but tonight, to her surprise, she found herself siding with Pam. If a sixty-something woman wanted to use her money to celebrate marrying the man she loved, why not?

How all that tied in with Trey was unclear right

now, but Elle would go to the wedding. She was very interested in seeing how Emmett adjusted to his bride's need to mark the occasion with public joy and extravagance. And Elle would dance with Trey if he still wanted her to. With that thought, she left the Christmas lights on, which was completely impractical and wasteful, and drifted off to sleep.

THE NEXT DAY she estimated that she'd probably spent more time dressing for the wedding than the bride herself. Because she traveled between Jackson Hole and Argentina every year, she kept her wardrobe simple. Yet she wanted to look good. No, not just *good*. She wanted to look amazing.

That left her with one choice—a cobalt-blue, knee-length jersey dress that could be dressed up or down. Today's event called for dressing it up, so she added a hammered silver necklace with large, irregularly shaped links, and earrings with the same type of asymmetrical loops. Her open-toed silver stilettos hardly ever came out of the closet, but now was the time.

She'd spent a good twenty minutes on her makeup, and she'd piled her hair on top of her head and secured it with several rhinestone hairpins. The glitter might be a bit much for an afternoon wedding, but she expected the reception to last into the night. She rummaged through her drawers and found the silver clutch she'd bought to match the stilettos.

Her small, utilitarian room didn't have a full-length mirror, so she could only see herself from her hips up. That much looked okay, so she'd assume the rest passed muster, too. As she walked down the stairs and into the guest area of the resort, she realized the dress code for a ranch foreman's wedding might be Western formal. Oh, well. She didn't own anything that fit that description.

The mellow sound of guitar music beckoned her to the room where the wedding was being held. Her stomach churned at the thought of seeing Trey again. Their night together hadn't ended well, mostly because of her.

He hadn't tried to contact her since then, even though they had each other's cell numbers. She'd reminded herself that he was no doubt busy with wedding activities, but that argument didn't wash. He was the guitarist for the ceremony and the reception, not a member of the wedding party.

That meant he could have texted or called this morning. He hadn't, but then she hadn't contacted him, either. Frankly, she didn't know what to say. She still worried that he'd created a fantasy that she could never live up to.

When she thought of him having his arm tattooed to commemorate her rescuing him, she shivered. Getting tattooed hurt, or so she'd been told. Maybe he'd done it after several shots of hard liquor, but still. He'd subjected himself to the process in her honor.

She didn't know what to do with that information. Her parents, the people who'd given her life, hadn't done much of anything for her major life events. Graduations were taken in stride, and when she'd won skiing competitions, they'd phoned to say it was nice. No flowers, no card.

Trey had allowed someone to stick needles under his skin and permanently alter his appearance because he believed she deserved to be honored. Not *her,* exactly, but the idea of her, the angelic vision he carried of that rescue. The guy was adorable, and wow, could he do the horizontal mambo, but the tattoo thing was intense.

She wasn't quite sure what to make of it. Even so, she yearned to see him, to be with him, to hold him close. He was Trey, the sexy guy who'd given her orgasms she wasn't likely to forget anytime soon. He was also fun, and caring and honest.... He could have lied to her about the tattoo. She gave him props for not doing that.

A sweet-looking redhead who couldn't be more than eighteen sat at a table just inside the door with a guest book in front of her. She looked up when Elle approached. "What a gorgeous dress!"

"Thank you. I'm Elle Masterson. I'm a ski instructor here. I don't know if Emmett had time to mention that he invited me, but I—"

"I know *exactly* who you are, Ms. Masterson." Her blue eyes shone with excitement. "You're the lady who rescued Trey Wheeler." The girl held out her hand. "I'm Cassidy O'Connelli. My sister Morgan is married to Gabe Chance, and my sister Tyler is married to Alex Keller. You gave Alex and Gabe ski lessons yesterday. Everyone had a blast!"

"Good! I didn't see you out there yesterday. Don't you like to ski?"

"I've never tried it, but I might tomorrow. Pam needed me to help her with a few things, and that was fine with me. I love weddings. I'm apprenticing to be the new housekeeper at the Last Chance. You should come and visit."

"Thanks." The blizzard of information from Cassidy combined with soft guitar music left Elle feeling distracted. She did her best to focus on Cassidy when all she really wanted to do was check out Trey's guitar performance. "I appreciate the invitation, and I'll try to make it out there."

"I hope you do. Here comes Jeb. He'll escort you to your seat."

Elle smiled at the freckle-faced cowboy who'd been one of her students the day before. He wore a smart-looking Western coat, a white shirt and a bolo tie. "Hi, Jeb. You're looking good."

Jeb offered his arm. "Pam wanted all of us to be stylin', so she helped pick out our clothes. I get to keep the jacket."

"Bonus."

"I *know.* I've never owned a jacket this nice. You're sitting on the groom's side, right?"

"I guess so. Emmett's the one who invited me."

"Then I'm putting you on the groom's side. Isn't this the fanciest wedding you've ever seen?"

"It's pretty fancy." To please Jeb, she glanced around at the greenery, wine-colored ribbons and white roses. Tiny white lights twinkled everywhere. Wine-colored poinsettias were clustered on tiered stands around the perimeter of the room.

"It's like a fairyland," Jeb said. "Well, here you go. This is your seat." He indicated a spot on the aisle in the fourth row. "You're gonna love this wedding. It'll be awesome. And cute. Little Archie, Jack's son, and Sara Bianca, Gabe's daughter, will be in it. And by the way, you look beautiful."

"What a nice thing to say. Thank you, Jeb."

"It's the truth. Oh, here's your program." He handed her an elegantly printed booklet. "If you'll excuse me, I have more people to escort."

"You go right ahead. I'll be fine." She would be more than fine in this spot. At last she had what she wanted—an excellent view of Trey. He and Watkins sat to the left of a greenery-covered arch that would serve as the focal point for the ceremony. Trey was not wearing his hat.

Watkins wasn't wearing one, either, so Pam might have made a no-hats decision. In any case, Elle loved being able to see Trey's expression as he played a gentle love ballad.

Although neither man was singing, Elle had no trouble filling in the lyrics. She knew the song well. She'd bet Trey did, too, and was repeating them in his head as he played. Watkins might be a better guitarist, especially because he'd had more years of practice, but in Elle's completely biased opinion, Trey put more emotion into the notes.

She'd been an idiot to ever think he could carry on an affair without becoming involved. He was an artist. Artists had to give rein to their emotions, whereas she was a ski instructor, an analytical teacher. She'd been raised by parents who believed in logic and efficiency. She believed in those things, too. Didn't she?

If so, she wasn't doing a very good job of being logical and efficient regarding Trey. Her breath caught as she watched him strum his guitar. Less than twelve hours ago, those strong fingers had been touching her, loving her, making her moan. She squirmed in her seat. She wanted him to make love to her again.

But was that fair to Trey? She'd been right all along.

He needed someone as romantic as he was, someone who would send him sentimental love notes and appreciate his flair for the dramatic. Speaking of that, how would he explain his tattoo to a future lover?

Although it was unworthy of her, she liked the idea that he'd have to. Perhaps he shouldn't have honored her with that angel's wing, but he couldn't do much about it now. Like it or not, he was stuck with this memory of her. That shouldn't make her smile. But it did.

The room gradually filled with happy people. Elle could feel the good cheer in the air, hear it in the muted laughter, see it in the glowing expressions and wide smiles. This was why Pam had insisted on a public celebration. It was a gift to all those who knew her and Emmett, all those who wanted to share in their joy.

But Elle couldn't help wondering how Emmett was holding up. About that time, he entered from a side door, accompanied by Jack, Gabe and Nick. Those brothers made an impressive trio, but Emmett was the guy Elle focused on.

She need not have worried about him. He looked magnificent. Tall and silver-haired, he carried himself with pride and assurance, as if he'd decided that this was, in fact, the most glorious day of his life so far, and he planned to enjoy it to the fullest.

Elle wasn't sure what she'd expected—maybe a hesitant man who had to be bolstered by the three younger cowboys at his side. Instead, he took the leadership role, and they served as his trusty companions.

Elle knew all would be well. Emmett had risen to the occasion and would make his bride proud. She barely knew Emmett and didn't know Pam at all, but her understanding of Emmett's dilemma had given her a stake in the proceedings. Happy anticipation made her glance in Trey's direction.

As if they'd choreographed it, he was looking back. He and Watkins had finished the last of the preceremony numbers, and Trey sat with his guitar in his lap and his gaze trained on her. He wasn't smiling. Her heart stuttered. Did he think their interlude was over?

She wouldn't blame him if he thought that. All things considered, he'd probably be better off without her. Selfish person that she was, she didn't want to let him go. Not yet. But perhaps he'd decided she wasn't worth the trouble.

Watkins leaned over and murmured something to Trey. With one last glance at Elle, he settled his guitar more firmly against his thighs. Together, he and Watkins began to play the "Wedding March."

The guests rose and turned toward the back of the room. So did Elle, which meant she couldn't see Trey anymore. But she was here for a wedding, and Pam deserved to be honored after all she'd gone through to plan this event.

Elle didn't know what to expect. It was doubtful that Pam's father was alive and could walk her down the aisle, and the three Chance brothers were all at the altar with Emmett.

First a little flower girl appeared. Her red hair indicated she was Morgan and Gabe Chance's daughter, Sarah Bianca. Basket of rose petals in hand, she surveyed the admiring crowd like the princess she undoubtedly thought she was in her frothy emerald dress and crown of rosebuds.

And no wonder. She was adorable, and every camera was pointed in her direction. Behind her, though, some fuss was going on.

Standing on tiptoe, Elle could see Josie Chance, elegant in a long blue dress, urging a small blond boy down the aisle behind Sarah Bianca. Elle pegged this tyke as Josie and Jack's son, Archie, the designated ring bearer. He was tricked out in a Western vest, coat, pants and tiny boots, but he seemed totally uninterested in his assignment.

With a martyred sigh, Sarah Bianca turned around and grabbed his hand. Then she proceeded to tow him down the aisle while he kept stopping to gaze in wonder at his surroundings. She wouldn't allow it. Her jaw was set and her attention was fixed on the goal.

Good thing the rings were tied to the pillow, because Archie clutched it to his chest like a favorite teddy bear. Deprived of a free hand to toss rose petals, Sarah Bianca swung the basket vigorously so they'd spill out behind her. She had everything under control.

Chuckles rippled through the gathering, but no one laughed out loud. That impressed Elle. Apparently everyone here recognized that Sarah Bianca was struggling to make things right the best way she knew how. That was worthy of admiration, not ridicule. These were good people.

Josie managed to keep her composure, too, as she followed the pair. Elle could see the combination of laughter and tears swimming in her eyes, but she took a deep breath and kept going.

Morgan Chance appeared next. She obviously was fighting the same battle to keep from both laughing and crying at the antics of her daughter and Josie's son. This, Elle knew, would be a moment talked about for many years.

Elle wondered if Dominique Chance, Nick's wife, would be next down the aisle, but then she noticed a movement at the front of the aisle. There was Dominique crouching down, camera in hand, as little Archie broke away from his cousin and ran to his father.

Jack scooped him up with a grin. It looked as if Jack would hold on to him during the ceremony, which also meant the rings would be available when needed. Dominique captured it all.

Elle could imagine how great those pictures would be, considering Dominique's photography skills. Maybe Dominique would preview them at the reception, or put some up on a website. Elle decided to ask about that later.

When a soft murmur passed through the group, Elle faced the back of the room again. At last, Pam stood in the doorway wearing a stunning burgundy velvet gown. On her left side was a blonde woman whose bone structure hinted that she might be related to Emmett. Elle guessed she might be his daughter. On Pam's other side stood a silver-haired woman with a regal bearing who could only be Sarah Chance, matriarch of the Chance family.

Elle loved it. No man was going to give this woman to her dashing ranch foreman. No, the women of the Last Chance owned this rite of passage. Elle, who was only barely acquainted with them, felt a moment of solidarity as they passed. She resisted the urge to give them a high five.

Once Pam and her companions had gone by, Elle turned to watch the bride approach her broad-shouldered groom. His eyes shone, and she moved toward him with the steady gait of a woman certain of her path. Elle's throat tightened and her eyes grew moist. She couldn't remember the last time she'd cried, but she was crying now.

God, it was beautiful, this joining of two lives, this celebration of all things precious between them. Tears slid down her cheeks. Someday…when she was ready…when she'd tired of the freedom to move unfettered about the world….

But that time had not come, she reminded herself gently. She was viewing an image of what was to be in the future. She shouldn't get too carried away by the emotional ceremony taking place today.

She wouldn't wait until she was in her sixties before she looked for a guy, but she had more to see and do. She'd given herself at least until she was thirty before settling down, which was more than two years away. She didn't want to jump the gun.

That was important to remember whenever she interacted with Trey. Most people had a mental timetable, whether they acknowledged it or not. His wasn't in sync with hers.

But thanks to him, she had begun examining the patterns she'd been taught as a child. Thanks to him, she'd discovered a capacity for pleasure that she'd never dreamed of having. Thanks to him, she was able to be part of a celebration that showed her that sometimes, pulling out all the stops could be wonderful.

The ceremony was classy and relatively short. It included one musical interlude when Tyler Keller sang, accompanied by Watkins and Trey. Emmett and Pam promised to love and cherish each other, and when they kissed, everyone in the room cheered.

Grinning like teenagers, the newly married couple hurried back down the aisle accompanied by lively guitar music. The guests streamed after them, bound for a reception in the ballroom down the hall. Everyone, that was, except Elle and Mary Lou, Watkins's wife.

When Elle noticed that Mary Lou was waiting for Watkins, she decided to take her cue and wait for Trey. No one had to know that she and Trey had exchanged sharp words the last time they'd seen each other.

Mary Lou motioned for Elle to come and stand with her. "Weren't our guys terrific?"

"They were."

"Tyler and Watkins made a recording last year, and Josie sells the CD at the Spirits and Spurs. I think they should make another one, don't you?"

"That's a great idea."

"I'm so glad Emmett invited you. I'm sure Trey was thrilled you could come."

"I hope so." She planned to act as if they had nothing to quarrel about. This wouldn't be the time to talk about the issues, anyway. But she couldn't completely ignore their less-than-happy parting. He was too much of a gentleman to reject her in front of Mary Lou and Watkins, but he might after they reached the reception.

He walked toward her, his guitar case in one hand. "Glad you came." He still wasn't smiling.

"I wouldn't have missed it. You and Watkins were wonderful."

"Thanks. It was fun."

She lowered her voice. "Trey, I'm so sor—"

"Never mind." He hooked his free arm around her waist and drew her in for a quick kiss. "We'll talk later."

"Good." She hoped they'd do a whole lot more than talk.

"You look amazing, Elle."

She sighed. "Thank you." It would be all right. Because he had a big heart, he'd forgiven her for running out on him and saying a few things she wished she could take back. But somehow she had to figure out how to keep from breaking that big heart of his. That would be a challenge.

11

WHEN ELLE HAD walked in, Trey had screwed up a chord, but he'd quickly recovered and didn't think anybody but Watkins had noticed. Then she'd actually waited for him to pack up so she could go over to the reception with him. He wasn't sure what it all meant, or what exactly she'd been about to apologize for, but at least she was here.

If she'd planned to tell him she was sorry, but it was over between them, he wasn't about to give her that opportunity. He couldn't let her break up with him before he danced with her. Dancing was bound to help his cause, especially if they moved as well together as he expected they would.

Amy had said Elle was susceptible to his music, so he'd use that during the reception, too. He'd grab every chance to convince her that throwing away something this great was a crime against nature. He'd use sex, too, because she responded well to that.

She'd admitted that she'd never had it this good. He wondered if she'd asked herself why that was. Sure, people talked about having great sex with a virtual stranger, but how often did that happen? In his view, the best sex took place between two people who were right for each other in many ways. Right for each other like Pam and Emmett were, for example.

"How did you like the wedding?" he asked as they walked hand-in-hand, following Watkins and Mary Lou down the hall to the reception.

"Loved it."

"Me, too. Everything went off like clockwork. I was worried that Emmett wouldn't throw himself into the occasion, but he was a stand-up guy in the end. He came through with flying colors."

"He did! He looked so proud and handsome at the altar. Maybe he finally realized how special the moment was, and how important it was to experience that moment with family and friends. Vegas would have been so...impersonal."

"Vegas would have been a disaster. Besides, Watkins said Pam would never have agreed to Vegas. He thinks she would have called off the wedding before she'd have agreed to get married there."

Watkins glanced over his shoulder. "Did I hear my name mentioned?"

"I was just telling Elle your opinion about how Pam would have reacted if Emmett had insisted on Vegas."

"Oh, he's right." Mary Lou paused and glanced back at them. "I talked to Sarah, who said that Pam was breathing fire over that suggestion. Good thing Trey changed Emmett's mind."

"Trey?" Elle glanced at him. "I didn't realize you were the magician who made this come out okay."

"It wasn't just me. Watkins said some good things, too."

"No, it was you." Watkins and Mary Lou turned around, and Watkins lowered his voice. "You helped Emmett understand why Mary Lou wasn't backing him up on the Vegas idea. That was the key."

Mary Lou directed her comments to Elle. "Emmett expected my support because Watkins and I got married on a cruise instead of at the ranch."

"Oh." After seeing how much everyone enjoyed this wedding, Elle was surprised.

"Which was fine." Watkins obviously wanted to demonstrate his loyalty to Mary Lou.

"It was fine," she said. "I didn't want a fuss, and it wasn't like we were young folks, like you two, for example."

Elle flinched. She hoped Mary Lou wasn't making assumptions.

"However…" Mary Lou exchanged a meaningful glance with her husband. "We probably should have gotten married at the ranch, shared the occasion with everyone and then gone on the cruise."

"Probably," Watkins said.

"It doesn't matter how old you are." Mary Lou sighed. "People want to be there, and now I understand why. I would have been devastated if Pam and Emmett had run off somewhere to get married."

"We could renew our vows," Watkins said.

"Excellent idea," Trey said. "I volunteer to play for it."

Mary Lou brightened. "That does sound like fun. Except aren't you supposed to do that for a significant anniversary? We haven't been married that long."

"Lou-Lou, every anniversary with you is significant."

"Aw. You are so full of it." But Mary Lou smiled and kissed him on the cheek. "We'll do it next summer, then." She turned to Elle. "And you should come."

"I'd love to, but I'll be in Argentina all summer."

"Really? All summer?" Mary Lou looked over at Trey. "That's a long way from Jackson Hole."

"Yep." Trey didn't need anyone to tell him that. He wasn't ready to accept the idea that Elle would go to Argentina in April. He wasn't planning to accept it until he had no choice. "Hey, we'd better get in there and start playing before the natives get restless."

Watkins nodded. "Right. We can plan our summer party later. Pam's expecting music at this shindig, and we're all she's got, poor lady."

"She's got the best," Mary Lou said. "Isn't that so, Elle?"

"It certainly is." Elle gave Trey a big smile. "Go on in there and do your stuff, cowboy. We'll both be watching."

He liked that big ol' smile of hers. He just wished she hadn't also reminded him that she intended to leave for Argentina as planned. He'd heard of relationships working out when the two people were separated for months at a time, but he'd never been a fan of the concept.

Once they entered the reception, Trey had to focus the bulk of his attention on entertaining the wedding guests. Dancing was a big deal at the Last Chance, and most everyone wanted danceable tunes. Trey and Watkins played and sang, joined every so often by Tyler.

While he was stuck on the makeshift bandstand, Trey had to put up with watching Elle dance with other guys. But he couldn't expect her to sit on the sidelines and wait for him to take a break. She looked good out there, but he reacted to having anyone holding her besides him.

Then someone asked him to play the song he'd written for Elle. "I'll have to ask the lady if it's okay," he said. "Don't want to embarrass her."

"Too late!" Elle called out.

That got a laugh, but he didn't consider her comment to be permission. Looking at her, he held out his fist, thumb pointed sideways. He hoped she understood what he was asking.

She must have, because she mimicked his gesture and turned her thumb up. He was more pleased than she could imagine. Although he'd love to serenade her with this song, he wouldn't have done it if she'd said no.

Settling down on the stool next to the microphone, he began strumming his guitar. The words had come to him so quickly the night he'd written them. No song had been this easy to write.

Holding her gaze, he sang to her about being lost and without hope. Then she'd come out of the darkness, his angel. He had to agree with her that the lyrics were sappy, but that was why he loved them. She'd saved his life, and if a guy couldn't get sentimental because a beautiful woman had come to his rescue, then why write songs at all?

Even from this distance he could see her cheeks turn pink. She was embarrassed, but she hadn't looked away. Not once. Instead, her attention had locked onto him as if they were connected by an invisible cord.

He milked the moment for all it was worth. If Amy was right, and Elle had a soft spot for country singers, then he'd work it. Her love of country music was another dead giveaway that she wasn't the hard-boiled realist she pretended to be. Country music was full of schmaltz.

At the end of the song, the crowd seemed to be holding its breath, as if everyone needed a second or two to absorb the last notes. He liked that. It was the sign of a good tune. Standing, he gazed at Elle, who continued to stand as motionless as a carved statue.

He blew her a kiss, and the room erupted in applause, whistles and stomping feet. Finally, in the midst of the commotion, she broke eye contact with him and ducked her head. But not before he saw her smile.

He propped his guitar in its stand and glanced at Watkins. "Can you take it for the next number? And make it a waltz?"

Watkins winked at him and covered his mike. "You got it, Romeo." Then he uncovered his mike again. "Tyler Keller, would you come on up and sing for us? At the request of my partner, I'm gonna treat you folks to a waltz, and Tyler sings a mighty pretty version of 'If I Didn't Have You in My World.'"

Perfect song, Trey thought as he climbed down from the temporary stage and moved through the crowd in search of Elle. Along the way people shook his hand and slapped him on the back. No doubt they thought he'd made a conquest by performing that tune of his, but he wasn't taking any bets on that. Elle was a tough nut to crack.

He didn't have to go far to find her. She was standing at the edge of the dance floor waiting for him. Her blue eyes sparkled as she stepped toward him. "I assume this is our dance?"

"If you'll do me the honor."

"I've been looking forward to it."

"Me, too." He drew her into his arms as Tyler began to sing. And the world slipped away. There was only Elle, moving with him as he'd known she would.

He breathed in her scent, a subtle flowery one that he didn't recognize. Maybe it was something she put on her hair when she fixed it this way. He leaned down and brushed his lips over her exposed neck.

"You'd better be careful," she murmured. "I'm a ticking time bomb."

"Oh?" He nuzzled her again. He didn't mind making her crazy. That seemed only fair, because holding her this close was making him crazy, too.

"I mean it, Trey. You are one sexy dude up on that stage. I keep watching you fingering your guitar strings. It gets me hot."

He whirled her around, and she followed him perfectly. "You like the way I finger my strings?"

She gazed up at him. "You know I do."

"Nice to hear. Do you have plans after this shindig is over?"

"I hope so. Do you?"

"I hope so." He looked into her eyes and wondered if she was listening to the lyrics of "If I Didn't Have You in My World." "Nice tune."

"Did you request it?"

"No."

"I wouldn't put it past you."

"I didn't think that far ahead. I just asked for a

waltz. Watkins decided on that one, but I agree with
his choice. It fits."

"Tyler sings it well."

"Mmm." He spun her around again. "Argentina,
huh?"

"That's the plan."

He didn't comment on that, but he nuzzled her neck
again, just because he could. Her small whimper made
him smile. She might think she was going to Argentina, but that was because he hadn't pulled out all the
stops yet.

ELLE COULDN'T DENY that Trey was one virile cowboy.
And she hadn't even seen him on a horse yet. After
their dance, which had added another sexy arrow to
the guy's quiver, he'd returned to the bandstand.

She'd spent more time than she'd like to admit sur-
reptitiously observing his long fingers moving up and
down the slender neck of his guitar. There was no better word for it—he fondled that instrument, using both
quick and slow movements that brought back vivid
memories of how he'd touched her.

The wedding guests enthusiastically applauded the
guitarists. They loved the added dimension of Tyler's
vocals. They wanted more.

A buffet was laid out and the liquor flowed. Elle
didn't begrudge anyone this celebration, especially
Pam and Emmett, who seemed to be having more fun
than anyone. But she wanted to be alone with Trey.

He and Watkins finished a rousing tune that had
everyone line dancing, and then Watkins spoke into
his mike. "Folks, we're going to take a break and get
something to eat. Our former professional DJ, Alex

Keller, has agreed to keep you company while we do that, and he's taking requests. We'll be back shortly."

As Elle wondered what constituted "shortly," Trey appeared by her side.

"Fill us a couple of plates while I get us something to drink. I'll meet you out in the hall in five minutes."

She didn't have to be asked twice. Looping the short strap of her clutch purse over her wrist, she crossed to the buffet table. Finger food seemed like the best choice, so she went with that—chilled shrimp, tiny quiches and elaborate petits fours.

Once she had two plates piled high, she made her way through the crowd and used her hip to open one of the double doors. Trey was already there, leaning against the wall looking gorgeous as he held two flutes of champagne.

"I hope you like the bubbly stuff. It was the quickest to grab."

"I like bubbly stuff. It fits the mood. Did you want to sit on the floor?"

"Hell, no. We're going to my room. We can make it there in a couple of minutes if we move fast."

"Okay, but I'm not sure that's a good idea." She fell into step beside him and walked as quickly as her stilettos would allow.

"Why not?"

"I'm liable to jump your bones."

"God, I hope so."

That made her laugh, which wasn't the best way to get two loaded plates of food transported quickly down the hallway and through the lobby. Her little purse swung wildly from her wrist, and a couple of cherry tomatoes bounced onto the carpet. "I'm dropping food."

"Ask me if I care."

"You don't want this food?"

"I'll cram a little of it down my throat after I've done what I've wanted to do for hours."

Her pulse hammered. "Lie down?"

"I don't care. We can lie, or sit or stand up, just so my cock is securely inside you."

She glanced around, but no one was in the hallway, thank goodness. "You might want to keep it down."

"I've been trying to keep it down for quite some time, and the damned thing keeps rising up on me whenever I look at you in that dress."

"This dress? There's nothing particularly suggestive about it!"

"That's what you think. There's just enough cleavage to remind me how much I love to suck on your—"

"*Trey.* We're still in the hallway, in case you hadn't noticed."

"I noticed, all right. Pick up the pace a little, will you, Masterson?"

"I'm walking as fast as I can in these shoes."

"I can see that. Did you know that walking fast in those things makes you jiggle? That's a bonus."

She stared at him. She'd never seen him quite like this. "Have you been drinking?"

"Not yet, but I plan to. I should have had you take the shoes off, except I have an image of doing you when you're wearing them."

"Trey, you're out of control." And she loved it.

"Sweetheart, you have no idea. How easy does that slinky number come off, anyway?"

"It just pulls over my head."

"Excellent. Once we're in the room, put down the plates and take it off. I'll handle things from there."

"So we'll have wild monkey sex and then walk back into the party like nothing happened?"

He glanced at her. "You have a problem with that?"

"Not at all."

12

If Elle had offered any protest, Trey would have dialed back his enthusiasm. But she was on board with the program, which gave him another dose of confidence for the future. Elle liked being a little wild, and that's why they were perfect for each other.

At the door to his room, he had to set down both champagne flutes while he dug out his key. But he got the door open, picked up the flutes, and followed Elle inside. The room looked pristine, because he'd let the maid have her way in here.

That had killed him, because he'd liked the rumpled sheets that still carried the scent of sex and Elle. But he'd picked up on Elle's desire for order, something she'd probably learned from her military parents. He could be orderly when it was important.

But she didn't seem to notice the crisp look of the room. Following his directions, she set both plates on his desk and pulled her knit dress over her head. The effect of Elle standing there in a skimpy bra, lacy panties and silver heels… He nearly dropped both champagne flutes.

She gazed at him. "Isn't this what you wanted?"

"Oh, yeah." He propped his butt against the door and pulled off his boots. "Don't move. Let me look at you while I get out of my boots and jeans."

"And your shirt." Her mouth tilted up at the corners. "You'll be up on the stage pretty soon. I don't want you looking as if you just had a roll in the hay."

"Why not?" But after he shucked his jeans and briefs, he took off his shirt, too. "Rock stars do it all the time."

"Is that what we're about to have? Rock star sex?"

"I have no idea what that is." He tossed the condom he'd carried in his jeans pocket as insurance—he'd had no idea whether she'd be up for this when he got dressed—onto the desk. Then he closed the distance between them and wrapped her warm body in his arms. "But any rock star in the world would be lucky to find you in his room between sets."

"Flatterer." She lifted her mouth to his.

"Nope." He leaned down and took a small taste, which required control because he felt like a starving man at a feast. "You're the real deal, Elle. You're incredibly beautiful without being a diva. You're fiery in bed, but I have the feeling that's a well-kept secret."

She wrapped her arms around him. "Very well kept. Only two people know it."

He groaned and rested his forehead against hers. "Do you realize how important that is? Dear God, Elle. You and I have opened ourselves to each other in ways that some people never do."

She heaved a breath. "Is this going to be a deep discussion? Because I don't think we have time for that before the next set."

"You're right." And he was officially an idiot, which came as no surprise. "We have time for one spectacular climax each, and then we have to go back to the reception."

"I'm still wearing the silver stilettos."

"So you are." He hooked his thumbs in the elastic of her delicate panties and drew them down over her incredible legs until he reached the floor. "Step out, please."

She did, with grace and style.

He tossed the panties over his shoulder and stood. "Rock star sex seems as if it should be up against a hard surface." He scooped up the condom and handed it to her. "Keep track of that for me."

"I don't think a rock star would make his date hold his condom."

"Maybe not, but I'm new at this." Catching her around the waist, he swung her up and around until she was braced against the door.

"The door? Really?"

"It has multiple advantages. While we're getting it on, nobody can force their way in."

"Is that likely?"

"You never know. Condom, please?"

She started laughing. "I feel like a character in a dark comedy." But she handed him the condom.

He desperately needed it for his aching cock, which was in danger of detonating before its time. She might think this was some sort of comedy, but seeing her clothed in nothing but a push-up bra and stilettos was playing havoc with his restraint.

He rolled on the condom and grasped her hips. His gaze traveled down to the silver straps and impossible high heels, and he wondered if he was into kinky, because seeing those things made his balls tighten painfully. "Wrap your legs around me and hold on to my shoulders."

"Now I feel like a performer in Cirque du Soleil."

He blew out a breath. "Just do it."

She did, and despite her smart-ass comments, her breathing was jerky and uneven. She might be into this as much as he was. When he looked into her eyes, he was certain of it. Blue flames danced there.

Her silver heels pressed against the small of his back, which made him aware of them, even though they were out of sight. He liked that. Yeah, he might be a little kinky.

Once he had her positioned properly, with her back firmly against the door, he eased forward, seeking that slick channel he knew awaited him. He wasn't disappointed. Judging by how wet she was, she'd been as impatient for this moment as he'd been.

Her breath caught. "I've never done it up against a door."

"Me, either, but I think I like it." He locked in tight and met her gaze. *Yes.* "Can you balance and unfasten your bra?"

"Why?"

"I want to watch your breasts quiver when I push into you."

"You're crazy."

"I want it all, Elle. Every bit of this."

Sucking in a breath, she let go of his shoulders long enough to flip open the front closure of her bra. The material fell away, revealing creamy skin and nipples tight with desire.

"Yeah. Like that." He drew back and rocked forward. Her body shook from the impact, giving him exactly the visual he'd been hoping for.

She moaned.

"Is that a good moan or a bad moan?"

She licked her lips. "A good moan. Do that again."

"With pleasure." He slid back, but not too far, and drove home once more.

"That's…nice." Her gaze lost focus, as if her concentration had shifted, moved to that locus of all things wonderful.

"Want more?"

"Yes. Please."

Sure of the territory now, he initiated a slow rhythm. She gripped his shoulders and met each thrust as they created a steady thumping noise against the door. At first he worried about that. But as the tension grew, he gave up worrying, closed his eyes and let himself feel—the delicious friction, the liquid heat, the surge of adrenaline when she tightened around his cock, signaling… Oh, yeah, she was coming, and so was he, in a furious rush of pleasure. She gasped and cried out. He shoved deep and stayed there, his cock pulsing, his brain spinning, his spirit soaring. *So. Good.*

He opened his eyes. The sight of her leaning back against the door, her gaze open and vulnerable, touched something so deep within his heart that he'd never forget this moment. Any second now she could pull up the drawbridge and lock him out.

But if she'd dared to leave the door open, then he would dare the perilous walk through it. "I'm falling in love with you, Elle."

For one shining moment, joy filled her expression. Then, as if she'd pushed a switch, the light dimmed. "It's too soon," she said gently. She touched his face with a trembling hand. "You were half in love with me before we met. You're falling for the idea of me."

His jaw tightened. "No, I'm falling for you, Elle Masterson."

"It's the sex."

"Of course it's the sex! And because we've had so damned much of it, I've found out you're warm, and giving, and funny, and adventuresome, and bawdy and incredibly…real."

She swallowed. "You are such a romantic. You're so good with words. You know exactly what to say to make it seem as if—"

"Damn it, don't dismiss what I've said because you've got it in your head that I'm some sort of crazy dreamer who's out of touch with reality."

"Trey, you are a dreamer."

"Okay, I'll own that label. But because I'm a dreamer, I pick up on things that other people might not. I *know* you, Elle. Every time we've been together, I've soaked that knowledge in through my pores. But do you know me? At all?"

Her expression closed down. "Maybe not. And we should go."

"Yes, we should." He wouldn't get anywhere with her now, anyway. She was blocking him, blocking the truth because it scared the devil out of her. She couldn't make the leap with him, at least not yet.

Easing away from her, he supported her until she was standing again. Then he turned and walked into the bathroom. She was right about one thing. It was too soon, but not for him. It was too soon for her.

She was right about something else, too. He had been half in love with her before they met, and for a very good reason. By rescuing him, she'd shown that she was brave and caring. He'd felt it in her touch. He'd recognized it in her determination to get him to safety.

And most of all, he'd heard the warmth in her voice. He'd fallen in love with the sound. Maybe he hadn't consciously analyzed why, but he could do that now. He was good with auditory cues, and her voice had been filled with compassion.

During that crisis, the soul of Elle Masterson had come shining through. She hadn't been cautious and logical when she'd come upon him in the snow. If she had been, she would have called 911. Instead, unwilling to depend on others when every second counted, she'd acted.

That was the woman he was falling in love with. Correction—he'd already fallen, but he'd decided to frame it differently so he wouldn't scare her so much. He'd scared her, anyway. Next time he'd give her the unvarnished truth.

And there would be a next time, he vowed as he walked back into the room. She was already dressed. She peered into the mirror over the desk while she tucked strands of blond hair back into the arrangement on top of her head.

"I like your hair like that."

She took a rhinestone hairpin out of her mouth and fastened it in place. "Thanks."

"Elle, I don't want to fight with you."

She turned toward him, her expression cautious. "I don't want to fight with you, either. I like you a lot."

He supposed that was something. "So you'll come back here with me after the party?"

"I'm afraid you'll get hurt."

He grabbed his clothes and started putting them on. "Look, if you're worried that I'll slip a disk, we can forget about the weird positions tonight. I admit that up against the door put a strain on my back."

"I meant—"

"No, really." He dressed quickly. "Missionary works fine for me. Or you can be on top, which is really easy on my spine."

She smiled and shook her head. "Okay, we won't talk about it."

"Good. Actions speak louder than words, anyway." He checked the time on his phone. "Wow, we were amazingly fast. Alex should have things under control for another ten minutes, at least."

"Then you should eat."

"I do believe I will. And drink." He crossed to the desk and picked up one of the champagne flutes. "Here's to great sex."

She glanced at him, as if wondering what he was up to. But she took her flute and touched it to his. "To great sex."

Elle tasted her champagne. "Wow. Nice."

"That's Pam Mulholland for you. She likes to go first-class, although I think she realized that caviar would be wasted on this bunch."

"Is she Pam Sterling now?"

"You know, I don't think so. I seem to remember hearing that she decided she'd keep her name, and

Emmett was fine with that." He picked up one of the miniature quiches and took a bite.

"Really? That's interesting."

"They're not going to be the typical couple living in a cottage with a white picket fence. Pam will stay at her B and B as usual, and Emmett will keep his little house at the ranch. They've been spending the night together off and on for years. Nothing much will change in their lifestyle." He gestured toward the plates. "You should eat one of these little sandwiches. They're amazing." He popped the rest of his into his mouth.

"So why get married?" Elle picked up a sandwich.

"Good question. From what I hear, Pam wanted to make what had been a private arrangement more public." He laughed. "And she wanted a party. I think a good part of it was staging this extravaganza. She runs a B and B for a reason. She's a very social person."

"Is Emmett?" Elle still hadn't taken a bite of her sandwich.

"Not as much as she is, but after today, I'll bet he gets into it more. They'll be good for each other." He glanced at the sandwich in her hand. "You'd better eat. We should leave pretty soon and this stuff will be trashed by the time we get back."

"Oh." She looked at the sandwich as if she'd forgotten all about it. "You're right." She ate it and reached for another.

"The veggies are good, too." He bit into a carrot stick.

She laughed.

"What?" He liked hearing her laugh, but he didn't know why she had.

"You sound like my mother. *Eat your veggies. They're good for you.*"

"Well, they are, but I damn sure don't want to be mistaken for your mother. I do, however, think you need to keep up your strength for later." He waggled his eyebrows as he popped a cherry tomato in his mouth.

The eyebrow routine made her laugh, too. "I'm sure you're right, but that's all I have time for." She drained her champagne flute and set it on the desk. "I need a couple of minutes to fix my makeup before we go back out there."

"That sounds like my cue to grab a kiss before you start doing that." He put down his glass.

"We're liable to be late."

"We won't be late."

"I don't know about this."

"It'll be fine." He drew her into his arms.

She flattened her hands against his chest. "Trey, you know what happens when you kiss me. I lose all sense of time."

"Not me. I'm a human stopwatch. We have thirty seconds on the clock. Go." He swooped in.

She was laughing when he connected with her mouth, so he had easy access for his tongue. He used it wisely, letting her know what they'd be doing after the party tonight. He cupped her head with care, not wanting to disturb the arrangement she'd fixed moments ago.

But he held her firmly, not allowing her to pull away, because he wanted to give her a kiss that would last for a couple of hours, at least. For the first few seconds, she refused to yield to temptation, but as the kiss heated up, she wrapped her arms around his neck and settled against him.

He deepened the kiss, and she moaned. Good. He wanted to leave her with a moaning kind of kiss. He wanted to leave her with a heavy breathing kind of kiss, too, and they were accomplishing that goal.

To finish, he pulled her in tight so she could feel his erection pressing against her belly. He wanted to leave her with that information, too, in case she needed reminding that while he was playing his guitar, he'd be thinking of what they'd be doing once they came back to his room.

Although he had no idea whether thirty seconds had gone by or not, he lifted his head and started to let her go. She wanted to fix her makeup, and only a selfish jerk would use up all her time so she couldn't do that. With a murmur of protest, she pulled his head down and kept kissing.

O-*kay*. He wasn't going to argue with that. If she was hungrier for his kiss than for that sandwich, so be it. His state of arousal increased exponentially. He massaged her cute little fanny through her skirt, and somehow it rode up, and now he was touching silk.

Not long afterward, he was stroking bare skin as she writhed against him. Then, with a groan of frustration, she wiggled out of his arms. She was panting. "See what I mean?" She pulled up her panties and smoothed down her dress.

"I do." He was secretly so happy that he wanted to punch his fist in the air, but he controlled himself. A victory dance right now would be in poor taste. He also wanted to ask her about Argentina again. He didn't do that, either. But if she thought she could leave this kind of passion and jet off to Argentina, she had another think coming.

13

ELLE REALIZED HER behavior was erratic, which was not like her. As she walked back to the party holding Trey's hand, the term *temporary insanity* flitted through her mind. She'd never met a man this compelling.

Although she'd had fun with those other guys she'd dated, they hadn't affected her as Trey did. He'd asked if she knew him at all, and she'd lied. From that first moment in his arms, she'd felt as if she'd known him forever.

But that feeling of connection had to be a result of sexual chemistry, right? She couldn't have bonded with him on any other level, not in the short time they'd spent together. And yet, being with him felt so right. They interacted with a kind of ease that should take much longer to develop.

Trey's attitude had a lot to do with that. He'd treated her as a good friend from the beginning, because after the rescue, he'd thought of her that way. His assumption that they belonged together was hard to resist.

She would resist it, though. Facts were facts. His

life as a ranch hand didn't mesh well with her life as a ski instructor. Her present career path spanned two continents. He might be willing to brush that barrier aside, but she wasn't. She hadn't known him long enough to justify rearranging her life.

Alex was still spinning tunes when they walked in, and Trey pulled Elle onto the dance floor. "One number."

"It's country swing. I'm not that familiar with—" But she laughed and gave in, because Trey wasn't going to take no for an answer.

Besides, only a person with no rhythm at all would have trouble dancing with Trey. His sense of the music traveled through his arms and his fingertips as he guided her through the movements. Soon she was twirling and two-stepping like a pro.

He grinned at her as she spun under his arm. "You're a natural."

"No, you're a fantastic partner."

"I'll take that, especially if it's a global statement."

"Global?"

"Covering all partner-type activities."

"I have no idea what you're talking about."

"Yes, you do. You're blushing."

She'd believe it. Between the fast dance and the sex they'd just had, she might have acquired a permanent blush.

When the music ended, Alex announced that the live music makers were back in the house. Trey planted a firm kiss on Elle's mouth before hopping up on the stage. Watkins followed at a slower pace.

Mary Lou walked up beside her. "We looked for you two during the break, but you disappeared."

Elle wondered if her cheeks could possibly get any hotter. "Oh. We, um, decided to—"

"That's okay, honey." Mary Lou patted her arm. "I was young once. In fact, even now, Watkins likes to be spontaneous, if you know what I mean." She winked. "And judging from your expression, I'm sure you do."

Elle struggled to think of a response.

"You look thirsty," Mary Lou said. "What do you say we get some champagne and sit for a minute?"

"Good idea." Elle didn't have a better one. She chose not to point out that champagne wouldn't quench a person's thirst. She suspected Mary Lou knew that.

Moments later they found a spot at a little table and sat down with their champagne.

"This is the good stuff," Mary Lou said. "Never pass up a chance to drink expensive champagne. That's my motto." She took a sip.

Elle swallowed a mouthful, and the bubbles tickled her tongue. "I think I'll adopt that motto, too."

"You're welcome to it. So, when are you coming out to the ranch?"

"I don't know."

"Now would be a great time, when there's plenty of room. In the summer the boys arrive, and then things are more hectic. Oh, I forgot. You might not know what I mean about those boys."

"I do, actually." Elle discovered that good champagne went down easily. "I looked up the ranch on the internet last night. It sounds like a great program."

"It is. You'd get a kick out of those boys. But you said you'd be in Argentina all summer." Mary Lou finished her champagne. "These glasses are pretty, but they don't hold much. Want a refill?"

Elle hesitated.

"Ah, come on. You're not driving anywhere. And remember the motto."

"Never pass up a chance to drink expensive champagne." Elle held out her empty flute. "Fill 'er up, Mary Lou."

"That's the ticket."

While she was off getting them more bubbly, Elle redirected her attention to the bandstand. Trey and Tyler were singing the country standard "Jackson," which was funny considering that the song was about Jackson, Mississippi, yet they had a town of Jackson right down the road. The two obviously had fun with the lyrics, as each taunted the other about making a splash in Jackson now that their love affair had burned itself out.

"That's real cute, isn't it?" Mary Lou set a full glass in front of Elle. "I've seen them perform that one before, and it's a crowd pleaser, since we have a Jackson right next door."

"They do a great job." Elle couldn't help paying attention to the lyrics, though, which described the danger of hooking up with someone because of hot sex, which in the case of the Johnny Cash song, faded fast.

When Trey and Tyler finished, she clapped and cheered like everyone else. But she continued to think about those lyrics. She turned to Mary Lou. "How long did you know Watkins before you married him?"

"A long time. I'll bet I've known him almost twenty years. And he was after me the minute he set foot on the ranch."

"He was?" Elle realized that sounded rude. "I mean, of course he was. You're—"

"Hey, it's okay. I'm gray and plump now, but twenty years ago, I could stop traffic. Well, that's not hard to do in Shoshone. We don't have much traffic and only the one light at the intersection."

Elle was fascinated. And slightly smashed. "So he wanted you, but you didn't agree to marry him for almost twenty years?"

"I didn't want to marry anyone, including Watkins. My plumbing's wonky and I couldn't have kids, so why get married? Besides, I liked being single."

"So do I." It was the answer she always gave, but she felt a twinge of resistance this time. Entirely Trey's fault, too.

"I pegged you for an independent woman from the get-go." She took another sip of her champagne. "Want some munchies? I could go for some munchies."

"Sure, why not?" If she intended to continue drinking champagne with Mary Lou, she needed more food in her stomach. The conversation was just getting interesting, though, so she wanted a reason to keep sitting there.

Mary Lou returned with plates of various kinds of cheese and more of the petits fours, plus a mountain of chocolate-dipped strawberries, which were a real luxury in December. "I'm in the mood to indulge," she said.

"So am I." Elle picked up a strawberry and took a bite. Champagne went great with chocolate-covered strawberries. "So after holding out against matrimony all those years, what changed your mind?"

"Watkins was pitiful."

Elle choked on her champagne.

"Easy, girl." Mary Lou patted her on the back.

"Didn't know you had a mouthful of champagne or I would have waited until you swallowed."

Elle dragged in a breath. "I'm fine. So you married Watkins because you felt sorry for him?"

"No, that's not right. I married him because he loved me more than life itself. And when I climbed down off my high horse and thought about it, I realized I'd loved him all that time, too. I'm not sorry I waited. Made him appreciate me more."

"I'll bet it did." Elle lifted her glass in Mary Lou's direction. "A toast to holding out."

"It has its advantages." Mary Lou finished her second glass. "One more?"

"Okay, but this is it. Someone will have to carry me out of here if I have more than that."

"I know someone who would volunteer for the job."

"So do I."

Mary Lou smiled. "Be right back. Don't go away. I have a point I want to make."

"You've already made a few, and I appreciate them all." Elle basked in the rosy glow of expensive champagne and the knowledge that Trey wanted her as desperately as Watkins had wanted Mary Lou.

But then there was that pesky Johnny Cash song to be considered. If Elle gave in, would the fire burn out? She ate another strawberry as she thought about that.

"Here we go." Mary Lou set a brimming champagne flute in front of Elle. "That bartender is a sweetheart."

"Amy? She is. I should go over and say hi. In fact, I should probably help her behind the bar."

"Not tonight. You're a guest, and from the looks of her tip jar, Amy will do very well tonight. The booze may be free, but the Last Chance folks are good tip-pers."

"I don't doubt it. There's an almost noble quality in the website. I get the feeling it's very good to be connected to the Last Chance Ranch. They're highly thought of in the area."

"They are, and I love working there. Which brings me to my point." She took time to drink more cham-pagne.

"Mary Lou, I don't think I've ever had better cham-pagne than this. Thank you for inviting me to sit and share a glass…or several."

"I had the feeling we might have some things in common. I get the sense you don't think finding a man is the Holy Grail, either."

"Hell, no." Elle clapped a hand over her mouth. "Whoops. I probably shouldn't be swearing in the mid-dle of a wedding reception."

Mary Lou waved a dismissive hand. "Don't worry about it. These are ranch folks. They're used to swear-ing. But back to the point I wanted to make."

"Which is?" Elle took another swallow of this most excellent champagne.

"The whole time I was holding Watkins off, and let me add that during that time we had some sexy inter-ludes, I was living right where he was living. He had to see me every day, and vice versa."

"That was convenient, but if you're comparing your situation to mine, I work as a ski instructor. In order to do that in the summer, I have to go to the opposite side of the equator."

Mary Lou nodded and swallowed more champagne. "That's fine, but I don't know if you can hold Trey off *and* spend six months in Argentina. If he doesn't see you all the time…"

"But if we're meant for each other, shouldn't he be fine with the separation?"

"In a perfect world, yes. But this is a man we're talking about. He'll get testy. You'll quarrel. It won't go well."

"Then I guess it won't work out." Elle felt a sharp pain in the region of her heart.

"Are you sure that's what you want? To have everything fall apart? Isn't there some work you could do in Jackson Hole for the summer?"

Elle gazed at Mary Lou. "How would that look? I change my entire schedule so I can hang around here and wait tables? Talk about pathetic."

"I see what you mean. I don't picture you turning into a groupie, Elle. You're better than that."

"Thank you! Finally somebody understands my position."

"But I also see the way Trey looks at you. He's as smitten as Watkins ever was." She leaned closer. "Woman to woman, that kind of devotion can be fabulous."

"So what should I do?"

Mary Lou shrugged. "Drink more champagne."

WHENEVER TREY GLANCED over at the table where Elle sat with Mary Lou, they had their heads together, and they seemed to be thoroughly enjoying each other and the champagne. Trey figured having Mary Lou and Elle buddy up could go one of two ways. Mary Lou might try to sell her on the idea of ranches and cowboys, or she might encourage Elle's independent spirit, which logically meant heading off to Argentina in April as planned.

In the end, Elle would do what she wanted, though. He just hoped that what she wanted turned out to be the same thing he did—for them to be together. Still, he couldn't help wondering what had transpired between the two women while he'd been stuck behind a microphone.

Mary Lou was a staunch feminist and Trey admired that. He'd never thought women should defer to men. Mary Lou and Watkins were a volatile combination, but they were devoted to each other. Come to think of it, Mary Lou and Elle had a lot of traits in common. No wonder they'd hit it off.

The party took a long time to wind down. Pam and Emmett left, but no one else seemed ready to give up. Tomorrow was a free day, with nothing on the schedule except a morning ski lesson and the after-lunch send-off for Pam and Emmett.

Pam had hired a limo to take them to the airport for their flight to Tahiti. Trey laughed every time he thought of Emmett lounging on a beach with an umbrella drink in his hand. He'd return a changed man.

Pam and Emmett's love story had come to a happy ending. Trey wasn't convinced that his and Elle's love story was bound for the same kind of bliss. They had many unresolved issues. Although he wished they could resolve them in bed, he doubted that would happen.

Even so, he was willing to try. The sooner this party ended, the sooner he could hustle Elle back to his room and continue to show her why they were meant for each other. But this was turning into the never-ending celebration.

Sometime around one in the morning, when Trey's fingers had grown numb from playing, Alex became his favorite human being of all time, excluding Elle, of course.

"You guys have gone above and beyond," Alex said. "This group isn't ready to quit, and it takes less energy for me to spin tunes than for you to play. Give it up."

"I appreciate that," Watkins said. "Years ago I could have plucked this guitar 'til dawn, but those days are gone."

"Nobody should play until dawn," Alex said. "I'll close the place down in another hour or so, but I give both of you permission to vamoose, along with the companion of your choice."

Watkins chuckled. "That sounds great. Come on, Trey. Let's go get our women."

"Amen to that." Trey was glad Elle wasn't there to hear Watkins's somewhat chauvinistic comment. Mary Lou would have given him hell for it, too. Neither of those ladies would consider themselves some man's *woman*.

Watkins knew that, but sometimes he liked to talk like the good ol' boy he'd been raised to be. He'd been around Mary Lou long enough to know when he could get away with it and when he couldn't.

Judging from the happy expressions worn by both Elle and Mary Lou, the men wouldn't have to worry too much about being politically correct tonight. Pam's champagne and good conversation had worked its magic and they were all smiles.

"I see you both have your guitars," Mary Lou said. "Does that mean you're finished for the night?"

Watkins nodded and sank into a chair next to Mary Lou. "Alex took pity on us."

"Want some champagne?" Mary Lou handed him her glass, which was half-full.

"Don't mind if I do." He polished it off.

Mary Lou motioned to Trey, who'd remained standing. "Take a load off, cowboy. There's plenty of champagne left. Pam ordered an ungodly amount of this stuff."

"And Mary Lou has taught me her motto," Elle said. "Never pass up a chance to drink expensive champagne."

Trey gazed at her. She was adorable. And slightly sloshed. "Thanks, but I'm ready to call it a night. You three can have my share." He wouldn't assume she'd want to go back with him. He hoped, but he wouldn't assume.

"You know, I've had enough champagne, too." Elle pushed back her chair, picked up her silver purse and stood.

He smiled at her. "Then I'll walk you home."

"That would be lovely."

Watkins laughed. "You two behave yourselves, okay?"

"Pay no attention to him," Mary Lou said. "Go have fun."

"Thanks, Mary Lou." Trey tucked his arm around Elle's waist, and his world clicked into focus again. "We will." He'd been aching to hold her for hours. The time had come.

14

ELLE MOVED DOWN the hallway in a sensual daze. She was desired by a sexy man who turned her on. She had reservations about the future, but none about the present. After consuming a fairly large quantity of champagne, she was ready to live in the present, at least for the next twenty-four hours.

But instead of guiding her through the lobby and down to his room, Trey was heading up the stairs in the direction of her room. She glanced at him. "Where are we going?"

"I have a plan, if you're willing to go along with it. How about packing up whatever you need for tonight and tomorrow morning and bringing it to my room?"

"You want me to stay in your room all night?"

"That's the idea."

She smiled. "I like it."

"I was hoping you would."

She climbed the stairs and wished they'd taken the elevator. She'd had enough of walking in these heels. "I can ditch these shoes while I'm at it."

"Uh, for now, sure, but I was hoping that you'd put them on later, when we—"

"Trey Wheeler, you are a wicked boy." Thoughts of stretching out in his bed wearing only her shoes sent a jolt of lust to all the places he'd soon be paying close attention to.

"Will you do it?"

"As long as I don't have to walk all the way back to your room in them."

"You can walk to my room barefoot and wearing a bathrobe for all I care. In fact, why not?"

"Sorry, cowboy. I'm not parading through the lobby in a bathrobe. It's one thing for the entire place to know we're having sex. It's quite another to flaunt the fact."

"Do we have to go through the lobby? Isn't there a service elevator we could use?"

She hadn't thought of that. She seldom took the regular elevator, let alone the service one. But the cleaning and maintenance staff wouldn't be using it tonight, now would they?

As she pictured herself riding the service elevator to the main floor, which would bypass the lobby, another image came to mind. She'd never had elevator sex. Either she was very inspired by Trey or very tipsy on champagne. Maybe both. Ordinarily she wouldn't consider such a thing.

"I'll change into my bathrobe and we'll take the service elevator." She grew damp thinking about what she had in mind. The concept seemed clandestine and daring. No one would come along, but someone *could,* which made the sex more exciting.

They reached her door, and she was ready with

the key. Now that elevator sex was on the docket, her adrenaline level had shot up. He might not go along with the idea, but she had a feeling he might. For this she might leave on the shoes.

Earlier today she'd scrounged an extension cord so that her Christmas tree was connected to the plug activated by the switch next to her door. That way she could turn on the tree whenever she walked in instead of using her bedside lamp. She'd become fond of the glow.

Trey followed her into the room. "Pretty little tree."

"Thanks." She grabbed a small duffel bag and threw some underwear and her ski clothes into it, along with her room key. Then she took some toiletries out of the bathroom and tossed those in, too.

"I thought you weren't into Christmas."

"I'm not really, but they give the employees trees every year, so it seems a waste not to decorate them." She took the pins out of her hair and laid them on her dresser before pulling her dress over her head and hanging it up in the closet.

"You look good in Christmas light."

She turned. The soft colors from the tree bathed him in a rosy hue that made her think of a fantasy cowboy. "So do you."

"Now I wish I had a Christmas tree in my room, so I could make love to you in this light."

"But you have that big ol' bed and I don't." She unfastened her bra and stepped out of her panties, but left on the shoes.

"God, you're beautiful."

"It's the light." She pulled her fluffy white bathrobe off its hanger.

"It's way more than the light, but those colors reflected on your skin are amazing." He glanced at the bathrobe in her hand. "Don't put that on yet. Give me a minute to look at you."

"Trey, I feel silly just standing here."

"You're not silly. You're a goddess. I've always been so intent on the sex that I haven't stopped to admire you. Humor me."

She let out a sigh of surrender. "Good thing I've had all that champagne or I'd be even more self-conscious." As long as he was going to study her, she might as well give him her best pose. Shoulders back, breasts out, stomach in.

"Wow."

Okay. Now that she'd gotten past the first few seconds of this, she realized that posing for him was turning her on. She was aware of his gaze traveling over every inch of her body, and she grew warm and achy as he continued to look.

His low chuckle sounded sexy and intimate. "Are you liking this better now?"

"Why do you ask?"

"Your breathing has changed and your nipples are erect."

"Maybe I'm cold."

"Or maybe you're hot." He drew in a ragged breath. "But even if you're not, I sure am. Either we leave or we make use of your little twin bed."

"Are you prepared for that?"

"Sweetheart, I've been prepared since that first night with you. I never leave home without those little raincoats. So which will it be? Stay or leave?"

"Leave." When she put on her bathrobe, the soft

terry made her skin tingle. She tied the belt and picked up her duffel bag. Walking reminded her of how damp her thighs were. "Let's go."

"Weren't you planning to take off those shoes?"

"Eventually. I'll leave them on a little longer."

"I won't argue with you on that. Watching you strut around in those shoes and knowing you have nothing on under your robe will be all the foreplay I'll need between here and my room."

She smiled as she thought about what would happen between here and his room. Up to now, he'd been the one with all the ideas. She would show him that she had a few of her own.

She directed him through another set of double doors on the second floor, and they were once more in the guest area. Fortunately, the hallway was empty. She'd rather not encounter anyone on their way to the elevator. After they reached it, they'd be fine. It opened not far from his room on the first floor.

"If anyone comes along, we're heading for the pool," she said.

"This place has a pool?"

"It's set up as an indoor pool this time of year, but in the summer, the glass canopy slides back. Or so I'm told. I'm never here then, so I haven't seen it that way."

"If this is primarily a ski lodge, what goes on in the summer?"

"Hiking, mountain biking, swimming, fishing. Serenity has tennis courts. There's an arrangement with one of the local stables if people want to ride."

"A bunch of summer sports, then."

"Exactly. But I don't do summer sports."

"Why not?"

She glanced at him. She knew why he was asking. Obviously there were jobs here in the summer for those who were into those things. "I love the challenge of skiing. I love the thrill of it. And I've put a lot of time into learning how to do it well. The summer activities seem tame by comparison."

"Makes sense." He was silent for a moment. "What about hang gliding?"

She couldn't help laughing. "Since I've never done it, I doubt I could get a job teaching it."

"Not right away, but I just—"

"You'd like me to find a summer job here."

"I would. I realize that's a lot to ask, but the plain fact is I wish you didn't have to leave in April."

"I know." She doubted that he really wanted to have this discussion now. She certainly didn't. "I don't know what the future holds for us, but…could we not talk about that tonight?"

His quick glance told her he realized they might be veering into difficult territory. "You're right. This is not the time or the place." His smile returned. "Or the outfit. A guy would have to be pretty dumb to talk about serious things when a woman is wearing shoes like yours."

She let out her breath in relief. "You like these shoes, huh?"

"Love 'em."

"Good. And look at that. Here's the service elevator."

"So it is. We're making progress." He stepped forward and pushed the button.

A current of excitement ran through her body, setting off little tremors of anticipation. He had no idea, poor man, but she was about to blow his mind. The doors rumbled open to reveal a spacious, utilitarian interior. Bright lights illuminated bare walls and no handrails. It was a stark cube, and all the more exotic to her because of that.

Trey gestured her forward. "After you."

She'd thought about her presentation ever since the idea had come to her. Sashaying into the elevator, she dropped her duffel to the floor and turned around to face him. As he stepped in and the doors began to close behind him, she untied her robe. Opening the lapels, she flashed him.

His gasp echoed off the walls. "What the hell are you doing?"

"Hit the stop button, cowboy. Then unzip and come on over here. I have something for you."

He whirled and smacked the stop button, but then he slowly turned back to her. "Are you serious?"

"Would I kid about something like this?" She cupped her breasts and fondled her nipples. That moment when he'd stared at her in the room had made her bolder. "See what a little champagne can do to my inhibitions?"

His set his guitar case down. "And I thought all we'd get was an elevator ride." He sounded short of breath.

"I have a different ride in mind." She slid one hand between her legs. "Care to mount up?"

Unfastening his belt and unzipping his jeans, he came toward her. "I'm going to find out what brand of champagne that was and order a case of it."

She licked her lips. "I did enjoy the bubbly."

"And now I'm going to enjoy you." Pulling a condom out of his pocket, he handed it to her. "Since this is your party, I'll let you do the honors."

"Be glad to." She ripped open the foil.

He planted one hand on either side of her head, caging her in as he leaned forward. "Put it on tight. This could get wild." Then he began playing with her mouth as he told her in great detail what he was about to do to her. After sucking on her lower lip, he used several four-letter words to paint a picture of his intentions. He ran his tongue over the bow of her upper lip and continued the litany of earthy predictions. He nibbled and promised. He lapped and suggested.

By the time she'd rolled the condom on, she was frantic to have him. Her breasts quivered with each breath. "You're ready."

"Oh, yeah. I'm so ready." He hooked his arm under the back of her knee. Leaving one hand braced against the wall beside her head, he raised her leg, probed her slick heat and pushed inside, groaning with satisfaction.

She was pinned to the elevator wall by his cock, and she loved it. He felt so damned good there—right there. "What was it you said you were going to do to me?"

"Lady, I'm doing it." He drew back and thrust forward again with firm deliberation. His hot gaze bored into her. "And I intend to keep doing it until you beg for mercy." He shoved in tighter, pushing her back against the wall. "I feel as if I could climb right inside you."

Her heart beat wildly. "Go ahead."

"Believe I will." He began to move, and each

stroke drove deep, touching her core, ratcheting up the tension.

She gasped with pleasure.

"Like that?" His eyes sparked fire.

She stared right back at him, unflinching. "Yes. Bring it on."

His breath caught. "Oh, Elle." With a noise that was nearly a growl, he surged forward, pounding into her without pause. The liquid sound of his cock driving into her created an echo that made the tiny cubicle resonate with passion.

Delirious with the untamed force of his body entering hers over and over, Elle surrendered to her orgasm with panting cries of delight. He kept going, and she came again, breathless with wonder.

"Now," he muttered. *"Now."* And he shoved her back against the wall one more time. As his cock pulsed within her, he lowered his head, and his gasps were punctuated with several colorful swear words.

Long seconds later, he lifted his head and looked into her eyes. A smile twitched at the corners of his mouth. "You continue to surprise the hell out of me."

"Glad to hear it."

"That was outstanding."

"I thought so. That's the first time you swore while you were coming."

He chuckled and shook his head. "Guess I did. I was out of my mind." He glanced around at the elevator. "I think it was partly the acoustics."

"The *acoustics?*"

"Yeah. The way the sounds bounced around in here seemed to amplify the sensation, sort of like a sex rock concert."

"Oh, my God." She started to laugh. "So this is what it's like to have sex with a musician. They're into how it sounds."

"Of course." He looked surprised that she hadn't figured that out. "I love the sound of sex. There's the moaning, the fast breathing, the lapping, the sucking, the incredibly erotic noise of my cock slipping in and out of your—"

"I get it." And her body wanted it again. The stirrings were unmistakable. "But we need to untangle ourselves. I'm losing feeling in my leg."

"Can't have that."

Putting everything to rights again took some doing, but they eventually managed. Fortunately, Trey was the kind of old-fashioned guy who carried a handkerchief in his back pocket. He said usually he carried a bandanna. The handkerchief was for special occasions like weddings.

"And having sex in service elevators?" Elle winked at him.

"Apparently so. I'll add it to my list of must-haves whenever I'm with you. Gotta make sure I have at least one condom and a handkerchief. Then we can do it anywhere."

"What a concept."

He gazed at her. "I know. Now I'm wondering what other places have interesting acoustics."

"So we're back to the acoustics?"

"Well, *yeah.*" He pushed the button and the elevator started back down. "Creaky beds are good. I'd love to find a set of those old-fashioned springs. A creaky old bed with metal springs, inside a small room with tile floors and no curtains, would give you a sexual symphony. I'd love to try that."

"Sounds loud."

"It would be loud, and wild. Then add in your voice saying naughty words in that husky way you have, and your moans, and little cries…" He reached out and ran a finger down her cheek. "I hope you're not sleepy yet."

"Please don't say we're going out in search of a tiled room with a squeaky bed."

"Not tonight. But even a cushy king-size mattress is capable of very nice sounds when two people are making love on it."

She realized that he'd switched the terminology from having sex to making love. Judging from the warm light in his brown eyes, he'd done it on purpose. They'd had plenty of wild sex. She suspected the next round would be about something else entirely. She might not be ready for that.

15

CREATIVE SEXUAL EXPERIENCES were all well and good, Trey thought as he opened the door to his room and ushered Elle inside. But tenderness was important, too, and they hadn't shared enough of that. He wasn't complaining. He'd remember that elevator ride for the rest of his life.

Time to dial back the frenzy, though, and show her a different kind of loving—his favorite kind. She walked in on those crazy shoes, and he decided those would be the first to go. He was responsible for her keeping them on, because he'd relished the fantasy of a woman wearing do-me shoes and nothing else.

He didn't need that anymore. They'd had that brand of fantasy sex in the elevator. He closed and locked the door before turning back to her. "You can take off your shoes if you want to."

Her blue eyes flashed with a hint of an emotion he couldn't identify. "You're sure?"

"I'm sure. In fact, sit on the bed and let me take them off for you."

She chuckled as she perched on the edge of the mattress. "Oh, I know where this is going."

"Do you?" He didn't think so. He sat cross-legged on the floor in front of her and took one foot into his lap. "These must be wickedly uncomfortable." He unbuckled the narrow strap.

"Not for the first couple of hours."

He winced. She'd been wearing them since before two this afternoon. No wonder she'd wanted to sit and drink champagne with Mary Lou. He took off the other shoe, and she sighed with relief.

"I shouldn't have asked you to keep them on." He took one of her feet in his hands again and began a slow massage.

"Yes, you should. That's the main reason this kind of shoe exists—to create a sexual fantasy for men. Women often wear them for that exclusive purpose." She moaned softly. "That's nice, Trey."

"I owe it to you." He deepened the massage.

"Hey, I'm the one who chose to wear them. You didn't force me to put them on today." She sighed again. "You're good at this. I shouldn't be surprised."

"Why?" He moved to her other foot.

"Because I already know you have talented hands. You can make that guitar sing. You can make me sing."

"Nice to know." Although that affected him, he wasn't going to indulge the demands of his cock right now. He continued to work on her feet. "Did you bring lotion?"

"There's some in my duffel bag."

Her bag was conveniently on the floor only a couple of feet away. Pulling it over, he handed it up to her. "Would you get it out for me?"

"I know what you're up to, Trey."

"Are you sure?"

"I'm sure." She handed him a tube of lotion. "You're making love to my feet, and then you'll work your way up my legs, and so on."

"So you think massaging your feet is a means to an end?" He squeezed out some sweet-smelling lotion and smoothed it over the arch of her foot.

She shivered. "I do."

"Well, you're right, it is." But he wasn't doing it to prepare her for his future satisfaction. He was doing it because she needed this more than she needed an orgasm. "Just lie back and enjoy it."

"Okay, I will." She settled backward on the bed.

"I like your gold toenail polish."

"The spa here does a nice job." She moaned again. "You could work there. You know your way around a foot massage, cowboy."

"You inspire me." He worked the lotion between her toes. Then he moved to her other foot and gave it the same treatment. He took his time, and the room grew very quiet. Too quiet.

Slowly releasing her foot, he rose to his knees and peered at her. Her eyes were closed, and her breathing was steady. She was asleep.

He chose to be complimented rather than insulted. He'd relaxed her with his foot massage, and she'd felt comfortable enough to drift off. She might be asleep, but they could still share a bed. That would be nice, too. They might not use the condoms he'd left in the nightstand drawer, but he'd be right there beside her all night.

Although he undressed as quietly as he could, he

probably didn't need to worry about waking her up. She slept on. But she couldn't stay like that with her legs hanging off the bed.

Surveying the situation, he mapped out a strategy. He drew back the covers on the far side of the bed. When he leaned over and scooped her up in his arms, she mumbled something and cuddled closer. It sounded like she said, "Has Santa been here?"

He might have misunderstood, but he decided to give her an answer anyway. "Not yet," he murmured as he carried her to the other side of the bed and laid her on the sheet.

Her bathrobe tie had loosened during the transport, and he didn't think she'd want to sleep in that bulky thing, anyway. Working carefully, he slipped each arm out of the sleeves. Getting the thick robe out from under her was a trick, but he finally succeeded.

Grabbing one stolen moment, he gazed at her. She was so much more than a beautiful woman. She had fire and intelligence to spare. If she'd only let him into her life, she'd be so easy to love.

She rolled to her side to face the wall, and he pulled the covers up over her bare shoulder. "Sleep well, sweetheart," he said softly.

"I want skis." The words were distinct this time, even though her eyes remained closed.

He didn't have to think very hard to figure it out. She'd been surrounded by Christmas decorations for days. Then he'd picked her up like a sleeping child and tucked her into bed. In her dream state, she'd asked Santa for a pair of skis. That memory had to have come from somewhere.

Yet she'd told him before that Christmas wasn't particularly important to her. It had been once, though. He'd lay money on it. But now she'd rejected everything that was even slightly sentimental, including Christmas.

Or maybe not. He had a sudden inspiration. If he could get her to spend Christmas Eve and Christmas Day at the ranch, he might revive her love of the holiday. He couldn't help thinking that once she surrendered to the joy of the season, she'd be open to loving him.

That wouldn't solve the problem of her heading down to Argentina for the summer months, but it would be a start. She craved the excitement of that sport, she'd said. All he had to do was present an option that was at least that exciting. Personally, he thought loving each other for the rest of their lives fit the criteria. But that was just him.

Turning out the lights, he climbed into bed beside her. He wished that he had a Christmas tree like hers to cast a warm glow as she slept. Her affection for that tree was another clue that she wasn't quite as immune to the holidays as she let on. But short of getting dressed again and stealing hers, he was out of luck on that score.

He gathered her close, because he couldn't help himself. Lying spooned against her, his cock close to her silky bottom, created a predictable result. He tried thinking of subjects that would tame his bad boy, but nothing worked, not even imagining himself naked in a snowdrift.

A snowdrift had started all this in the first place. Now he was in bed with his angel, someone who'd been only a fantasy three days ago. He'd had hot, creative sex with her. Yet in some ways, even though she was lying right next to him, she seemed out of reach.

His cock twitched because that's what cocks did when they were denied what they wanted. He wasn't going to wake her up so he could get relief, so he rolled to his back with a sigh of frustration. This could be a really long night.

"I'm awake." She rolled to her side, facing him.

Excitement warred with guilt. "My fault. Sorry."

She laid a hand on his chest. "This wasn't supposed to be a slumber party." She stroked him with those tantalizing hands, those provocative, arousing hands.

"I know, but you're tired. You need—"

"You." Reaching down, she circled his stiff cock with sure fingers. Sweet torment. "And you need me," she said. "We decided on this big bed for a reason, and it wasn't so we could sleep better in it."

He turned his head to look at her. "You're mighty persuasive, lady." And he was a sucker for the times when that husky note crept into her voice.

"One more climax apiece," she said. "Then we'll sleep."

When he hesitated, she scooted closer, put her mouth next to his ear and told him what she wanted in two succinct words. He was a goner.

But he refused to take her with the reckless abandon he'd allowed himself before. "Turn me loose, and I'll do exactly what you said." He gently removed her hand from his cock. He wouldn't do exactly what she'd said, though. He had much more in mind than the raw coupling those two words implied.

"Lie back." He reached across her. "Are you okay with the light?"

"Yes." She lifted her head and kissed him full on the mouth, her lips warm and pliant. He got so lost in that kiss that he nearly forgot what he'd been about to do. Her openmouthed, eager kiss shot messages down to his groin. Ah, yes. First the light. Then a condom from the drawer.

He fumbled for the light switch and found it. He'd be damned if he'd love her in the dark and miss watching her expression. Then he grabbed a condom and held on to it while he continued to explore her luscious mouth.

How he loved doing that. She might act skittish when they talked about commitment, but she put her whole heart into her kiss. He tended to believe her kiss more than he believed her words.

He wanted to be inside her, though, and the condom wasn't going to magically attach itself to his cock. Ending the kiss with reluctance, he pulled away long enough to put the doggone thing on. Someday, when his world was arranged the way he'd prefer, he wouldn't have to use them. But that was getting way ahead of the game.

As he moved over her, she looked up at him and seemed about to say something.

"What?"

She shook her head and closed her eyes. "Nothing."

"Please don't close your eyes."

Her lashes fluttered and she looked at him again. "What if I need protection?"

He remembered telling her why he usually wore his hat during a performance. "You don't need to protect yourself from me."

"Are you sure?"

"Absolutely sure." He entered her slowly. This time wasn't about speed and agility or multiple orgasms. This was about celebrating the connection he'd felt since that first moment when he'd discovered her standing in the gift shop.

She sucked in a breath. "When you look at me like that, I…I get scared."

"I told you before." He eased back and slid in again, still moving gently. "You don't have to be afraid of me."

"It's not you I'm afraid of." Her gaze held his. "It's what you make me feel."

"Could that be love?" He stroked her with subtle movements of his hips, arousing her by tiny incre-ments, building the emotion he wanted from her.

"I don't…I don't know."

"I do." He rocked gently within her. "It's this, Elle. This connection between two people."

"It's not that simple." Tears welled in her eyes.

"Yes, it is." He kept loving her, wanting her to feel what he felt.

"No."

"Yes. Two people, finding each other, recognizing each other. The rest is details."

"Oh, Trey." She swallowed. "I wish I could be-lieve you."

"I wish you could, too." He shifted his angle and felt her tighten. "Believe this. We're in tune, Elle. Do you know how rare that is?"

She nodded as tears leaked from the corners of her eyes.

"Then stay with me." He sought the rhythm that

would bring them both joy, and she arched against him as he knew she would. "Stay with me, Elle."

She came apart in his arms, and he followed soon after. But when it was over, he knew that one crucial thing was missing from their special moment. She hadn't promised to stay.

TREY HADN'T PRESSED her for an answer, and for that Elle was grateful. If anything, he pretended that he hadn't said those fateful words "stay with me." He kissed her tenderly before leaving the bed, and when he came back, he turned out the light and gathered her close. In minutes, he was asleep.

But she lay wide-awake, staring into the darkness. She couldn't lead him on anymore. Although she'd warned him from the first that she wasn't interested in anything long-term, he hadn't really accepted that. Instead, he kept trying to find reasons for her to stay in Jackson Hole instead of leaving in April. And tonight he'd made his romantic, loving plea. *Stay with me.*

She wouldn't do that. She wouldn't let herself be carried away by good sex and sweet words and sentimental songs. She wasn't that type.

But he was, and he needed someone who *would* allow herself to be carried away, who'd agree with his romantic belief in soul mates and destiny. Maybe he'd find another musician who could share his fascination with acoustical sex. They could have fun singing duets like the one he'd performed with Tyler.

Elle had toyed with the idea of continuing to see him after this long weekend was over. But when he'd asked her to stay, she'd faced reality. They had different goals.

The longer she indulged herself with this hot affair, the tougher life would be for Trey when she broke it off. He'd mourn losing her the way he'd mourned losing Cassie, which would sideline him for weeks or months. If she cared about him, she should minimize his pain, not prolong it.

But telling him that now, when he was celebrating with his friends, also would be cruel. He'd need some private time to work through the disappointment, and he wouldn't have that opportunity until the group went back to the ranch. She'd have to pretend all was well until he left on Tuesday. That wouldn't be particularly easy, but she'd do it for his sake.

She wondered if stress would keep her awake all night, but she was already sleep-deprived, and finally exhaustion claimed her. When she woke up a few hours later, Trey was in the shower, whistling. That broke her heart.

He was so cute when he was happy, and she wanted him to be happy. That meant exiting his life and leaving space for someone who fit into his world and his dreams. Someone who wasn't her.

Toweling himself off, he came out of the bathroom and grinned at her. "Better move it, sweetheart, if you still plan to teach a bunch of yokels to ski this morning."

She scrambled out of bed and pulled her phone out of her duffel. "Yikes." It was later than she'd thought, but that was better. No time for conversation about delicate topics.

"I thought I'd let you sleep a little longer, so I took first shower. It's all yours. I'm finished in there."

"Thank you." As she passed by him on the way

into the bathroom, he caught her around the waist and pulled her close.

"Good morning to you, too." He gave her a quick kiss and looked into her eyes. "Listen, about what I said last night, I probably shouldn't have—"

"Don't worry about it." She managed a smile. "You got carried away."

"Right." His gaze searched hers, and he gave her a little squeeze. "You'd better hop in the shower."

"Yep!" She heard the note of false cheer in her voice and hoped he hadn't noticed. She hurried into the bathroom. "I forgot to ask if you have ski pants for today," she called over her shoulder.

"Rented them yesterday morning. And a jacket. All the guys will be in better shape this morning. You'll be impressed."

"I'm sure I will." She turned on the shower, which cut off any further discussion. So far, so good.

But it was still early in the day. She had to get through the rest of it, including tonight, without giving Trey a hint that she was planning to end their affair tomorrow. Given how perceptive he was, she might be asking the impossible.

16

HE'D BLOWN IT. Trey had been afraid that he'd over-played his hand by asking her to stay. But the love-making had been so sweet, and he'd thought the timing was right. Obviously it hadn't been and might never be. He wouldn't ever know, because he'd been impatient, exactly what Watkins had warned him about.

Impatience was a failing of his, with the exception of his work with horses. He could be patient as all get-out with horses, because he made allowances for the language barrier. But communication should be easier between people.

It wasn't, though, and his lack of patience with that might have cost him Elle. All through the ski lesson he berated himself for not taking things slower. He'd had until *April,* for God's sake. Rome wasn't conquered in a day, as they said. He shouldn't have tried to capture Elle's heart in a weekend.

But he'd pushed the issue, and she'd decided her answer was no. She probably wouldn't tell him until tomorrow. She'd want to give him a chance to go home and lick his wounds.

That gave him a choice of pretending right along with her and sharing a bed with her tonight or breaking up with her now. Both options sucked. If he went along with her game, he'd get to hold her for one more night. But the whole time he'd be waiting for the ax to fall.

Debating the issue while trying to control a couple of skinny waxed boards on a very slippery slope meant he fell down a lot. He used up his entire vocabulary of swear words and invented a few more. Jack came gliding by when Trey was berating his *pucking foles*.

Jack executed a perfect hockey stop. "What the hell are pucking foles?"

Trey struggled to his feet, yet again. "It's from the Latin."

"Doesn't sound like Latin to me." Then his frown cleared. "Okay, I get it. Your pucking foles are driving you nucking futs. Am I right?"

Trey stood in the pizza slice position and adjusted his goggles. "You are so right, my friend."

"Listen, it might be my imagination, but you seem a little off this morning."

"I'm fine."

"If you say so. But Elle doesn't seem quite herself, either. I'm thinking there might be a connection."

Trey gazed at Jack. "I know you're my boss and all, but…"

"You wish I'd mind my own business?"

"Something like that. I was trying to find a more diplomatic way of saying it."

"I wouldn't be butting in at all, except that I already sort of did."

Trey's chest tightened. "Like how?"

"Trying to be Santa Claus. Seeing how well you two were getting along, I checked with Carl about Elle's work schedule, and he's fine with her taking Christmas Eve and Christmas morning off. So I invited her to the ranch for the night."

"What—" Trey had to stop and clear his throat. "What did she say?"

"That she couldn't make it. Too many obligations here. I told her I'd spoken with Carl, and then she made some other lame excuse about needing to call her folks that night, and they're over in Germany, and it's complicated, blah, blah, blah."

"I guarantee she made that up. She doesn't want to come to the ranch."

"Why not? I thought you two—"

"Nope."

"Since when?"

Pain sliced through his heart. "Last night. Technically, early this morning." That's when he'd opened his big mouth and killed his chances.

"I'm sorry." Jack sighed. "That sucks." He glanced at Trey. "You sure? Because sometimes a woman acts as if she wants one thing, but she really wants something else."

"I wish that could be the case, but it's not. Anyway, thanks for trying." He desperately wished to change the subject. "Nice outfit, by the way."

"I'm rather fond of it, myself." Jack's ski pants and jacket were solid black except for a red stripe down the side of the pants and along the length of each sleeve. He'd chosen to go with a red-and-black headband instead of a hat, which suited a guy who was part Shoshone. His iridescent goggles must have set him back a tidy sum, but they made him look like an Olympian.

"Are you thinking you'll get into this skiing thing, then?"

"I just might. I'm usually a little bored in the winter. I've considered building an indoor riding arena, which would help, but I couldn't do that until next summer. If I drove up here a couple of times a week and practiced with Elle, I might get the hang of it."

"You might." Trey cursed himself all over again. He could have done the same exact thing and taken his time wooing Elle.

"You could ride up with me."

"That won't work. Not now."

"Hellfire, cowboy. You must have really put your foot in it."

"Yeah, I did." Trey glanced over at Elle, who'd acquired a new pupil this morning. Redheaded Cassidy O'Connelli, wobbly on a pair of skis, moved slowly down the slope with Elle skiing just as slowly right beside her. It hurt to watch Elle, who was at her best teaching a beginner to ski, so he looked away. "And I don't think there's a damned thing I can do about it now."

ELLE HOPED THAT Trey's inability to concentrate on the skiing lesson was from lack of sleep. She didn't think it was. He knew something had changed with her, and he was no dummy. He could figure out why.

She also hoped Trey hadn't been behind Jack's invitation to the ranch. Asking if Trey had requested that invitation would have opened up a can of worms, so she hadn't. In any case, Jack was certain to relay her response, which would give Trey further proof that the relationship was about to end.

If he'd put Jack up to asking, then she was definitely doing the right thing by backing away. She wasn't going to be pressured by Trey or the Chance family. She'd built a life that suited her, and abandoning it on a whim wasn't her style.

The lesson ran long because nobody was ready to quit, so it was late morning before everyone started packing up. Cassidy still wanted more instruction, but Elle thought the girl needed a break between sessions. As they worked out a time to meet that afternoon, Trey approached, his skis balanced on one broad shoulder. She'd bet he could hardly wait to get rid of them. If today was any indication, skiing wasn't his thing.

He waited until Cassidy left, but once she did, he wasted no time on pleasantries. "Do you have some free time this afternoon?"

Judging from his expression, he wasn't asking because he wanted to race to his room and have sex. "I have a little time. Cassidy wants to come back out around three."

"After lunch, then?"

"Not right after. There's the send-off for Pam and Emmett. I'm sure you want to be there for that."

"Yeah, I do. I'd forgotten about it."

That he'd forgotten the send-off was another sign that he was very distracted. She had a bad feeling about why he wanted to see her this afternoon.

"So after Pam and Emmett leave, are you free?"

"I should be. Alex and Jeb want another lesson, and we settled on four, if the weather holds. But I'm not booked between the send-off and Cassie's lesson at three." She sounded like a CEO juggling appointments, but that couldn't be helped. Now that the stay was almost over, a few people wanted to cram in more time on skis, and she was thrilled about that.

He gave her a wry smile. "Glad you can fit me in."

"Could this wait until after I'm finished with Jeb and Alex?"

He hesitated. "Not really. I thought we might take a walk, if that's okay with you."

"Sure. That sounds nice." Whatever this discussion would be about, she could tell he wanted it over with. A knot formed in her stomach.

"Great. If you're going to the send-off, we can meet up there."

"I thought I'd go. They won't care if I'm there, probably, but…yes, I'd like to see them off."

"I'll meet you afterward, then." He started to leave.

"Trey?"

"Yeah?" He turned back to her, and there was a tiny spark in his eyes, as if some unnamed hope had been momentarily ignited.

"Did you ask Jack to invite me to the ranch for Christmas?" She couldn't help asking. Before they took that walk, she needed to know.

The spark died. "Nope. That was all his idea."

Although she was relieved to hear it, she hated seeing the light leave his dark gaze. "I appreciate being asked, but I can't make it. It's complicated, but I—"

"I understand, Elle. See you after Pam and Emmett leave."

When he was gone, she stared at the snowy hillside for a long time. She felt like such a louse. If only she'd followed her instincts in the first place and steered clear of this man, they'd both have been spared a lot of pain.

A few minutes later, as she was headed back to the lodge, Jared called out to her.

She turned around. "Did I forget to put something away?" In her current frame of mind, that was possible.

"Nope. Everything's shipshape. Did you eat breakfast?"

"Never got around to it."

"Me, either. Want to go see if there's anything left in the kitchen?"

"Sure." She might as well. Although she wasn't particularly hungry, she ought to eat. It could be a long day.

Jared fell into step beside her. "So, everything okay with you?"

"Yes." She glanced at him. "Why?"

"Just wondered. A while ago you were staring off into space as if there'd been a death in the family. And Trey didn't smile much this morning."

"I'm sure he wasn't smiling. He wiped out a lot today."

"I noticed. But you two are okay, right?"

"We have some issues, but it'll be fine."

"I'm glad to hear it, because he's really good for you."

Elle blinked. Jared wasn't in the habit of making personal comments. "What's that supposed to mean?"

"Don't take this wrong, but you keep people at a distance. You're different with him, though. It's nice to see."

She stared at him. "I do not keep people at a distance."

"Yeah, you do, Elle. You're sweet and friendly and a good teacher. But it's like there's an invisible force field around you. Except this weekend, not so much. I figure that's because of him."

Her chest tightened. If that was true, then she'd made a big mess for herself as well as for Trey. But she didn't want Jared to know how his comments had rocked her back. "You're scaring me. Since when did you turn into Dr. Phil?"

That made him laugh. "I know, right? Totally out of character. Blame it on the fact that I watched *The Muppet Christmas Carol* last night on TV. Now I'm all introspective about the meaning of life."

"You're not comparing me to Scrooge, are you?"

"*No.* Nothing like that. Forget I said anything. Sheesh. This is why I don't get into the touchy-feely stuff."

"We'll pretend it never happened." As if she could. Now she'd be obsessing over what he'd said, damn it.

"Good. By the way, they want us to make another teaching video whenever we can work it in. I'm thinking this week would be good. Maybe Wednesday afternoon. The schedule's kind of loose on Wednesday."

"Wednesday would be great." She welcomed a change of subject, and filling her calendar with activities was a good idea. If Jared was right, and she'd let down her guard and fallen for Trey, even a little bit, then she had some recalibrating to do. Keeping busy would be her salvation.

Trey stood with Watkins and Mary Lou in the crowd of well-wishers gathered in the front driveway of the resort. A long black limo sat under the portico and a uniformed driver stood by the passenger door, waiting. Everyone had been given a bottle of bubbles as a send-off gesture.

The bride and groom had not yet arrived, so Trey had time to scan the crowd for Elle. She wasn't here. She'd said she was coming, though. And after the limo drove away… He swallowed hard when he thought of the discussion ahead of him.

Mary Lou put a hand on the sleeve of his sheepskin jacket. "Where's Elle?"

"Don't know."

"She's coming, isn't she?"

"She said she would."

"Trey, look at me."

That almost made him smile. Mary Lou had adopted a parental tone with him, and he loved it. He glanced down at her. "Yes, ma'am?"

"Did you two have a fight?"

"No."

"Well, *something's* wrong. I can tell by the—oh, wait. Here she comes."

Trey had spotted her, too. She hurried out of the resort entrance door, pulling on her ski jacket as she came. He would love to say that his heart didn't ache like hell at the sight of her. He couldn't say that.

She smiled as she walked over to where he stood with Watkins and Mary Lou. "I'm glad I didn't miss them. Time got away from me."

"You don't have any bubbles," Mary Lou said. "They handed them out earlier."

"Take mine." Trey held out his bottle.

"That's okay. I'll—"

"Take it, Elle."

She met his gaze. Something in his voice or in his eyes must have communicated his frustration with this entire situation. She must have decided he was nearing the end of his rope, because she took the bottle. "Thanks. That's generous of you."

A cheer went up, and Trey broke eye contact with Elle. "Here they come." Then he gasped. "Good Lord, she's got him in a white linen suit and a Panama hat. I can't believe it."

Mary Lou laughed with delight. "I love it! Look at Pam, all in pastels. They're ready for the tropics. That's just the cutest thing ever."

"I don't know," Watkins said. "Emmett's never worn anything but jeans and cowboy shirts. He's not gonna recognize himself in the mirror."

"Give him a week," Mary Lou said. "Don't forget that you were wearing shorts and gaudy shirts by the second day of our cruise."

"Yeah, but Emmett's not even there yet and he already looks like he owns a sugar plantation."

"I think it's great," Trey said. "Good for Emmett. Two days ago he was ready to ditch the ceremony and head for Vegas. Now look at him."

"He's doing it for love," Mary Lou said.

"And for nooky," Watkins added.

"Watkins." Mary Lou punched his arm, but she laughed all the same.

"Nothing wrong with having a double motivation." Trey glanced sideways at Elle. Hard to tell what she was thinking, but she didn't seem to be enjoying the conversation the way the rest of them were.

Emmett and Pam stood on the top step giving hugs

and handshakes to family members clustered around them. Then they turned toward the limo.

"Get your bubbles ready," Mary Lou said. "It's time."

The driver opened the door. Hand-in-hand, Emmett and Pam hurried down the steps in a shower of iridescent bubbles. Once they were tucked inside the limo, everyone followed the car a little ways down the drive, waving and blowing more bubbles.

Throughout the send-off, Trey kept track of Elle. She'd blown bubbles along with everyone else, but her shouts of good cheer had sounded hollow to him. That might be his mood, though.

After the limo pulled away from the resort, he glanced down at her. "Ready for that walk?"

"Sure." She started to tuck the bottle in her jacket pocket. "Oh, do you want these back?" She took the bottle out again.

"You can keep it."

"All right. Some of the younger skiers might have fun creating bubbles going downhill. Where are we walking?"

"I'd hoped you'd make a suggestion. You know the area better than I do." Their careful formality sliced him to ribbons.

"This way, then." She started across the driveway.

He walked beside her in silence. He'd rather not say his piece where they might have an audience. Within about five minutes they'd entered a groomed trail that wound through the trees.

"This is for cross-country skiing," Elle said. "We have a few guests who've asked for that over the years, so Carl built a small trail for them. Nobody will be on it now."

"I wonder if cross-country would suit me better." His boots crunched on the packed snow, but he didn't sink in.

"It might, at that."

"I don't suppose you care much for it, though. Too tame."

"It's okay for a change of pace." Her steps kept time with his.

"Maybe I'll check it out." He didn't know why he was discussing this. Procrastination, probably. They were out of sight of the resort. The air was still and cold. Then a breeze sighed through the pines, and ahead of them, a branch showered snow onto the path.

He stopped and turned to her. "Elle, I pushed you with that request last night, and I realize it set you off. You've decided there's no hope for us, and if that's the case, I'm ready to cut my losses." He watched her eyes, hoping against hope that he'd see denial there.

Instead, she gazed at him with sad resignation. "It's for the best, Trey. I'm not the one for you. I pray that you find her someday, and that she's as romantic and loving as you are. You deserve that."

So that was it, then. He wished an avalanche would come along and bury him under it. But he wouldn't want her to be buried under it, too, so he couldn't really wish that.

Instead, he had to man up and get through this. Except he wasn't sure what to do next. Shake hands? Give her a farewell kiss? No, that was out. One kiss and he was liable to do something stupid, like beg her to change her mind.

She looked away and cleared her throat. "Maybe we should walk back."

"Uh, yeah. You go ahead. You have that lesson with Cassidy. I'll stay out a little longer."

She glanced up, her blue eyes moist. "You're sure?"

"Elle, I won't get lost."

"Okay, then. Goodbye, Trey." She looked as if she might touch him, but then she didn't. "Goodbye." She walked away from him, her pace faster this time, her feet making a noise like a popcorn machine.

He stared after her, his whole body aching. Then he turned and walked in the other direction, because that was easier than standing still. He'd promised her he wouldn't get lost. But he'd never felt so lost in his life.

17

ELLE MANAGED TO avoid Trey for the rest of the time the Last Chance folks were at the resort. Doing that kept her on edge. She didn't sleep well, either, knowing he was there. She woke up in the middle of the night, certain he'd knocked on her door, but no one was outside when she looked.

She told herself that once Trey had left, she'd be able to relax. Instead, she got the flu, or what felt like the flu. She didn't run a fever or get sick to her stomach, but she ached all over. A soak in the hot tub didn't help. A massage didn't help. Getting drunk with Amy didn't help.

As the two of them sat in Amy's room working on their second bottle of wine, Amy listened to Elle describe her peculiar symptoms. "Is there a chance you're in love with the guy?" she asked. "Could that be what ails you?"

Elle's head jerked up. "Hell, no!"

"Don't look so horrified. That would explain why you feel so rotten. You're in love with him. It's possible."

"No, it's not possible. Not after four days."

"So you don't believe he's in love with you, either?"

She shook her head violently. Too violently. She had to put her hand over her eyes and take a deep breath. "Whoa. Dizzy."

"Not to mention that you overreacted to the question. I think maybe—"

"Nope, nope." Elle held up her hand like a traffic cop. "Trey is not in love with me. He's in love with the angel who came to his rescue. He's a romantic dreamer who fell in love with an idea, not a flesh-and-blood woman."

"Hmm."

"What?"

"I watched him at the reception. I watched both of you. If he wasn't a man in love, he gave a damned good impression of it. You seemed to be into him, too."

"Amy, you were seeing what you wanted to see."

"That is so not the case. First of all, I wish he hadn't been so stuck on you, because I would have dated him in a heartbeat. Second, I was fascinated by the change in you. You can deny it all you want, but you acted way happier when he was around. More open, somehow."

Elle frowned. That sounded too much like Jared's comment. "So I've been closed in the past?"

"That sounds bad. I didn't mean that in a critical way."

"Jared said I don't let people get close to me."

Amy's gaze was filled with compassion. "That's sort of true. Part of it is that you're only here for six months. I just start getting to know you again, and you're gone. But…I have the feeling that's on purpose.

By going somewhere else for six months, you don't get too attached to the place or the people."

Elle didn't know what to say about that, especially because Amy might have scored a bull's-eye. "It's… it's what I'm used to."

"I know, hon. When you grow up like that, always on the move, it becomes a habit. But if you've fallen for this guy, and I think you have, then maybe it's time to break that habit."

"That scares me to death."

"I'll bet."

Elle held out her glass. "More wine, please. I'm not ready to examine this concept sober. Not yet, anyway."

Amy poured wine for both of them. Then she picked up her glass. "Here's to facing down fears."

"Maybe." Elle raised her glass. "To quote Scarlett, I'll think about that tomorrow."

But she didn't. The next day she rejected the idea that she was jetting between continents because she was afraid to let herself become attached to people and places. What nonsense. Unfortunately, her mysterious aches and pains refused to go away. She took aspirin and pretended she was fine.

Three days before Christmas, Dominique Chance emailed a link to the wedding pictures along with a chatty note about the fun they'd had at Serenity. Elle put off opening the link for another day. She wanted to see the pictures, but also knew Trey would be in them.

When she woke up at four in the morning on Christmas Eve Day with a burning desire to look at those pictures, she surrendered to the urge to click on that link. For the next hour, she sat on her bed and watched a slide show of the wedding.

Some shots made her laugh, but others…well, she had to hit Pause, climb out of bed and grab the tissue box. It wasn't only the pictures of Trey that made her cry, either. She teared up at the tender scene of Jack holding Archie at the altar, and the loving expression on Emmett's face as Pam walked toward him down the aisle.

She got weepy when she came to the image of Pam and Emmett dancing at the reception. And then…there she was in Trey's arms when they'd waltzed to "If I Didn't Have You in My Life." Dominique had several shots from different angles, as if she hadn't wanted Elle to miss the message.

She didn't miss it. Trey gazed down at her in the same way Emmett had looked at Pam. But that wasn't all. Dominique had captured the emotion on Elle's face with stunning clarity, too.

It was a portrait of a woman in love. Jetting from continent to continent hadn't worked this time. She'd become attached to Trey Wheeler, and if she ever wanted this horrible ache to stop, she had to admit that attachment and honor it. Her roving days were over.

TREY VOWED THAT he was going to enjoy his first Christmas at the Last Chance and put all thoughts of Elle clean out of his mind. Around four in the afternoon he left the bunkhouse. The other hands were taking their sweet time getting showered and dressed for the big night, but Trey was eager to join the party.

A light snow fell as he took the short walk uphill to the massive two-story log structure that was the heart and soul of the ranch. According to Watkins and Mary Lou, the house had begun as a two-story box shape.

As the family had grown, a wing had been added on each side, canted outward so the house seemed to be reaching out its arms in welcome.

A covered porch ran along the entire length. In summer, the porch was lined with rockers and became a good spot for socializing. But winter was not the time for rocking on the porch. Winter meant gathering around the giant stone fireplace in the living room, and that's what Trey looked forward to.

Most folks had arrived, judging by all the vehicles parked near the house. Although the Chance brothers each had a house of their own on ranch property, they'd all driven the few miles to the main house and would spend the night here, along with their wives and kids.

They'd be the only ones to stay overnight, but there'd be plenty of other guests. Josie's brother, Alex Keller, and his wife, Tyler, would be here. Trey wanted to ask her about recording a few songs, just to see what would happen if they put them out there. He planned to train horses for the rest of his life, but a little extra income never hurt.

Nash Bledsoe's truck was parked with the others, so he and his wife, Bethany, had driven over from the Triple G, a small ranch that bordered the Last Chance. Bethany wrote motivational books. Trey didn't know her well yet, and he'd had no opportunity to talk with her at the wedding, either. But gatherings like this one were a good place to get acquainted.

No doubt other members of the Chances' extended family would show up, too. Jack's half brothers, Wyatt and Rafe Locke, along with their wives, had promised to make it. Neither couple had been able to attend the wedding, so they were adamant they'd be at the Christmas Eve party.

Trey figured he was forgetting several other folks who would be there, too. Good thing the house was big and Mary Lou had cooked a whole bunch of food. Watkins said she'd been cheerfully slaving away in the kitchen for two days. Apparently, she liked nothing better than preparing for a party.

Lights glowed from every window, and as Trey approached, snatches of Christmas music filtered outside. A huge wreath hung on the front door, and two miniature trees with sparkling lights stood on either side of it. When the temperature dipped lower tonight, those little trees would be brought in so the lights wouldn't pop in the cold, but Sarah loved making the entrance festive.

Trey had told himself not to think about Elle, but damn, he wished she could see this. She might not fall in love with him, but she'd have to fall in love with this big old ranch house and the wonderful people inside, celebrating the season. She wasn't here, though, and that was her loss.

Taking a deep breath of crisp air, he walked up the steps and opened the door. Inside, the scene was even better than Trey had imagined. The noise level was high, with a mixture of Christmas music, conversation and laughter—it was a happy noise. A few people sat on the comfortable leather furniture, but most of them stood so they could move around and talk to everyone.

A graceful wooden staircase spiraled to the second floor. Trey noticed little Archie navigating his way down the stairs, a Barbie doll clutched in his pudgy fist. About the time he reached the bottom step, Sarah Bianca raced down the upstairs hallway. "Archie! No!"

Archie looked at Trey, pure mischief in his expression, before taking off toward the crowded living room.

"Archie!" Sarah Bianca pounded down the stairs in hot pursuit.

As Trey watched the drama unfold, Jack snatched up his son and took him over to admire the lights on the giant tree in the corner. While Archie was distracted by the lights, Jack quietly took the doll away. Gabe put a hand on Sarah Bianca's tiny shoulder, steered her toward Jack, and retrieved the doll. His daughter marched back upstairs, and all was well.

Trey had often wondered if Jack and Gabe's work with horses carried over to their method of child care. If so, he might turn out to be a pretty good dad himself. But that thought reminded him of Elle and their failed love affair.

"Hey, cowboy, no long faces tonight." Watkins approached him, a beer in each hand. He gave one to Trey. "Merry Christmas, son."

Even though Watkins's use of *son* put a lump in Trey's throat, he wouldn't ever want the older man to quit saying it. He smiled. "Same to you, Watkins. Cheers. How's Mary Lou doing in the kitchen?"

"Just fine, but I'm fixing to go back and help her and Cassidy. I wanted to make sure you had a beer, though, before I left the area."

"I'll come and help, too."

"Nah, you don't have to do that. Stay out here. Have fun. Get you some munchies."

"I can do that in a little while. Let's go." He started

down the hallway that led to the dining room and kitchen area.

"Okay, if you insist." Watkins walked along beside him. "This is a big crowd, bigger than usual, so Sarah's asked Mary Lou to set up a buffet in the dining room instead of trying to serve the food in the living room, like they used to do."

"Makes sense. I— Whoops, there's my phone. I don't know why I brought it. Habit, I guess. If we hadn't walked down here I doubt I would have heard it." He couldn't imagine who'd be calling him. Maybe some cowboy from his old job, wanting to wish him a happy holiday.

Then he stared at the readout in disbelief. "Oh, my God."

Watkins's swift glance was filled with concern. "What's wrong?"

"I don't know. Elle's calling. Excuse me a minute." Heart pounding, he put the phone to his ear. "Elle?"

"Trey, I can't believe this. I'm stuck in a snowdrift."

His heart beat faster. "Are you okay?"

"I'm fine, but this truck isn't going anywhere without a tow."

For the life of him, he couldn't figure out why she was calling him. "Where are you?"

"On the road to the Last Chance."

"What?" Then he said the first stupid thing that popped into his head. "What the hell are you doing there?"

"I was coming to see you, and I don't know the road, and it's dark out here, and it's snowing, and I somehow lost track of where the road was."

"You were coming to see *me?* Why?"

"Because I—listen, instead of telling you all this on the phone, could you come and pull me out? Then I can follow you to the ranch."

"Yeah, sure. I'll be right there. See you soon." He disconnected the phone and looked at Watkins. "She's stuck out on the ranch road."

"So I gathered." Watkins clapped him on the back. "Looks promising, son."

"Maybe." Trey was afraid to hope for too much. "I need to go pull her out. I know I offered to help you and Mary Lou, but—"

"Don't give it another thought. But can I offer a suggestion?"

"Like what?"

"Don't take your Jeep out there. You'll be fumbling around in the dark, and when you're done, you'll still be in one vehicle and she'll be in another, which isn't very romantic. Save the towing for when it's daylight."

"And do what?"

"Rescue her the cowboy way. Ride out there on a horse and bring her back tucked in front of you. You have the advantage, son. Maximize it."

ELLE PONDERED THE irony of her situation as she watched for headlights on the road. Maybe it wasn't ironic, after all, but fitting. Supposedly she'd saved Trey's life last spring, but by doing so, she'd apparently saved her own.

Without realizing it, she'd blindly followed a pattern stamped into her by her parents. They'd adjusted to constant moves by becoming detached from people and places. Or maybe they'd chosen their life paths because they preferred to stay detached.

She wasn't like them. Trey had shown her that by jolting her out of a numbing lifestyle and making her feel again. She'd needed a dyed-in-the-wool romantic to accomplish that, and she'd found him.

But getting to him tonight had been more of a challenge than she'd anticipated. Honest to God, they needed streetlights on this road. She'd never driven in such total blackness. If Trey hadn't answered his cell phone, her predicament could have been dire.

He had, though, and he should arrive any minute. She'd left her headlights on so he'd see her. Beyond the reach of those beams, she searched for evidence that he was coming in her direction.

Then her phone rang. Why the hell was he calling her? She pushed the connect button. "Where are you? I have my lights on. I shouldn't be hard to spot."

"I decided to warn you that I'm not coming in my truck."

"What do you mean, you're not coming?" She sounded panicky, but she couldn't help it. Darkness surrounded her, not to mention snow, and she needed to be rescued, damn it!

"I'm heading toward you, but I'm riding a horse. I didn't want to scare you."

"A *horse?*" She wondered if this was a crazy dream. "What is it, a Clydesdale?"

"No, just a regular horse named Inkspot. We're going to leave your truck here until tomorrow when it'll be easier to see what we're doing. Inkspot and I will take you to the ranch."

"You're kidding, right?"

"Nope." And he rode into the beam of her headlights.

She stared at this broad-shouldered cowboy wearing a sheepskin jacket and a Stetson. He'd come to her rescue, not like the Lone Ranger, but like a knight in shining armor, mounted on a magnificent black-and-white horse.

Grabbing her duffel, she opened the door and climbed out as he dismounted. They met in the beam of her headlights, and she launched herself into his arms, knocking his hat into the snow.

He didn't seem to notice as he gathered her close and kissed her. His mouth was cold at first, but it warmed up fast. And all the while, she was thinking that this was the man she would be kissing for the rest of her life, and that was beyond wonderful.

Although he couldn't seem to stop kissing her, he managed to lift his mouth long enough to murmur a few words about needing to get her back to the ranch. Maybe that was so, but she had what she wanted right here.

Finally, he cupped her face and put some distance between her lips and his. "Seriously. We have to get back. It's cold out here."

"I hadn't noticed."

"Trust me, you will. Let's turn off your headlights and lock your Jeep."

"Not before I say what I came to say." Suddenly it seemed more important than anything else.

He went very still. "Okay."

"I love you, Trey Wheeler. I've never been in love before, so I didn't know what had happened to me, but you happened to me, and I've been an idiot, and—" She didn't get to finish because he started kissing her again. But she'd said most of it, at least.

Moments later, he came up for air. "That's the most beautiful speech I've ever heard."

"There's more."

"And I can't wait to hear it. But if we don't get back soon, they'll send out a search party, and that will louse up everyone's Christmas Eve celebration."

"I don't want that."

"Me, either."

"But I just need to hear one thing from you before we go."

"Anything. I'll say anything you want me to."

"Come on, Trey. You know what it is. You write songs about it."

"Are you talking about saying that I love you? Isn't it obvious?"

"Yes." She laughed. "But that doesn't mean a girl doesn't want to hear those words when she's driven all the way out here in the dark on Christmas Eve."

He cupped the back of her neck with one gloved hand and gazed into her eyes. "I love you, Elle Masterson. I love you with everything I have, everything I am and everything I will ever be."

"Oh." Tears filled her eyes. "That's…beautiful."

"Not nearly as beautiful as the life we're going to have together." He brushed his warm lips over hers. "Starting right now." In moments he'd locked her Jeep and hoisted her into the saddle in true hero fashion.

And although they rode off into the snow instead of into the sunset, Elle had no doubt they would have a very happy ending.

Epilogue

"GUESS WE WON'T have to spend Christmas Eve delivering a foal, after all." Regan O'Connelli stripped off his rubber gloves and got to his feet.

Timothy Lindquist, head trainer for the Marley Stables, sighed. "Sorry to bring you out here for a false alarm, Doc. I thought for sure she was in labor. The boss has high hopes for this one, up to and including the Triple Crown, so I can't take chances."

"I completely understand. But my fiancée will be very happy not to spend Christmas Eve alone."

Timothy grinned. "Same with my wife. She knows how important this foal is, but she still grumbled when I informed her that this was the night."

"Not from what I see, but I'd keep an eye on things if I were you." Regan picked up his bag.

"Don't worry. I will. But coming down here every few hours is a hell of a lot better than spending the night in the barn. Thanks, Doc."

"You bet." Regan shook the trainer's hand. "Call me if you notice any changes."

"Got your number in my phone. Merry Christmas."

"Same to you." Regan left the barn and glanced up at the clear sky. No snow in sight. Too bad.

In Virginia, you never knew if you'd have snow for the holidays or not. Jeannette was hoping for a white Christmas, and it didn't look promising. But she'd probably trade snow for having him around tonight. He'd told her he'd probably be gone for hours, maybe all night.

On the drive home he pulled out his phone to call and let her know he was on his way. He was in the habit of doing that. Then he thought better of it. Since it was Christmas, he'd surprise her. That would be more romantic.

But now that he had his phone out, he could call his sister Cassidy in Wyoming and wish her a Merry Christmas. So far she seemed to love apprenticing as the housekeeper at the Last Chance, plus she got to see Tyler and Morgan a lot, and Cassidy adored her big sisters.

With seven siblings, plus his parents, Regan had to space out his holiday calls. He'd contact both Tyler and Morgan tomorrow, when he had more time. He wanted all the details on the wedding, especially Tyler's performances with Watkins and Trey Wheeler.

Talking to Morgan would take a while, too, because it would undoubtedly include a long conversation with his niece Sarah Bianca. He smiled. He was crazy about that little redhead.

Cassidy answered right away. "Regan! Merry Christmas! I can't talk long, because we have this *huge* party going on. I'll text you about it later."

"Great! So you're having fun?"

"Are you kidding? I *love* it here. Love, love, love

it. You should move out to Jackson Hole, Regan. Nick keeps saying he needs a partner in his vet business."

Regan laughed. "Yeah, he mentioned that when I was there last summer, but Cass, I have a partner, remember? Drake wouldn't appreciate having me bail on him, and I wouldn't, anyway. He's my best friend."

"I know." Cassidy sighed dramatically. "But it would be so cool if you were here, too. You and Drake could both come!"

"'Fraid not. His folks live here, and they helped us build our practice. Then there's Jeannette. Her family's here, too. I guarantee she wouldn't want to move to Wyoming."

"Well, bummer. Promise you'll come out for a visit soon, okay? Bring Jeannette. Maybe once she sees the place, she'll be hooked."

"I'll see what I can figure out, sweetie." But he didn't know when he'd work in a visit to the Last Chance. He and Jeannette were deep into wedding planning. He'd suggested Jackson Hole for their honeymoon, and she'd made a face.

"Gotta go, brother of mine. Mary Lou needs me. Merry Christmas!"

"Merry Christmas, Cassidy. Love you." As he disconnected, his chest tightened with longing. He could imagine how festive the ranch house was tonight.

But he couldn't be in two places at once, and he had a hot woman waiting in the town house they'd rented temporarily until they decided for sure where they wanted to buy. He was almost there. She'd be so excited to see him.

As he turned down the street, he noticed Drake's SUV parked in front of the house. Huh. Then he chuckled. Drake had dropped by with his last-minute gift. Typical of the guy. Drake bragged about his Christmas Eve shopping marathons. Jeannette had probably offered him a beer.

Regan parked in the street instead of pulling into the drive. This would be fun. He'd surprise them both, and then the three of them could have a Christmas Eve drink together. Perfect.

Pleased with how the evening was turning out, he strode up the walk, climbed the steps and unlocked the front door. When he walked in, he expected to see both of them sitting in the living room, but it was empty. Maybe they'd gone back to the kitchen, although it was really quiet back there.

Then he heard a sound he knew quite well, one that he'd become fond of in the past six months. The wail drifting down from their upstairs bedroom was unmistakable. Someone had just given his fiancée an orgasm. And the odds were excellent that it was the same person who drove the SUV parked outside.

* * * * *

Twelve military heroes.
Twelve indomitable heroines.
One UNIFORMLY HOT! miniseries.

Mills & Boon® Blaze®'s bestselling miniseries
continues with another year of irresistible soldiers
from all branches of the armed forces.

Don't miss

THE RISK-TAKER
by Kira Sinclair

A SEAL'S SEDUCTION
by Tawny Weber

A SEAL'S SURRENDER
by Tawny Weber

THE RULE-BREAKER
by Rhonda Nelson

UNIFORMLY HOT!

The Few. The Proud. The Sexy as Hell.